Carved

To Pat —

Hope you enjoy this sequel with Elberton & St. Simons landmarks.

Happy Reading!

Martha

The sculptures and other art presented in this book are real and used to enhance the plot of the fictional story. Most characters, names, houses, schools, etc., are fictional. Homes, businesses, and streets specifically assigned to the fictional characters exist in my imagination. (I purposely made up streets and gave them names.) Any likeness or familiarity to any person or happening is totally coincidental with the exception of Bunny the Tour Guide.

Many thanks to the Elberton Granite Museum and Exhibit for permission to use the Sea Lion as a part of this story, and to Keith Jennings, artist extraordinaire, who sculpted several art-filled spirits described in this story. Bunny Marshall really is a great tour guide. She brings the past to life in an entertaining and informative way.

First printing: August, 2013

ISBN-13: 978-0-9859255-3-6
ISBN-10: 0-9859255-3-1

Front and back cover designed by ThomasMax (photography by Martha R. Phillips).

Published By:

ThomasMax Publishing
P.O. Box 250054
Atlanta, GA 30325
www.thomasmax.com

Carved

by Martha Phillips

Martha Phillips

ThomasMax

Your Publisher
For The 21st Century

Acknowledgments

Allison Floyd not only did a great job editing, she made me feel that my characters were believable and worthwhile. Thanks Allison.

Writer friends are invaluable. Pat Adams and the Writers' Group at the Oconee Cultural Arts Center in Watkinsville, Georgia, listened to my progress with this sequel and encouraged me greatly.

Lou Aronica continues to support my writing endeavors. Without his suggestions, this book would be inadequate in so many ways.

I send many thanks to family and friends for their support and all the stories they inspire and all the books they sell. You're the best.

My water aerobics buddies, Paula Schwanenflugel and Debbie Hamby, patiently listened to my creative craziness as we exercised. They gave me confidence to push on.

A special thanks to Peggy Hancock, for sharing numerous funny stories with me for more than thirty years – what fun we've had.

Thanks to two local artists, Claire and Bob Clements, who support and encourage me in all my artistic undertakings.

Thanks to Pat Priest for suggesting I use nature stories in my book. Her hosting the nature writing classes at the Athens Land Trust resulted in my writing about our funny, loveable Huey – aka Suede.

Thank you, Keith Jennings, for sharing your artistic creations (sculpture of whales and tree carvings). Thanks, too, to Bunny the Tour Guide, for letting me use your version of the history of an island off the coast of Georgia. I love sharing your Southern personality with my readers.

Elberton residents, businesses, and landmarks have impacted me most of my life and helped make my first novel, *Written on a Rock*, successful. I thank them all.

Even though Weaver Lineberry, Phillip Smith, and Matthew Harper have many interests of their own, their love and support keep me going. Their encouragement has no bounds. Thanks guys.

Dear Readers – WOW! Spending your hard earned money and giving your precious time to read my books mean a lot to me. Thank you many times over.

This book is made possible by ThomasMax Publishing. Thanks, Lee Clevenger!

Dedication

Dedicated to the world's artists
who use their hands and imagination
to give shape to history and myth,
and share their hearts in the presentation of their art.

Inspiration

Mrs. Geraldine Smith of Elbert County, a cancer survivor, ignored her chores of the day to read my first novel, *Written on a Rock.* She told me she enjoyed it so much she read it again and wants to be the first to read my second book. I needed her inspiration to commit to this fictional sequel. Thanks, Geraldine!

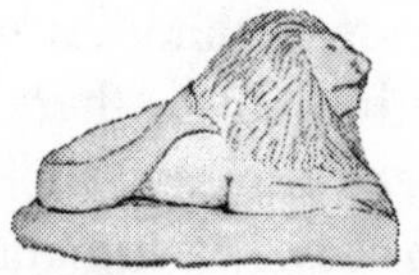

Chapter One – A New Year

The cold air enveloped Dee Dupree Jackson as she sat on a granite bench at Ben Sutton Square in Elberton and thought about how clairvoyance affected her life. Her mother hated the word and said it brought back bad childhood memories. Growing up, Dee knew better than to bring up the subject with her mother even though her little girl ears stayed tuned to whispers about a great-aunt's ability to predict births and deaths as well as local disasters. By the time Dee went to college, she knew Mr. Webster's Collegiate Dictionary's meaning of clairvoyance: *1: the power or faculty of discerning objects not present to the senses 2: ability to perceive matters beyond the range of ordinary perception.* By the time she finished college, she knew her mother's sister, Connie, saw beyond the norm. Dee sat there wishing she could see the future or at least understand the cause for her current anxiety. For almost a decade, she felt happy in this small northeast Georgia town. Creeping back into her life like a slow-moving snake, anxiety reared its ugly head even as she sat peacefully waiting for her husband's sister, Emmy, to arrive.

She rested her elbows on her knees. The winter sun beamed down on her dark hair as it hung forward, partially covering her light complexion. She sat up, pushed her hair behind her ears, and pulled the hood of her thick black jacket over her head. Her green eyes focused on the tall Confederate soldier high on his granite pedestal as she contemplated her life with her eight-year-old daughter and loving husband. Thinking about her tall red-headed husband's distinctive deep laugh mixed in with her young daughter's light giggle as they left the house an hour earlier, made her smile.

She never considered herself a clairvoyant person even though she experienced visions for a short time several years earlier. On her daughter's third birthday she realized Sara shared her Aunt Connie's gift. Sara said, "Mama Anna can't come to my party. She's sick." Dee didn't think much of it until her father arrived a half-hour later with the news that her mother had a migraine headache.

Dee tried to hide Sara's extraordinary ability to see the future. Sara picked up on the need for secrecy and normally managed to disguise or hide what she could see and hear that others couldn't fathom. Dee shook her head, trying to clear her thoughts and focus on landmarks carved from Elberton granite. The newly renovated stone courthouse looked majestic as a backdrop to the bicentennial fountain with Elbert County's history engraved on granite panels encasing its base. A sculpted American eagle perched on top of the narrow spire in the center of the fountain.

After graduating from the University of Georgia, Emmy helped her get a job teaching history at the local high school and introduced her to her brother, Dan. Within a year, she and Dan married. She quickly adapted to small-town life. She had become a part of the inner workings of Elberton in the past ten years and couldn't imagine living anywhere else.

The loud dong from the old courthouse clock rang in the noon hour. Where was Emmy? She pulled her cell phone from a metallic purse that matched the blue in her jeans and pressed the direct dial number for Emmy's cell phone.

Almost immediately, Dee heard the University of Georgia's fight song from her sister-in-law's phone. Before Dee turned around, Emmy touched her shoulder.

"Dee." Emmy laughed. "Caught you daydreaming again, huh?"

"Hi." Dee stood up and leaned over to give Emmy a hug.

They walked arm in arm, crossed the street, passed the local newspaper office, and turned left onto McIntosh Street.

"Sorry I'm late," Emmy said. "James spilled milk all over himself just as I was leaving Mom's house, which means I'll have to do laundry before we head back home tomorrow. Mom stopped cleaning the collards and helped me with the mess. I should've called you, but ended up spending the time trying to calm James down. He was afraid he'd miss out on today's plans with Dad."

The cold air made Emmy's cheeks rosy red within her white freckled face. Her strawberry blonde curls peeked out from a dark blue knitted cap with a white circle and a dark blue logo of a blue devil's head in the center. The local high school's initials, ECCHS, were stitched in white below the logo. Her matching blue winter jacket hid her three-month baby bump.

Dee looked at Emmy's hat and said, "Love your hat." Dee knew it was a keepsake from Emmy's years of attending and teaching at the Elbert County Comprehensive High School.

"Yeah. I'm a Blue Devil through and through." Emmy said.

More than once, Dee had heard her friend tell someone that she'd been born and raised a Blue Devil.

"What's Sara doing?" Emmy asked.

"She and Dan are having their father/daughter day. They're spending the day at the Mall of Georgia. Lunch and a movie. I wouldn't be surprised if Sara doesn't talk him into one of those create-a-bear sessions."

The circles under Dee's eyes prompted Emmy to ask, "Are you okay?"

"Sure. Why?" Dee tried to think of something about her herself that would cause Emmy to be concerned.

"You look tired." Emmy took a step to the right to make way on the sidewalk for a couple of former students to walk by. She smiled and waved as they passed.

When Emmy stepped closer, Dee answered. "I hardly slept the last few nights. Remember the nightmare I had after Dun Dunsman tried to kill me – the one that haunted me for so long? It started again last week, only this time it's worse than before. I haven't told Dan about it, even though I woke him up tossing and turning."

"Alright. Tell me about it over lunch," Emmy said as she wrapped her arm around her friend's waist.

"Does Mom Jax need help with those collards?" Dee referred to her mother-in-law and purposely didn't promise to share details of the nightmare.

"She seemed to have it under control. I told her I'd cut out the veins and chop the leaves when I get back. She knows we all need our black-eyed peas and collard greens to start the New Year off right. Can't believe tomorrow starts another year. I'm not leaving here until I get my share. I don't want to be broke all next year."

Dee laughed at the way Emmy seemed to believe in the Southern superstition that eating black-eyed peas and collard greens would ensure both change and dollar bills for the coming year.

What are you bringing?" Emmy asked.

"Squash casserole and chicken strips," Dee answered, happy to leave the memories of the nightmare behind. She didn't want Emmy to know about all the uncertainty creeping into her life. Emmy had enough to worry about with two boys and a baby on the way. Her friend didn't need to be reminded of all the horrors of the recurring nightmare. She opened the door for Emmy to enter the McIntosh Coffee Shoppe.

Two nights later, the screaming demons in the familiar black hole crawled over each other, anticipating Dee's falling body. Each ugly character fought to be the first one to grope her and pull her into the darkness. The most aggressive one reflected Dun Dunsman's distorted facial features. A lock of pewter gray hair across his forehead blew backward, exposing gray thin skin stretched across his skull face. Cold black eyes narrowed as a large hand reached toward her face – the movement revealed bulging muscles in his arms and shoulders. She woke up fully expecting to find blood on her cheek left from the touch of a pointed sharp fingernail.

She turned on the bedside lamp. The nightmare seemed too real. She touched the pillow beside her, expecting to find her husband sleeping, until she remembered he left the day before to work in Texas. She ran her palm across her right cheek. No blood. No pain. To ensure the nightmare had nothing to do with reality, she pushed the covers to the end of the bed, checked her light blue flannel pajamas, and found them spotless. *Aaaah.* Relief flooded her mind. She tried to push the nightmare away.

The huge black hole reminded Dee of the granite quarry that Dun Dunsman intended as her final resting place ten years earlier. Her visions of a sixteen-year-old girl's 1960s death initiated a chain of events that changed Dee's life. They started when she moved to Elberton to teach. Facts from the visions of Mollie's kidnapping and murder brought negative reactions from local authorities as well as her own mother. In the visions, the kidnapper referred to Mollie as Rotten Tamale, then followed with physical abuse. Dee felt the hurt and pain that Mollie experienced, making her more determined than ever to pursue Mollie's killer.

The visions continued until she found Mollie's remains in the trunk of a 1957 Chevrolet, abandoned in the woods of the Dunsmans' neglected estate. The patch of hardwoods and pines near the old brick two-story house hid the horror of Dun's evil actions and his doting grandfather's cover up. It took Dee months to uncover the dark secrets within the old house with high columns spaced across a porch that stretched from one side of the house to the other and wrapped halfway around the sides. Dun Dunsman's atrocities were not confined to his interaction with Mollie. He had raped his sister. The grandparents who raised the two of them blamed the sister for enticing her brother. Dee wondered how many victims suffered at the hands of what Dee thought of as "the monster."

DNA found with Mollie's skeleton matched Dun Dunsman's. He added rape victims to his list before and after moving to California. Even though he had never been convicted of rape, a 1980 charge placed his DNA in the national offenders' file. The local newspaper ran an article mentioning Dee's visions and how she assisted in finding Mollie's remains as well as Mollie's killer. Once the authorities connected him to Mollie's death, Dun placed a homeless man about his height and weight behind the steering wheel of his car and parked the car in front of an oncoming train. His lawyer identified the mangled body as Michael (Dun) Dunsman, III. His obituary ran in the Elberton newspaper. Everyone thought he was dead until he showed up in Elberton, kidnapped Dee, and took her to a quarry with the intention of raping and killing her before throwing her into the quarry. He had misjudged her. In the end, she was able to put him into the huge black hole. Her quick response and stubbornness saved her life. *Stop thinking about this,* Dee told herself. *Count your blessings.*

Most of her friends and family had forgotten her efforts to find justice for Mollie. And, since she no longer received visions from Mollie, the traumatic experience hid in the back of her mind where it belonged – until recently. She shivered and wondered why the demons came back to haunt her.

The following Monday, Dee and her daughter walked from the dress shop on the north side of Sutton Square on their way to the pizza parlor on the south side. They crossed a side street and stepped onto the sidewalk flanked by a wall of brick.

"This is where Mollie walked as a teenager, right here," Dee said. "A glass wall stood here where the brick is now." Dee motioned to the wall beside them.

"How do ya know, Mommy? Did Mollie tell you about it?" Sara touched the solid brick wall. Sara not only knew about this great-aunt, she'd claimed Mollie as a friend since she was two years old.

"No, honey. I saw it in a vision Mollie sent. Mollie walked by the glass window with 'Rose's 5-10-25 Cents Store' written in gold and red lettering. An awning hung overhead, as Mollie walked down the sidewalk to the drugstore, right here." Dee pointed to the next area of solid brick wall. "It's where Mollie and her friends enjoyed a cherry Coke. A bank was there where the newspaper office is, on the corner."

Dee noticed how the blue in Sara's eyes turned a dreamy gray. "I wish I could've had a cherry Coke with Mollie."

They crossed North McIntosh Street, stopped to let a white pickup truck go by before crossing Heard Street, and made their way toward the pizza parlor on the other side of the Square.

As they walked by an art gallery, Dee told her daughter that in the 1960s Mollie would have seen a men's store instead of the art gallery and two doors down, the dress store once housed a Woolworth's five and dime store. They crossed South McIntosh Street to eat pizza in a restaurant that had, at one time, been part of a Gallant Belk store.

On the way home Sara said, "Mollie sure lived a different life from ours."

"It was," Dee agreed, thinking how she planned to share the ugly facts about Mollie's death – someday – when Sara could handle more of the dark side of life. Dee desperately wanted to shield her little freckle-faced daughter from the prejudice and hurt she felt when she shared her visions of Mollie.

Dee glanced in the rearview mirror at Sara sitting in the back seat of their silver Prius working on her latest drawing of their dog, Suede. Sara's shoulder length red hair touched the collar of her long-sleeved lavender blouse.

Many of Dee's college classes covered child development and she often caught herself judging her daughter's physical progress. Sara never developed the baby fat that many girls carried. Her birth statistics seemed to have been a forewarning of things to come with a length of twenty-one and a half inches. The tall genes that came from both Dee and Dan were passed to Sara. The pediatrician's records always found her in the hundredth percentile of height, yet her weight was average. Except for one boy, Sara was the tallest child in her class.

The only real conflict between Dee and Sara happened a year earlier when Sara insisted she had to have her ears pierced. Dee asked her to wait until she was at least ten years old. Two months later, when Dan and Sara returned from a Saturday's father/daughter outing, Sara sported small diamonds studs in each ear. Dan refused to say how much they cost even though he knew Dee would see the amount when she paid their bills. He also bought a set of expensive fourteen-carat gold hoops and a small jewelry box. Dee accepted the fact it was a done deal and never confronted them openly about being left out of something she considered important. Sara's determination to get what she wanted and Dan's failure to include her in the decision or discuss the purchases made her feel insignificant. After the credit card statement arrived, verifying the expensive purchase, she kept her mouth shut. She hated confrontations.

Sara was a loner, hiding her special gift, yet using her height as a symbol of pride. Dee seldom saw Sara's thin shoulders slumping. Sara ignored her classmates' pressure to change in order to be a part of the in-crowd. She often supported shy classmates and those with disabilities. Dee was proud of Sara's sensitivity to others and hoped the trait would not diminish when her daughter approached thirteen – "the year of transformation," as her daddy called it when she turned thirteen.

Within a few minutes, the view of their home made Dee appreciate how she never got tired of their brick ranch house on the hill – a safe haven from a day's work at school. In a few months, the brown grass would be green, and tulips and daffodils would have pushed their green spikes out of the brown, mulched earth. The barren bushes in the yard would be a showcase of color from a variety of azaleas and camellias in bloom. She loved her students, but at the end of the day she happily came home to spend time with her only child.

Sara added the date in the bottom right corner of her picture as her mother pulled into the garage. The colored pencil slipped off the edge of the paper and left a black line on her denim jeans. As soon as the car's engine stopped, she threw her pencil and pad on the beige leather seat and scampered out of the car, ignoring the cold air.

Suede's short tail wagged a greeting. His strange yellow eyes watched intently as Sara made her way to the gate. He danced as he waited, making tapping sounds on the brick pathway. Sara didn't remember life without Suede. She was three years old when her daddy brought the six-week-old silvery tan-colored Weimaraner puppy home. She remembered that her mother had named Suede, because his ears felt like the suede boots she and her mother wore that winter.

Dee watched as Sara took the thumb latch off the gate of the chain-linked fence. The thumb latch proved to be a necessity as soon as Suede could place his nose on the gate's handle and push upward – a feat accomplished before his first birthday. He had watched Dan lift the handle, go through the gate, close it, and push the handle back down. Suede repeated Dan's actions. Dan walked to the garage, turned around, and almost bumped into the dog.

Dee left those memories behind as she watched Sara and Suede. She knew that no amount of training or discipline would stop Suede from jumping on people. His nostrils twitched in the air and often meant trouble. If his keen sense of smell led him to a morsel of food on the counter or floor, he devoured it immediately. If it happened to be a pie cooling on a rack, it was his. His enthusiasm and energy seemed boundless. Other memories of Suede as a puppy made her smile. He had attached himself to Dan, until Dan started spending more time out of town. Suede suffered separation anxiety. He waited at the gate for hours each evening. Sores appeared around his mouth. His almost invisible eyebrows twitched inward and created a sorrowful expression. Eventually, he chose Dee as his master with Sara as his second choice.

Dee watched Sara step into the back yard, replace the thumb latch, and run toward the hammock that was attached to two oak trees. Suede reached the hammock first; his short, cropped tail wagged back and forth.

Dee took her purse and tote bag from the front passenger seat, closed her door, and gathered Sara's blue-jean jacket, pencil, and a drawing tablet from the back seat. She used her hip to push the passenger door closed. In order to get in the house, she was forced to place Sara's stuff on the single step at the back door. She searched for the key in her purse. The metallic sound of the keys made her realize they were dangling from a finger on her right hand.

When she got to the kitchen, she placed her purse and bag on the kitchen counter and went to retrieve Sara's things. She held them in her hand and was almost in the house when two drawings fell out of the pad. Dee picked them up, took them to the kitchen, and placed them with Sara's jacket on the table. She took a closer look at the pictures, recognizing the first one – the Sea Lion Sara drew after a visit to the Elberton Granite Museum and Exhibit. The granite statue had the head of a lion and the tale of a fish.

The second picture showed a young strawberry blond-haired woman with two boys walking towards a store. An older woman, with a large bag, followed them. Sara gave the youngest boy yellow hair and the older boy sported dark brown curls. The older woman's brown hair hung below her ears. Sara's artistic abilities were advanced for her age except when it came to drawing people. She still drew stick figures to get shapes and height before adding hair and accessories over what Sara called "the bones." A bad feeling crept into Dee's mind as she focused on the older woman. Her hand shook when her index finger traced the outline of the young woman. Dee thought of Emmy. She continued looking at the picture. Emmy's dark curly-haired husband wasn't included in the picture. *Was Fred out of the picture because he was working?*

Dee unlocked the den door and called Sara. Suede bounded in ahead of Sara, ran to the kitchen, and returned to the den in seconds.

"Sara, honey, sit down." Dee motioned to a chair beside her. "This is an interesting picture. Tell me about it."

"It's not finished. Mollie said I should draw it."

"Do these people remind you of anyone?" Dee knew she needed to confirm the characters' identities if she wanted to understand the significance of the picture, even though she probably wouldn't like Sara's answers.

"Oh. It's Aunt Em and James and Hank." Sara stated matter-of-factly.

"That's what I thought. Did Mollie say anything about the woman with the bag?"

"Just that she's up to no good." Sara left the table.

"Did Mollie say anything else?" Dee needed and wanted more information.

"Nope." Sara replied. She called Suede, turned back to her mother and added, "Mollie didn't say for sure what the woman wants. Maybe she don't know yet."

"Wait. It's 'maybe she *doesn't* know yet.'" Dee automatically corrected her daughter's grammar. "Wear your coat. It's on the table."

Sara turned around, retrieved her jacket, and ran out the back door. The door slammed shut, barely missing Suede's short tail.

Unlike Dee's rare encounters with Mollie, Mollie communicated with Sara easily and often. Before Sara was old enough to articulate her words, she said Mollie was her guard on the angels. Dee knew Sara considered Mollie her guardian angel. She also knew the drawing wasn't a coincidence and she made a decision to talk with Emmy, soon. Emmy knew about Mollie – the ghost. *What message was Mollie trying to send?*

On an Island off the coast of Georgia, Nan Jones thought, *January 15, another birthday without him.* Her mind went to her most recent trip. Other than the purchase of a black Honda, her trip to Jacksonville proved to be a failure. She used the trade-in value of a dark blue Nissan as a down payment. The old car served its purpose. Disappointment in her inability to find Timmy in Jacksonville faded. She sat for hours in the hospital, choosing different locations – watching and waiting. Her boy never showed up. When she delivered him, the doctor called it a tragic stillbirth. She didn't believe him then. And, she wouldn't believe him – ever. Her Timmy survived, and she would find him.

Two days of sixty-five degree weather and blue skies, in the middle of winter, made her head to the beach. She stepped out of her brown walking shoes, took off her white socks, and stuffed them inside the shoes. Her small brown eyes darted back and forth, in a perpetual state of assessing her surroundings. Still damp from her morning bath, her brown hair hung limp and barely covered her ears. Her sallow complexion exaggerated her small dark eyes.

She rolled her khaki colored pants' legs up to her knees and walked across the packed wet sand. The ivory neckline of her blouse disappeared as she buttoned a beige hip-length sweater. Purposely walking a few feet into the surf, she turned and walked in the water at the edge of the outgoing tide. The gray cold water lapped at her feet and ankles. Pushing against the resistance of the water made her walk more productive and her ankles stronger. There was no way she'd jeopardize her future by not exercising or eating well, unless it fit a need toward fulfilling her dreams. She enjoyed having the beach to herself. She had lived on the island for more than a year and figured out when the least number of locals would be on the beach. She wanted to be alone on the beach or lost in a crowd.

The cold water was bearable. Her thin lips smiled as she thought about how tough she could be. She laughed to herself and thought, *A little cold water won't keep me from a walk in the water on a sunny day.*

She kicked her feet and created a spray of water with each step. She watched a myriad of water drops fall back into the ocean. The different sized drops looked like diamonds sparkling in the winter sunlight. How she longed to have her son by her side. He'd be delighted to share the water diamonds with her.

A flock of Sanderlings, wintering over on the Georgia coast, flew in ahead of her. The small birds, from the sandpiper family, pecked in the sand for some unseen food source and clipped along in different directions on their short thin legs. She counted twenty-five. She walked on until the beach disappeared. The waves ahead slammed against huge boulders and crashed against the barnacle-encrusted rock at the edge of the ocean. The deeper water around the jutting rock forced her to turn back.

The cooler weather almost always made the psoriasis on her arms and legs worse. The hateful crusty spots made people notice her. Even in the summer, she hid the skin condition. She didn't want to bring attention to herself. Her mousy brown hair, nondescript clothing, and sallow skin tones were purposeful.

The Sanderlings chirped a warning of her return. They all flew into the air at the same time. They stayed together for several seconds, separated into three groups, and flew into the blue sky.

Nan had started a walking regimen twice a week after her mother's death the year before. She forced her mind away from memories of her mother, picked up her shoes and socks, walked towards a set of wooden steps, and sat down to put them on. When she finished, she climbed the steps and walked to the pier.

A young bearded white man, clad in dark jeans and a black jacket, threw a circle of netting into the air. For a few seconds, the net floated outward before landing in the water. The weights, sewn into the hem of the net, pulled it down into the water, trapping the creatures of the sea.

With one strong pull, the young man lifted the net out of the water, hauled it over the rail, and shook his captured items loose. Two red fish rolled out. He placed them in a pail before separating the small shark from the heavy strings. It landed on the pier's flooring with a thud. He held the netting in the air and shook it, forcing the weights down. The hem of the netting slid across the boards of the pier. Swish! Like a broom, the weights swept the shark back into the ocean.

When he turned and looked in her direction, Nan immediately turned away. She learned years ago to keep to herself. Making eye contact often led to conversations. She avoided both.

Nan left the pier, walked toward the lighthouse, and took the first wooden railed boardwalk to the beach. The outgoing tide enabled her to walk home via the beach. Frustrated, but determined, she thought about her original plan and how she put The Plan into action on her thirtieth birthday, when she lived in Atlanta. She checked her monthly cycle and knew exactly the best time to get pregnant. She trolled the local bars looking for a blond, green-eyed man, the one she called her Dream Man, to help fulfill the first item on her list of things to accomplish – a blond, green eyed baby of her own. She'd been at it for months without success, until the night she decided to try one more time.

She looked at several fashion magazines before choosing the Marilyn Monroe look, hoping it would bring her good luck in the pursuit to fulfill The Plan. Her dyed blond hair, impeccable makeup, and low cut red dress were eye-catching. She knew her thin red lips represented the only flaw in her do-over. Without succeeding, she'd tried to make her lips fuller by adding lipstick outside her bottom lip line. Disgusted with the results, she'd slashed red lipstick across her cheek with a tissue, forcing her to start over with the lip liner and soft makeup around her mouth. She practiced holding her lips in a pout, trying to make them look full and inviting.

Three bars into her evening's hunt, she stopped at a narrow brick building and walked up two steps. The pink neon sign to the left of the glass door proclaimed the name, *Two Step Bar and Grill.* Laughter, coming from a group of men playing pool, caught her attention as she walked in. Her eyes immediately found her Dream Man, who stood a head taller than those around him. The lights shining through the stained glass fixture above a pool table caught the blond highlights in his hair. Her small brown eyes checked out the area near the pool table as a couple vacated a polished chrome pub table with two matching stools. She pushed through the crowd, determined to make her way to the table and chairs before anyone else realized they were empty. She sat on one of the black vinyl stools and leaned her shoulders against the wall. Her Dream Man stood a few yards away and glanced in her direction as she hiked the skirt of her red dress above her knees and practiced her pouty smile.

God, she thought as she took a deep breath. *He's worth the trouble and the wait. Those green eyes. The dimple in his chin? A bonus. My dream will come true tonight.* She checked her purse for the drug she planned to put in his drink. It would make him pliable and easy to manipulate. She could see by the smile he directed at her that she had his attention.

The Plan worked. She took him to a nearby motel room she'd rented that afternoon. Within an hour of seducing him, she gave him a strong sedative and took him back to the Two Step Bar and Grill and dumped him in the parking lot. From the rear view mirror, she could see him crawling after her as she drove away.

A few weeks later, she knew The Plan was working, and rejoiced when she woke up with morning sickness. The first time the baby moved within her belly, she stayed still for the longest time enjoying the feathery feeling of new life moving inside her. She continued working at a neighborhood drugstore and told her co-workers that her boyfriend abandoned her when he found out she was pregnant. By the fourth month, she knew her shape had changed enough that her mother would know she was pregnant, so she made up stories to tell her mother why she couldn't visit: she had a cold; the boss made her pull double shifts at work; her car wouldn't start. The list went on and on.

The morning the contractions started, she drove herself to the hospital and waited in the car until the pains were ten minutes apart. Once inside, things happened quickly. The nurses and doctor started working with her immediately. Before they gave her medication for the pain, she thought she heard the doctor tell the nurse to have a surgeon and a pediatrician waiting. She felt the panic in the room.

Afterwards, Nan remembered waking up and the doctor telling her she'd delivered a stillborn baby boy. She screamed at him, insisting he bring the baby to her. He said she shouldn't see the baby. She threatened to sue him, the hospital, and the nurses. When they brought the baby to her, his shriveled, purple veined body with an indention running from the middle of his forehead to the nape of his neck, as though his scull had divided underneath the skin, made her nauseated. She turned her head away. They brought her a freak. Following the doctor's orders, the nurse injected a calming drug into Nan's IV. Nan remembered saying over and over, "That thing is not my baby. That thing is not my baby."

The following day, Nan left the hospital. While in a wheelchair on the way out, she asked the nurse to stop at the window of the nursery. A perfectly formed baby boy in a basinet near the window opened his eyes. Nan felt certain he smiled at her. She knew he was her baby. They gave her someone else's monster and pretended it was hers. She knew differently. She knew she'd found her baby. It was just a matter of time before she'd have her Timmy in her arms. The nurse wheeled her to the lobby, placed the brakes on the chair and waited. Nan told the nurse her mother was on the way and pretended she left a jacket in the closet of her hospital room. As soon as the nurse left to retrieve it, Nan left the hospital.

Three weeks later, she'd moved into a small brick rental house two blocks off Flat Shoals Road in Decatur, made possible because she'd duped her mother into sending money to her each month. Her mother believed she had suffered a nervous breakdown.

Nan knew the baby in the nursery at the hospital was her baby, even though it took time for her to follow the leads to where he lived and find out how she could get her hands on him. Within a few weeks of leaving the hospital, she merely walked to the back deck of a house in south Decatur and took the baby from his infant rocker while the mother stood inside the double glass doors with her back to the deck. Nan never knew what the woman was doing. She only knew it was her first opportunity to take her baby from the woman who thought she was the mother.

She created a very believable birth certificate and records from a doctor's office stating the baby's progress since birth. The first few months with him were heavenly. She changed his diaper, made formula, talked to him, held him constantly, and rocked him to sleep each night. When her mother retired and purchased a house at the beach, the money stopped coming. Nan had to go back to work.

The closer the time came for her to get a job, the less patience she had with the baby. She couldn't work and take care of a baby who had started to cry a lot. Her Timmy would've laughed and giggled. This baby looked at her as if she were a stranger; his wrinkled brow meant a crying spell that seemed to never end. Her Timmy wouldn't have been a crybaby. She started thinking of ways to make him stop crying. It was easier than she imagined. The night he cried from seven o'clock in the evening until seven o'clock the next evening, she simply helped him go to sleep – forever – with an adult dose of sleep medicines. The medical examiner issued a death certificate for Sudden Infant Death Syndrome. The lack of symptoms or any prior history of illness matched the finding.

The ability to keep the baby's death out of the newspaper and to keep her mother and others from knowing what she'd done gave her pleasure. She felt certain the numerous deceptions she pulled in her lifetime prepared her for fulfilling The Plan. With cremation and no funeral service, she spent very little money. Her obsession to detail finally paid off. Her neighbor next door brought her a casserole when the baby died. She was an old softy – an old fool for sharing her income tax refund. The woman believed anything.

Getting her old job back enabled her to use the cash register at the drugstore to steal money and finance The Plan. A year later, she found the perfect little boy. He and his mother came into the store. His green eyes and blond hair caught her attention and when he smiled at her, she knew he was her Timmy. Like before, she waited and watched until the opportunity presented itself. This time, she followed the woman and the child from the drugstore. It happened as she left work for the day and wouldn't be back for a week. She felt certain that it had been preordained for her to have the child. After all, everything fell perfectly in place when the woman left the boy in the car and pushed the grocery cart two lanes over and parked it with the other empty carts. Nan quickly took the boy from his seat and ducked behind a truck blocking the woman's view. She placed the boy in a child's safety seat in the back passenger seat of her car. Nan saw the woman running amongst the cars and heard her screaming as she drove out of the parking lot. Nan took two-year old Timmy to her small house, called the drugstore, and told her boss she was quitting,

She fooled the old woman next door into believing she had a twin sister named Ann with a two-year-old son, Jimmy. As Ann, she visited the neighbor, dressed in bright reds, blues, and yellows. Makeup and a different hairstyle completed the disguise. With the two-year old on her hip, she talked about her mother and how fragile she had become. Her fake outgoing personality convinced the woman that Nan had allowed her sister and nephew to move in with her. It took a lot of effort on Nan's part to remember to call the boy Jimmy and refer to herself as Ann.

A few weeks later, dressed in her old clothes and no makeup, she visited her neighbor and told her how unhappy she had become because her sister's boy reminded her of her baby. When she moved, the old woman believed Nan couldn't stand living in a house with so many memories.

Little Timmy was too cute. Everybody said so. Months later, he was still unable to talk with her. He was more than two years old and mean. He held his breath and turned blue if he didn't get his way. Her Timmy would never do that. Within a year of pretending to be her sister, she and the boy disappeared in the middle of the night. The Plan failed. Revisions became a necessity.

She considered her marriage to Joe Jones a huge sacrifice towards motherhood. The new Revised Plan reflected the need to have a common surname and more money than she could make as a sales clerk at a mall drugstore in Atlanta. Several moves hid her trail of deceit. Getting lost in the crowd took no effort in a city as large as Atlanta. Changing jobs often and never getting close to her co-workers, helped her keep her secrets.

She attended several churches that offered rehabilitative programs for alcoholics and drug addicts. When she found Joe Jones, with no known relatives, it was a no brainer. With his stringy gray-streaked brown hair cut and cleaned, and clothes she purchased from a thrift store, Joe Jones became a somewhat respectable looking man. His insecurity and dependence on whoever would or could help, made him an easy target. As soon as they married, she took out a large insurance policy on him. Within a year, drugs and alcohol took their toll. Joe hardly knew where he was or what he was doing. After the minimum time clause attached to the insurance policy passed, Joe's death came quickly. She remembered how she laced his morning orange juice with Vodka and painkillers. He never felt or saw the needle slip into his vein. To ensure he'd get the blame, she cleaned the syringe carefully and placed his fingertips exactly as she had held it.

She hadn't counted on the side benefits of her new role of widow and reveled in sympathy from church members and co-workers at the drugstore. They all thought Joe's backsliding into past bad habits killed him. No one questioned his death. She called the insurance money her *seed money* that would help grow the family she wanted. Without a sufficient money source, the Revised Plan to be a mother would fail. The Original Plan already proved she needed money and a house of her own. Her mother never knew about Joe Jones or the imposters. She never knew about the birth of her daughter's baby.

The thought of Joe Jones made Nan feel nauseated. She could almost smell his body odor, hear his unceasing complaints and whining, and see the partially chewed food slipping from his open mouth. She pushed the gross memories of him back into a dark place somewhere in the back of her head where she buried secrets – the ones that couldn't live in the light of day – where the imposters and Joe Jones found a home, helping erase them from reality.

She left the beach and walked through an overgrown vacant lot to her small house. Her mind went back to the Revised Plan as she approached the small white framed house she inherited from her mother. *Timmy will love the beach*, she thought as she opened the screened door.

Her nightly ritual included lying quietly in bed, trying to recreate the feeling of the first time her baby moved within her all those years ago. Dressed in an old white cotton nightgown, eyes closed, hands spread open and resting on her abdomen, she could almost feel the movement – light as a feather, teasing her from inside, letting her know he was well and alive. Before drifting off to sleep she made the decision to go north to try and find her Timmy. Tomorrow, she'd be thirty-eight years old. Time was running out.

The next day she drove off the island to I-95, took the north exit, and arrived on Hilton Head Island before noon.

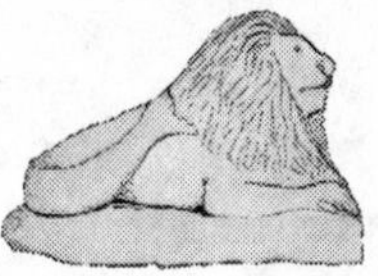

Chapter Two – Clairvoyant Significance

Dee loved her sister-in-law Emmy like the sister she never had, long before she married Dan. She would never say something so corny out loud, but she often thought of Emmy as her sister-in-love. As roommates after college, they shared almost everything. When Dee, an only child, married into the growing Jackson family she adjusted quickly.

As soon as Emmy's husband graduated from UGA's College of Environment and Design with a bachelor's degree in landscape architecture, the Rafferty family moved from Elberton to Hilton Head Island, with their son, Hank. James arrived a couple of years later. Their third baby was due in the summer. Emmy's declaration about limiting the size of her family was memorable.

"I'm having my tubes tied after this one," Emmy said when she and Dee found a few minutes to talk without their children hovering about.

"Just be sure it's what you want."

"I use to think it took sex to have a baby, but I believe I can get pregnant if Fred hangs his pants on the bedpost." Emmy shared her hearty laugh with Dee, the one that reminded Dee of Dan's distinctive laugh. Emmy continued, "I'm also going to get serious about getting some of this weight off. One more baby to feed and these jugs will get smaller. I've never been skinny like you, but this baby-making business hasn't helped me control my weight."

Dee didn't say a word. She didn't want to share her anxiety over her own failure to get pregnant since Sara's birth. She noticed Emmy had put on a few extra pounds and agreed that she should do something about it after the baby arrived. Her friend's petite frame showed the least bit of weight gain. They were opposites in so many ways; yet, their friendship and love for each other and their families bonded them completely.

Dee couldn't help but think how strawberry blonde Emmy was becoming more and more like Emmy's and Dan's mischievous maternal grandmother, Granny Nida, who loved to tell jokes, especially dirty jokes. She also liked to misuse clichés and metaphors – for the fun of it. It was harmless; but it was difficult to get away from Granny Nida, who insisted on telling another funny story or joke.

Many years ago, Dee was present when Granny Nida reminded Emmy that she had promised to provide great-grandchildren. Thinking of it, made Dee smile. Granny Nida said, "Yore mama did her part, now you gotta do yore's."

When Granny Nida found out about Emmy's third pregnancy, she said, "Now Emmy Lou," Granny Nida made up names for everyone, "I didn't mean to create a monster here. I hope you're gonna git yore little girl, but after this one, you need to remember to put that aspirin between yore knees and keep it thar till the fe'vah of love goes away. Lordy mercy, girl, it's the best prevention I know of."

On Emmy's next visit to Elberton, she told Dee how she felt like she was being watched while she was shopping in Sun City near their home on Hilton Head Island. The feeling was so strong on one shopping trip that she held onto James' hand the entire time she was in the grocery store. She said she left the store without several items on her list.

Hearing about her experience, Dee decided to tell Emmy about Sara's drawing of a woman following Emmy and her children around the island. Emmy listened. She and Dee were roommates during the months Dee dealt with visions and saw first-hand how psychic phenomena worked. She had known Sara since she was born and was not shocked that Sara possessed extraordinary abilities.

Sara's drawing and Emmy's own experiences with Dee's visions, made it easy to encourage her husband, Fred, to take a landscape architecture position in Athens near her hometown of Elberton. Emmy hoped they could avoid a disaster by moving to Elberton.

The move took place during the March spring break, a few days after Sara's ninth birthday. Dee and Dan helped the Rafferty family move.

Dan's and Emmy's parents, known as Mom and Pop Jax, had always named their cars and trucks. Emmy and Dan continued the tradition by naming Emmy's van Long John Silver and Dan's white truck became Casper. Wascal's crate filled the space where the bench seat had been folded away, in the back of Long John Silver. The black Labrador watched as Dee and Emmy placed houseplants on one side of the cage. Boxes of Emmy's precious family photos filled the space on the other side. His empty water bowl and a partial bag of dog food went in last.

The family vehicles pulled out of the Hilton Head Island driveway with Fred's blue truck, Elvis, in the lead. The outdoor potted plants sat near the cab of the truck, catching Fred's attention as they waved in the wind. The boys' bicycles lay against the pots ensuring the pots stayed in their assigned places. He planned to catch up with the moving van before it reached the new house, even if meant skipping lunch.

Dan's white truck, Casper, loaded with a glass patio table and breakable yard art, followed Fred. Emmy's van completed the convoy as it headed to the Sweet City Community just outside Elberton near Dee's and Dan's house.

Non-threatening white clouds floated in a powder blue sky as the entourage made its way off the island. Dee felt the perfect weather was a good omen. With eleven-year-old Hank and six-year-old James buckled safely in the middle seats of the van, she wondered, *Have we managed to avoid a catastrophe? Or, will it follow us to Elberton?* She hoped the white-framed house near Nickville Road and familiarity with the area would bring back a sense of security and normalcy to Emmy and her family.

Fred arrived at the new house about the same time as the mover's van pulled into the driveway. Within the hour, all the family vehicles were parked in the yard and driveway. Mom and Pop Jax and Sara arrived after the movers left.

Dee watched as Mom Jax smiled and smiled. Finally, she asked, "What's up, Mom Jax? You look like the cat that swallowed the canary."

"I want to tell everybody at the same time. I'm so excited." She squeezed Dee's hand and called out, "Hey y'all. Let's take a break. I've got snacks and drinks set up, out here in Pop's pickup truck. Come on." She took Dee's arm and led her to the truck.

When they had gathered around the truck, Mom Jax stood on the runner board and announced, "Your Pop is going to build us a pool." She hesitated, waiting for the news to make its impact. "Tell them, Pop." She looked at her husband.

Embarrassed by the attention, his ruddy complexion turned red, making his blue eyes more prominent. His normally shy voice boomed, "I'm building a pool for us. It should be ready by the time the weather warms up."

Everyone clamored around him, laughing and slapping him on the back. After the others drifted away, Dan asked, "What's up, Dad? I thought you said it would be a snow day in hell before you'd do such a foolish thing."

"Son, I didn't have a choice. Your mama has her heart set on it, and the city folks are talking about including our street in a request to put the whole damn area on the Historical Register. If I don't do it now, and they get their way, we won't be able to change anything."

He said he believed in preserving history and went on to describe how some houses, a few blocks away, are deteriorating fast and the owners can't afford to abide by the strict guidelines imposed on historical buildings.

"You were a baby when we took the wood siding off, bricked the house and built the garage – without getting approval from every Tom, Dick and Harry. Besides, a pool will make your mama happy. She said if we don't do it while the grandkids are little, she doesn't want it done at all. She can be mightily persuasive." He winked at Dan. "My daddy built our house when a man could build a home without asking permission from a dozen people. Nowadays, you can't do nothing without approval from somebody in the government. Damn shame."

Dee noticed her husband and his father talking, and then glanced at Emmy hugging her boys before letting them climb into the back bench-seat of Pop Jax's pickup truck to make the trip to their grandparents' house to spend the night. She watched Sara take Wascal to the fenced back yard. After closing the gate behind her, Sara returned to the van, pulled the bag of dog food and Wascal's bowl from Long John Silver and returned to the back yard. The dog waited, his long tail wagging vigorously. Dee wondered again, *Have we managed to avoid a catastrophe?*

The smell of spring flowers and the lacy shapes and pale greens in the new growth of hardwood trees reminded Dee of the promise she made to Sara during the winter months and prompted a trip to the secretive and mysterious Georgia Guidestones on Highway 77, north of Elberton. When she saw the huge granite slabs on a hill, Dee told Sara to look to the right. Immediately, she heard the girl draw in a quick breath.

The May sky matched the deep blue in Sara's eyes. The sun shining through the car's window created shadows that moved across her white cotton blouse as the car slowed. Her eyes sparkled when she saw the enormous blue-gray granite slabs of the Georgia Guidestones standing majestically inside a designated area within a large pasture.

Dee turned onto a short side road and parked the car in a graveled area near the stones. She and Sara stepped over wooden railway ties partially buried in the Georgia red dirt. The ties separated the parking area from the open space reserved for the stones, the historical marker, and the large slab containing specific information about the languages, structure, and dimensions of the stones. Evergreen shrubs partially hid the fencing bordering the remaining three sides of the park. Beyond a fence bordering the park, cows grazed in a nearby pasture.

Dee put her arm around Sara's shoulders as they made their way across the grass to the stones. Dee's shoulder length, dark hair contrasted with her daughter's natural red curls. Their light complexions and perky noses left no doubt about the family connection. Sara's intensely blue eyes didn't match the dark green and brown in Dee's eyes or the blue-green of her father's eyes. Only one other member of Dee's family could lay claim to those startling blue eyes – Dee's clairvoyant Aunt Connie.

The way Sara ran to the huge slabs of granite and slowly walked around them, letting her fingers brush each one as she passed it, reminded Dee of the first visit she made to the stones. Sara stopped when she arrived at the stone bearing the English version of the message. She backed away in order to see the entire message. Shading her eyes with her hand, she started reading out loud, "Maintain human-i-ty under . . . How many is that?"

Dee walked closer, "It's five hundred million, sweetie." Because Sara worried too much, her mother chose not to tell her the world population already exceeded that number. Dee didn't want Sara to have a difficult time dealing with the message on the stones.

"That's a lot." Sara added, "A whole lot of people." She continued, "with nature. Guide re-pro . . ."

"Reproduction. It means having children and says to have children in a wise way. Want me to finish reading? It's really hard for you to see way up there."

"Sure," Sara agreed.

Dee's tight-fitting black jeans stretched with her when she stood tall, her frame reaching its full five feet, seven inches. She read, "It says to improve on health, talks about including diversity, which means to involve all the different people of the world. The next one says to create a new language for all of us to use. The fourth one says, reason should rule over passion, faith or tradition. I think that means be fair to everyone, regardless of the church they go to or if they don't go to church at all. It also means that just because we've done things one way all our lives, we shouldn't try to make others be just like us."

Dee watched as Sara walked closer to the stones and used her index finger on her left hand to follow the letters cut in the stone.

Dee continued, "The fifth one wants us to protect people by making good and fair laws and the sixth one follows that, saying we should rule our nations ourselves, but set up a world court to resolve world disputes. The seventh one tells us not to waste time with petty laws and useless officials. The eighth one goes on to say we should balance personal rights with social duties. I think that means we are all responsible for making things right, and we should take care of each other."

"Mommy, it sounds like it's hard things for us to do."

"Some are hard, but others are easy. Like this next one. It says we should value telling the truth, beautiful things, and love. Now, I like that don't you?" Dee smiled at Sara.

"Yeah." Sara leaned against her mother.

"We're almost finished. It says to seek harmony with the infinite. I think that means we should appreciate our lives and try to understand where we came from and appreciate being created. The last one says we shouldn't do bad things to the earth. It reads, 'Be not a cancer on the earth.' It also says that we should leave room for nature. It says that twice." Dee looked at Sara to get her reaction.

"I know what that cancer on the earth thing is. It's like when the oil people let all that oil out in the ocean. Remember how the white sand turned orangey brown and the oil killed those turtles?"

"You're so smart." Dee took Sara's hand and led her to the slab of granite on the ground to the right of the stones. "Look here. This says there's a time capsule buried under here. This huge slab was probably put here the same time as the Guidestones in 1980. But look at this." Dee knelt down and read. "To be opened …" She looked up at Sara.

Sara knelt down beside her mother. "No date. When will they open it?"

"I don't know. There's a lot of mystery about the stones. No one knows who wanted them so much they paid lots of money to have them put up. Opening the capsule is another mystery. Maybe somebody has it in a will. When they die, their will just might state the day the capsule can be opened. I bet all the secrets are in the capsule. Maybe we'll have all the answers then."

The sound of tires crunching on gravel made Dee look up in time to see a van pulling into the parking space beside her Prius. A dozen people piled out. The tour guide separated herself from the crowd, held up a book with a picture of the Georgia Guidestones on the cover, and led the group to the English version of the message. After discussing each of the ten guidelines within the message, she went back to the top one listing five hundred million people as the number that should inhabit the earth. She talked about another group of people who believed the message meant that the current world population of more than a billion would necessitate the killing of many people to get back to the desired number.

Dee and Sara stood up and walked toward their car. Dee hesitated when she heard the tour guide explain how the interpretation could mean five hundred billion instead of five hundred million if the message had been translated from a different numerical system, such as Sanskrit. This particular theory came from a Middle Eastern man who participated in one of her tours. He drew the formula for her the day of the tour, and it made sense that the number changed during translation.

Dee listened as the guide told the group how some people associate the message with the apocalypse and believe the message is intended to guide the survivors of the apocalypse to an age of reason.

The guide explained rumors that Ted Turner may have participated in some way with the stones or a Rosicrucian individual or group may have financed the message. She talked about how their beliefs didn't match those of the Roman Catholic Church, forcing them to go underground.

Dee could hardly wait to look up the Rosicrucian movement. It was her first encounter with the name. The tour guide's next theory came as a complete surprise to Dee. The guide said some people connected the name, Rosicrucian, with the person using the pseudonym R. C. Christian, who made a visit to Elberton to choose the site, enable payment, and ensure the message reflected the intent of the financiers.

Bored and restless, Sara shifted her weight from one foot to the other and tugged on her mother's short-sleeved khaki jacket. Dee looked down into Sara's face and realized her daughter's interest ended a while back.

As Dee and Sara turned to leave, the tour guide asked Dee to take a picture of the group. The guide and her people quickly lined up in front of the stones. Sara walked towards the car, kicking clumps of dirt and grass on the way. Dee took a couple of pictures with the guide's camera. Several tour participants also asked Dee to take photos with their cameras.

Sara continued kicking clumps of dirt and grass. Dee caught up with her just as Sara kicked a fire ant hill. She pulled Sara back from the red mound as the ants scattered in every direction. Dee bent down and swiped several ants from her daughter's shoes. Some made their way inside her socks, and Sara jumped up and down as the ants bit her legs and ankles. Dee swooped her up and placed her sideways in the back passenger seat of her car. With Sara's legs dangling outside, Dee pulled off her daughter's socks and shoes. The red bumps appeared immediately.

Sara whined and fidgeted over the ant bites. The more she scratched, the more they burned and itched.

"I hate these things. Mommy, do something." Sara's unhappiness was obvious as her complexion turned red from anxiety.

To try and keep the ants out of the car, Dee stepped back, shook Sara's socks, and banged the shoes together. Several ants fell on the gravel.

On the way home, Dee tried to get Sara's mind off the ant bites. Even though she knew she was pushing her luck on the subject of the Guidestones, she pointed to a highway road sign. She told Sara how seventy-seven seemed to be a theme around the Guidestones, especially since they were located 7.7 miles from Elberton on Highway 77.

"I understand there's a 7.7-acre farm around here somewhere." Dee watched Sara in the rear view mirror. Her serious expression surprised Dee.

"Did you see those bad words somebody wrote on the stones?"

"I saw the graffiti," Dee answered. She hoped Sara hadn't paid any attention to the crudely drawn phallic symbol and ugly words.

"Are they evil?" Sara continued her questions about the stones.

"The stones aren't evil. Some people think they cater to bad witches and have some evil intent. But, you saw the message. It's about taking care of the earth. Some people find evil in lots of things, because they're looking for it." Dee looked into the rear view mirror again. "When we get home, we'll look up Stonehenge and you can compare the stones in Elberton to England's stones."

Sara alternated scratching the ant bites and balling her hands into fists. Her noisy whining made the trip through Elberton to the Sweet City Community miserable for both mother and daughter. Dee let out a sigh of relief when she saw their brick house on the hill. It was the only home Sara knew. She and Dan bought it just before Sara was born. Dee pulled into the drive and pressed a button above the rear view mirror. The garage door opened slowly. Normally, Sara would walk to the backyard fence, open the gate, and pet Suede. His huge yellow eyes watched as Dee and Sara entered the house through the kitchen door. They ignored the silver brown dog with its wagging tail. Suede flopped down on the grass.

Sara sat on a stool at the island in the kitchen. Her feet kicked back and forth under the edge of the multi-colored granite countertop that separated the kitchen from the breakfast area. She beat her right fist on the earth tone swirls of the countertop and used her left hand to scratch the ant bites. She squirmed and made faces as if she were dying. Dee found anti-itch medicine for the ant bites and smeared the cream on the inflamed spots. She took Sara's hand, led her to the brown leather sofa in the den, and placed the television remote in her hand. Sara immediately started channel surfing.

By the time Dee was back in the kitchen, she heard the chime announcing the opening of the outside door. Dee assumed Sara finally remembered Suede and let him inside. Shortly after, she heard the music and introduction of a comedy television show, followed by Sara's laughter. Dee thought about how Sara's clairvoyant gift made her seem more mature than her nine years; yet, her childish response to the ant bites left no doubt about her daughter's immaturity. Dee took the time to glance into the den. Suede lay on his side in front of Sara's chair, his long legs stretched toward the television set, with his back propped against Sara's chair. Sara's bare feet moved back and forth across the dog's back.

Dee took her phone from her purse. She felt certain Dan would love to have a picture of Sara giving Suede a foot massage. Sara, totally immersed in the funny videos, and Suede, completely content with Sara's attention, never acknowledged Dee's presence. She took the picture, sent it to Dan's e-mail address, and walked back into the kitchen.

A stack of Sara's drawings lay on the kitchen table. Dee sat down and pulled the stack closer and smiled at the huge sunflower covering the entire page of the top drawing. As she looked closer, she saw how the brown center of the flower consisted of letters from Sara's name in lower case, repeated again and again filling the center and framed by yellow petals. The second picture in the stack, a three-headed woman with their torsos coming together at the waist and only one set of legs, made her shiver. Each head sported a different hair color and style. Narrow empty eyes looked out from each face with identical turned-down, narrow lips. The shape and size of the eyebrows changed from face to face.

After the show was over, Sara came into the kitchen for a snack. Dee asked her about the picture. Sara pointed to the woman, touching each head, and explained to her mother how the three heads were the same woman. She said the woman was evil.

Dee looked at Sara and asked why she thought the woman was evil instead of just bad.

"It's 'cause the mean ole woman can't have a boy of her own. She wants somebody else's little blond headed boy." Sara added, "Mollie said I should draw this ca. . ca. . . million." Sarah titled the picture, "Mollie's Evil Woman" in the bottom right corner. She considered it a work in progress.

"Honey, I think you mean chameleon. You know, it's the little lizard that can change colors. We saw one at the park not long ago."

The following day, the picture still haunted Dee. It was hard to forget the woman who morphed from a dark haired person to an overweight blond woman to a small woman with short auburn hair and masculine features. Dee knew Sara had completely forgotten about the woman with three heads. Dee remembered. She walked into the den and looked at the blond-haired boy in the family photograph on the mantel. Dee knew the drawing of the three-headed woman had psychic significance. She wondered, *How significant? And, what can I do about it?*

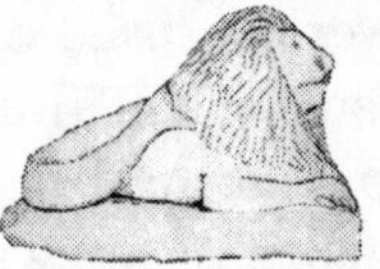

Chapter Three – The Jackson Pyramid

The refrigerator attested to the family's love of Suede. Sara's drawing of the dog and a limerick she wrote about him hung on the door. Magnets held several photographs in a haphazard display on the lower part of the door – below the dog's picture. Dee couldn't resist reading Sara's limerick, a recent school project. Sara's English teacher's large red A+ in the top right corner made Dee proud. She couldn't help but hear the cadence of the poem, even as she read silently:

His After Dinner Dance

After his dinner he comes through the door
His paws a tapping on the kitchen floor
He sniffs around
No food is found
He's had his dinner, but he still wants more

Ready for a comfortable night at home, Dee showered and dressed in old red sweat pants and a worn gray T-shirt. She placed leftover meatloaf and macaroni and cheese in the oven to heat before stepping into her small office and switching on her computer. Her laptop died several months before, leaving her dependent on the desktop computer. The screensaver came up with one of the Jackson family's beach photographs from their vacation the summer before. Dee's fingers hovered above the keyboard, reluctant to move on. She loved the title she gave the group of pictures: *The Jackson Pyramid*. The background of white sand dunes, green seaweed, and blue skies made the perfect setting.

Dee's mother-in-law, Emily Jackson, had arranged for a professional photographer to take pictures with the girls dressed in white sundresses and the guys dressed in white shirts and khaki pants. Mom and Pop Jax sat on the top step. Ron Jackson's soft blue eyes contrasted with his ruddy complexion, thick neck, and crew cut gray hair. He looked the same as the day Dee met him for the first time more than ten years before. Weekly visits to the hairdresser kept the gray out of Mom Jax's hair, leaving it an artificial auburn, close to her natural hair color. Mom Jax rested her arm on her husband's leg, her light green eyes looking adoringly at her children and grandchildren while her husband looked at her.

Dee, Dan and Sara sat below them on the second step. Sara smiled at her five-year-old blond cousin, James, her hand resting on his shoulder. He sat one step below Sara, with his mother, Emmy, and his father, Fred. Hank sat on the step below them, holding a seashell in the air. He appeared to be handing it to his mother. The photographer did an excellent job making the family look natural instead of posed. Dee loved the entire set of photographs. She purchased almost all the pictures in the portfolio. Dan gave her a hard time about buying so many.

She seldom argued with Dan, letting him have his way about most things; however, she reminded him of how his recent credit card charges played havoc with the family's budget. She told him if he could buy clothes from an expensive store when he was in Texas, she could certainly afford family pictures.

The screensaver photo made Sara's red hair look darker than it really was. Sara's childhood games almost always reflected age appropriate behavior regardless of any gift she inherited. She still enjoyed "knock-knock" jokes. She failed dismally in trying to show James how much fun the jokes could be.

Smiling at the memory, Dee recalled Sara telling a knock-knock joke to James, "Knock. Knock."

James turned his blond head to look at Sara, waiting for her to say something else.

Sara waited, too. Finally, she told him, "You're supposed to say, 'Who's there?'"

Irritated, he asked, "Who's there?"

"Barbie."

"Barbie's not a joke. She's a stupid doll."

Sara said, "You're supposed to say, "Barbie who? And, then, I say 'Barbie, Doll.'"

"I'm not your doll." James made a joke of his own. "Knock. Knock." He waited for Sara's response.

"Who's there?"

"James."

"No. It's not like that. You don't say your own name."

"I can if I want to, Sasa." He used the nickname he gave her when he first learned to talk. "You tell poopy jokes." His green eyes narrowed to ensure she understood just how much he didn't like her knock-knock jokes.

Sara interrupted Dee's trip down memory lane when she came into the room and reminded her mother about the promise she made to let her read about England's stones. Dee typed Stonehenge into the computer's search engine and within seconds she left Sara looking at one of England's most popular destinations.

Dee checked on dinner and sat on a stool at the kitchen's island. She propped her elbows on the counter. The cliché, *familiarity breeds contempt,* came to mind. She thought familiarity might grow into a lifelong relationship of love that ebbs and flows like a river. Dee's thoughts centered on her family and how she loved Dan Jackson the first time she saw him at Emmy's graduation ceremony at the University of Georgia. At the time, he was in a relationship.

Disappointed and certain she didn't have a chance to be an important part of his life, she tried to forget him. A year later he was free, and when Dee discovered Dan was as interested in her as she was in him, her life changed. Like the river, their relationship had ups and downs. For her, familiarity with Dan certainly didn't breed contempt. His red hair changed to a darker brown within the past five years. The few gray strands at his temples made him look distinguished. The slight tummy bulge above his belt changed his shape; otherwise, her Daniel, as she liked to call him, remained the same man with whom she fell in love.

She had never been so physically drawn to anyone before Dan. The unimaginable visions almost ruined her future with him and jeopardized the deep love growing between them. *Mollie's disappearance in 1960,* Dee thought as she remembered how it took many months of visions from Mollie and investigations in two states for Dee to find Mollie's remains and her killer. In the end Mollie, from her grave, gave Dee something no one else could – completion of her family tree. Dee's father, adopted as an infant, left a short biological branch on the family tree. Mollie and her family filled the void. Dee's thoughts went back to Dan and Sara.

With her hands held as if she was praying, she softly said, "Thanks,

Dan, for giving me Sara. What a blessing." She raised her face to the heavens and added, "Thanks for not letting the 'Mollie experience' compromise my job." She loved the history of the granite business and passed on Elberton's rich background to the local students in her history classes.

"Mommy?" Sara hopped on the stool beside her mother.

Dee looked at her daughter and wondered if she said her prayer out loud. Sara immediately confirmed Dee's suspicions.

"Who you talking to?" Sara asked. "You said Daddy's name, but he's not here."

"Oh. Just trying to be thankful for all my blessings. You're one of those. I'm thankful for you, my love." Dee got out of her chair at the kitchen's island and walked toward the pantry. "You hungry?"

Sara nodded her head up and down in answer as she quietly watched her mother drain a can of green beans. Dee cut half an onion in small strips, dropped them into a skillet with a splash of olive oil, and added the green beans. The room filled with an appetizing aroma as she sautéed the mixture. When all the liquid disappeared, she switched off the burner, took the meatloaf and macaroni and cheese from the oven, and placed them on the stove top with the beans. She saw Suede watching and waiting, with his nostrils sniffing in the air and drool moistening his big pink lips.

"How's about we eat right here?" she asked and handed Sara two plates. Sara took one plate and placed the other one nearby for her mother. Dee gave Sara the forks and napkins. As Dee served their plates, Sara asked if she could call her daddy after dinner.

"Sure." Dee turned just in time to grab Suede's collar and pull him away from the meatloaf. "You need to feed Suede before we eat."

Sara took a treat from the pantry and held it in front of Suede's nose to draw his attention from the smell of the meatloaf so she could lead him outside. She filled his bowl and added water to the dog's large metal water pail before joining Dee inside.

A half-hour after dinner, Sara let Suede back inside where he climbed into Dan's favorite chair, turned around twice and curled up between the leather arms. Almost immediately, his droopy eyelids closed and he was asleep before Sara made the call to her father. Lightly rubbing Suede's soft thin ears, she heard the ringing of her dad's cell phone. She listened to his message and waited for the tone before asking him to call her back. She told him she loved him and said goodbye. She fell asleep on the sofa waiting for him to call. She barely remembered her mother waking her, helping her to the bedroom, and tucking her in.

Dee used the quiet time to find out about the Rosicrucian people she heard about when she and Sara visited the Georgia Guidestones. She did a search on the computer for "Rosicrucian." The results were confusing. The cross with a rose theme seemed to be consistent. From there, the paths diverged in so many directions she knew she'd never have time to sort them out in one evening.

She decided to use the theories she learned about the Georgia Guidestones as a part of class curriculum, which would require further exploration. She could assign homework to the students with the intent of finding a link to Ted Turner, the Apocalypse, a time capsule, and the Rosicrucian people. She felt certain that many of her students would feel challenged. She certainly felt excited to learn something new and interesting. She put Suede out for a potty break.

Dan called at ten o'clock and explained how he left work late and gone to dinner with his boss. When he hesitated, Dee said, "Okay, I'll —"

Dan interrupted, "See you tomorrow night."

She heard the dial tone. As she placed the receiver in its holder she wondered if he thought she would give him a hard time and accuse him of neglecting Sara. Dee felt the chill of the night air as she opened the door to let Suede in for the night. He made his way into the utility room, ran inside his crate, and flopped down on his large doggy cushion. Dee closed the metal-framed door and latched it. The cool air followed her through the house and down the hallway to her bedroom.

She wanted to tell Dan about Sara's drawing of the sinister woman. She wouldn't tell him how sure she was that the woman would impact their family in some way. She knew he didn't appreciate her intuition and he denied that Sara inherited a special gift.

Dee knew about loss, not only from the death of her father two years before, but from Mollie's short life too. Dee felt the same fear Mollie experienced. Dee stopped talking about how she knew things about Mollie. She learned fast that no one wanted to accept the visions she'd seen. Long ago she stopped telling people how Mollie intervened to save her life.

Years ago Mollie, in a dream, told Dee to use the same stubbornness she used to survive a vicious attack from Dun Dunsman to accept Dan's apology for not being there when she needed him. He found it difficult to understand her visions and distanced himself from her for several weeks. The visions subsided after she found Mollie's remains and obtained justice against Mollie's rapist. Resting in peace, Mollie didn't need to send visions of the past to Dee. Dee and Dan married in less than a year after finding Mollie's remains.

Thinking of loss brought her thoughts back to losing her father. He had always been her rock. When she moved to Elberton, she never dreamed the change would lead to finding her father's biological family, including his dead sister, Mollie, and a brother living in South Carolina. The blood kin to Mollie through her dad's side of the family and the genes from her mother's side enabled her to receive visions from Mollie.

Dee's mother ignored her own sister's psychic ability and chose to pretend that Dee's propensity to see visions didn't exist. Dee longed to tell her mother how concerned she was when Sara talked with Mollie. Sara's imaginary friends didn't always act like typical childhood imaginary friends. They often shared true and believable information. Like Dee, Sara kept that side of herself private, even though they were open with each other about Sara's extraordinary gift.

Dee often talked with Aunt Connie about ways to keep the negative side effects of Sara's ability to a minimum. She and her aunt considered Sara's clairvoyance a gift to be used carefully. *Would Connie know how to protect Emmy's family? Could she interpret Sara's drawings?*

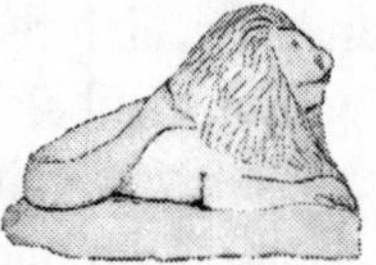

Chapter Four – The Sea Lion

Several envelopes and magazines on the island countertop caught Dee's attention as she walked from the back door into the kitchen. Dan's note, letting Dee know he and Sara had gone to the Pizzeria and would soon be home with dinner, sat on top of an envelope from her mother. Dee had spent two days helping Emmy set up a nursery, moving James' belongings to Hank's room – a room the boys would share. Emmy said that if James was unhappy, they would move Fred's office into the dining room, and James would have his own room.

Fred worked in the middle of Marcie's room, setting up the crib, while Emmy and Dee worked around him. Considering Emmy's condition, Dee didn't allow her to lift or move the boxes. She kept that chore for herself. By the time Dee arrived home, every muscle in her body screamed for relief.

Thankful for not having to make dinner, she flopped down on the den sofa with the mail and opened her mother's envelope first. The invitation read, "The Q-tips are having a party and you're invited!" *What on earth?* Dee's brow wrinkled as she puzzled over the information. The invitation stated a date and time to celebrate her mother's and her aunts' "Early Summer Party."

Dee looked inside the thick envelope to see if she had missed something. She pulled out a picture and laughed at the four white heads of hair. The picture didn't show their faces or how The Girls shared the same light complexion, freckles and smile. In the past, their hair color, height and sizes reflected their individuality. That is until they got to be senior citizens. As the picture showed, age made them look so much alike that some of their grandchildren got them mixed up, especially after they all left off the hair dye.

Dee wouldn't have known which white head belonged to her mother if their names weren't included. Her Aunt Becky, at the top left was the oldest, with Aunt Connie, just below her. Aunt Pat's head was below Dee's mother's head, Anna Marie, the youngest. The picture, with a view of the backs of their heads didn't show that Anna Marie stood taller than the others. It was a funny invitation. A smile lingered on Dee's face when Dan and Sara walked through the back door with a pizza. She met them in the kitchen.

"Thought you'd be tired and grumpy. Instead, here you are with a smile on your face. What's up?" Dan asked.

She handed Dan the invitation from The Girls and gave him a quick kiss on the cheek, followed by a hug for Sara. "Mom sent this funny invitation." She waited for Dan to read the invitation before handing him the picture.

"It's good they put the names on those heads. They all look just alike." Dan handed the picture to Sara. "Look at Mama Anna and her sisters. Aren't they funny?"

"Yeah. She said they'd have to do this – 'cause I called 'em Q-tip heads on Mother's Day. Remember Mommy?"

"No. I don't remember." Dee answered, knowing it had to be recent since her mother and her sisters stopped coloring their hair only two years before.

"I remember Mama Anna telling me she liked it. Guess she liked it a lot. Big Q-tip heads," Sara said as she touched each head. She handed the picture to Dee.

"Ummm. Thanks, you two, for making a pizza run. I don't think I could do one more thing today." Dee gave Dan a sideways hug and a kiss on the cheek, and thought, *Thank heaven. He's going to be home for a whole week.*

The old saying about not being able to go back home because things won't ever be the same didn't apply to Emmy. She missed her hometown and the friends she'd known for a lifetime. As soon as her family settled into their new house on the Athens Highway, she picked up where she left off with the volunteer work at the old Elbert Theatre, spending time with childhood friends who still lived in Elberton, and enjoying her close knit family.

Fred's fantastic raise with an annual bonus at the end of the calendar year made the Raffertys' lives easier. Emmy loved being a stay-at-home mom. She considered it a real blessing to be able to stay home with the boys. Knowing she didn't have to go back to work after the birth of their third child made her pregnancy easier.

Having time to taxi them from place to place helped her keep the boys busy in a constructive way. The Elbert County Library became a favorite hangout for Hank and James. They seldom missed a children's author's reading or a game day planned by the staff.

Hank grew up around all sorts of cultural events at Hilton Head Island. He had been especially fond of plays and enjoyed a small part in "Oklahoma" at a local theater on the island, just before the move back to Elberton. His love of acting started in the third grade when his teacher encouraged him to sing in the school's rendition of "Oliver." Like his daddy, his curly dark hair, black eyebrows, and long eyelashes highlighted his light complexion. His good looks and ability to sing made him a natural for the theater. The pride she felt made her smile.

Emmy, excited about Hank's most recent audition at the Elbert Theatre where he earned a leading role in a play called "Our Rocky," committed to the many trips she'd have to make to the theater for play practice. Hank would be one of three boys who taunted a mute man with Down syndrome as he walked home from his job at his uncle's store in town. Emmy began to see a difference in Hank's attitude as he learned the lines of his character. In the past, she corrected him for being insensitive when he called a handicapped person a retard or retarded. She noticed, except when practicing his lines for the play, he never referred to Rocky as a retard. Hank's solo part included singing a verse of "*Ma, I Wanna be a Man*."

Rocky's character, played by a young Down syndrome man named Eli, required him to add padding to his middle and get a short haircut. He adopted the awkward gait of the character. After the third play practice, Emmy and Hank stopped by Mom and Pop Jax's house to get James.

Emmy overheard Hank ask his grandparents if they remembered Rocky.

Mom Jax answered first. "I remember him, but didn't really know him. When I saw Rocky, he was always with his mother. He lived on the other side of town and we didn't know much about Down syndrome. I had no idea what kind of person he was. I just knew he was strange. He seemed old, but Down syndrome children don't usually live to be old."

"I remember him," Pop Jax entered the conversation. "He was friendly and almost always smiled. I gave him a ride home a couple of times. Normally, he seemed happy to be out and about. I saw him angry once, but his mother knew how to calm him down." He took his glasses off and proceeded to clean them with the edge of his shirt. "She worked at the hospital. Answered the phone there, I think."

"Did he scare you?" Hank looked at his grandfather when he asked the question.

"No, not at all. A huge sports fan, he never missed a Blue Devils football game. Somebody always brought him to the Granite Bowl. Or, maybe he walked. Back then people walked more than they do now. It wasn't unusual to see him at out-of-town games with his uncle." He adjusted his glasses as he put them on.

"What happened to him?" Hank asked.

"I think he and his mother moved into a retirement community after she retired. I heard he passed away a year or so after they moved."

"How will they arrange the stage for this one? I can't imagine how they'll make that work." Mom Jax shook her head and shrugged

"It'll have a tree house on one side of the stage. They're making plans now. It'll have a road across the front with a street that turns at the tree house to Rocky's house at the back of the stage. Me and the other two boys will be in the tree house. We'll throw rocks at 'im ..." Hank placed emphasis on the fact that the rocks weren't real, "Pretend rocks."

"That's mean," James piped in.

"No it's not. You're too little to know – baby," Hank said.

"Am not. You not suppose to throw anything at 'im." James' eyes narrowed.

"It's all pretending." Hank looked at Emmy. "Mom, tell 'im. It's not real."

"James, you'll see. When we go to the play, you'll see how the three boys learn how to be nice to people, even when they're different." Emmy reached into her purse for the car keys and addressed her mother, "Thanks, Mom. I know James enjoyed hanging out here instead of running errands with me." She was almost to the door when she realized the boys weren't following. She kept walking as she called back to them, "Hey, guys. Let's go. Put a move on it."

On the way home, Emmy stopped at the traffic light at the corner of North Oliver and College Avenue. She signaled a left turn as an old black Honda stopped behind her. The driver sat low in the seat. Emmy watched in the rear view mirror and got a glimpse of the driver's face – a face that seemed slightly familiar. The car stayed behind her until Emmy turned into their drive.

Emmy watched until the black car was out of sight. Something familiar flitted through her mind. *What?* She couldn't quite decide. She wondered if she'd become paranoid.

The weekend before school closed for the summer, Dee got up early to go to her mother's for the Early Summer Q-tip Party. Anna Marie still lived in the house on the golf course her husband loved. Her three sisters lived in neighboring counties, so she felt no need to move even though the golf course didn't hold the same importance for her as it had for Sam.

Before getting on the road, Dee looked through the sliding glass door into the screened porch to make sure there were no unsuspecting birds. Then, she let Suede out. The screened door was always left open to ensure Suede a cool place out of the sun. The storms of the night before gave Dee reason to let him stay inside in his crate. Movement in the far right corner of the porch caught her eye. Two short fat birds scooted across the floor. They looked too heavy and compact to fly well. She slipped out the glass doors. Unlike most birds, they didn't fly high to escape. She shooed the songbirds out through the open screened door. She waited and watched from inside the house. The cute birds made their way into the shrubs, safely away from Suede before she let the dog out. Shortly after, she and Sara left for Marietta.

Dee enjoyed the drive through her mother's neighborhood. Knock Out Roses, in pink, red, and white bloomed in the yards. A few azalea blooms, left over from spring, dotted the edges of the golf course. Shades of green sprinkled the landscape. Large oak trees lined the streets and created lacy green canopies. Dee and Sara arrived before most of the cousins. Dee laughed out loud when she saw how all four women sported short haircuts with bangs. The teased and combed-over hairdos carried the Q-tip theme well. Light makeup gave each face a similar white complexion.

Dee looked around the room while Sara headed straight to her grandmother and gave her a hug. Dee thought about how the similarities of the sisters, stopped at the neck. The Girls' outfits were as different as could be. Anna Marie wore bright red pants with a rainbow colored open shirt over a white fitted sleeveless blouse. Her bright red and black earrings with a matching necklace fit her artsy personality.

Dee waved to her mother on the other side of the room as she walked toward Aunt Becky. Her aunt told her how difficult it was to date after being married and divorced. Dee invited her to visit Elberton if she wanted to get out of the Atlanta area for some time away from the singles' scene. Dee complimented her on her ability to keep off the fifty pounds she lost after a divorce from a narcissistic husband ten years earlier. A yellow and blue scarf floated down her aunt's torso over a yellow blouse that was tucked into white slacks. Single life suited Becky.

Dee's Aunt Pat's weight gain in the past few years showed in her round face. Her light pink short-sleeved jacket and matching pants blended with the white hair and makeup. Compared to her sisters, she looked sedate and non-descript. Dee had noticed how she stayed in the background when she and Sara arrived. Dee made it a point to visit with her until her children arrived.

After saying hello to her Aunt Pat's children, Dee made her way to Aunt Connie, who wore brown slacks with a long beige blouse. A wide brown leather belt hung around her waist with the buckle draped low to one side. Her Native American jewelry of turquoise set in silver complemented the outfit. Dee was surprised when Sara peeked from behind her great aunt Connie.

"You scared me, you rascal," Dee said.

Dee knew her daughter and aunt shared many character traits beyond the clairvoyance. Dee couldn't help but smile when Sara laughed and reached out to touch the turquoise stone resting on Connie's wrist. As a baby, Sara showed a preference to using her left hand over the right. Sara and Connie were the only left-handed people in the room. Their relationship gave new meaning to kindred spirits. After receiving a promise from her aunt for a private conversation, Dee left in search of her mother and found her in the kitchen.

Dispensing with the usual greetings of affection, Anna Marie asked, "Where's Dan?"

"Probably flying into the Atlanta airport as we speak." Dee pushed a strand of hair behind her ear.

"Is he coming to the party?" Anna Marie continued her questions.

"No. He said he'd be too tired." Dee avoided looking directly at her mother.

"Well. I never. He didn't come see me at Christmas either," Anna Marie complained.

"He's spending a lot of time on an important project in Texas. It's too bad he left his truck at the airport. I could've picked him up. I know he would have enjoyed your Q-tip party." Dee hugged her mother. "You guys are too funny. What did the Q-tips make for us to eat?"

"White stuff," Anna Marie responded as she handed Dee a plate of coconut candy.

"What's that?" Dee pointed to a platter in the middle of the table.

"Cheese balls made with white flour and white cheeses like Parmesan. We call them Q-tip balls." Anna Marie poked one in her mouth. "Ummmm. You'll love it. Tastes very Italian. Becky made those and white peach punch."

"It is good." Dee agreed and reached for a second cheese ball. "What's on the Ritz crackers?"

"Swiss cheese. It's rather simple. A slice of stuffed olive on the cracker, Swiss cheese cut out to fit the cracker and placed on top of the olive. Then, you melt the cheese. It doesn't take long. Leave it in the oven for a minute. I made it. It's an original," Anna Marie boasted.

Dee sampled a cracker and picked up a cucumber and cream cheese sandwich with the crusts cut away.

"Ummmm. Good. Who made these?" Dee took a bite of the white sandwich.

"Connie. Pat made the chicken salad sandwiches. I know Sara won't want the fancy stuff, so I baked French fries and chicken nuggets in the oven for her and the other children. She'll like the fluffy white candy Pat made. I'll save her a couple of pieces." Anna Marie opened a cabinet and took out a small plate.

"Thanks. I'll tell Sara." Dee left the kitchen. The living room was full of cousins. She spoke to several as she walked through the crowd.

Connie smiled as Dee approached.

"Do you know where Sara is?" Dee asked her aunt, placing her arm around thin narrow shoulders.

"She's looking for golf balls – over there," Connie pointed toward the trees separating the lawn and the well-kept golf course. "She's with Pat's grandson. She told him the golfers often hit the balls into her Mama Anna's yard." Connie looked back at Dee, "What's up? You said you wanted to talk."

"Let's go out back. I need to give Sara a message from Mom – about the food." She took her aunt's arm, leading her through the Florida room that also served as her mother's art studio with its large windows overlooking the golf course.

Sara and her cousin met them at the back door, holding handfuls of golf balls. Dee told them about the chicken nuggets and French fries. They hurried inside as Dee turned to Connie. "Sara's drawn a woman with three heads. Each head has a different hair color and style. Her narrow eyes are empty and haunting. Each head has the same turned-downed mouth. The eyebrows are different on each face. The picture is disturbing. I don't want to upset Sara by making a big deal of it. But, I don't want to ignore it either."

"Did Sara say anything when she drew it?"

"She says the three heads are the same woman. The woman has no children but wants someone's little boy. She said Mollie told her to draw it." Dee guided her aunt to a small black wrought iron table with two matching chairs, and sat down. "I meant to bring the drawing with me, but left it on the kitchen counter."

"E-mail a copy. I'll try and find out if Mollie wants Sara's help. That can happen. Or, maybe she's a threat to Sara or someone Sara loves. Or, it may be nothing. Try not to worry about it until we can get a handle on what it means."

"Thanks. You're the greatest. I suppose we better get inside before Mom comes looking for us." Dee's chair scraped the brick patio as she pushed it away from the table. She and Connie stood up.

As they walked back into the house, Dee thought about the times Connie used her psychic abilities to help the Decatur Police Department solve several crimes. Tired of worrying about the picture, she hoped her aunt would find it meant nothing at all. Still, the features of the faces in the picture floated through her mind's eye, making her uneasy. Dee wondered, as they made their way across the lawn, *Should I tell Aunt Connie that I believe it's James the woman's interested in? Nope. Too much information may bias her – or would it help?*

The day after the Q-tip party, Dee stood in her pajamas at the kitchen sink listening to a chorus from outside. Two birds outside the screened porch perched on a bird feeder bellowing their morning song. They looked like the songbirds she rescued from the screened porch. Prolonging the moment of beauty and song, she lingered at the sink.

Later that day, Dee and Emmy sat in pool chairs at the edge of Emmy's parents' new pool. The afternoon sun shimmered and sparkled on the water. A couple of feet away from their mothers, Sara and James bobbed in the water.

"I took Sara to the Elberton museum a while back. She loved it, especially the Sea Lion with its tail of a fish and head of a lion." Dee looked at Emmy and asked, "Do you think Hank and James might like to go?"

"Maybe I can take them before the baby comes." Emmy didn't sound excited about adding something to her "to do" list.

Dee offered, "I can take them when you're in the hospital. It'll give them something to do. I think Hank will like seeing Dutchy, the first soldier carved and erected on the Square. He'll like hearing how he was roped and pulled off his pedestal in the middle of the night. Dutchy's story is far more interesting than the Georgia Guidestones. Imagine people hating a granite statue enough to try and destroy it."

"That's a better plan. Thanks." Reaching over her large stomach, Emmy gathered the material of her white maternity pants, pulled the pants legs upward towards her cobalt blue blouse, and exposed her white legs to the sun. "Uuuugh. Like you, I should've worn shorts." Emmy looked enviously at Dee's sleeveless white and black striped top and white Bermuda shorts. She gazed wistfully at Dee's flat stomach. Maternity clothes were boring. She announced, "I'm going to the shade. It seems to be hot sooner than normal this year." Emmy grabbed the arms of the chair, hefted her pregnant body out of the chair, and moved to the shade under an umbrella.

"Mommy. Tell James about the Sea Lion," Sara requested as she clung to the side of the pool.

Dee told James the statue had been carved in an Elberton shed, by an Italian. It was a custom for Italian people to have a statue placed in the front of their house for good luck. For years and years the statue sat in the yard near the front door of the shed owner's house. After the man died, his daughter inherited the Sea Lion. She took it with her to her home in Alabama and, like her father, kept it in her front yard. When the woman fell ill and had to be hospitalized for several days, a thief took advantage of her absence and stole the family's good luck charm.

Sometime later, a local reporter heard the story of the Sea Lion's disappearance and ran an article in the newspaper asking for information leading to the whereabouts of the statue. An antiques dealer responded, saying he bought it. He returned the Sea Lion to its owner. In the meantime, the Elberton Granite Association built a museum and granite exhibit in Elberton. The nice lady decided it would be safer in its hometown and donated her family's Sea Lion to the museum.

Sara ended the story. "I saw the Sea Lion. It's carved from rock and was stolen. Because of good people, it found its way back home."

"I like that, Sasa," James said.

They all heard the gate open and saw Mom Jax with Granny Nida. The gate slammed shut as the two women stepped away from it. Granny Nida's walker scrapped the concrete as she made her way to the shaded table near Emmy. Granny Nida and her daughter continued arguing as they made slow progress across the patio.

The sun made Granny Nida's thin white hair shine and exposed the pink scalp between the curls. Bent over the walker, she came to a complete stop after each step. Her light blue slacks barely touched the tops of her white shoes. Even on a sunny day, she required long pants and sleeves to stay warm. The quarter-length sleeves of her white and blue striped blouse contrasted with old age spots and dark red bruises on her exposed lower arms – constant reminders of her age. When they finally made it to the table, Mom Jax held a chair for her mother.

Emily Jackson addressed her mother. "It's cur-mudgeon. Not crud-mudgeon."

"I said that old man at Elsburg Towers is a crudmudgeon, 'cause he's cruddy, not a cur. Curmudgeon makes him sound like a dog. He ain't that bad." Granny Nida looked at Emmy and ordered, "Tell yore mama that crud is a word and that makes crudmudgeon a word."

"I don't know. Never thought about the word in that context." Emmy was reluctant to get into a word battle with her grandmother.

Hank came out the back door, ran to the pool, and jumped in. The water splashed into the air like liquid fireworks and fell on everyone and everything within several feet.

Emmy shouted, "Henry Jackson Rafferty, if you do that again, you'll have to sit out for a long time. First of all, don't run. Second, if you want to jump in, jump at the other end where your splashes won't bother anybody." Emmy rolled her eyes and shook her head. She didn't realize she called him by his full name, Henry, after Fred's stepfather and her maiden name, Jackson.

In a much quieter voice, Emmy addressed the group at the table, "I don't know what I'm going to do with him. Since his twelfth birthday is coming up in a few weeks, he calls himself a *pre*-teenager. All he wants to do is hang out with his friends. You'd think he's a teenager already. He's certainly acting like it." Emmy shook her head again. "It's scary."

"Have you told him about the birds and bees?" Granny Nida asked.

"No. And that aspirin thing won't work on him," Emmy replied. "Besides, that's Fred's job. If this baby's a girl, I'll tell her. Fred can tell the boys."

"I know the aspirin won't work. It could've worked for you, missy, if you just listened to yore granny," Granny Nida looked at Emmy with impatience. "But, you shore need to tell Hank to keep it in his pants."

Emmy wondered how she got on Granny Nida's wrong side. When Granny Nida called someone missy, it meant trouble.

"Shhhh. Sara and James will hear you. It's hard enough having to deal with Hank's hormones. I don't need James asking questions. He's asked enough about this baby," Emmy admonished her grandmother. "The other day he asked me how she got in my stomach. I told him I'd have to think about that and get back to him. I'm trying to figure out just how much to tell him. I don't think he's ready for the full details."

"Granny Nida," Dee wanted to take the conversation to a less controversial topic, "What did the doctor say yesterday?"

"He says I'm fit as a fiddle."

Mom Jax looked at Dee, "Want to help me with some drinks? And, maybe a snack?"

Dee helped her mother-in-law bring out chocolate chip cookies and lemonade. She made a trip back to the kitchen for paper towels. With the roll of paper towels in her hand, Dee pushed the glass storm door out just as Emmy reached for it from the outside.

"Gotta make a pit stop." Emmy rubbed her large stomach. "I forgot just how pregnancy affects the bladder." Emmy stepped past Dee. She turned around, "Wait, Dee. I wanted to ask you if you'd noticed an old black Honda in town or on our road."

"No. Why?"

"I saw one the other day as I left town to go home. I could see the driver was a woman, but that was all. She drove behind me all the way to Sweet City. Then, she went on towards Athens. It spooked me. That's all. I'm easily spooked these days. It was probably nothing."

Emmy made her way to the hall bathroom. As she sat on the toilet thinking, she realized she should have told Dee about her last visit to her obstetrician. When she checked in, the receptionist mentioned her phone call the day before – a phone call Emmy didn't make. At the time, Emmy felt certain the girl had gotten her mixed up with someone else. Uneasiness seeped into her veins and spread through her body like a drug. She chided herself for being suspicious.

Emmy's question about the black Honda bothered Dee. Her mind put the question together with Sara's drawing of the woman with the three faces. When she got home, she attached the picture to an e-mail and sent it to Connie.

Early the following morning, Dee checked her e-mail and found a reply from Connie, saying she was certain the picture was connected to some action the woman was planning. She ended the message by mentioning a doctor's appointment, but didn't elaborate on the reason. Dee quickly e-mailed her back, thanking her for looking at the picture and asking her aunt to let her know why she was going to the doctor.

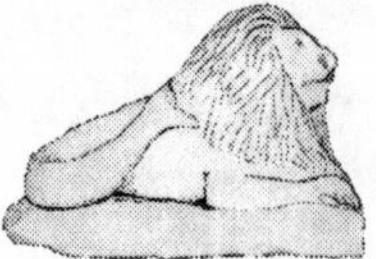

Chapter Five – Nan's Plan

"Nanette, darling. It's all right. Mother will make it okay." Nan woke up with her mother's words ringing in her head. Her short blue nightgown had bunched up around her waist above her white cotton panties. Wispy brown hair stuck to her cheeks and forehead.

The night hours brought back the dream of her mother giving her a hug when Nan told her she wanted to be a mother. She felt her mother's presence lingering long after the dream disappeared. She knew her mother wanted her to have whatever her heart desired, making Nan more determined than ever to have Timmy – regardless of what she had to do to make it happen.

When she was growing up, her mother covered for her when she got caught lying or stealing. If Nan wanted it, Nan got it. If she got in trouble at school, Mother took care of it. Once when a neighbor's dog chased her and made her fall, the dog disappeared. Nan knew her mother killed and buried it in their backyard. Nan needed a house for herself and her son. She knew exactly how to get it. She thought motherhood had eluded her because she didn't have the right home for Timmy. The lack of her own house spoiled her past chances of becoming a mother. She learned a lot from her mother.

Her mother constantly told her she gave her the prettiest name because she was the prettiest girl. Nan discovered she could be whatever she wanted, be it pretty, homely, or in between. She changed her looks on a whim. She did it for fun. She did it to get what she wanted. She did it to keep from getting caught for taking what she wanted.

The next step in planning her future included owning a house. Nan placed a picture of a small blond-haired boy on her mother's corner table in the living room of her retirement house. When her mother asked about the boy, Nan told her it was a boy she planned to adopt. Nan went on and on about the boy. Her Mother became excited with the thought of being a grandmother. Nan didn't want her mother's friends to be surprised when she showed up with Timmy.

Nan told her mother's friends and neighbors about her mother's diseased heart and told them it would upset her terribly to talk about it. They promised they wouldn't do anything to upset her mother. The secret was safe. No one questioned Nan's inheritance of the house on the island, or the fact that her mother died suddenly. There was just enough believability in Nan's story for it to work. Time was running out. Nan's thirty-eighth birthday was coming in the fall. She didn't want to be an old woman with a young child.

Her visits to the hospitals along the coast finally paid off. She saw her Timmy in the children's ward when he was in the hospital in Hilton Head Island recovering from a severe reaction to a wasp sting. She waited and watched the woman who sat with him, and hatched a plan when she saw the woman's baby bump. She followed them home. Later, through a map search on her computer, she found the homeowners' names. She used several locator programs to learn the names and ages of their children. When the family moved from the coast she thought she'd lost all hope of getting Timmy.

Early morning was Nan's favorite time of day. Dressed in thin beige slacks and a white blouse with three-quarter-length sleeves, Nan sat at her desk in the corner of her small living room. She typed Emmy Rafferty's name into the search box on the Facebook social network. The page came up showing where and when she finished high school. Nan searched classmates for the year Emmy finished high school until she found a classmate with a common first and last name. She managed to copy the picture and edit it slightly, then, use it as her own when she set up a new Facebook page. Just in case the woman was already a friend on Emmy's Facebook account, Nan filled in the profile information using a made up married name. The Rafferty woman had so many friends; she'd probably never notice a near duplicate. She gave herself a family, and added a few pictures she scanned from magazines, and sent the friend request.

Within twenty-four hours, Emmy responded, accepting the bogus information. When Emmy Rafferty accepted her as a friend, Nan was ecstatic. The woman's profile information still listed her residence as Hilton Head Island, South Carolina. Nan read Emmy's entries on Facebook several times every day, following her progress with the pregnancy and learning details about the Rafferty family and their friends.

When Nan saw Emmy's children's full names, she felt certain that divine intervention sent this family her way. The boy, James, fit her idea of the perfect son. Her own mother gave her the middle name of Jamie. James would be the male version of her name. *Timothy James, s*he thought, *I love it. It sounds perfect – just like my Timmy.*

It took a couple of months for everything to fall in place. Nan's plan for kidnapping her green-eyed boy revolved around the birth of the new baby.

When Emmy updated her profile information on Facebook, Nan learned where the Raffertys had moved. Not long afterwards, she made her first trip to their small town. She watched their house and followed the family into town. As soon as she saw Emmy Rafferty getting out of the car at the grocery store, she felt certain her old plan would work. Emmy Rafferty's baby bump of a few months before looked like a baby mountain as she stood by her car. Nan's heart raced when she saw the blond haired boy get out of the back passenger seat and take the woman's hand.

As a stranger in a small town, she knew she would stand out eventually. Disappointment at seeing Elberton didn't stop her scheming mind from working on other ways and places with the least chance of getting caught.

Her thin lips curved into a smile as she remembered the hours she spent on the computer checking out obstetricians in the area. A few phone calls verified her theory that most women do not deliver their babies in small town hospitals. Just when she thought she'd run into a roadblock, she saw a Facebook entry that told her what she wanted to know. Emmy Rafferty was on her way to see a doctor in Athens. Within a few days Nan not only knew Emmy Rafferty's doctor, she knew her choice of hospital as well as a projected delivery date.

Nan thought about how hard she worked to make her dreams come true. *This time, I'll have all I need.* She clicked them off in her mind: *Money to live on, a house to live in, and a precious little boy with whom I can share it all.*

Dee, Dan and Sara drove to Dee's mother's house to celebrate her mother's birthday with The Girls and their families. Dee took ham and potato salad, and made it back home with some of the ham left on the ham bone. The potato salad bowl came home empty.

The leftover ham had been put away before Suede was allowed in the house – the spiral slices of ham cut away and placed into plastic bags for sandwiches later that evening. The hambone was safely stored away, waiting for Dee to take it to Mom Jax to be used as seasoning for pinto beans. Even though Suede ate the scraps earlier, the lingering smell of ham led him to sniff every inch of the kitchen, with the hope of finding a morsel of forgotten food.

The next day, Dee opened the refrigerator with the intention of retrieving the hambone to take to her mother-in-law before she drove to her dentist's office. When she pulled out the large plastic bag, the hambone slid out and fell to the floor, leaving bits and pieces of ham scattered on the tile

After rescuing the hambone and rinsing it off, she realized the cleanup time was going to cause her to miss the appointment. *Suede,* she thought. She let him in and within minutes all the ham scraps disappeared. Suede licked the floor clean. Dee delivered the hambone to her mother-in-law and arrived for her dental appointment – on time. When she got out of the car, she saw an older model black Honda turning the corner. She wasn't close enough to see the tag. She watched as the car blended in with the traffic. She thought of Emmy asking her about a black Honda. It gave her the creeps.

Chapter Six – A Hot Summer Day

Dee's and Dan's anniversary, Saturday, the twelfth of June, fell on a hot sultry summer day. Dan chose to celebrate with a family gathering rather than their traditional intimate dinner for the two. Without asking Dee's opinion, he asked his mother to host a dinner to celebrate. His insistence on including his family disappointed Dee.

He left a card and bag from an upscale store in Houston, Texas, on the kitchen table earlier in the day before leaving to run errands. When she pulled out a fancy box of Beautifully Bold for Women perfume spray from the bag, she knew it was expensive. She tried to feel excited about it. It smelled vaguely familiar even though she knew she never owned any fragrance with such a large price tag attached. *How thoughtful*, she thought. *Just when I felt he was taking me for granted he gives me a special gift. I love Daniel Jackson.*

Her gift of a new wallet with a recent picture of Sara tucked inside seemed small. She decided to thank him for her perfume spray and give him his gift later that evening. Feeling the need to spend time with the most important man in her life, she planned to wear the fragrance, hoping to make it a night to remember – a toe curling-night. She smiled, thinking of the times his lovemaking had curled her toes and lifted her to the heavens.

Dan's assignments for the day included getting Granny Nida to the party. Halfway listening to her chatter, Dan helped her onto Casper's wide seat. "Up you go," he said as he lifted his grandmother into the truck. He pulled the belt across her rose-colored blouse, reached across her dark pink slacks and buckled her seat belt. He stored her walker behind the driver's front seat and said, "You look pretty in pink today." He closed her door, walked around the truck, and slipped into the driver's seat.

"You don't look bad yoreself." She smiled. He always made her feel good. As Dan buckled himself in, she asked, "Is my little Sara Lee still making up knock-knock jokes?"

"Yep. Some of them are pretty good, but some aren't too easy to follow."

"Knock. Knock." Granny Nida gave Dan a teasing look.

He responded, "Who's there?"

"Frank."

Dan wondered where this was going. "Frank who?"

In her best Rhett Butler voice she replied, "Frank-ly my de-ah, I don't give a damn."

Dan laughed his hearty laugh and added, "You probably don't want to share that joke with Sara. She might repeat it in Sunday school tomorrow."

"Oh no. I wouldn't do that. I'll think of another one for Sara Lee."

They arrived at his parents' house just as the Raffertys were getting out of Long John Silver. James came running to Dan, "When's Sasa gonna get here?"

"I thought they'd be here by now," he said as he reached behind the seat for his grandmother's walker.

"I want her to draw me the Sea Lion," James said.

Dan's cell phone rang. "Hi, Dee. Where are you?"

"I'm not far away. I stopped for gas. Will you ask your mom if she needs a bag of ice? I can get it here."

"Give me a minute. I'm helping Granny Nida get in the house. I'll call you right back." He placed his phone in his shirt pocket, looked at James and said, "They're on their way. Won't be long."

James ran ahead and held the glass storm door open.

Dan placed the walker at the top of the steps. To ensure Granny Nida didn't fall backwards from the step, he walked behind her and held both her elbows. He felt the door close behind.

"Gonna wait for Sasa out . . ." was all Dan heard as James ran toward the picnic table near the pool.

"Hey Fred-er, have I ever told you about how I like my bacon?" Granny Nida cornered Fred as soon as she got inside the house. Dan knew the story. Busy making Granny Nida a bacon and egg sandwich a couple of weekends earlier, she told him she preferred old man bacon. He asked, "What's that mean?"

She answered, "Not too stiff. Limp will do." Dan heard those same words directed at Fred and saw the grin Granny Nida couldn't hide. Dan chuckled when he saw his brother-in-law's face turn bright red. He heard Granny Nida's laugh as he walked away to find his mother.

In the kitchen, he sneaked up behind Mom Jax who jumped when he tapped her on the shoulder. He thanked her for hosting the party.

"Dee wants to know if we need ice." He sneaked an egg from the white porcelain deviled-egg dish.

"That would be nice," she said, giving him a playful slap on the hand for stealing the egg.

Dan pulled his cell phone from his pocket. It didn't take long for Dee to answer, "Hi, Daniel. What did she say?"

"Yes. We need more ice. By the way, tell Sara that James wants her to draw him a picture of the Sea Lion. Hope she has her markers and some paper."

"Not to worry. Mom Jax always has a good supply. Love —"

"See you in a little while," he interrupted and hit the end button on his phone.

Dee closed her cell phone, and then paid for a bag of ice. With the ice stored away behind the passenger seat, she relayed James' request about the Sea Lion to Sara as they drove through town. They arrived at the Jacksons' house with the ice and homemade potato salad. Dan sat in a chair to the left of the pool near where Pop Jax was turning hamburgers on the grill. Dan's funny grin made her smile as he got up to meet her. He grabbed the ice from its resting place, walked around to the driver's side of the car, gave Dee a quick kiss on the cheek and ruffled Sara's red curls. He explained how the hot weather forced the party inside as he opened the back door for his wife and daughter.

Laughter and noisy kitchen sounds greeted them as they entered. James ran to Sara chatting excitedly about her promise to draw the Sea Lion.

Sara confirmed the promise. "Soon as we eat, I'll draw the Sea Lion. And Mommy's promised to take us to the museum soon, so you and Hank can see it." She walked to a shelf below the television in the den and started looking through Mom Jax's stash of paper and pencils.

"Cool," James chirped.

"Sara, wait till after we eat, sugar," Mom Jax ordered. "Food's ready." She placed the deviled eggs on the dining room table.

They were almost finished with the meal when Mom Jax realized Emmy had eaten very little. "Emmy, you okay?"

"I'm not feeling that great. My back hurts."

"Does it feel like labor pains?" her mother asked.

"No, not really. It's more like a backache. I don't remember my labor pains starting with a backache with Hank and James." Emmy hesitated, "Ooooh! Yep, the hurt is low, but moving to the front."

Fred jumped up, ready to go. "It's almost an hour to Athens. Let's go."

"This is different," Emmy said. "I've carried her differently from the beginning. Ouch. Why would that change now?"

Fred looked worried, much more than Emmy. He pulled her chair back and tried to hurry her.

"Wait. I can't move this giant belly so fast. Slow down. We have to stop by the house and get the suitcase. Thank goodness it's packed and ready," Emmy said calmly.

"Go ahead," Mom Jax looked at Fred as she stepped to the other side of her daughter. "Call us when you get checked in at the hospital. Dee, you and Dan want to go with them? I'll keep the children. I'm sure they'd like to play in the pool for a while. Just keep me posted."

"We'll get your suitcase. We won't be far behind. It'll save you time." Dee said to Emmy as she unzipped the side pocket of her purse for her key to the Raffertys' house. "Got the key, right here." She dangled it in the air.

Mom and Pop Jax walked out and watched as their children and their spouses left for the hospital. Emily Jackson knew the process could take some time. Her daughter might not have this baby until tomorrow or the next day. The Jacksons held hands as they went back in the house. Mom Jax took the dishes from the children's table and replaced them with colored pencils and paper. Sara drew the Sea Lion for James and colored it light gray. She used a pencil to add darker gray speckles above the tail and lines around the face, creating the lion's thick mane.

"Lions ain't that color. They more yellowish and brown," James said as he offered her both yellow and brown colored pencils.

"Not this one. It's carved from rock. Like a lot of the rock you see around here." Sara picked up an ink pen, leaned over the paper, signed her name in the bottom right corner, and added the date. Before giving him the drawing, she wrote his name in big black letters in the top left corner. "Keep this one just for you, James Rafferty." She looked at him, "Keep it. Remember, I made it just for you." She pushed the paper across the table and wondered why she felt the need to emphasize James' name, or how she knew the Sea Lion would hold such importance in James' future.

"What's that thing in the tree?" James pointed to a spot to the right of the Sea Lion.

"Ummmm. It's the face of a beautiful princess. It was carved there to help the Sea Lion. I think." Sara tried to make sense of the face in the tree, where a limb once grew. She often saw images she didn't understand. It was part of her life, and the urge to pursue a matter – whether by drawing a picture or listening to Mollie – seemed natural.

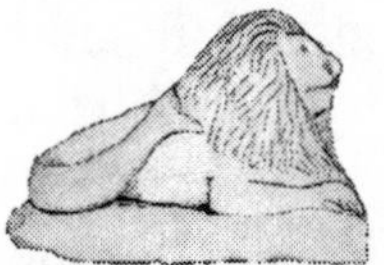

Chapter Seven – Little Timmy

Nan did her homework well, keeping track of Emmy Rafferty's visits to the obstetrician with just a couple of phone calls pretending to be Emmy. That's also how she knew which hospital Emmy would be in when she delivered the baby. Pretending to be Emmy made it possible to verify Emmy's choice of hospital, as listed in her records. Two weeks before the projected delivery date, Nan started calling the hospital every day asking if Emmy Rafferty had checked in. She knew the Rafferty woman wouldn't be chatting with friends on Facebook when she went into labor. Her tenacity paid off in less than a week.

She envisioned the time and effort it took to bring a newborn into the house. Little Timmy would be ignored. With an older brother and a new baby at home, there wouldn't be enough time for him. He would be so glad to have a mommy who could devote all her time to his every need. If he didn't show up at the hospital in Athens, she would have to go to Elberton to get him. She knew the window of opportunity would be very small. She planned to be creative and take advantage of a time when no one was watching. It was on a Saturday, after dinner, when she called the hospital in Athens and was told that Emmy Jackson Rafferty had checked in.

Wearing a long sleeved blue shirt and ankle length black pants for traveling, she thought of Timmy. *The perfect size. The perfect age. The perfect little boy.* To ensure success, she would have to change her look. As planned, she used her weight gain, the padding she would place around her middle and in her bra, as well as large non-descript clothing, to her advantage. The crusty dry spots of psoriasis forced her to cover her arms and legs. She finished dressing, added thick makeup and a blond wig to her overnight bag, and set the alarm clock to ring at four a.m. She slept in her beige recliner, dressed and ready for travel.

She left the island before the sun came up. The old black Honda served her well. Once again, it made the trip through Brunswick to I-95, to I-16 near Savannah, where she headed west. Three hours into the drive, she turned north on Highway 15 toward Athens. She used several older cars at different times in the past five years, to cover her tracks, and found they didn't draw attention and could be replaced easily. The old Chevrolet she owned before she became Nan Jones was a distant memory.

If the opportunity to take Timmy didn't come in the next day or two in the hospital, she'd go to her alternate plan and follow the family to Elberton. The love of her life waited. Years of dreaming about the green-eyed boy kept her working and scheming.

Dee noticed how Dan jumped at the chance to leave the hospital in the middle of the night when Fred told them the doctor said Emmy had dilated only a few centimeters and predicted mid-morning delivery.

Tired and sleepy, they fell into bed a few hours before dawn. Dee curled up behind her husband, absorbing the warmth from his familiar muscles. She placed her arm around his torso. Sleep came fast.

Dee woke to find Dan watching her sleep. He smiled as soon as he realized she was looking back at him.

"Morning," he said and looked away.

The phone rang. Dee heard her mother-in-law's excited voice as soon as Dan answered the phone. She waited, listening to the one-sided conversation.

"Marcie arrived at nine thirty-four, just as the doctor expected," Dan said as he placed the phone in its holder on his side of the bed. "I need to get on the road. I'm driving this time. Remember? I'm taking the boat with me. I'll stop by and see my new niece on the way. How about some breakfast. You mind cooking while I pack?"

"Sure. Eggs and bacon okay?" She asked absentmindedly while thinking of Emmy.

"I'd love one of your pour omelets, as you call them. Maybe some bacon on the side?" He turned and opened a dresser drawer. "Where's my underwear? They're not all here." His annoyance at not having everything at his fingertips showed.

"They're on the dryer. I've not gotten around to putting them away. I'll get them," she answered his last question first. "Oh, and I'll have your omelet ready by the time you finish packing." She handed him several dress shirts from the closet.

The smell of coffee greeted Dee as she entered the kitchen, making her wonder how long Dan had been awake. She walked through the kitchen to the laundry room and returned to the bedroom with a stack of underwear.

When she got back to the kitchen, she pulled out a container of no-fat, cholesterol-free eggs. She forgot that the omelet was his favorite. He often teased her about cooking with the eggs she poured from a carton. She had switched to the healthier eggs when his last checkup showed high blood pressure. After sautéing chopped red peppers and onions in a splash of olive oil, she poured the egg mixture over them, added pepper, and purposely left off the salt. The cheese would add enough sodium to make the omelet taste right. With a light sprinkle of garlic granules, she waited until the eggs were almost solid and flipped it like a pancake. She added shredded cheddar cheese to one side, folded the other side on top, slid the omelet on to a plate, and placed it in the oven to keep it warm. She placed several strips of bacon in the microwave and returned to the bedroom.

When Dan left the room to collect his shaving gear from the bathroom, she slipped his anniversary present and a card into his bag beneath his shirts.

A nurse handed Emmy an antibiotic for a urinary infection caused from a buildup of fluids during the last eight weeks of her pregnancy. As soon as Emmy placed the capsule in her mouth, the nurse handed her a sip of water in a paper cup. The nurse turned to leave and almost bumped into Dan as she headed out the door. Dan stepped back to let her through.

"How's our little mama today?" Dan's deep voice reached Emmy's ears before she saw her older brother in faded jeans and a white short-sleeved shirt.

"Uuugh. I'd be better if I hadn't gotten an infection," Emmy answered as Dan leaned over and placed a kiss on her cheek.

"Where's Fred?" Dan asked, glancing around the room.

"He's gone home for a nap. He's bringing Hank and James to see Marcie. I can hardly wait to see my rascals. I talked to Dee earlier. She said you were on your way."

"I'm driving to Texas instead of flying. I'm taking the boat with me. Plan to do a little fishing next week. It'll probably slow me down. Mom and Dad are on their way. I don't know if Dee's coming."

"She's not. I asked her to go to the house and move a couple of James' things out of Marcie's room. I thought there would be plenty of time to do it myself."

"Where is my little niece?" Dan peeked under Emmy's sheet. "You hiding her somewhere?"

Emmy laughed, "She made a mess. They're cleaning her up. She should be back any minute now."

"Are you going home tomorrow?" Dan stood by the bed, never making an effort to sit down.

"I hope we're home by mid-afternoon." Emmy looked at the slowly opening door.

Dan stepped aside when the nurse walked in with Marcie.

"Here she is," Emmy said with a smile.

The nurse placed the baby, wrapped in a light pink-and-white-striped blanket, in Emmy's arms and left the room. Emmy pulled the blanket away from Marcie's arms and legs. "Marcie, meet your Uncle Dan. See. She has ten toes and ten fingers. Everything a little girl needs, she's got. She's an alert little thing – when she's not sleeping. Want to hold her?"

"I'm not good with newborns. They scare me." Dan didn't make an effort to touch Marcie.

After saying goodbye to his sister and her baby, Dan left the room. On his way to the elevator he passed a brown-haired woman sitting in a chair near the entrance to the maternity ward. He noticed the pink scaly spots on the hands clutching a large beige handbag. A brown and beige tote bag leaned against the legs of her chair. A stuffed monkey peeked out from the bag; his bright fake eyes seemed to follow Dan as he passed by. Dan stepped in as soon as the elevator door opened. His thoughts immediately went to Texas, hoping to drive straight through to Brownsville without stopping overnight.

Nan learned a long time ago how to maneuver around a hospital without looking out of place. The day before, she made an effort to be inconspicuous when the tall red-headed man left Emmy Rafferty's room. Focused on the stuffed animal in her tote bag, the man hardly looked at her. Later in the day, Timmy came in with the Rafferty man and a boy she assumed was the brother. She couldn't take the chance of approaching him with that irritating older boy by his side. The father had been distracted. The brother stuck to Timmy like glue. If Timmy didn't come to the hospital today without the brother, she'd follow the family home. Sooner or later an opportunity to talk with her boy would happen. That's all she needed.

She was careful not to stand out too much. Sneaking in and out of buildings and changing her looks had become second nature. She knew the locations of all the cameras in the maternity ward, elevators and the hallways involved in her elaborate plan. She waited patiently the day before and considered the time well spent as a learning experience. She knew exactly where to sit without being noticed. She watched as other families came and went through the maternity ward. She witnessed the vulnerability of parents when they were under stress. Time and circumstances were on her side.

This time, my plan is working well. Soon, I'll have my little boy in my arms. I'll be able to stay at home with Timmy and be a good mother. Nan made herself stop daydreaming. She pushed the stuffed monkey aside and pulled a small cooler from her tote bag. It had been hours since she ate the sausage biscuit she purchased on her way to the hospital. She took a pimiento cheese sandwich from the cooler. Slowly, she ate the sandwich, finished off a bottle of water, and waited.

Nan's heart raced. Her hands became clammy when she saw them walk through the door opposite the hallway from where she sat waiting near the elevators. She saw him holding his daddy's hand as they walked toward the maternity wing. She watched the small boy as he sat down on a short sofa in the waiting room. She watched and waited just like the night before when she wasn't wearing the blonde wig and makeup. She watched as the boy adjusted his red baseball hat and ran his small hand over his red and white jersey. As he turned to look up at his father, she saw the white lettering above a number on the back of his shirt. A smile curved her lips. When the father's cell phone rang, he walked into the hallway to get better reception.

Concealed by a huge concrete column, she watched the boy's father carefully. When she felt safe, she took a step forward and pulled the large Seeking Sam monkey from her tote bag. She asked the boy if Seeking Sam could wear his hat. James moved his head up and down, took his hat off, and handed the hat to her. She placed the hat on the stuffed animal, took the boy's hand, helped him off the sofa, and replaced him with Seeking Sam. She took a few magazines from a nearby table and slipped them under the stuffed animal to make it as tall on the sofa as James had been.

Pretending to get a better look at Seeking Sam wearing the hat, she held James' hand and backed away from the sofa, pausing behind the huge concrete column that separated them from the hallway where his daddy was talking on the phone. Just as she hoped, when the boy's daddy looked around, he saw his son's hat. Nan knew the man assumed his son was sitting on the sofa.

She talked quietly with James as they left the waiting room near the maternity wing of the hospital and walked toward the elevators. She said, "I'm here to take you to get an ice cream. What's your favorite ice cream?"

"'nilla," he said.

"Okay, let's go just down the street. They have really good vanilla ice cream. You like a cone or a cup?" Nan asked as she adjusted her tote bag, letting it hang from her elbow and cover most of James' body.

"Cone, please. Where's my daddy? He wants a ice cream too."

"Maybe we can get him an ice cream."

"Okay. We're gonna see my baby sister and take her home. I don't think she can eat ice cream."

"You're so right. She won't be able to eat ice cream for a long time. Let's be sure we don't get ice cream on your shirt." She took a dark green shirt out of her large purse and placed it over his head. She kept herself between the boy and the camera on the wall behind them, concealing him with her large body, her purse and the tote bag. As she pulled the shirt down over his shoulders she continued, "And, since you gave your hat to Seeking Sam, I want to give this one to you." She placed a black cap over his head and tucked his blond hair into the hat. "You look so handsome, Timmy."

"My name's James." He looked straight into her eyes.

"That's right. We'll have to talk about that. Don't you like the name Timmy?" She watched his reaction.

"Yeah. I like it. But, I like my name better. I'm James."

"Maybe I can call you Timmy James," she said with a smile.

"That sounds funny."

Nan and James exited the hospital through the crowded emergency room. She smiled and skipped with joy. They were only yards away from her car.

"Where's the ice cream?"

"Down the street." She placed her bags on the pavement to free a hand to open the door. She held onto James with the other hand, determined to force him into the car if necessary.

"My daddy wants 'nilla ice cream, too. Just like me," James said, looking up at her with the afternoon sun in his eyes.

"And what kind does your mommy want?"

"Choc'late. Always choc'late."

"Okay. Do they want a cup or a cone?" Nan asked, keeping him talking.

"Daddy wants a cup. Mommy wants a cone."

"You're such a smart boy. Your mommy and daddy are very proud of you. They'll think you are a big boy for remembering what kind of ice cream they like." She gave him a hug, took the keys from her purse, and unlocked the door.

He looked up at the hospital. "Won't they miss me?"

"Oh, no. By the time your daddy finishes talking on the phone, we'll be back with the ice cream." She placed him in a car seat purchased just for him. Her slow purposeful movements kept him calm. She was able to buckle him in without any protest. Calmly unzipping a small cooler while keeping an eye on him, she retrieved a colorful spill proof cup with apple juice laced with antihistamine. The cup was decorated with a popular cartoon character with a big head, skinny body, and thin arms and legs. James' little hands reached for it immediately.

As soon as they were out of the parking lot, Nan took off her blonde wig and pulled a wet washcloth from a zip lock bag. Within seconds, most of the makeup was wiped away. She looked in the rear view mirror at James, who asked, "Do you like 'nilla ice cream, too?"

"I do," she said smiling. She watched via the rear-view mirror as the medication made him sleepy. The black Honda headed south on Highway 15. Nan pulled into a side road south of Greensboro and removed the cardboard tag she created to cover her permanent car tag. The pine trees' shadows crept over the car and stretched to the middle of the dirt road creating an alternating pattern of sunshine and shadow. She easily pulled off a Destin, Florida decal she had placed on the left side of the bumper a few days before. A folded corner of the sticker on the right bottom side ensured easy removal. The quiet tree-lined side road made the perfect cover. The only noise came from the crackling sound of the sticker as Nan pulled it away from the bumper. Her Timmy was sound asleep. She smiled as she thought about the police wasting their time looking for her in Florida.

She crossed I-16, staying on Highway 15, purposely taking a different route back to the coast with the hope of bypassing any cameras that might be on I-16 or I-95. She smiled as she headed home to the house where Timmy would grow up. She would finally be the mother of her precious little boy. They would laugh and play. She would be the perfect mother.

Chapter Eight – Naked Fear

As Nan Jones made her way south on Highway 15, Emmy sat on the edge of the hospital bed dressed in light peach-colored pants and a matching blouse, ready to go home. She thought about how lucky she was to have packed her suitcase well ahead of time since Marcie came almost two weeks early. A shower made her feel better and surprisingly energetic considering she gave birth the day before. Her plans to be home by mid-afternoon were falling apart. She didn't understand why the pediatrician had not released Marcie.

It was almost noon when Emmy watched the pediatrician press the baby's abdomen. Emmy saw the yellow tint in the skin when he lifted his finger. He explained that many babies experienced some symptoms of jaundice at birth. Normally, the jaundice disappeared within the first twenty-four hours. He told Emmy he needed to run a bilirubin test before they left the hospital.

When will they bring my baby back? She thought the nurse or doctor would have returned with Marcie by now. She picked up the baby's tiny white dress from the open suitcase beside her and smiled as she touched the crocheted collar Granny Nida had so lovingly stitched. *Where is Fred?* Hours ago, he called to say he was running late. Her smile faded when she heard Fred's voice outside the room. He sounded upset and agitated.

The naked fear she saw in his pale face as he entered the room scared her. Something was terribly wrong. She recognized the nurse who came in with him, but didn't know the man dressed in green scrubs. A hospital security officer followed them in. She felt panic rising from the pit of her stomach.

"Em," was all Fred got out, before tears started down his face. He approached her from the left side of the bed where she sat facing him.

The man in the green scrubs moved toward her. Emmy felt the panic spreading. She looked from Fred to the stranger beside him.

"Mrs. Rafferty, Dr. Sorenson." He held out his hand without smiling. Emmy automatically shook hands with the doctor.

Fred moved closer, took Emmy's hands and forced himself to look into her eyes. "I have to do this, doctor," he said. "Em, I . . . James came to hospital with me and now we can't find him. We hope he's still in the building, but I . . ." He watched and waited, expecting her to get angry and scream or something. Her lack of reaction surprised and puzzled him. She always had a quick comeback regardless of the situation.

Emmy took her hands from his. She turned, absent-mindedly pushed the suitcase to the side, and lay down on the bed. The nurse caught the suitcase before it fell on the floor. Emmy couldn't control her thoughts. Questions jumped around in her head; before she could consider the answer to the first one, another question formed, and then another. *Who would want to take James? Why isn't Marcie back from her test? Is jaundice life-threatening? Where is James hiding? This can't be happening – can it?* Finally, she got out one word, "Where?"

Just outside the room, in the lobby. We aren't sure where he is," Fred admitted, wringing his hands.

"He's just hiding somewhere," she heard herself say. She knew it wasn't that simple and tried to focus. "He's at that age. You know how Hank used to play hide and seek all the time when he was James' age."

"I'm so sorry." Fred reached for her hand and held it close to his heart. "We have reason to believe that someone took him." Fred didn't want to tell her about Seeking Sam. His mind wandered to the Seeking Sam books Hank and James loved. His mother saved them from his childhood and gave them to the family when Hank was born. Like his mother, he and Emmy read the Seeking Sam books over and over to their children: *Sam Wants to Help; Sam Falls in a Well; Sam and the Mama Bird.* The irony of the stuffed animal with James' hat perched on top felt like a punch in the stomach. He let go of Emmy's hand, swayed slightly to the left and then to the right toward Dr. Sorenson.

Emmy silently watched the doctor steady Fred. She saw a nurse come to the door with Marcie in her arms. She saw the nurse take a couple of steps backward before the doctor told her to bring the baby to her mother.

Emmy felt tears run down her face as she reached for Marcie. She cupped her baby's nearly bald head and held her close. Emmy expected to be dressing Marcie for the trip home. She focused on the new baby as she tried to push away the thought that someone had taken James. Unable to do so, she demanded, "Tell me. Just tell me why you think he was taken."

Fred told her about how he kept looking at James sitting on the sofa and assuming if he could see James' hat, he was wearing it. He went on to explain how the Seeking Sam monkey was wearing the hat and that hospital security had contacted the local police.

Marcie's pediatrician walked in. He heard the story about James and told Emmy and Fred that unless Emmy was breast-feeding the baby, she could go home; however, it would be necessary for Marcie to stay for phototherapy treatment for at least twenty-four hours.

"I *am* breast-feeding Marcie. Even if I wasn't, I AM NOT LEAVING MY BABY." Emmy almost screamed, leaving no doubt in anyone's mind about the decision she'd made.

Dr. Sorenson asked Fred to go into the hallway with him. However, he stopped when he heard the pediatrician explaining the treatment to Emmy. He and Fred turned back toward the bed. They lingered long enough to hear the pediatrician tell about the procedure.

Marcie would be placed under a special fluorescent blue light in a warm enclosed crib with temperature control. Her eyes would be covered while the remainder of her body, except for a diaper, would be exposed to artificial light. The pediatrician looked toward Fred, then back at Emmy. He said the good news was that Marcie's jaundice was moderate to severe. He said if it had been more severe, she would have to stay in the hospital much longer. He felt certain the twenty-four hour treatment would be sufficient.

Emmy felt like she was in the Twilight Zone watching Fred and Dr. Sorenson walk out of the room with the pediatrician. They stopped just outside her room. Dr. Sorenson told Fred that under the circumstances, and with the baby's jaundice condition, it would be best for Emmy to stay another night in the hospital. Marcie's pediatrician agreed.

A uniformed policeman walked into the lobby accompanied by a hospital security guard. The policeman introduced himself and told Fred and the doctor that agents from the Federal Bureau of Investigation were on their way.

Fred interrupted, "Why the FBI? Surely, no one believes James has already been taken out of state."

The policeman explained how all kidnappings have to be investigated by the FBI under a federal law that became effective after the abduction of the Lindbergh baby back in the 1930s. He asked Fred to join him in looking at the videos from the hallway cameras. As they walked toward the elevator, Fred noticed several lengths of tape blocking entrances to and from Emmy's room. Security guards stood at all the entrances and exits, making Fred understand that a nightmare he never anticipated had just begun.

The lead agent in the FBI's Athens office sighed. Her long dark hair, held back by a wide tortoise-shell barrette at the nape of neck, hung over the collar of her navy blue blazer. Her white camisole accentuated her summer tan. Special Agent Lois Crandall, didn't want to spend time with Thomas Kidd. Calling him The Kid seemed the right thing to do since he was the youngest agent in the unit. It wasn't that she thought twenty-eight was so much younger than her thirty years; it was his charming personality. It didn't help that he had one of those baby faces whose ID would be checked when he was forty-eight. His wavy black hair, tight fitted shirts, and designer jeans added to the youthful look. She thought of him as The Kid, even though he asked her several times to call him TK.

Agent Crandall knew he came to the Athens FBI satellite office from Atlanta before being assigned as her partner. She was told to take him under her wing and show him the ropes. She looked him up in the database only to find that he had been an agent for a very short time. She didn't have time to research his background further. She also couldn't figure out why she felt threatened by him. Every time he walked through the door the muscles around her stomach tightened. She wanted to run the other way. He gave her a crooked smile as he sauntered toward her car.

"Ready ta go?" he asked with a strong Northern accent as he opened the passenger door of her work car.

"Doesn't matter," she said. "Ready or not, we need to get to the hospital as soon as possible. The sooner we get the details about the kidnapping, the better chance we'll have of finding him alive."

While settling in the passenger seat and pulling the seat belt across his chest, he asked her what she knew about the situation.

"Only that it happened at the hospital." Agent Crandall turned her head, looked to see if anything was behind the car, backed out, pulled forward, and continued the conversation, "The kidnapped boy and his daddy were there to take his mother and baby sister home."

"You know, if I was gonna kidnap a child or commit any other crime, I can't think of a better place," he offered.

"Why's that?" She asked, giving him a sideways glance.

"Think about it. It's not far from I-85. The kidnapper can go north or south and be in another state within a few hours. Georgia ta Alabama. South Carolina's not that far away. Tennessee ta the north."

She didn't want to give him credit for assessing the situation so quickly. After all, she was supposed to be training him, and she just found out about the kidnapping.

He continued, "Could be, that's too simple. Maybe she or he is purposely staying away from interstate roads. That's what I'd do."

She sneaked another look at him and felt she may have judged him too harshly and too quickly. She decided to concentrate on driving.

He saw her glance his way and felt she would have been surprised to know how he thought their ages were not a factor in their working relationship. She would have been even more surprised if she knew he fantasized the last two weeks about her in ways that had nothing to do with work. He smiled at the thought.

"Sound track from the Jersey Boys?" he said as he reached over and picked up the empty plastic CD box lying on top of the console.

"My favorite. My sisters and I saw the play in New York last fall. I love those oldies. Want to hear some of it?" She pushed a button on the dashboard and almost immediately it sounded as if Frankie Valli sat in the car with them singing *Sherry, Sherry, Baby.*

They listened to several songs before he turned the volume down and said, "You know I'm from Jersey don't you?"

"Yep. Sure do, Kid," she lied. She could tell from his accent, dark hair, and olive complexion that he was Italian. She hadn't connected all the dots leading to New Jersey. He was the spitting image of the actor in the play. He could have been Frankie Valli – the Frankie Valli who could sing like an angel. She was certain The Kid was no angel.

Agent Crandall turned into the parking lot of the hospital. Her thoughts turned to the kidnapped child.

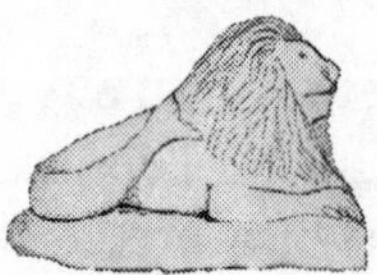

Chapter Nine – The Guilt

"Mommy," Sara poked her small index finger into Dee's upper arm.

"Mommy," she said again.

Dee looked up from her book to see Sara standing by the sofa. Sara started shaking Dee's arm. "Mommy. Aunt Em's crying. Aunt Em needs you."

"Aunt Em's at home with Uncle Fred and Baby Marcie. Uncle Fred went to the hospital to bring them home this afternoon. We're going to see them first thing tomorrow. Remember? Hank and James are with Mom and Pop Jax."

"I know. I remember. But, I don't see James. Aunt Em can't see James either and that's why she's crying."

"Sweetie, I'm sure Aunt Em would call me if something was wrong." Dee purposely had left Emmy and her family alone, believing they needed a few hours to settle in. She left their dinner in the refrigerator. All Fred had to do was heat the barbequed pork and stew. The slaw was ready. She planned to visit the next day and make sandwiches from the leftovers.

"I saw the po-lice. They —" The sound of the ringing phone interrupted Sara's sentence.

Dee knew Sara was right. Something was terribly wrong. "Hello."

"Dee, Em asked me to call you."

Dee hardly recognized Fred's voice.

"It's James." Fred could hardly talk. "We went to the hospital to bring Em and the baby home."

"I thought James and Hank stayed with Mom and Pop Jax."

"They were supposed to. But, James begged to go with me. Em and I have been worried that he felt left out, so I gave in and brought him with me. I was talking with Mom on the phone . . . Dee I didn't even turn my back to James. Not really. I don't know how someone got to him and left his hat on a stuffed animal. I kept my eyes on him the whole time. At least I thought it was James under the hat. It was his hat. I don't know . . . I . . ."

"Did someone kidnap James?" Dee bolted straight up and patted a spot beside her for Sara to join her. Sara accepted the offer, crawled up beside her mother, placed her small arms around her mother's torso just below her breasts, and squeezed her tightly.

"Yes. Yes. I don't know how it happened. I've racked my brain trying to put it together. The police are getting the recordings from the cameras all over the hospital and we hope to find out who did it." Fred's voice cracked, "I didn't even see another person in the room."

"Have you told Mom and Pop Jax?" Dee asked.

"Yes, I've called the Jacksons and my mom and Henry. Will you call Dan? I didn't want to alarm anyone. At first, I was sure he would be found in the hospital. Now it's been several hours and the police believe someone has had time to take him out of the area."

"Fred, I'm so sorry. I can be there in less than an hour, but I'll have to bring Sara." Dee added, "Or, take her to a neighbor's."

"That's OK. Mom and Pop Jax and Hank are on their way or leaving soon. Emmy will need you later. So will I. The doctor sent in a prescription for her nerves. They're trying to be careful about what she takes since she's breast-feeding Marcie. Oh heck. I forgot to tell you that Marcie is jaundice. She and Em will be staying an extra day."

"I've heard about infant jaundice. How bad is it?" Dee wondered what else could go wrong.

"It's bad enough for treatment. But her doctor says it's not too severe." Fred continued, "My folks are coming tomorrow."

"Mom Jax said she never saw Emmy more happy than she was yesterday when they were there to see Marcie. And James loved having his picture made with his baby sister and Hank. This is unbelievable." Dee leaned over and kissed Sara's forehead.

"I know. I know." Fred sobbed and broke down again. "I'm sorry. I can't believe this has happened. It's all my fault."

"No one would have expected this to happen in a hospital, especially with an older child instead of an infant. Someone planned ahead. Please try not to drive yourself crazy over this. Emmy is going to need you more than any other time in her life." Dee heard the call waiting beep on her phone and dreaded the next conversation. She was sure it was her mother-in-law.

"I know, but what if she hates me for it?" His voice quivered. "Did I hear a beep? Do you have a call coming in?"

"Yes. But, that's okay. It can wait." Dee felt relief when she didn't have to answer Fred's question about Emmy hating him. She knew Emmy's difficulty with letting a grudge go, much less something this monumental.

"It may be Mom Jax. You'd better take it," Fred advised.

They said their goodbyes. As soon as she hung up, the phone rang. Mom Jax's strained voice asked, "Dee, have you heard?"

"I have and I'm so sorry."

"Mom will be going to bed soon. I can't let her go to bed with this on her mind, and I'll have Hank with me tomorrow. Would you go and tell Mom for me – first thing in the morning?"

Dee thought her mother-in-law sounded like an old woman with the weight of the world on her shoulders and quickly agreed to be the one to tell Granny Nida. She listened as Mom Jax repeated details of the kidnapping and she tried to calm Sara by wrapping her arms around her daughter's thin shoulders. She felt the dampness of Sara's tears soaking through her pajama top.

After the phone calls, she and Sara talked until Sara was ready to go to bed. Dee allowed her to sleep with her that night. Neither of them slept well.

Fred's question kept making its way back into Dee's mind. Would Emmy hate him? Dee's thoughts went back in time. Emmy's mood swings started while planning the wedding. After a short honeymoon, and in order to save money, Fred moved into the small duplex apartment she and Emmy shared. His plan to commute to and from Elberton to the UGA campus in Athens allowed him to sublet the apartment in Athens for the few remaining months before graduation.

Two weeks after the wedding, Emmy found out she was pregnant. Dee overheard their initial conversation when Fred found out. "Em, I thought we agreed we wouldn't start a family until I've had time to get a job and get established. I have several more months of classes. Now you tell me you're eight weeks pregnant?" Fred made no effort to keep his voice down. He spoke loud enough for anyone in the apartment to hear.

"I *am* telling you that. And I didn't do it by myself," Emmy said. Dee heard Emmy's voice tremble and knew she was trying to hold back the tears. "Have you forgotten it takes two?"

"You told me you were taking the pill."

"I was. I don't know what happened. I don't remember skipping one. Don't you want our baby?"

"That's not the point. We agreed to wait." Dee remembered how Fred's voice became louder.

"I know and I feel really bad about it happening so soon. I would rather have waited, too. But, I'm not unhappy about having your baby."

Dee had walked to her room. Even though she was concerned, she didn't want to hear more. Still, she couldn't shut out the conversation because of the thin walls in the apartment.

Emmy continued, "I am happy you and I don't smoke and we haven't had anything much to drink in months. I plan to do everything I know to make this a healthy, happy baby."

Dee had heard enough of what should have been a private conversation. She rummaged around in her dresser drawer looking for earplugs.

The conversation in the other bedroom continued. Emmy said, "My God, Fred, you don't want me to get an abortion do you?"

"No, I —" Fred was interrupted.

"I don't care. I know I'm a pro-choice person and my choice is I will not now or ever have an abortion."

"Em, stop. Stop right now. I said no and I mean no. I would never harm our child. I'm just trying to get used to the idea of a new job, a new marriage, and a baby. How are we going to afford it?"

"I'm sure my folks will help us as much as they can. They will be so excited. We'll not have to worry about the cost of the baby. And the other stuff we would have to worry about anyway. I'll be able to finish out this year teaching and I've managed to put a little in the bank for an emergency. Besides, your mom will be so excited." Emmy had included Fred's stepfather. "Henry will love our baby too."

"That's true." Dee imagined that Fred took Emmy's hand and looked into her green eyes.

"Are you going to call your dad and tell him?" Emmy asked.

"No. Henry *is* my dad. He was there for me. It was Henry who gave me a hug when Granny died. Dad didn't even come to his own mother's funeral. A genetic pool makes a biological father. A daddy is made on a daily basis. It will be Mom and Henry who will love this baby."

"Want to call them now and tell them?" Emmy asked hopefully.

"No. Let's tell them in person this weekend. I want to see their faces when they find out about our baby."

"Our baby will be loved by so many people," Emmy said.

The next day Emmy told Dee about the pregnancy and relayed details of the conversation Dee already heard. She described Fred's concerned look fading to happiness and how he held her close and kissed her. "If he felt any regret about the baby, he never expressed it again," she said.

Dee didn't tell her she knew how Fred reacted. She teased Emmy and asked her why she didn't take Granny Nida's advice and put an aspirin between her knees when the *fe'vah* started.

Emmy laughed and said, "You sound just like Granny Nida. *The fe'vah of love.* The aspirin thing certainly would have been more effective than the pill. But you know, it's like mother, like daughter."

"What does that mean?" Dee asked.

"Ooops. I shouldn't have said that, but you'll probably find out anyway. Mom and Dad have always played down their anniversary date. I realized it when I was a teenager. I started checking. Mom was pregnant with Dan when they married. Believe me, the subject is not discussed. I expect the same will happen with our little *fe'vah* child."

Dee hoped Emmy forgot the bad times and wasn't obsessing over Fred's reaction to her first pregnancy or about the time he broke up with her just before she graduated from UGA, telling her he wasn't ready to make a permanent commitment. Dee knew, better than anyone, that Emmy never stopped loving Fred. A year after the breakup, he got in touch with Emmy and the past was history. Dee wondered if the hurt of James' disappearance would be stronger than the marriage.

Pondering facets of Emmy's and Fred's relationship brought Dee back to the present where Sara's picture appeared in her mind's eye accompanied by her aunt's premonition that the images were connected to some action the woman was planning. Dee tried not to feel guilty. She processed the information and kept telling herself over and over that she didn't know enough to stop the kidnapping. *Should she have asked Sara more questions? Should she have pushed Aunt Connie to pursue the psychic connection to the picture*? She tried to rationalize why she shouldn't feel guilty. The guilt already consumed her. It was growing like a cancer.

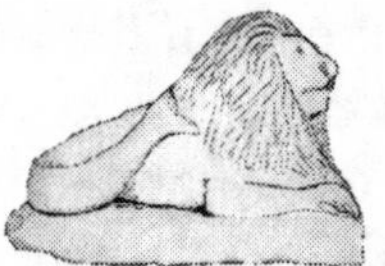

Chapter Ten – Ten Ice Creams

Waking up in an unfamiliar car left James disoriented and puzzled. He felt someone lifting him from the car seat. His brow wrinkled as he tried to make sense of where he was. He thought, *Who is this woman?* Then, he remembered. *She's the one buying my daddy and me an ice cream. Mommy, too.*

He wiggled until the woman let him down. She took his hand and led him into the house. "Where are we? I don't see no ice cream man here. I'm hungry. Where's my daddy? I want . . ."

"Well, Timmy, you went to sleep on the way to the ice cream shop, so I just brought you home so you could sleep here and spend some time with me before we go —"

James interrupted her, "I told you. I'm James. Not Timmy. Why's your hair dif'rent?"

"Okay. I keep forgetting. I hope you'll learn to like living here." She purposely ignored the remark about her hair, thinking he'd forget about it soon enough.

"I don't live here. I live with my mommy and daddy," James said emphatically, backing away from her. He looked at his shirt, trying to remember why he was wearing a shirt that wasn't his. She grabbed his wrist, forced him into the kitchen, and sat him in a chair at the end of a rectangular table.

"Well, you know your mommy and daddy are taking your little sister home – right now. And, they are really, really busy." She gathered bread, cheese and mayonnaise from the refrigerator and placed them on the white kitchen counter. Timmy's hunger pains didn't surprise her at all. He had slept for hours. She turned back to the refrigerator, took out a half-gallon jug of milk, and bumped the refrigerator door with her elbow to make it close.

She continued, "They don't have time to take care of you and a new baby. They want me to take care of you because I have lots of time." Nan hoped the explanation would be enough. She placed the cheese sandwich on a small plate and put the plate in front of the boy.

She watched him closely as he sat quietly eating his sandwich and felt sure he was trying to figure out if the woman was telling the truth.

James remembered his mother and Aunt Dee moving his things from his room. He saw his daddy putting together a baby's bed in the middle of his room. He didn't remember having a baby's bed. Hank wasn't happy about sharing his room and called him his *baby* brother. James remembered screaming at Hank, telling him he wasn't a baby. He figured the woman was right. He took the glass of milk she had placed on the table in front of him. He frowned, not knowing that his frown confirmed what she thought all along.

Nan smiled and thought about how the Raffertys didn't deserve this child. She planned to make him so happy he wouldn't even think about the mommy and daddy with whom he once lived. After all, he was her little boy now.

When he finished eating, she led him into the living room, took a puzzle from a shelf, and dumped it on the rug in front of the coffee table. She sat down beside him and showed him how to place the A in its correct slot and handed him the C.

He sat on the floor and in no time at all finished placing each letter of the alphabet into the correct slot. When he looked up at the lady, he saw a huge smile on her face.

"Smart boy. I think somebody underestimated you." She had asked the store clerk specifically for puzzles that would interest a six-year-old. Now, she was sure her little boy was smarter than most six-year-olds. The clerk assured her the puzzle would be appropriate. *My Timmy is smarter than most six-year-olds*, she thought again with pride.

She could see that her Timmy was getting bored. He reminded her, "You said I could have a ice cream cone. You said so."

"Sweetheart, you're so right. You can have all you want. I always keep my promises. It's too late now, but tomorrow we'll go to the Dairy Queen and get an ice cream. Now, dear boy, let's go to the bathroom. I have a surprise for you." She took him by the hand, walked with him to the end of the hallway to the only bathroom in the house. She closed the lid on the toilet and motioned him to climb up. She opened the medicine cabinet and reached for a package of brown hair color. She and Timmy would both have brown hair until it was safe to change his back to the natural color – one of the things she loved about her son was his blond hair. *Maybe I'll become a blond too*, she thought. *After all, it's not uncommon for a son to favor his mother.*

The chirping birds woke James the following morning. He sat up in the unfamiliar room, looked around, and wondered how he had gotten here. When he remembered the strange woman, he slipped his hand inside his pillowcase and pulled out the drawing of the Sea Lion and the face in the tree. He unfolded the sheet of paper and ran his finger over the lion's face. A noise outside the room prompted him to put the picture back into the pillowcase. The woman came through the door talking.

"And how's my little man today?" The woman didn't wait for an answer; she took an outfit from the closet and helped him dress. She said, "Timmy, how would you like ice cream for breakfast?"

"Ummmm. I never had ice cream for breakfast. Can I have ten ice creams?" He thought she might let him have ten ice cream cones if he ignored the fact that she called him Timmy.

"That might be a little too much, dear boy. We don't want you to get sick, do we?"

He wrinkled his nose when she combed his hair. He didn't like the fragrance of the dye she'd used the night before.

They walked a few blocks to the Dairy Queen where she ordered James a vanilla ice cream cone. He frowned at her when she ordered herself a chocolate ice cream.

They sat in a corner booth away from the crowd and watched the workers make shakes and dip ice cream, until the teenage boy who took their order called their ticket number. When she returned with his vanilla ice cream in a cone and her chocolate ice cream in a cup, he said, "You said you like 'nilla ice cream."

Nan remembered lying to him. She never dreamed he'd remember such a minute detail.

"Oh. I like to try different things some times. Don't you?" She handed him his cone. As she expected, he licked the curl off the rounded scoop of his ice cream cone and forgot about her choice.

She watched the people around her, trying to block their view of Timmy. When they finished, she wiped the ice cream from his face before leaving. They walked across the side street toward Murphy's Tavern.

He pulled on her hand, trying to force her toward a tree. From his vantage point, a face seemed to have grown out of the tree trunk. He could see the nose, the chin and the forehead. James recognized the woman's face carved in the tree. It was the same one Sara drew beside the Sea Lion in the drawing he kept hidden.

"See. See. It's the woman in the tree." He jumped up and down. "She's a princess." He continued pulling Nan toward the tree. He liked it when she lifted him up so he could get a better view and stood with him as he stared at the face carved in the tree. He didn't like it when lowered him to the ground, took him by the wrist, and forced him to walk away.

They arrived in the village just in time to hear the trolley's bell ringing. Nan steered clear of the parking area near the pier. Each morning at 10:30 the trolley parked across from the small playground and waited for the day's tour customers to arrive. Several times, Nan watched Bunny the Tour Guide leave the trolley and walk down the street to get a coffee or a soda.

It didn't take long for Nan to know that Bunny knew more than the history of the island. She was certain Bunny could easily separate the visitors to the island from the permanent residents. Nan made it a point to stay away from the park area when the trolley was scheduled to arrive and depart. She didn't want to attract Bunny's attention. The woman's natural instincts could ruin all Nan's plans. Long before she brought her Timmy to the island, Nan did whatever was necessary to ensure she stayed off Bunny the Tour Guide's radar screen.

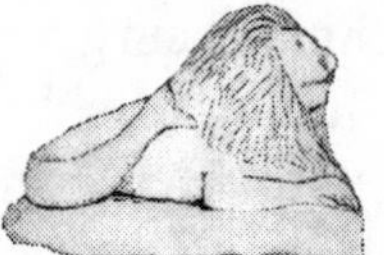

Chapter Eleven – Secrets

As Mom Jax requested, Dee waited until morning to tell Granny Nida about James' disappearance. Dee thought about how everyone in this small town knew the Jackson family. Their friends and neighbors would want to help. She wished Dan could go with her to Granny Nida's; but all the wishing in the world couldn't get Dan home before late afternoon. She left him a message on his cell phone and hadn't heard back from him.

How does one tell an old woman that her great-grandson has been kidnapped? Procrastination set in; she changed clothes three times, finally deciding to wear jeans and a T-shirt. She made herself walk out the door. She didn't want Granny Nida to find out about James from someone else.

Dee knocked on the door of Granny Nida's apartment and heard, "Come in. Door's unlocked."

When she walked through the door and caught the scent of the cleaner the home health care person used to mop the linoleum-tiled floor, she knew she'd always associate the smell with the day of bad news. The pine oil fragrance permeated the small handicapped-accessible apartment. Although she thought Granny Nida couldn't possibly have any beauty routines as bizarre as the Preparation H she had used to get rid of the bags under her eyes, the scene she saw as she entered the room surprised her. Granny Nida, still in her pink flowered cotton gown and housecoat, sat in her brown lift chair with a headband tucked under her chin, pulled up over her forehead and framing her face. The black and white checkered stretch band covered her ears and contrasted with her thin white hair.

Granny Nida said, "I'm fixin' to take this thang off, sugar. I only got ten minutes left to wear it. You know, you might want to try this yoreself. It pulls my jowls up, and it's gonna git rid of this double chin. If I leave it on long enough, I'm sure I'll look a lot younger. I try to wear it at least thirty minutes a day."

Dee smelled coffee before she saw the large brown mug on a tray table to the left of the lift chair. A small daily devotional book, a box of tissues, and a Bible were within Granny Nida's reach. A walker, opened and ready for use, stood on the other side of the chair, attesting to the old woman's deteriorating health. Her grand-mother-in-law had lived in the senior citizens' home for many years and moved into the adapted apartment only four years earlier. Its beige linoleum floors, emergency pull strings in the kitchen, bedroom and bathroom, and the walk-in shower, enabled the old woman to live alone.

Dee smiled at her grandmother-in-law's antics, wishing she didn't have to be the bearer of such bad news. She pulled a chair from the nearby table, sat in front of Granny Nida, took the old woman's hands, and told her everything she knew about James' disappearance.

Dee pulled a couple of tissues from the box, as tears formed in the old woman's light blue-green eyes. Granny Nida took the tissues and balled them up in her fist. She let the tears run down her cheeks and into the headband. "My pore little Emmy Lou. Bless her precious heart and Jamie James' too."

During the night at the hospital in Athens, Emmy slipped back into her bed after another visit to the nursery to check on Marcie, a trip she made every thirty minutes. The nursing staff let her in to see the baby as she lay in a crib with a light above her. Emmy hadn't been allowed to touch her baby except for feeding times.

Shortly after the visit to the nursery, Emmy's nurse came in and tried to get her to take something for her nerves. Emmy, afraid the medicine might make her drowsy, shook her head. No way would she take such a chance with this baby. She knew she would never sleep the same again. She couldn't imagine a life without James.

At dawn, a nurse brought Marcie in for feeding. Emmy kissed her beside each eye. The raccoon look from the eye mask used during the treatment left the areas around the eyes a lighter color than the rest of her face. She knew Fred watched from his makeshift bed, listening to the baby's nursing sounds. She heard him turn over when the nurse came back for the baby.

A couple of hours later, Fred still faced away from her. She felt certain her was faking sleep. After the sleepless night of going over and over the events of the day before, Marcie's jaundice, and talking with the Athens police, Emmy didn't regret her decision to take the doctor's advice and stay in the hospital an additional night. She looked at her husband. *How could he? How could he be so careless with my baby boy?* As if on command, Fred turned over. His mussed hair and wrinkled clothes reminded Emmy of a red-eyed homeless person.

She could tell that Fred knew what she was thinking and knew that she blamed him. She saw his effort to smile and watched as he pushed the footrest under the chair and slumped back against a pillow.

Marcie's nurse came in and placed the baby in her mother's arms. Fred stood close by the entire time the baby nursed. He lovingly stroked her head. At one point, he pulled back the blanket, removed a sock and touched her tiny toes. He said, "I forgot how tiny they are."

Soon after, the nurse came back to take Marcie for the remainder of her phototherapy. Emmy looked longingly after them. Separation had become agonizingly painful.

Mom and Pop Jax and Hank arrived mid-morning. Hank's quietness added to the strangeness of the situation. Emmy knew he was hurting, and knew she hugged him too hard and held him too long. She reminded her mother to take Hank to the theater for play practice the following day. Shortly after her parents and Hank returned to Elberton, she cried and wondered how she could think of such a trivial thing at such a horrible time.

The streaming tears left Emmy's face blotchy and swollen. She paid no attention to her appearance and her thoughts jumped around in wild and crazy patterns. One thought came creeping back again and again. *Had Fred really wanted their children?* Her wandering thoughts stopped when she recalled her conversation with Dee about someone following her and the boys when they lived in Hilton Head Island.

Once they moved, the strange feelings disappeared for a while and she felt safer in the same town in which she had grown up. Everyone knew her and her family. She remembered how Fred made a name for himself in the landscape architecture world and could easily have found work anywhere in the Southeast. He didn't have to agree to move back to Elberton. She loved him for agreeing to the change, even though he didn't completely understand why they were moving. She kept trying to remember how much she loved him. She wondered if she loved him enough to forgive him.

She never told him about the black Honda in Elberton because she convinced herself she was paranoid. The feeling that she was being followed had hung on like a bad case of flu. Now, guilt took its place.

Any illusion of safety she got from her new home was gone. James was gone. “James. I know you’re alive. I know you’re alive,” she said out loud. She kept thinking those words, over and over. She felt certain she would know if her little boy was dead.

“I agree, Em. I believe James is alive. I think the kidnapper really wanted a little boy. He’s so adorable. I can’t blame someone for wanting to take him.” Fred stared into space. “I have to believe that if he wanted him enough to carry out such an elaborate plan, he’ll take care of our little boy. I have to believe it or … I won’t … I’ll spend the rest of my life trying to get him back.” He leaned over, elbows on his knees for support, and studied the floor.

At the sound of the words *he* and *him*, Emmy's thoughts ran amok to the barrage of stories of child molesters that seemed to be around every corner these days. But deep down, Emmy knew that wasn't right. “Why did you say ‘him’? Did somebody tell you it was a man?” Emmy frowned when she asked the question. “Fred Rafferty, did you see somebody take my boy and you’re hiding something from me?”

“No, Em. I swear. I said ‘him’ like it could be anybody.”

“Well, it’s a *her*. Remember, I tried to explain one of Sara’s drawings of a woman following us in Hilton Head? It’s her. I know it’s her. She’s got my baby boy, damn her.” Emmy’s chin quivered.

An uneasy quietness filled the room until Emmy broke the silence. “Dan came by Sunday on his way to Texas. I forgot to tell you. You went home to get … bring Hank and James …”

“Yeah. Something’s going on with him,” Fred didn’t want Emmy to finish her sentence. “I’ve never seen him so distant with everyone. Did he tell you what’s on his mind?”

“No. I wondered why he didn’t take Dee to Athens to eat at DePalma’s. They’ve celebrated all their other anniversaries there. Mom said he insisted he wanted everyone to celebrate with them. Does Dan know about James?”

“I don’t know. Want me to call Dee and ask?” Fred asked, knowing it would give him something to do. *Anything would be better than sitting here going over and over the events of yesterday,* he thought as he waited for Em’s answer. Before she could speak, Fred’s mother and stepfather walked into the room.

Emmy prepared herself to hear and help tell the story again. She wondered how she survived. Each telling of the kidnapping made it more real. She wanted to escape reality – not face it.

The phone rang as Dee opened her kitchen door. Breaking the sad news to Granny Nida hadn't been easy. It didn't seem right for a woman of her age to have to deal with the possibility that she'd lost a great-grandchild.

Dee's uncle's name, Frank Tremane, appeared on the display. When she answered the phone, his wife, Nancy, told Dee they wanted to make the trip from Easley, South Carolina, to Elberton to change the flowers on Mollie's grave in the Elmhurst Cemetery. She asked Dee to join them for lunch.

Dee told her how James was missing and Marcie was jaundice. Nancy didn't speak for a few seconds. Dee waited for her aunt to put her thoughts into words.

"I'm so sorry. Hope their baby is okay. As you know, the kidnapping brings back a lot of unhappy memories. I'll have to think about it before I tell Frank," Nancy said.

"I understand. Uncle Frank knows better than anyone how it feels to have a sibling kidnapped. You don't have to tell him if you think it'll upset him too much. He can't help but think of Mollie."

"I just hope Emmy's little boy is found soon, and found alive. I'll think about telling Frank. I still want to see you and your family, if you can spare the time. I know you're busy helping out. How's Wednesday of next week?" Nancy asked.

"We'll make it work. Sara asked me not long ago when we'd see you again. We haven't been to the cemetery ourselves in months. We can meet at the cemetery or here at the house," Dee gave her a choice.

"Let's meet at the cemetery, then go somewhere on or near the Square for lunch. Any suggestions?"

"My favorite place is the McIntosh Coffee Shoppe. The chicken salad and quiche can't be beat."

"Sounds good. Shall we set a time?" Nancy asked. "Maybe meet at Mollie's grave at eleven o'clock? That way, we can still be at the restaurant before the noon crowd comes in."

Dee agreed. Before hanging up, Nancy gave Dee an update on her boys and their families. Dee told her how her mom was coping since her dad's death. She dated a widower neighbor twice in the last month and declared there was nothing to it – just a couple of dinner dates.

When the phone call ended, Dee thought about her father's biological mother who lived and died not knowing that Sam had survived. When her daughter disappeared at the age of sixteen, her grief was unimaginable and led to many writings she called "Ramblings of Grief." They were haunting, and created a picture of a strong Christian woman grieving over the disappearance of her sixteen-year-old daughter while trying to be a good mother to her son, Frank. She lived the rest of her life thinking that only one of her three children lived to be grown. She never knew that Dee's father, Sam Dupree, was mistakenly switched at birth and later adopted.

Her father's adopted parents gave him a good life and taught him to be a strong, dependable person. Dee loved them for teaching him to be honest and loving. She missed him so much and felt her biological grandmother had been cheated. His siblings, Mollie and Frank, were cheated. Yet, Sam made it clear that he thought his life turned out exactly as meant to be. Anytime Dee questioned her father, he never backed down about how much he loved his adopted parents. Yet, once he found his brother, Frank, and knew about Mollie, he constantly thanked her for solving Mollie's murder and bringing Frank into his life. She often heard her dad's voice saying, "Deedle Bug, you can do this," giving Dee strength to tackle the next problem.

She wished she could tell her daddy just how thoughtless Dan acted about their anniversary. Dan never called to say he found his new wallet with Sara's picture.

Dee's mind stopped wandering when Sara came into the living room with a pink and green tote bag and said, "Let's go. Mom Jax is waiting for me at James' house." Sara placed her hand over her mouth.

"It's okay, honey. It is James' house." Dee hugged her daughter and kissed the top of her head. "Mom Jax plans to stay there until they bring the baby home."

The drive to Emmy's house didn't allow Dee much time to talk with Sara about James. She made a mental note to spend more time talking with Sara about how she was feeling since James disappeared. Sara loved James like a brother. Mom Jax met Sara at the back door of the Rafferty home.

"Do you need me to help with anything before I go to the hospital?" Dee asked her mother-in-law.

"No, sugar. I'm fine. Hank is on the side porch reading. Sara and I will hang out 'til you get back. Give them all my love."

Dee left the Sweet City Community with a heavy heart. She thought about the numerous times she made the drive to Athens never dreaming there would be a day she'd make the trip to console her best friend. A few days ago, she expected to make the trip to celebrate Marcie's birth. She wondered if she could hold Marcie. She wanted to hold her close and let her feel the love she deserved regardless of the heartbreak going on around her. *Will this baby ever know James?* Dee's thoughts rambled around in her head. *We should have been more careful.*

In the hospital room, Dee listened while Emmy explained Marcie's jaundice and waited for the right time to tell her that Dan knew about James' disappearance. He called that morning while she was visiting with Granny Nida and left a message saying he would be back in a few days. She didn't tell Emmy how Dan said he wouldn't be coming back immediately, since there was nothing he could do. She kept that to herself, justifying it because she couldn't bear to have her best friend know how little empathy Dan had for his sister.

Dee's secret paled in comparison to Emmy's. Emmy continued thinking about the black Honda. Still, she didn't tell Fred about the guilt she carried for ignoring her nagging suspicions about the woman and the car. She kept trying to remember if she saw that old Honda when they lived on Hilton Head Island. Her mind closed down rather than accept any guilt for ignoring the signs of a stalker or any responsibility for James' kidnapping.

Early the following morning, Emmy woke up with the hope of taking Marcie home. When the nurse came in, she told Emmy and Fred that Marcie was having another test – the one that would determine whether they could take her home. She told them the doctor wanted to ensure Marcie didn't have any side effects from the jaundice. Trying to be optimistic, Emmy took Marcie's clothes out, ready to dress her baby girl for the trip home as soon as the nurse brought her back to the room. Once again, she sat on the hospital bed dressed in her peach colored pants and matching blouse – waiting.

Emmy and Fred heard Granny Nida's walker clanging and scraping the tile floor outside the hospital room. They heard the metallic rattle each time she picked up the walker, set it down, and slid it one step at a time. Fred opened the door. Mom Jax pushed the door a little wider to accommodate her mother and the walker. She placed a gift bag on the windowsill before wheeling Emmy's bed tray out of the way to make room for her mother and the walker. Fred moved the tray farther away and leaned against the wall.

"Hey, you two. Mom insisted on a visit this morning. Pop and Hank are hanging out in the shop working on some project for Marcie's room. Mom and I won't stay long. She has an appointment with the eye doctor – just down the street. We'll soon be out of the way." Emily Jackson leaned over and kissed her daughter.

"Whar's that baby, Emmy Lou?" Granny Nida asked impatiently.

"She's having another test for jaundice. The phototherapy should have done the job," Emmy said. "She'll be back any minute now."

"What's that? Oh. I remember. Didn't one of yore babies have that?" Granny Nida said as she shifted her weight and looked at her daughter.

"Emmy did. I'm surprised you remember that. Remember how we left her in the hospital an extra day? They put her under fluorescent lights as a treatment. They didn't call it phototherapy back then. I never quite understood how that helped. But, it did," her daughter said as she tried to maneuver Granny Nida to a chair.

Granny Nida wouldn't budge. Her white knuckles showed as she clung to the metal rods of the walker. Determined to be near her granddaughter, she ignored the suggestion that she sit down.

"My goodness, I hope they don't have to keep our Baby Marcie any longer," Granny Nida said.

"Me too." Emmy and Fred agreed.

"She should be okay today. She did the treatment for twenty-four hours. That's supposed to be enough," Emmy added.

"Git me that bag over yonder," Granny Nida made a slight turn to the right without moving her feet and without letting go of the walker. She nodded her head toward the bag on the windowsill.

Her daughter held the bag while Granny Nida reached inside and removed a small package wrapped in white paper with a pink ribbon and gave it to Emmy who pulled the ribbon and wrapping away and opened the small white box. A silver baby spoon with Marcie's initials on the handle lay on soft white padding.

"Thanks. This is lovely." Emmy handed the box to Fred.

"That's nice, Granny Nida. I'll put it in her diaper bag and make sure it doesn't get left behind," Fred offered.

Everyone in the room chose to ignore the one thought they all shared – James. A quiet moment ticked by.

Granny Nida broke the silence. "I don't want to go out of the tree here, but I have to ask if there's any news about Jamie James."

"It's out on a limb, not out on a tree," Emily corrected her mother.

"No, sugar. When it's this awful, it's out of the tree. The limb gave way a long time ago."

Special Agent Lois Crandall sat at her desk looking at an open file. She talked with the missing boy's parents separately and together, making numerous notes and finally dismissing them as suspects. She long ago learned the sad fact that many kidnapped children were taken by parents or extended family members.

The organized file made her job much easier, and she was happy with the local police work and her unit's handling of the evidence. The hospital security guards cordoned off the waiting room and elevator hallway. No one was allowed into the area until she and TK arrived, bagged the stuffed animal, the boy's hat, the magazines placed under the stuffed animal, as well as any crumbs on or around the short sofa. They bagged flakes and a breakfast bar wrapper from the area near the entrance to the waiting room. It made sense since the boy's father stood in the opposite hallway and the only way out with the boy was near the elevator entrance. It also made sense that a man, maybe dressed as an orderly or doctor, might have enticed the boy to leave with him. She'd make sure they checked the pedophile registry list for those living in the area.

It took almost a week for information to come back from the lab. The evidence helped her recreate the kidnapper's movements within the hospital. The flakes from the nearby doorway matched the DNA of the numerous skin cells found on the stuffed animal. Agent Crandall thought about the book she could write about how Seeking Sam helped solve the mystery of the kidnapped child. With the perpetrator's DNA, they knew he or she had an advanced case of psoriasis. Even though the cells from the psoriasis scabs may have been damaged, enough good cells survived, enabling the laboratory to get sufficient DNA results.

Agent Crandall sent The Kid on a mission to run the DNA through the national registry for pedophiles. He found no match. When she told the parents it was good news, they didn't understand. She explained how a match would lessen the chances of finding their son alive. Pedophiles almost always molested or hurt the child, often killing them. She explained that children taken by others had a greater chance of survival. She was careful not to mention the horrible people who stole children for the sole purpose of selling them.

She and Fred Rafferty looked at the videos from the hospital but saw no definite leads. Once she found out about the psoriasis from the evidence, she looked at the videos again. Looking through the third CD, she spotted a woman near the elevators, placing a large shopping bag on the floor, and bending over as if to tie her shoes. The long sleeves, long wide pants with shoes and socks caught her attention. She backed the video and ran it forward, stopping when she saw the image of the hand on the bag. She enlarged the picture on the screen and zoomed in until she could see a good picture of the back of the woman's hand. There it was! A dark pink crusty circle about the size of a dime, just below the cuff of her sleeve, revealed an acute case of psoriasis.

The video also confirmed her suspicions that the woman was wearing a wig. They had found two short pieces of synthetic blonde hair hidden under Seeking Sam's arm. Seeking Sam was giving up all his secrets.

While looking through the inventory of CDs, she found several of the hospital parking lots. She chose one, recorded about the time of the kidnapping. The same blonde woman placed a child in the back seat of a car while making sure her body shielded most of the child. Feeling a bit of a charge from the progress she was making, the agent zoomed in on the car tag. Disappointment clouded her face as she saw a handmade sign instead of a tag. It looked like the kind of tag a dealer would give a buyer to use until he could get a permanent tag for a new car. How did the woman get from the hospital hallway to the parking lot? The agent couldn't find any CDs from the elevator cameras. She knew she'd have to go back to the hospital and ask for them.

After making the call about the elevator videos and receiving a promise to get back to her about them, she placed the CD from the parking lot back into the machine, remembered something she wanted to check out, and fast-forwarded to the picture of the cardboard tag. She zoomed in on the lower left side of the bumper, where she could make out a bumper sticker advertising Destin, Florida. She wondered, *Does she live there or vacation on the Gulf Coast?*

Chapter Twelve – Water Diamonds

Nan's happiness seemed complete. Her smart green-eyed son turned out to be everything a mother would want. She didn't let him out of her sight. She hugged him often. Her hands constantly smoothed his now-brown hair. The smell of the dye she used to turn his blond hair darker caused him to wrinkle his nose. Nan felt certain he would forget the smell he called "yucky." To ensure he didn't think about it, she took the mirrors from his room. If he couldn't see the brown hair, he wouldn't miss his blond hair.

When they went grocery shopping at the local store, she bought anything that interested him. She loved spoiling him. *I can tell he loves me,* she thought each time she gave him something she knew he liked. She planned fun activities and complimented herself for being such a good mother.

The first time Timmy saw a shrimp boat, he pulled at her hand, pointed to the boat and the birds surrounding it. He jumped up and down, screaming, "Look. Look. The birds. Lots of birds."

He was so excited that she made an extra effort to make sure he saw them often. There were times when the brown-haired boy fell asleep while they sat on a bench at the edge of the park and waited for the shrimp boats to pass by the lighthouse near the village. When his head leaned against Nan's upper arm she stroked the brown hair and smiled. She looked around at the other mothers with their children and thought, *I'm just like them, except I love Timmy much more than they could possibly love their children. I love being a mother. This is what it's all about. My precious Timmy is all boy. I'll have to rein in the independent streak he's exhibiting; otherwise, he's the perfect child.*

The following day when the tide was going out, she dressed him in his new dark green shorts and a matching green-and-white-striped shirt and took him to the beach. She held his hand as they walked into the surf. She kept him on the outside, closer to the sand, protecting him from the waves. She showed him how to kick the water in the air and watch the drops fall.

"See how the drops look like diamonds?" Nan kicked at the surf as it came in. "The sun shows through them and makes them shine and sparkle."

"I ain't seen them like that before."

Nan stopped walking. She wanted to be sure he could hear her well. "Don't say 'ain't.' Say you haven't seen those before. You have seen them. Just not lots of them falling down like these drops of water. Real diamonds are in rings and jewelry."

"I know. It's like the ring my mommy wears. Daddy gave it to her. He said he gave it to her 'cause he loves her. Then, they got married."

She didn't like the direction the conversation was taking. She didn't want him to remember his past. She stepped out of the water and pulled him along with her.

He knew she became unhappy with him and was trying to figure out why. The night before, she got that mean look when she gave him a couple of crackers and he said he wanted peanut butter on them, because his mommy put peanut butter on those kind of crackers. Each time she got that look, he felt frightened.

"Want to go somewhere for lunch?" Nan asked.

She didn't wait for an answer. They walked back home. She bathed him and changed his clothes. She took Timmy to the Fourth of May Restaurant in the village, arriving before the noon crowd. They made their way to the tables near the windows. She didn't want the wait staff to see his face, so she placed him in a chair facing the street and sat across from him watching the waiters and the customers.

An energetic teenage waitress appeared, her blonde ponytail bounced as she approached Nan and Timmy. She placed herself facing the side of their table, between the two of them.

"Well, hi there, handsome," she addressed Timmy and leaned slightly into the table to see him better. "What's your name?"

"James."

Nan broke in quickly before James could add another word, "His name is Timothy James." She tried to keep the girl's attention. She didn't want her to see the scowl on the boy's face.

"That's nice. I like that. And, what can I bring the two of you to drink?" The waitress looked at Nan.

"I'll have water with lemon. He'll have milk." Nan pressed her lips together and narrowed her eyes, warning the boy to be quiet.

When the waiter brought their drinks, Nan ordered pot roast, green beans, and macaroni and cheese. Knowing the helpings would be generous, she ordered an extra plate to share her food with Timmy.

Timmy looked down at the table when the waiter brought their food. He didn't want to take a chance on making the woman across from him angry again. Earlier, when he refused to get out of the tub, he watched her smiling eyes change to the mean hateful look again. That look scared him more and more.

He ate all the macaroni and cheese she put on his plate. Without success, he tried to eat the beans and pot roast. In his mind, he'd already started thinking of her as the mean mommy.

The mean mommy looked at his plate. When she looked at him, he saw the cold mean look creeping into her dark eyes. He placed a forkful of greens beans in his mouth. When the waiter brought their ticket, he looked down at his almost empty plate.

The mean mommy held his wrist as they stood in line to pay at the register. He looked down at his tennis shoes, the only personal item she'd let him keep.

Nan followed his gaze. *Tomorrow, I'll get rid of those shoes. We'll go shopping. Maybe he'll forget about being James if he doesn't have James' shoes to remind him*, she thought.

They left the restaurant and walked toward the pier. The smell of soap drifted in the air as they neared the entrance to a souvenir shop. Nan picked up the wand from a pan filled with a soapy mixture. She slowly swished the wand back and forth in the soapy water. She lifted the fluid filled wand. Swoosh. A long bubble formed and floated toward Timmy. He stepped back, making space for the bubble to move with the air current. He smiled as the huge bubble changed into a circle and traveled past him into the tree at the edge of the sidewalk. He turned toward Nan just in time to see the second bubble make contact with his shirt. Poof! It was gone.

Nan watched him watch the bubbles she produced. She handed him the wand.

Her Timmy reappeared with his look of wonder and his sweet smile. She allowed him to play with the bubble wand for several minutes before rewarding him even more by taking him a few doors down to the local bookstore.

She nodded her head to the proprietor as they walked by the counter. Holding tightly to Timmy's hand, she led him to the children's room in the back of the store. After he sat down on the floor surrounded by books left there by other young readers, she walked a few steps away and looked through the stacks of books on the sales table.

He knew the mean mommy was watching as he reached for a Miss Pugg book titled *Some Little Oink Oink*. He loved the story about a family of pigs who could talk. The small pigs were always getting in trouble. He remembered his daddy and mommy reading the book to him – many times. He couldn't read the words. He remembered them. His little fingers went from word to word as he turned the pages.

Some Little Oink Oink

Some little Oink Oink got into trouble. Who could it be?
Could it be Oink Oink One, Two or Three,
or, maybe Four, Five, Six, Seven, Eight or Nine?
so many little piglets to keep straight and in line.
So many little piglets for one mama to feed,
she didn't even miss little Oink Oink Three,

Oink Oink Three went visiting where his snout would lead.
His snout took him to the hen house where noisy chickens feed.
They screeched and fluttered and pecked at his snout,
Oink Oink Three ran. He was glad to get out.
He peeked around the barn and saw a boy at play.
He thought and thought about what he could say.

He said to the boy, "My name is Oink Oink Three.
I'm one of nine piglets. I'm from a big family.
I'm wondering if you could tell me your name?"
The boy said, "Andrew. Want to play a game?"
Oink Oink Three answered, "I'd love to play with you."
Oink Oink Three was happy to have a friend named Andrew.

They played with Andrew's cars and pushed them all around,
Until Mama Oink Oink spotted her piglet – then he was found.
She said, "I have to know where you are and where you'll be.
I'm your mama, and I love you Oink Oink Three."

It was James, not Timmy, who remembered his mommy hugging him when she read, "*I'm your mama, and I love you Oink Oink Three.*"

His thoughts and his mind were back in Elberton, in his room at his house with his mommy, daddy and his older brother. James didn't understand why he couldn't go home to his family. He was in a dark place and longed to be held by loving arms. His real mommy never looked at him with cold mean eyes like the mommy walking into the room.

"Timmy, it's time to go," Nan said.

He picked up the book and tucked it under his arm. She took his free hand and led him to the front area of the store. Timmy saw a postcard on the floor.

"Look. Look. It's the princess in the tree," Timmy pointed to the postcard. He slipped his hand out of Nan's and picked up the card with pictures of several tree carvings. He pointed to the face enclosed within circles.

"Since you like her so much, I'll buy that for you," Nan offered. "The book too." She took the Miss Pugg book and placed it on the counter. She turned to the woman behind the counter, "How much?" she asked.

"That's 30 cents for the card." The woman turned the book over and said, "The book is $10."

Nan paid for the postcard and book, took Timmy's hand, and was almost to the front door when the clerk asked if she knew about the faces in the trees that had been sculpted in the past few years. Nan said no, and the clerk gave her directions.

Nan and Timmy walked back up the street to the Fourth of May Restaurant on the corner where they had eaten lunch and turned left. They passed several buildings and veered left again, arriving at two large white columns on the right – the entrance to a future subdivision.

As soon as they entered, Timmy saw a sad face on a tree near the right side of the road. He ran to it, stretched up to reach it and lost his balance. He fell into the grass, looked up at the face, and thought it smiled at him. He smiled back. He felt the mean mommy lift him up and heard her scold him for running away from her. He was surprised she allowed him to touch the carved face. His small fingers lovingly touched the nose and moved across the old man's hard wooden cheeks.

Nan put him down. She held his hand as they meandered through the vacant subdivision and looked at other faces in the trees. She pointed to a tree with a green fern growing above a carved face. "Look, see the fern growing above his head. Looks like he's wearing a green hat."

Each face seemed to give James a message of hope. One face, with wild hair, a beard and a mustache, reminded him of the Sea Lion. It also reminded him of his real name. He looked at the mean mommy. He thought about the picture of the Sea Lion Sara drew for him. He knew exactly where he hid it.

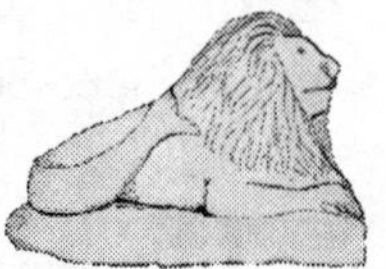

Chapter Thirteen – A Quiet Unhappiness

Emmy's neighbors and members of her Sunday school class delivered dinner every night the first week after they brought Marcie home. Dee and Mom Jax took turns being there to accept the food and clean up afterwards. Every time Dee visited, she thought Emmy and Fred looked exhausted. A quiet unhappiness crept into each room of their house, growing and replacing the loud noisy exuberance normally filling their home.

As the weeks went by, Dee continued checking on Emmy. Twice a week she took Hank to play practice at the theater. When she took Hank and Sara to Chucky E. Cheese's on the Atlanta Highway in Athens, Hank seemed able to push the grief aside as he put all his energy into the games. Once, after rehearsal, instead of taking him home she drove to the Jacksons' house for a surprise pool party. Several of his friends from school and children in the upcoming play greeted him enthusiastically.

Eli, the young man portraying Rocky in the play, arrived with a big smile. Hank approached him and asked, "Hey, what was wrong with you today? You're always talking. Today, you didn't say a word. You just looked at me when I talked to you. What's up?"

Eli replied, "Just practicing my lines, buddy. Just practicing my lines."

"You don't have any lines," Hank said. Several others chimed in, agreeing with Hank.

Eli waited for his words to sink in, smiled and said, "Exactly." His fingers moved left to right across his mouth, pretending to zip his lips closed. All the kids laughed. It would have been the perfect party if worry about James hadn't hovered in and around the pool.

Late that afternoon, Dee heard the phone ringing as she entered the back door. Her aunt, Nancy Tremane, called to tell her the kidnapping story appeared in the Anderson, South Carolina paper. She told Dee she'd been waiting for the right time to tell Frank about how Emmy's son had disappeared when he read it in the paper. He hadn't slept well since. Nancy hoped the visit to Elberton would help him cope with all the memories of Mollie's disappearance. Seeing her grave often helped him put the past in perspective.

The following day Dee marked off another box on her calendar, with no break in James' case. The days had turned into weeks. The dark clouds hovered over their houses, adding gloom to an already dreary day. She and Sara made a trip to town to pick up Emmy's favorite food, hoping to entice her to eat. Rain started pelting the windshield as Dee pulled into the Raffertys' driveway with two servings of chicken salad from Richard's Restaurant and chicken nuggets from McDonald's for Sara and Hank. Sara jumped out of the car and into the rain before Dee opened the umbrella. She heard the squishy sounds of Sara's flip-flops as her daughter walked away.

Sara, balancing a cardboard container with two cups of lemonade in one hand and a bag of food in the other, darted to the right side of the house when she spotted Hank lounging on a brown wicker sofa on the side porch, hunched over a handheld video game. His wrinkled navy blue shorts and white T-shirt looked as though he had slept in them. He gave no indication he was aware of her presence. As soon as Wascal smelled food, the dog got up from the shade beneath the picnic table and greeted Sara, his tail swishing back and forth. He nudged the screen door from inside, providing Sara enough space to squeeze in without dropping anything. Sara placed the rain-splattered bag of food on the end of the table near Hank, who looked up and grunted a greeting. She separated her food from his, opened a box of chicken nuggets, and offered Wascal half of a nugget. It disappeared quickly. Wascal sat, patiently waiting for another bite.

As soon as Dee stepped on to the covered deck, she closed her umbrella and placed it beside the back door. Through the glass in the storm door, she could see Emmy in her favorite recliner. Surprised to see a bottle in Marcie's mouth, Dee said, "Thought you were breast feeding." She noticed the picture, taken in the hospital, of James, Hank and Marcie, sitting on a table beside Emmy's chair.

"I hoped to, but I'm not making enough milk to keep her happy. I never had such problems before. I'm sure it's the stress."

"That's understandable." Dee couldn't believe how much weight Emmy had lost. Her pullover shirt hung off her shoulders. Her normally tight jeans needed a belt. She knew Emmy wanted to lose a few pounds, but not like this.

"Excuse me just a minute. I'll put her to bed." Emmy bent over and kissed Marcie's forehead. "She's so beautiful."

"I agree." Dee hoped Emmy would be able to eat the chicken salad and sweet potato fries. She couldn't believe she had to entice her to eat.

When Emmy returned, Dee noticed her pulling up her loose jeans and seemed more interested in talking than eating. Dee couldn't help but see that Emmy's normally healthy strawberry blond hair hung lank and oily and needed shampooing. The dark circles under Emmy's eyes prompted Dee to ask, "Are you getting any sleep?"

"Not really. I keep thinking there's something I should be doing to find James."

"We all wish we could do more." Dee couldn't think of anything else to say.

"I can't get past Fred letting it happen." Emmy said.

Emmy's growing anger made Dee want to defend Fred.

Emmy added, "He said he didn't turn his back on James. But, he did or it wouldn't have happened."

Dee listened as Emmy rambled on about how she first found out about how James was taken, even though she'd heard the sad story many times. Emmy, again, got to the part about questioning how Fred could have let it happen.

When Emmy stopped talking, Dee handed her a tray with the chicken salad and sweet potato fries. Emmy ignored the food and went on to say she knew she was being unfair to Fred. Dee ate her chicken salad as Emmy told her how Fred cried when he thought she couldn't hear him. Still, she couldn't understand how he could have left James sitting in the waiting area by himself. She kept repeating herself.

Dee wondered if Emmy would ever be able to forgive Fred. Each time she said something positive about him, she followed it with a bigger negative. Her anger grew with each statement.

Emmy picked up a sweet potato fry and slowly ate it. "Ummmm. These are good. Thanks for picking up lunch for us. I assume Hank and Sara are somewhere having lunch."

Dee was happy that Emmy took a bite of chicken salad and assured her friend that Hank and Sara were having lunch on the side porch. They sat in silence for a few minutes giving Dee time to think of something that might help Emmy see Fred in a better light. Her eyes went to the small red and black tattoo on the inside of Emmy's foot. She asked Emmy to look at the inside of her left ankle. Emmy frowned as she lifted the recliner's footrest.

"See the tattoo?" Dee asked.

Emmy stared at the black outline of a butterfly with the ampersand as its body and the red initial "F" on one wing and "M" on the other. She didn't say anything. She kept staring.

Dee broke the silence. "Remember when you had Fred's pet name for you and his initial placed in that butterfly? M and F." She waited for Emmy to nod her head before she continued. "Remember, too, how you wanted it off when he broke up with you? Yet, you loved him so much you forgave him a year later. You two were meant for each other. I know your heart is broken about James. Don't add more heartbreak. Fred is hating himself for letting that woman take James."

Emmy moved food around on her plate, and refused to look at Dee. Dee gave her a kiss on the forehead, went into the kitchen, emptied the dishwasher, refilled it with the dirty dishes from the sink, and wiped the counters clean. When she finished in the kitchen, she made her way to the side porch to check on Sara and Hank.

She wasn't surprised to see wrappers and spots of ketchup littering the table except for the space where Sara was drawing. She watched as Sara's left hand moved quickly over the shape of what looked like a large gray rock with a smaller rock on top. She noticed that Sara had put water around the rock. Dee learned long ago not to get too involved in Sara's drawings before they were finished. Her interpretations were almost always wrong. Dee turned her attention to Hank.

"How's the play coming, sweetie?" Dee asked as Hank looked up from his video game.

"It's okay. Thanks for lunch, Aunt Dee."

"You're so welcome." She picked up the used napkins and other litter, placing it into the McDonald's bag. She leaned close to Hank and asked, "You really okay?"

Hank shrugged, "Yeah. Guess so."

Dee gave him a hug and whispered, "Call me if you need me. Night or day." More than ever, she realized just how vulnerable twelve going on thirteen could be when things were normal. These days were far from normal. Until James was found, normal wouldn't exist. She hoped Dan would spend time with Hank the next time he came home.

She walked into the kitchen with the trash from the side porch, deposited it in the garbage, and stepped into the den to talk with Emmy, who sat staring into space. She didn't respond when Dee asked her if she had finished lunch. Emmy's depression scared Dee.

Shaking Emmy's shoulder brought a response from her. Emmy pulled a sheet of notebook paper from its hiding place beside the cushion in the chair. She handed it to Dee. The words, written in pencil, said it all:

My heart
is hiding
from the truth
My mind
is knowing
the truth
My hands
are reaching
to touch your face
My spirit
is longing to
communicate with
you somehow
The truth is
you are gone

Emmy told Dee if she didn't have Marcie and Hank, she'd never be able to go on. "I know I have to think of my children who didn't get kidnapped. They are just as important as James." She went on to tell Dee she feared a future without James and envisioned seeing him at different ages, imagining him as a teenager, wondering in old age if she would see a young man with a family and believe he was James.

"Dee, I swear to you I'd kill myself if … I ...." She didn't finish the sentence. Dee bent over and held Emmy against her chest and smoothed her oily unruly hair.

"Shhh. It'll be okay." Dee said.

Mom Jax heard Dee's words as she opened the back door. She announced that she had brought Granny Nida for a visit. It took a while for Granny Nida to make it across the room, moving with her walker one step at a time. Dee brought in a chair from the dining room for the old woman, knowing the height and arms of the chair would be more comfortable and would help her get out of the chair later. Dee heard

Mom Jax telling Emmy how Granny Nida insisted she needed to see her Emmy Lou.

The raindrops had left dark water spots across Granny Nida's shoulders, making her light green blouse two-toned. Mom Jax guided her mother into the seat and placed a light sweater around her shoulders. Ignoring her own wet hair, she ran a paper towel over her mother's white curls. Granny Nida's feet barely touched the floor and dangled below the hem of her brown pants.

Granny Nida interrupted Mom Jax to tell a joke. "I just want to tell Emmy Lou about that cat that died and went to pet heaven. St. Thomcat asked 'im what he wanted, and the cat asked for a large cushion. Right away the saint placed 'im on a large soft cushion and told 'im to thank about what else he wanted or needed and he'd check back with him in a day or two." Granny Nida paused.

"The very next day three mice arrived at the pet door to heaven. They were a'fixin' to step into heaven when St. Pet-her, in charge of animals that day, asked if they wanted or needed anythang. The three mice, all together, told 'im 'We want skates.' The largest mouse added, 'We've always wanted skates. We've run and run to keep from getting kilt.' The saint replied, 'Y'all will get yore skates for shore. I can get them for you right now.' They got their skates, and St. Pet-her placed them in the same room as the cat. When St. Thomcat arrived a few hours later, he asked the cat if he knew what it was he needed or wanted. The cat replied, 'I've got all I need. I got meals on wheels.'"

Dee and Mom Jax laughed. Dee heard the joke before, but Granny Nida, as always, added her own spin. Emmy gave her grandmother a weak smile, asked her guests to excuse her, and made her way through the master bedroom to her bathroom.

"My pore Emmy Lou. She hardly said a word. Remember how she used to talk non-stop?" she asked her daughter. She looked at Dee, "Dee Dee, sugar, when Emmy Lou was a little girl she talked all the time. She'd talk to a stick, even if it couldn't talk back to her." Granny Nida stopped wringing her hands, placed them quietly in her lap and bowed her head.

Dee knew that James' disappearance was taking a toll on everyone. The thump, thump, thump of rain hitting the roof seemed to add a new level of grief in the room. Dee wondered, *Is James in a dry safe place?*

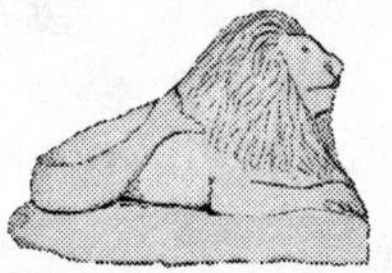

Chapter Fourteen – The Clown

Robert hadn't planned to be a clown. Fate took him in that direction when he visited his grandfather in New Jersey and listened to Granpa's adventures.

As a teenager in the 1960s, his grandfather bought a unicycle. He said he picked up clown paraphernalia after the skinned knees and bruises from falling off the cycle had faded away. Back in those days, his red hair resembled his grandson's. He told Robert how he let his hair grow out and wasn't happy with his slight natural curl. He thought he'd look like a real clown if he had curly hair, so he talked his sister into giving him a home permanent.

Robert laughed as the old man described the plastic pink rollers that looked like small bones with clamps. Granpa told him how he sat at their family's kitchen table while his sister rolled his hair on the curlers. He said she sang songs as she wrapped his hair around the curlers. In his old raspy voice, he sang one of the songs for Robert, *"Yankee Doodle went to town, riding on a pony, went into a beauty shop and came out with a Toni."*

Robert didn't remember Grandpa's sister. She died when he was a baby. "What's a Toni?" he asked.

His grandfather replied, "Son, that was a brand of home permanents. It gave me more curl than I wanted. Actually, it was quite kinky and took forever to grow out. After that, I got a wig to wear with my clown outfit. The Toni Yankee Doodle song wasn't her favorite though. It was, *'Yankee Doodle went to town, riding on a turtle, turned the corner just in time to see a lady's girdle.'"*

"A girdle?" Robert questioned, his green eyes twinkling.

"Aaah. Ummmm." Granpa hemmed and hawed. "It's a woman's underwear. Well, not exactly. It's this elastic underwear worn over regular underwear to make a woman look skinny. At least your Granma wore one over her real underwear. It was tight. I never understood why a woman would do that to herself."

"I get it. He was riding on a turtle, low to the ground, and saw the woman's panties when he looked up. Right?" Robert laughed.

"That's right. It was funnier back then. Women never let us boys see anything. It was a time when two-piece bathing suits were becoming popular, and certainly long before bikinis existed." He thought a while, laughed and added, "You just had to be there." He went on to tell Robert how his favorite place to ride the unicycle was in a small grocery store where the owner let him juggle oranges and apples as he rode through the aisles and entertained the customers.

Robert came home to the Georgia coast with a fake red nose, a clown suit that was way too large for his thirteen-year-old frame, a unicycle, and a head full of funny clown stories. He spent hours maneuvering around the house balancing himself on the unicycle before taking it to the yard and finally to the sidewalk.

Eventually, he added juggling to his act, starting with two tennis balls, adding one at a time until he was juggling five. Within a year, he was entertaining his parents and their friends in their backyard. His little longhaired Chihuahua jumped through a hula-hoop and used her nose to push a ball around the yard so fast no one could catch her. Robert made a big to-do over trying to keep up with her. When Robert wasn't on the unicycle, he found ways to trip and fall as part of the clown act. On Halloween, he juggled apples and oranges before giving them to the trick-or-treat children.

By mid-July, a few days after his fifteenth birthday, Robert knew he was ready. With a few adjustments that his mother made, the clown suit fit him well. He refused to perm his hair. Like his grandfather, he wore the red wig. He painted his clown's face, placed the red bulbous nose over his own, and cycled down Mallery Street. He passed the Dairy Queen and rode into the village. The locals watched his progress as he made his way to the pier.

Tourists crowded the streets and stores in the village, blocking him from the streets and sidewalks. He felt much safer when he arrived at the park where children and their parents made way for him.

He rode past the swing set and slide. He made his way down the walkway from the parking area past the picnic tables, by the sculpture of the mother whale with her baby on her back, to the lighthouse and back to the small playground near the pier. He entertained the children as they waited in line for the next swing or an opportunity to enjoy the slide.

Robert's tired muscles in his arms and legs forced him to take a rest. He sat on a bench with a woman who was correcting a brown haired boy about six years old. When the boy turned to look at his clown suit, the woman jerked his head around and made him look at her. Robert heard her say, "Look at me. Now. Say, Mommy."

Robert saw the angry look in the boy's eyes and saw the child look down at the ground, pinch his chin, and mumble, "Mamamommy."

Trying not to be too obvious, Robert continued observing the strange woman as she pursed her thin lips together, stood up, pushed the boy's hand away from his chin, placed her hand behind his shoulder, and forced him to walk with her to a swing. She lifted him into the swing and started to walk behind him to give him a push. The boy jumped out of the seat, fell in the sand, got up, and ran toward the sidewalk. She wasted no time catching up with him.

Robert watched as she grabbed his arm and forced the boy to walk beside her. He assumed they were tourists, since he hadn't seen them before. Her long sleeves and pants looked out of place. A feeling of unease stayed with him long after she and the boy were out of sight.

Nan's dark thoughts showed in the scowl on her face. *That stupid clown. That dumb, stupid clown. I'll have to be more careful. He watched us too closely.* She squeezed the boy's hand harder as she pulled him along beside her.

They walked away from the playground, got into her black Honda and drove to Ocean Boulevard, passed the stores and restaurants on the left side of Mallery Street, and were headed toward the Dairy Queen when James made a noise from the back seat. She knew he wanted to stop here. The tree fascinated him.

Nan learned from talking with the owner of the bookstore in the village that the same artist who carved the faces had also sculpted the mother whale with her baby on her back, in the 1990s, and recently sculpted the faces in the trees in the vacant subdivision. She pulled in beside the huge tree across from the Dairy Queen and talked as she helped him get out of the car.

"An old sailor from a pirate ship put that face in the tree," Nan lied. "His ship sailed right up to the pier a hundred years ago. They needed the limb of the tree to make a post to hold the sail way up high to catch the air and make the ship move across the ocean. After they cut the limb, the old sailor took his knife and cut and cut until he made this face." Nan enjoyed the satisfaction of seeing Timmy's perpetual scowl leave his face for just a few seconds. She continued, "The face is his long lost love. She died. He couldn't forget her."

"Weeweeweally?" James questioned.

"Really. Timmy, it's really, not weeweeweally. Now you just stop that nonsense." She grabbed him by his right wrist and forced him back into the car. She knew he could talk correctly. He certainly talked right when she first brought him home. He was doing it just to irritate her. She would show him. He looked longingly at the entrance to the Dairy Queen, raised his left hand and pinched his chin.

"No. No ice cream for you, until you quit that nonsense and talk to me like the intelligent boy I know you are." She hated the bad habits he picked up in the last few weeks.

Chapter Fifteen – A Woman in the Tree

Arriving at Mollie's grave ahead of her uncle and aunt, Dee walked to the backside of the monument and looked at the word TREMANE centered at the top. Musical notes rested just below the name and above the words, "*Singing with the Angels*."

She walked to the front side of the headstone and read Mollie A. Tremane on the top line, glanced at the birth and death dates. She read out loud the line below the dates, "*She came back to us . . .*" Dee stopped reading when she heard the hum of a motor nearby.

Frank and Nancy Tremane's truck pulled up behind Dee's car a few yards from Mollie's grave. Dee smiled as they walked towards her. Her uncle's shy smile reminded her of her dad. The silver hair at his temples mingled with his thick black hair. He looked different from the Frank Tremane she met more than a decade earlier. He no longer sported a ponytail, and age had softened his features. Her heart skipped a beat when she recognized her dad's walk in his younger brother's slow gait. His rough brick-mason hands felt gentle as they touched her face in greeting. His quiet strength continued to impress her. He looked comfortable in blue jeans and a white T-shirt.

She stood in the same spot ten years earlier looking at Frank Tremane and one of his three sons. The young man seemed quite familiar even though she knew they had never met. Later, she compared her father's picture as a young man to a picture of the Tremanes' son. The seed of finding her father's biological family had been planted here at Mollie's grave. Finding Mollie's remains took a lot of strength and stubbornness, and led her on another journey. She insisted her father and Frank Tremane have DNA testing. The verification came back quickly.

She felt good that her father, Sam Dupree, was able to spend the last years of his life enjoying the brother he never knew before. Dee's smile widened as she embraced her uncle.

Nancy walked past her husband and Dee, took the faded purple silk tulips from the front of Mollie's monument and replaced it with a pot of bright red artificial geraniums. Balancing the old arrangement on her left hip, she gave Dee a right-handed hug.

"Where's Sara?" Nancy handed Frank the old flower arrangement and brushed soil from her khaki pants and blue cotton pullover blouse. Crumbs of dirt landed on her right foot. With one hand on her husband's shoulder for balance, she took off a stone studded flip flop, shook it, placed it back on her foot, and listened to Dee's answer.

"She's in town. Her piano lesson is over in about ten minutes. I'll stop and pick her up on the way to lunch. She'd be one unhappy little girl if she got left out. She made me reschedule her lesson so that she didn't miss you two today."

Nancy turned around to face Dee and said, "We aren't sure where the McIntosh Coffee Shoppe is. I expect we could find it. The last time we were in town several stores on the Square were empty."

They went over the directions as they walked to their vehicles.

Back home, after her uncle and aunt had gone back to South Carolina, Dee left Sara at her drawing table in the front room near a window and went to the kitchen to prepare a Greek casserole for the Raffertys' dinner. She sprayed a casserole dish with olive oil and layered the dish with diced raw chicken sprinkled with oregano, salt, and pepper. She pressed a layer of fresh spinach over the chicken, added sliced onion and more seasoning, followed by a drained can of petite diced tomatoes, and topped it off with feta cheese crumbles. She put foil over the dish, placed it in the oven, and set the timer as a reminder to take the foil off in forty-five minutes so it could cook the last fifteen minutes without a cover.

Dee walked to Sara's small table and saw her daughter working feverishly on a drawing of a huge tree with a limb stump, cut at an angle. Erasure crumbs attested to the fact that she was struggling to create a picture of a face carving. Dee watched her wipe the erasure crumbs away.

"What is that, sweetie?" Dee bent down to get a better look at the drawing.

"It's that woman in the tree," Sara answered reluctantly. She seemed annoyed at the interruption. "You know, the one I drew for James. The picture with the sea lion."

Dee propped on her knees beside Sara's chair to get even closer to the drawing. She understood Sara's short retort when she saw her struggling with the picture. She watched as another erasure took away a nose, leaving a blank spot.

She waited until Sara redrew the nose before asking, "Why is the woman in the tree?"

"I don't know. Some man put her there. James likes it. He calls her a princess. He sees her almost every day. Sometimes he sees a tree with a man's face that looks kinda like a lion. The faces in the trees are James' friends."

Dee almost fell the rest of the way to the floor. *James.* She closed her eyes and prayed for strength. Sara's strong clairvoyance was different from the visions she experienced. Her visions from 1960 were sent by Mollie. It was Mollie's need that initiated contact with her, enabled by blood kin and the family clairvoyant gene. Sara saw current events. Sara saw the same things as James. Dee wondered if Mollie was sending messages? Or, was Sara's ability so strong she could see these things without any help from Mollie?

"Knock. Knock." Sara looked at her mother, waiting for her to join the game.

"Who's there?" Dee responded.

" Color."

"Color who?"

"Color me blue. I miss James, Mom. He didn't like knock-knock jokes."

"I miss him too, sweetie. Mom? What happened to Mommy?"

"I'm too big to call you Mommy. Mommy's a baby's word. Right, Mom? I'm not a baby anymore." Sara sat straighter in the chair, hoping her mother could see a difference.

Dee smiled. "Sure. I like Mom. Want me to help you get packed to go to Mama Anna's?" Dee offered. "She'll be here soon." Thinking of her mother didn't make Dee feel better. Her mother almost always found fault with something she said or did. Her mother's fault-finding got worse as she grew older.

"Mom. Don't worry. Mama Anna loves you. She just hides it a lot," Sara said as she closed the pad and placed her pencils in a wooden box.

Dee laughed, thinking, *Leave it to Sara to cut to the chase.* "You are too smart, little girl."

"Mama Anna misses Granddaddy so much it makes her sad. I'll draw her a picture and ask her to draw one for me. She told me I got the drawing from her. I like those paintings of leaves. Cousins … or something like that. You know, the pictures that look like green animals or people."

"I know the ones. It's kudzu vines. Kudzu leaves, in the shapes of animals or people."

"Yeah. That's it. She'll show me all the picture books of you." Dee could hear her mother's voice as Sara added, "She says you were a stubborn child." Sara shook her head, "But she didn't mean it like a bad thing."

Dee hugged her daughter. "You're the one who shouldn't worry. Believe me, I know my mother. She's not a bad person, just opinionated. Come on, let's go check your bag." She took Sara's left hand, kissed it and pulled her up from the chair before they walked down the hallway, hand in hand. "I'll miss you, sweetie. But, I know Mama Anna will love spending time with her favorite granddaughter."

"Yeah. Her only granddaughter." Sara laughed.

"Daddy and I will come get you on Thursday. Okay, sweetie?"

"That's good." Sara said and handed Dee her well-loved purple stuffed bear. Dee stuffed Purple Burple into the bag. Sara named the large bear soon after she received it. When she burped, instead of asking her mom or dad to excuse her, she laughed and blamed the noise on the bear saying, "Purple Burple, you're excused."

They were in Sara's room when the doorbell rang. Sara zipped her bag, left it on her bed, and joined Dee at the garage door to welcome her grandmother, who walked through the door dressed in lavender slacks with a matching jacket over a red blouse.

"Red Hat Day, Mom?" Dee asked with a smile.

"Yep. You should see the hat I wore with this. We looked good when the photographer at one of those specialty shops in the Mall of Georgia took our picture. The others went back to Marietta after lunch." Anna Marie leaned towards Dee for a kiss on the cheek before giving Sara a hug and asking, "How's my girl?" Without waiting for an answer, she asked Sara, "Ready to go?"

'Mom. You just got here." Dee's disappointment showed in her voice.

"I know, it's a long drive back home and I don't want to be on the by-pass during rush hour."

Dee insisted they all sit at the kitchen table and have a drink and a snack. Dee and her mother drank sweet tea and Sara devoured a glass of milk. Sara served the last of the Girl Scout chocolate chip cookies straight from the package.

Anna Marie and Sara left for Marietta soon after. Dee sat at the kitchen table wondering, not for first time, why her mother never spent a night in their house. Even when her daddy was living, her mother always found some excuse to get back home.

Dee looked around her Sweet City house. She loved the high ceilings in the living room, kitchen and breakfast room. When they moved into the house, life was sweet. How could so many things change in such a short time?

She walked to the bedroom and sat on their bed, looking around and remembering the love shared in this room. Daniel had been a great lover. He would laugh when she told him how her toes curled when they made love. Sex by itself never appealed to Dee. Sex with love felt like a potent drug. *Had been.* It had been a long time since she felt her toes curl.

Questioning when his interest waned and why he found excuses to leave town often, left her with no answers. She knew he felt threatened by her family's unusual gift, and as Sara's clairvoyance became stronger, he withdrew from both of them.

The shocking truth about why he no longer initiated lovemaking, hit her hard. *He doesn't want me to get pregnant. He doesn't want another child with me*. The revelation left her feeling weak and devastated.

James' absence and Sara's response to it made Dee want to protect her daughter. She assumed Dan's guilt and helplessness were making him feel inadequate, also.

With Sara's clairvoyant gene and blood kin to James, Sara more than likely would know things no one else knew about the kidnapping. Dee knew Sara could get hurt. She didn't know how to stop it. She didn't know if she should try to stop it. Sara may be their only hope of finding James.

When Dan arrived home from Texas, Dee served lasagna and his favorite salad: stacked sliced tomatoes, layered with basil, a slice of paper-thin onion, and soft mozzarella cheese sprinkled with balsamic vinegar. The single basil leaf placed on top completed the Mozzarella Caprese. She knew the bottle of Italian wine she chose would perfectly complement their meal.

After dinner, they talked about his company's on-going engineering project in Texas. She showed him Sara's picture of the face in the tree and tried to explain its significance. She didn't have long to wonder how he felt about Sara's involvement in finding James. He told Dee he wanted Sara left out of it.

The anger in his voice surprised Dee. "We've lost James. Our family can't survive losing another child, and this could affect her mentally. There are more ways than kidnapping to lose a child. Sara needs a normal life. I know you think Sara has inherited this strange ability, but we're just going to have to ignore it for her sake. My God, she's only nine years old. If she wants to pursue this thing when she's older, then okay. It needs to be her choice. You shouldn't lead her on about this."

"Do you honestly think we have a choice in whether Sara has this special gift?"

"Special gift? Remember how haunted you were with those visions from Mollie. I loved you; but that was a nightmare, in more ways than one. She'll get over it. You did."

She heard him use love in the past tense and chose to ignore it. Grabbing his arm to make sure he didn't walk away, she said, "You're missing one really big point here, Daniel." This time, her tone wasn't endearing. "Those visions didn't go away until after Mollie was found and after her rapist and killer were no longer threats to anyone else." A pain shot through Dee's stomach. She remembered how her visions bothered him and recalled how he left town on one of his trips without calling her for weeks – he couldn't handle the role she inherited. They weren't married back then. She didn't choose the visions any more than Sara did.

"Sara won't stop seeing the same things James sees just because you want her to," she said. By the time she finished, tears ran down her face. He didn't back down. The tears stopped when the anger started. The abandonment she felt ten years before crept back in. She called him narrow minded and hateful. He accused her of not making good choices for their daughter.

"I didn't make a big deal out of you insisting that Emmy and her family move back to Elberton just because Sara felt that some crazy woman was following them around. But, this is going too far," he said.

"You shithead. Do you actually believe it's a coincidence that someone followed Emmy and the boys in Hilton Head Island, and now

James has been kidnapped, even though they moved? Think about it."

"I have thought about it and damn well will not cater to or have my child's life ruined by your craziness."

Dee went to the hall closet, chose a sheet and a pillow, threw them at him, and told him he could sleep on the sofa.

She watched him walk past her, headed to the bedroom, and heard him say, "I've not slept in my bed for weeks. You can sleep where ever you want to, but I'm sleeping in my bed tonight."

The hateful words they said to each other came back again and again as Dee tossed and turned. The list of questions kept growing. What happened to him? How could he be so adamant when his own sister's child needed Sara's help? She wasn't happy about the situation either. She knew Sara's pictures from James would continue regardless of Dan's opinion – or hers. She would never willingly choose to jeopardize Sara. Never! It hurt that he thought she would.

She moved from the sofa to Sara's room for a couple of hours. Unable to sleep, she returned to the den. After tossing and turning all night, she felt tired when the sun's rays woke her the following morning. Sara's trip to her mother's felt like a godsend. Dee would never want Sara to hear or see them fighting.

She knocked on their bedroom door before entering. The small suitcase he carried on his last trip lay on top of the unmade bed, along with the larger black suitcase. Partially opened dresser drawers caught her attention, their emptiness telling their own story. His pajamas lay discarded on the floor. She turned toward the walk-in closet as he came out with an armload of shirts.

"Who is she?" Dee asked.

"Who's who?" Dan came back at her as he placed the shirts on the bed and turned away.

"You know what I'm talking about. You've been distancing yourself from me and from your family for a long time. Who is she?"

"It doesn't matter. You know why I'm leaving. I can't take this mystic hocus-pocus crap anymore," he said without looking at her.

"I remember what you called it last night. My craziness. You're such a coward. Make up your mind. What about your daughter? Her gift is a hundred times more powerful than any gift I've ever possessed. Are you going to dump her, too?" Dee stood rigid waiting for his answer.

"Sara will always be my daughter. I will always be her daddy. I think a jury wouldn't like or understand your telepathic junk any more than I do," he said with a sneer of superiority.

"You piece of shit. You aren't leaving because of my craziness. Who is she?" Dee asked again.

"I said it doesn't matter. Let it go, damn it."

"All those trips to Brownsville weren't all business. Were they?"

He didn't respond.

"How long?" She asked and then waited. He kept piling clothes into the large suitcase.

"Three years," he said without looking at her.

Dee went to the closet, took hangar after hangar of pants and threw them on the bed. She stripped his side of the closet, threw his shoes into the bedroom, followed by stacks of jeans and shorts. Everything he owned came out of the closet in a fury.

"Now I know why you brought home very few new clothes from the mall in Brownsville. You bought her more clothes than you bought yourself. I thought the pants you brought home were pretty expensive. I helped you pay for your mistress' gifts. I don't even shop at L&L for Sara and me. You make me sick. Leave me the name of your lawyer. There's nothing left for us to talk about."

"There's Sara," he added. "I'll have to think about her best interest in all this. I may let you have custody if I have generous visiting rights."

"Oh. You *may* let me have custody? You're so kind," she added sarcastically. "You are not and will not be making the decisions alone."

She could see the surprise in his eyes when he finally looked at her. She knew he had forgotten how stubborn she could be.

She continued, "If you think I'll lay down and play dead for you while you decide on my future or the future of our daughter, you don't know me."

She looked for something to throw at him. Instead, she turned and left the room, made her way to the utility room in the garage, retrieved several cardboard boxes, and carried them to their bedroom. "Here. Don't leave anything that's yours. I can't promise I won't throw it out."

She could see that he was stunned at her reaction.

"*You* should tell your parents." she said from the doorway and waited for an answer. When he didn't respond she asked, "Are you going to?"

"I hadn't gotten that far. Don't you think you're rushing things?" He asked without looking at her.

"You said three years. No, I'm not rushing things. I've waited long enough." She took a couple of steps to the chest of drawers near the door, reached for the bottle of Beautifully Bold perfume spray he gave her for their anniversary, and removed the cover.

"This was never me. Is it the perfume she wears?" Dee sprayed the expensive perfume over his clothes before he could grab the bottle. She would have poured the entire contents into his suitcase if she'd been able to remove the spray top.

"Hey. Stop wasting that. You have no idea how expensive that is." Dan tried to take the bottle from her hands. She sprayed towards his face. The scent went into his hair. She threw the bottle into his suitcase.

"After today, I hope it makes you sick every time you smell Beautifully Bold." Holding back the tears, she grabbed a pair of jeans, a Georgia Bulldog T-shirt, her shoes and socks, and left the room. She changed clothes in the hall bathroom, took her purse from the kitchen table, and left the house.

Her heart ached when she realized Dan planned to use Sara as a way to negotiate a settlement in his favor. She knew he had no intention of providing a home for their daughter. The smell of Beautifully Bold perfume spray filled her nostrils.

Her stomach turned upside down when she remembered how many times the same fragrance drifted from Dan's clothes when she washed them. Believing the smell came from the hotel's soaps and shampoos, she hadn't questioned him. He did not deserve her blind faith – ever. His thoughtlessness amazed and shocked her. She stopped the car, jumped out, ran behind the car, and threw up on the tough roadside grass. The relief she felt from her body's reaction to the perfume and Dan's attitude surprised her. She stood tall as she walked back to the driver's side of the car, leaving the noxious bile on the side of the road.

Many miles away from Athens, Robert spotted the woman from the park. It had been two weeks since he watched her walk away with the little boy. He remembered the scene and how he felt that something wasn't right about her and the boy.

He hoped she wouldn't recognize him without his clown outfit, so he followed her and the boy to see if they lived in the village. They walked down Mallery Street, crossed Kings Way, and entered the restaurant on the corner. Robert watched as she opened the door and let the boy go through first. Everything seemed normal. He felt he would be the weird one if he went into the restaurant with his fishing pole and tackle box. He walked on past the art galleries, bookstore, and souvenir shops towards the pier.

When he got to the pier, he told his friend, Dale, about the strange woman and the brown-haired boy. As he told the story about seeing them earlier, he told Dale how neither of them seemed to have a natural hair color. Finally, he knew why this haunted him. The boy's hairline showed blond roots. *Little boys do not willingly dye their hair.*

The next day Robert and Dale whizzed through the parking lot of Brogan's on their skateboards. When Robert saw the woman and the boy at the small playground near the parking lot, he motioned for Dale to come closer and quietly asked Dale to take a look at the strange pair. They picked up their skateboards, walked past the playground, and leaned against a car in the parking lot just a few yards away.

When the woman's eyes darted their way, they decided to put some distance between them and her. They sauntered toward the pier. Dale spoke first, "You're right. She's weird. She's constantly checking out her surroundings, like she's paranoid or something."

"Yeah. Let's walk on. You look at her and tell me what she's doing. Then, I'll take a second look. I think she spotted us and thinks something's up," Robert said as he bent over pretending to be interested in a dog lying in the hot sun before walking towards an old fisherman with a bucket of fish.

They nodded to the old fisherman and walked on. Dale walked faster while Robert looked back at the woman. Robert caught up with Dale and said, "I think we spooked her. Look, she's on the run again. I hope she hasn't caught on that I'm the clown from the other day."

They watched as she forced the little boy to leave the playground and walk to the corner store past Brogan's. She turned the corner and mingled into the summer tourist crowd. By the time Robert and Dale got to the main street, there was no sign of the woman and the little boy.

Meandering down Mallery Street toward the Dairy Queen, the boys caught a glimpse of the woman, at the beachwear store. By the time they passed the shop, she and the boy had disappeared again.

"This is not the route she took the last time I followed her. She walked towards the Dairy Queen, took a right and disappeared into an overgrown vacant lot just past the park." Robert added, "I think she's trying to outmaneuver us."

"Or, she lives nearby and has no idea we're following her," Dale said.

"She weighed a lot more the first time I saw her. It's not normal to lose that much weight in such a short time," Robert shared his observation. "I think she's changing her look on purpose. She knows we're watching; otherwise, she wouldn't be disappearing so much."

"Hey. I got an idea. Let's bring our camera and take a picture of her and the boy. We could take it to the police and see if there's a boy missing – one that looks like him," his friend suggested.

"Yeah. Like she's gonna let us get that close."

"I can take one with my phone," Dale said with determination. "She'll never know."

Nan walked faster, pulling Timmy along. She knew she tended to repeat her route to and from home. She found it difficult to throw the boys off her track. *They think they're so smart*. Her thin lips curved into a half smile as she congratulated herself for recognizing that the red-haired boy's shoes were the same ones the clown wore a few weeks before.

Timmy's short legs tried to keep up. It took two of his steps to make one of hers. When he lagged behind, she jerked him forward.

Her disappointment in Timmy left her with a dilemma. Soon, it would be time for him to start school. His identification papers and fake birth certificate waited in the middle drawer of her desk in her bedroom. His new clothes hung in his closet, with each shirt placed with matching pants. The shelf below the shirts and pants held socks, their stripes mirroring the colors in the outfits above.

If she let him start to school, he couldn't just disappear, unless she made up a story that his father had custody during the school year. It would be easier if he didn't get into the system. By the time she meandered around several backstreets trying to avoid the pesky boys, she had made up her mind – she wouldn't let Timmy start school.

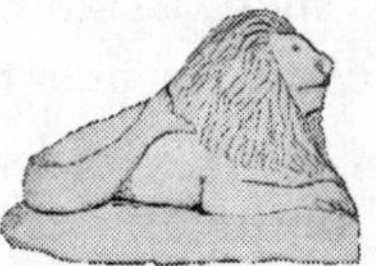

Chapter Sixteen – Sing, Smile and Pray

Dee hardly saw the Elberton city limit sign as she drove into town. Her thoughts centered on the last twenty-four hours and how many times she deliberately pushed away the thought that Dan had found someone else. Until today, she never let herself accept that he was pulling away from her. She wondered just how much this would affect her relationship with Emmy and her in-laws. She missed her daddy. She could have talked with him and he would have known how to help.

She thought, O*h hell. I'll have to tell Mom when I get Sara tomorrow.* She felt certain her mother would side with Dan. Not understanding or not wanting to understand the family clairvoyance was the one thing Anna Marie and Dan had in common. Her mother couldn't forget how hard it was on her family when Connie's strange behavior started. Connie wasn't the only one to suffer. All four girls were picked on in school because Connie was different. Their parents spent a lot of money sending Connie to psychiatrists and mental health clinics. Dee lived in fear that her mother would see those same traits in Sara. She knew she would have to deal with the problem eventually. She would never admit her breakup with Dan had anything to do with Sara's abilities. Dan's weak character caused this heartbreak. She didn't want Sara, under any circumstances, to carry any guilt.

She drove to the park across the street from the Catholic church and managed to get the car parked before the tears blurred her vision completely. She felt as though she had loved Daniel Jackson all her life. How would she survive without him? The strength she showed earlier was dissipating. She dreaded facing Emmy and her in-laws.

Drying her tear-streaked cheeks with the hem of her T-shirt, she got out of the car and walked briskly for thirty minutes. She took her time driving through town, stopped at the Dairy Queen for a milkshake and at the last minute, changed the order to Sprite. Her normally good appetite vanished earlier, with each hateful word she and Dan uttered. She needed something to settle her stomach.

How long will it take him to load his things? If he's still there, I won't go in, her thoughts ran together as she made her way home. His truck was gone. With a heavy heart, she pulled into the empty garage. Any energy left over from the fight with Dan disappeared with the tears.

The quiet house added to her loneliness. The unhappiness hovered around her, closing in like a fog after a summer rain. Their room looked as if a whirlwind drifted through the window and played havoc with the hangars and debris Dan left scattered around. She wasn't sure she could sleep in their room that night.

She felt like a stranger walking through her own house. Again, she wondered who she was without Dan. In the den, his stuffed fish hung above the fireplace and reminded her of one of Janet Dayson's songs. Janet, her former college roommate, left Athens before she graduated from the University of Georgia and moved to California to start her acting career – that never took off. She called it her long distance detour since she wound up in Nashville, Tennessee, writing and singing country songs.

To Dee's knowledge, Nashville had never seen a young black woman as determined as Janet. She sent Dee a copy of the demo CD more than six months ago when she was pitching it in Nashville. Dee looked through two stacks of CDs before finding the one she wanted. She placed it in the player. Janet's smooth voice filled the room. Dee sang along to the lyrics printed inside the CD box.

It Doesn't Matter Anymore
It doesn't matter anymore
if you walk right out the door.
Take your diamond; take your ring;
take your clothes and take your things.
It doesn't matter anymore.

My love for you was, oh, so "true."
But "true" is not a word for you.
Oh, the hurt went on and on,
Gave me words for this sad song.
It doesn't matter anymore.

It doesn't matter anymore
if you walk right out the door.
Take your diamond; take your ring;

take your clothes and take your things.
It doesn't matter anymore.

I asked you to leave her alone
And help me make a happy home.
Oh, you couldn't stay away.
She was with you every day.
But, it doesn't matter anymore.

Dee screamed the next three lines:

Take your stuffed fish off the wall
I don't want it at all,
Like the fish, you don't matter anymore.

She sang the remaining lines:

So many times I'd cry and cry.
It hurt so much I thought I'd die.
You killed all my love for you,
Now I don't care what you do,
It doesn't matter anymore.

"You killed all my love for you,
Now I don't care what you do,
You don't matter anymore."

She knew her love for Dan would die slowly. Each part of the life they shared would be like the limbs of a dying tree, dying one limb at a time. The song would be her song – *for how long?* It would be a while before he really didn't matter anymore. As hurt and angry as she felt, she knew he still mattered. She moved a chair from the breakfast room to the den, placed it in front of the fireplace, stepped into it, and reached above the mantel. The stuffed fish almost fell off the wall and into her hands.

Berating herself for choosing the easy way out and ignoring the signs didn't make her feel any better. Tomorrow she'd make the trip to her mother's. She didn't know how she would tell Sara about Dan, or if she could possibly muster the courage to tell her mother. She couldn't put it off. Tomorrow she'd have to drive to Marietta.

Before switching off the computer that evening, she looked up the name of the perfume he gave her. The gift cost almost $900 – as much as a house payment. She felt certain he had lost his mind. The new woman in his life had expensive taste and her influence on Dan changed him. He left without seeing his parents or visiting with Emmy. He didn't even mention the new baby. He had no interest in anyone – except himself.

I'd have been better off if he died. That way, he wouldn't have chosen to leave, she thought as she turned off the bedside lamp. Immediately, guilt washed over her like a stream of water moving over a bed of pebbles. The thought of Sara not having or knowing her father for rest of her life, made her want to take the thought back, leaving her with the question: *How does a person undo a thought? Uuuugh. Go to sleep,* she kept telling herself. An hour later she climbed out of bed, searched for a book she bought a few weeks earlier, and spent most of the night reading.

It was after nine o'clock the following morning when she finally pulled herself out of bed and unlocked Suede's metal crate. He darted to the glass door that opened onto a screened porch. A small concrete frog doorstop held the outside screened door open to make sure Suede had a dry safe place at all times. It gave Suede the freedom to come and go; however, birds had gotten trapped inside the porch and had difficulty finding their way out. More than once, Dee had used a broom to force a bird to the open door to freedom. Suede waited impatiently for Dee to open the inside glass door. As was her habit, she looked into the screened porch to make sure a bird wasn't trapped inside. She didn't see one, so she pushed the sliding glass door open.

As soon as Suede ran out, Dee heard wings flapping. She realized that Suede had seen the movement of a large bird long before Dee saw the bird fly over the door. As soon as she saw its plump body and tinge of red, she knew it was a female cardinal. The poor bird never realized that escape could be found inches below the doorframe. Dee tried to give the bird a chance by holding Suede's collar. His strength amazed her and he pulled away easily. She commanded him to stop. The bird flew back to the other side of the porch – away from its chance of freedom. Suede ignored Dee. The sound of beating wings preceded Suede's jump into the air. He grabbed the bird between his jaws, and came down on the screen at the floorboard, pushing the screen out and leaving a gaping hole.

She watched in horror as Suede ran out into the morning sun, his head held high. With the limp bird clamped between his teeth, he ran across the concrete walkway. Back and forth. He pranced like a well-bred horse. She'd never seen him so proud of himself and knew he acted on instinct. Tears filled her eyes. Just thinking of the bird made her want to punish Suede. But, how could she punish the dog for fulfilling the role his ancestors passed to him? She remembered how he cleaned up the mess from her dropping the hambone, allowing her to be on time for a dental appointment. She knew she had to accept Suede just as he was and remember that no person or animal is perfect. She still couldn't make herself stop and pet him. She hoped she'd be able to do so when she got back home from her mother's.

Before leaving home, Dee used more makeup than normal, trying to hide the effects of lack of sleep the night before and the tears over the dead bird. She hoped her mother wouldn't ask too many questions.

On the drive to Marietta, she couldn't help but compare Suede's hunting skills to Sara's instinctive talents. Could Dan forgive Sara for having traits he didn't like? It made her see Suede more clearly. Of course she loved her beautiful, active, and crazy dog even if she didn't like his natural hunting instincts. For the first time that day she smiled.

Breathing deeply, Dee tried to prepare herself for a confrontation with her mother as she pulled into the driveway. There was no doubt in her mind that her mother would place all the blame on her for Dan leaving. Her father always acted as a buffer for her mother's harsh comments, finding some excuse for Anna Marie's negative attitude. He tried to make up for her mother's insensitivity.

Just before Dee touched the doorbell, the front door opened and Dee saw her mother's smile fade quickly.

"You look like death warmed over. Did you have a wreck on the way over here? Where's Dan?"

"No Mom. I didn't sleep well last night. Dan was too busy to make the trip." Dee leaned around her mother, looking for Sara.

"She's out back in the studio. By the way, Connie asked me to tell you she's having gallbladder surgery." Before Dee could comment, her mother continued, "Did you know just how gifted your daughter is?"

"Well. Yes. She's ... she's always been gifted." Dee wondered what gift her mother was talking about.

"For her age, her drawings are amazing." Anna Marie bragged on her granddaughter as she led Dee to the studio.

Sara's hug made Dee believe her daughter had already picked up on the fact that something was not right.

"Hi, sweetie. How's my girl?" Dee hugged Sara again.

"I'm fine. Me and Mama Anna had a good time painting. See my picture?" Sara handed Dee a watercolor painting.

Normally, Dee would have corrected Sara's grammar. Today, she didn't have the energy to worry about it. She looked at the still life painting of pink Knock Out roses in a green vase. She wasn't surprised to see the real thing on a table near the easel where Sara was working. Her mother's easel stood a few feet away, with her artistic interpretation of the Knock Out roses. Shades of pink filled the entire canvas. Sara's smaller version almost mirrored her mother's artwork.

"See what I mean?" Anna Marie asked Dee. "She's good. Most children her age have no idea how to mix the paint to match colors. She's a natural." The smile on Anna Marie's face reflected her delight in Sara's artistic ability.

Dee hadn't seen her mother this happy in years. She couldn't bring herself to tell her about Dan. If her daddy had been there to comfort her mother afterwards, she would have shared the bad news. Grateful that her mother didn't pursue her earlier comment about the circles under her eyes or Dan's not making the trip, Dee began to help Sara gather her clothes.

Anna Marie asked if she could keep Sara's painting. She wanted to show it to her sisters the next time they got together. Sara smiled and agreed.

Sara waved to her grandmother as her mother backed the car out into the street. As soon as they were on their way home, Sara looked into the rear-view mirror and asked, "What's wrong? Why didn't Daddy come with you?"

"Sweetie, do you mind if we talk about this when we get home? It's complicated and I really need to focus on driving. I didn't sleep well last night. I'm really tired. Okay?" Dee looked in the rear-view mirror, hoping to see Sara's face when she responded.

"Umm, okay. I'm sorry you're sad. But we can talk about it later."

"Thanks. Want to choose a CD?" Dee hoped to divert Sara's attention to something more positive. She passed a case of CDs to the back seat. Sara took the case, unzipped it, and pulled out her favorite, made just for her by her mom's friend, Janet. She handed it to her mom who inserted it into the CD player. Janet's voice filled the car with one of Sara's favorite songs, one Janet wrote for Sara's Sunday school class.

Sara used hand motions to match the words, placing her opened hands beside her mouth for singing, pointing to the corners of her mouth for smiling and pressing her hands together in front of her chest for praying. *"We need to be singing enough; we need to be singing enough; when life is hard and times are tough."* Sara raised her fist beside her when she sang "hard," and then brought them together in front of her when she sang "tough." *"We need to be singing enough."*

Dee glanced up at Sara's reflection in the mirror as she started the second verse: *"We need to be smiling enough; we need to be smiling enough; when life is hard and times are tough, we need to be smiling enough. We need to be praying enough; we need to be praying enough; when life is hard and times are tough, we need to be praying enough. So sing and smile and pray. So sing and smile and pray, your life will be brighter today."* She swung her arms in a giant circle and ended with a huge sun shape as she repeated the last words, "*Your life will be brighter today.*"

Dee wondered if Sara chose the *Sing, Smile and Pray* song for herself or for her. Maybe those lyrics were meant to help them both as they made their way into a hard and tough time ahead.

Dee's mind went back to the problem of how to tell Sara about the present situation without turning her against Dan. She knew she needed to be careful not to say derogatory things about Dan. To hate Dan would sound like she hated a huge part of Sara.

She heard Sara singing along with Burl Ives' old rendition of *The Ugly Bug Ball,* her favorite song at Sara's age.

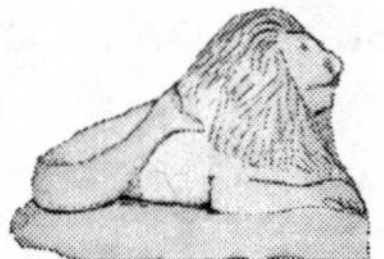

Chapter Seventeen – He Really Left

In her mind, Dee perfected the conversation she planned to have with Sara about Dan's leaving. Over and over, she tried to put a positive spin on the situation. Dee watched Sara gathering her colored pencils and paper and decided she couldn't postpone the inevitable. She prayed for the right words. She took Sara by the hand, led her to the sofa in the den, and turned to face the little girl who knew too much by instinct. More than ever, Dee knew Sara's sensitive nature left her more vulnerable than the average child. Pushing aside her protective instincts, Dee took a deep breath.

"You know your daddy has spent a lot of time in Texas lately."

"I know, Mom," Sara agreed. "He's always going to Texas." She placed her pencils on the sofa and reached for a drawing pad.

"This time is different. He took all his clothes and will be living in Texas all the time. I'm sure he'll miss you and want to see you. We'll work it out so he can see you as much as possible." Dee watched Sara's face as her little girl absorbed the words.

"You said he'd miss me. Won't he miss you too?" her eyebrows squinted and created a furrowed brow.

"It's hard to explain. I don't understand it myself. Your daddy doesn't want to be married to me. He's found someone else. But, that doesn't mean he doesn't want to be your daddy. He loves you so much." A tear ran down Dee's cheek. Before she could brush it away, Sara reached up and wiped it away.

"Mom, we'll work it out. Remember Cathy? Her mom and dad divorced. She said it's great at Christmas. Santa Claus brings her things at two houses now. Besides, Daddy still loves you a little bit. I know he does."

Dee chose not to argue with Sara. If Sara had seen him and heard his words she'd know Dan despised her and everything she stood for. *So much for trying to be the "good" wife*, she thought.

Sara kissed Dee's cheek, bundled her colored pencils on top of the drawing pad, and headed toward her small desk near the window. Dee made her way into the kitchen determined to make the call she dreaded even more than telling Sara about Dan's leaving.

Her fingers tapped nervously on the granite countertop as she waited for her mother to answer.

"Hello."

"Hi, Mom. How are you?" Dee asked and made her fingers stop tapping.

"I'm fine. I suppose you've called to tell me why you were wearing bags under your eyes today when you came to get Sara. I didn't want to make a big deal of it in front of her."

Well that was a surprise, Dee thought before she said, "Thanks. I appreciate that." Her mother had put on a big front – the light-heartedness she showed during the visit wasn't completely real.

"It's that son-of-a-bitch. Isn't it?" Anna Marie didn't waste any words about how she felt about Dan.

Dee decided to be short and truthful, "It is. He's gone."

"After Sara was born, your daddy said this time would come. He said he could see a change in Dan. I know how close you and your daddy were. I hope you'll let me know when you need help. You've always been so independent. We haven't always seen eye to eye on things, but I love you. You okay?"

Surprised, again, at her mother's words, Dee hesitated before responding. After a few seconds she said, "Thanks Mom." Her voice quivered. "I have no idea what I'm going to do. I just told Sara, and she said the funniest thing. She seems to think Santa Claus will visit her here and at Dan's new place."

"Don't be fooled. Sara was just trying to make you feel better. She's the smartest nine-year-old I've ever seen. She really is talented even if she is my granddaughter. Or, could it be it's *because* she's my granddaughter?"

Her mother surprised her again with her attempt to bring a little levity into the conversation. "Thanks Mom. I hope Sara can visit you more often. She loves doing artsy things with you. She can learn a lot from you."

"Before we hang up, you promise me you'll let me know if you need help of any kind. Okay?"

"Sure. Love you. Bye now."

"Bye, Dee."

Dee sat at the kitchen counter pondering her mother's words, and the promise she made to let her mother know if she needed anything. Her mother's concern comforted and surprised her. She couldn't imagine having to ask for help. But, she also never imagined a life without Dan or being a single parent.

She found Sara in the den totally consumed with an art project. She walked back into the kitchen and picked up the phone with the full intent of letting Mom and Pop Jax know about Dan's leaving. Just before their phones connected, she pushed the off button on her phone, convinced that Dan should tell his family. She told her family. He should have to break the news to his family.

She heard Sara, in the other room, asking about supper. Dee had completely forgotten. Food was of no interest. She was happy when Sara said she wanted a pocket bread toasted cheese sandwich – one of Dee's own recipes.

It didn't take long to prepare Sara's supper. Dee sliced a pita loaf in half, opened each one, and filled them with thin slices of cheddar cheese. She sprayed olive oil with butter on the bread and browned both sides in a non-stick skillet. Dee placed the melted cheese sandwich and milk on the table for Sara.

Dee sat down with her bowl of cereal and milk, making every effort to have a normal evening. They chatted about the new school year coming up, knowing their lives were upside down, and changes were coming. Dee's appetite certainly wasn't normal. Her cereal sat in front of her getting soggy.

After eating, Sara went back to her art project. Dee sat at the kitchen table pondering her decision not to tell Mom and Pop Jax about Dan's leaving, more than two days ago.

When the phone rang and the Jacksons' name and number appeared on the display, Dee answered, fully expecting Mom or Pop Jax to share the news that Dan called them. She reluctantly answered the phone.

"Dee, has Dan left yet?" Mom Jax asked.

"Hi, Mom Jax. He's gone. Didn't he call you?"

"No. The last time I heard, the two of you were going to your mom's to get Sara. Your mom okay?" Emily Jackson picked up on Dee's hesitation to answer. She knew something wasn't right.

"Mom's fine. I went to Marietta by myself. Dan left early yesterday morning. I thought he would have called you by now." Dee waited.

"No. He didn't call. What's going on?" Mom Jax said as she held the phone to her ear with her shoulder and dried her hands on her apron.

"Dan left. I mean he really left. Took his clothes and everything." Dee didn't want to tell Dan's mother about his girlfriend – the one he had for three years.

"What happened?"

"You'll have to ask him." Dee stopped talking.

"Well, I would if he'd answer his phone. I've tried calling his cell several times today. It goes straight to his voice mail. Even though I've left several messages, he hasn't called me back. That's why I called the house tonight." Emily Jackson waited for Dee to respond. The silence continued.

"Dee, sugar. I'm so sorry. You and Sara all right? Pop and I can come over if you need us."

"Thanks. We're okay. I'm … I'm sorry he hasn't called you." Dee really did feel sorry for Dan's parents. They were good, loving people.

"It's not your fault. Surely he'll call soon and let us know what's happened to him." Emily Jackson's voice quivered.

"I haven't told Emmy. I can't bear giving her more bad news. Could we tell her together?" Dee sat with one hand holding the phone and the other one cupping her forehead.

After her mother-in-law agreed to be there when she shared the bad news with Emmy, Dee said goodnight.

She left the kitchen to check her e-mail. As she sat in front of her computer, she wished for the umpteenth time that she owned a laptop so she could be with Sara in the den and work on lesson plans for the coming school year. Her finances were more complicated than ever, and money would be more of a problem. She felt certain there would be no laptop in her near future.

While Dee considered their financial future, Sara stared at the clown forming in her picture. The colorful clown outfit floated in the air. Sara struggled with drawing a bicycle underneath him. She sat with a colored pencil in her hand trying to remember what she had seen in her vision of James looking at the clown. Large fat curls of red hair took shape above the clown's face. She placed the red pencil on the table, picked up a yellow pencil, and slowly drew balls in the air, placing one in each of the clown's hands. She added a slight touch of green to the balls, making them look a little more like tennis balls.

After pondering the bicycle, or lack of it, she picked up the picture and took it to her mother's small office behind the kitchen. "What's a bicycle that doesn't have two wheels?" she asked.

"I don't know. Is this a riddle or a joke?" Dee finished typing before looking at her daughter.

"It's not a joke or a riddle," Sara looked at her mother with disappointment.

"I'm sorry. I don't understand." She put her arm around her daughter. "Let me take a look."

Sara placed her picture on top of the keyboard. "Here. See this clown? He's on a funny bike. It doesn't have two wheels like my bike."

Dee looked at the drawing. The clown, juggling greenish yellow balls, with one foot higher than the other as if he were peddling an invisible bike, sat on a short horizontal line that represented the bike's seat with two short vertical lines dropping below the seat. Dee pictured the bike wheel below the seat.

"I know, sweetie. It's a unicycle and doesn't have two wheels, only one. A big one." She pushed back from the computer table to give Sara her full attention.

"James watched him ride his bike. And the clown watched James."

"Do you know where the clown is?" Dee couldn't help herself. She asked, hoping Sara could give her clues about where James now lived.

"At the playground. James' new mommy made him get into the swing. James didn't want to so he tried to run away from her. The clown saw James run away." Sara reached for the drawing.

Dee knew better than to push Sara. She waited patiently as Sara retrieved her drawing,

Sara turned around when she got to the door, "How can a clown ride a bike with one wheel?"

"It's a balancing thing. People have to practice a lot in order to stay on the bike. Your clown is good. He not only stays on the bike, but is able to juggle the balls at the same time."

"He's James' clown. He's James' friend too," Sara said with conviction and walked away. She heard her mother's words as she walked through the kitchen.

"Get ready for bed, sweetie. It's later than I thought."

Exhausted from the events of the day, Dee expected to sleep like the dead. Sleeping alone had become ordinary with all Dan's traveling through most of the years of their marriage. It felt different now that he moved out. The nighttime was lonely and sad. She turned and tossed, reliving the departing scene. She kept trying to find something he said to give her hope that he would return.

She was thinking about getting out of bed and watching television when she felt the covers shift. Sara didn't say a word. She slipped under the sheet and curled up next to her mother.

Dee's arms closed around her daughter. She kissed Sara's head and sleep crept in.

Dee kept a mental calendar of the days since James' kidnapping. The days were piling up, one on top of the other, with no progress. She put off calling her aunt even though she hoped Aunt Connie would give her some direction in deciding how to handle Sara's pictures and conversations about James. There was no one else to ask.

Dee's home number showed up on Connie's display when the phone rang. "Hi, sweetie. How are you?"

"I'm fine. Just need some advice from my fabulous aunt," Dee made the effort to start the conversation on a light note.

"I've missed you, girl. When are coming to visit?" Connie asked.

"I don't know." Dee hesitated, not wanting to put pressure on her aunt about James' kidnapping.

"I know things must be crazy in Elberton. Have you heard anything at all about Dan's nephew?" Connie asked.

"No. Not officially. Sara has drawn more pictures. She keeps saying they're what James is seeing. I believe her. I hate to bother you, knowing you're having surgery tomorrow."

"Not to worry. Your mother is taking me really early in the morning. The surgery's scheduled for eight. She'll have me home by mid-afternoon. I did tell you it's laparoscopic, didn't I? It's not as invasive as the old way." Connie said, listening as she made her way to the small kitchen table and sat down.

"You told me. I hope it goes well. That's one thing I called you about. The other is, do you think I should insist that the FBI agents take Sara's pictures seriously?"

"By all means. Someone, somewhere will recognize the place or people. It could mean finding him," Connie advised. "If they don't have any answers, call me. In a few days, I'll be able to drive. I'll come over and look at them. I don't expect to be of much help. Lately, my psyche hasn't been much help to me or anyone else. I suppose all abilities dwindle with age. Health issues seem to impair my ability. Maybe my mind and spirit will be stronger as soon as I get this diseased gall bladder out."

"Thanks, Aunt Connie." Dee then asked about family news and Connie told her how The Girls were planning another Q-tip party.

Dee ended the conversation. "Thanks again. Good luck tomorrow. I'll call Mom tomorrow afternoon and check on you. Bye, now."

"Wait, don't hang up. Your mother told me about Dan and I'm so sorry."

Dee heard Connie's words and put the phone back to her ear. "I didn't want to bother you with my problems, especially just before your surgery."

"Sweetie, don't worry. You're stronger than you think. You just might find out you're happier without him. I know that's not what you want to hear when you're still hurting. Take it from me, the voice of experience, you'll do fine."

"Thanks. I hope you're right. I don't feel strong right now. But, it helps to know you think I am."

Dee felt better after talking to her aunt. She decided to make copies of some of Sara's drawings, knowing she'd have to ask Sara which ones involved James and might help in finding him. The connections weren't always apparent to Dee.

A few miles away at the Jackson's house, Emily Jackson placed a ham sandwich and a glass of tea on the table in front of her mother. As she handed her mother a napkin, the phone rang. She breathed in deeply when she saw the name on the display. It was the call she desperately wanted. Until now, Dan had ignored her calls to him. She picked up the phone and mouthed a message to her mother, "It's Dan."

Granny Nida took a sip of tea, watched and listened as her daughter answered the phone. She placed the glass on the table when Emily reached for the back of a chair to steady herself. The one-sided conversation left Granny Nida wondering what in the world Dan could say to Emily that would cause such a reaction. Her daughter's wrinkled brow and pursed lips concerned the old woman. When Emily's chin trembled, Granny Nida became worried.

Emily sat down across the table from her mother. When she ended the conversation, she covered her face with her hands and said, "You're going to be a great-grandmother again."

"You mean Dan?"

"Oh, how can things get so complicated? Yes, it's Dan. He's got a girlfriend." She placed her hands palms down on the table and shook her head.

"Well, that explains a lot. I wondered why he left Dee Dee and Sara Lee." Granny Nida added, "That turkey butt. He shore made a mess. Didn't he?"

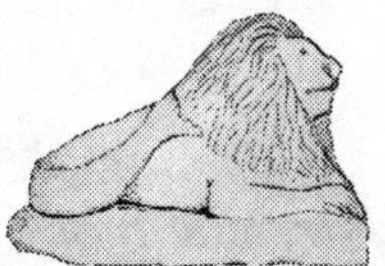

Chapter Eighteen – Ekphrastic Collection

The new book by a Georgia author who published Emmy's favorite poem, *Don't Put Me on a Pedestal*, lay on the table ready to be wrapped and delivered to Emmy. Emmy had used the poem to tell Dee she kept Dan on a pedestal and warned her that someone would get hurt when he fell off. Emmy's prediction proved too true. The ripple effect of Dan's leaving affected everyone in the Jackson family. Dee knew she wasn't the only one hurting. They all felt abandoned.

Dee watched Sara pack colored pencils and several sheets of paper and knew her daughter's goal was to have a project she could share with Hank. Dee didn't discourage her, but wondered if Hank would have any time for his younger cousin. He hung with his friends during their last few visits and paid no attention to Sara. She wondered if he was just unable to deal with James' kidnapping and Sara reminded him of James. He showed a lot of patience with Sara in the past and treated her like a little sister. Hank refused to talk about what everyone else referred to as James' disappearance.

Dee couldn't resist looking through Emmy's gift before wrapping it. She made a copy of a haunting essay about the North Atlantic Right Whale's extinction and reread it:

Whales in the Park

It's the same trip her mother and her mother's mother made to birth their babies. She is confused when the life-giving waters no longer cater to the needs required for the birthing process.

Against the odds, she manages to complete the birth, sings to her baby riding on her back, and smiles as only a North Atlantic right whale can – knowing it was worth the trip to the south to birth this wondrous creature in the warm waters off St. Simons Island. She teaches her baby all she knows about nature's survival skills.

Pollution, traffic and environmental changes work against them –

endangering the new life trying to develop the strength to make the trip to the north with its mother.

Each year the number of survivors making it back to the northern, cooler waters, becomes smaller. The mother's natural survival instincts no longer suffice. The baby's struggles come to an end.

The mother grieves – haunting sounds of mourning go unheard above the deep waters. The trip north is cancelled. Extinction creeps toward reality.

Sadness engulfed Dee when she read how the word "right" became a part of the whale's name because it was said to be the "right" whale to kill. Most the entries in the collection covered environmental issues. The words, "Ekphrastic Collection," in the right top corner of the cover, weren't familiar. She looked up "ekphrastic" and found that it's the process of combining two art forms – in this case – the written art with visual art. The picture of a mother whale and baby accompanied the poem and created the perfect example of ekphrastic. Dee wrapped the gift. At the last minute, she placed it on a shelf. Emmy didn't need sad stories. All the poems weren't sad; however, she didn't want Emmy to read about the whales just yet. She planned to give the book of poems to her later.

Trying to juggle all her responsibilities, along with her mounting troubles, forced Dee to change priorities often. She almost forgot to call her mother to check on Aunt Connie. She told Sara it was time to leave, pulled her cell phone out of her purse and pressed her mother's direct dial number. The call went straight to voice mail. Dee left a message asking her to call back.

Sara joined her in the garage. Dee placed her purse in the passenger seat as Sara strapped herself in. After checking to be sure Sara's seat belt had clicked, she backed out of her driveway and headed to Emmy's.

Mom Jax's car sat in the driveway and Dee decided it was time to tell Emmy that Dan had left. Wascal waited at the back door. Sara rubbed the dog's head before following her mother inside and shooed the dog back as she closed the glass storm door.

Sara disappeared into the den where Hank was watching Animal Planet. The television screen showed several large elephants on their way to a watering hole with their babies in tow. She liked elephants, especially baby elephants, and didn't hesitate in finding a place on the sofa to curl up. Sinking deep into the comfortable sofa and hugging a cushion, she forgot about the art project she'd planned.

Dee sat in the kitchen with Mom Jax and Emmy, as Emmy lovingly watched Marcie finish a bottle of diluted apple juice. A lull in the conversation gave Dee a chance to talk about Dan's leaving. She started off by apologizing for not telling her sooner. She explained how she thought he would get back to Texas and miss her and Sara so much he would want to come back.

Mom Jax told Dee that Dan called. She didn't mention the baby, hoping to find a time when she could talk with Dee alone. Emmy made no comment at all. Dee and Sara left soon after sharing the bad news.

On the way home, Dee felt relieved knowing that Mom Jax and Emmy both knew that Dan had left. She spared them the details of the hurtful words he said. She thought how normally vivacious, talkative Emmy sat at the kitchen table showing no response to the news of Dan. In another time she'd have called Dan a shithead or worse. In another time, Emmy would have phoned Dan and told him what she thought of him. Emmy's silence frightened Dee. James' absence left a big gap in their lives with Dan's leaving adding to the emptiness.

Momentarily, Dee pushed Dan and her problems aside as she thought about how Special Agent Lois Crandall needed to see Sara's drawings of the faces in the trees. Dee planned a trip to Athens to visit Agent Crandall with the hope that the agent would use Sara's drawings to help find James. Agent Crandall didn't sound enthusiastic about using psychic abilities in her investigation when Dee suggested it earlier. Her words were, "I'm not interested in the drawings of a child." Dee knew she had a battle ahead of her.

Puzzling over the records of interviews she and The Kid recorded, Agent Lois Crandall felt his presence even before he said, "What's up, Beautiful?"

She looked up at him, "What's up – who?"

"Beautiful."

"Where the hell did that come from?" She got out of the chair; instinctively knowing she was at a disadvantage as he stood towering over her.

"Just thought you looked especially pretty today. Did ya wear that low cut undershirt just for me?" he teased.

She saw him looking at the pink lace triangle covering her cleavage.

"No. I did not. For your information this isn't an undershirt." She crossed her arms – ready for battle.

"Looks like one ta me, with that little piece of lace right there." He said as his finger moved toward the lace.

"That's sexual harassment, you little piece of shit." She slapped his hand away.

"Nope. Not really. If I were your boss, it would be sexual harassment. But, since you're my boss, I can't be held accountable. No one would hold me accountable anyway if they saw you like this. You're a foxy lady when you're mad. I'll just try to keep you that way."

As he sat down in the chair opposite her desk, she wondered if he was right about the boss business. She planned to look up the department's sexual harassment policy as soon as she could get him out of her office. She glanced at an open file on her desk.

"Gonna tell me what you're looking at, boss?" He purposely changed the subject.

"The Seeking Sam monkey seems to have given up all his secrets, but there's a bunch still out there, and now I'm supposed to take this nine-year-old girl's psychic ability seriously. Her mother is insisting I look at the child's artwork. I haven't gotten that desperate." She sat down, happy the topic of conversation changed to work.

"Lois. Lois. You're gettin' your panties in a wad, and your prejudice is showing. First of all, a nine-year-old hasn't learned to lie well enough to pretend ta be psychic. Second, you call me The Kid, even though I'm only eighteen months younger than you. You definitely have a prejudice against young people, including me." He watched her brow knit and thought, *Homerun. I've scored here.* He couldn't stop, "You scared you might like me if you get ta know me?"

"Look, Kid. Two years, not eighteen months."

"See. You're still doing it. Your prejudice is also hampering my ability ta learn my job. You don't share with me like you would another partner. And, it's eighteen months. You're rounding off just to make it easier ta ignore me."

She knew he was right. She hated it, but she knew he hit the proverbial nail on the head. She swiveled around in her chair with her back to him, stood up and looked out the window. She heard the door close behind her. *Well, he needed to leave. The tension had gotten too* *thi*ck.

She felt his touch and it made her jump. Instead of leaving, he had closed the door to prevent others from seeing him walk up behind her and put his arms around her. She turned around, into his embrace, fully prepared to be angry. Instead, the touch of his lips sparked a need she had pushed far, far away. Her arms went up, touching his jeans, belt, and the muscles underneath his tight fitted green shirt. Her hands found their way to the nape of his neck and into his thick black hair. She was losing control, and it scared her.

Her hands came down to his chest. She pushed him away. "I can't do this. I … I just can't do this."

His silence was unexpected, so she continued, "I'm sorry. I'm still sifting through the garbage left over from my divorce. It's not fair for me to let anyone else deal with the mess. But, I promise I'll try not to let my prejudices get in the way of you learning your job." She opened her office door and watched him leave.

The past two years, since the divorce, had moved slowly for Lois. She joined the guys from the department for a drink a few times. If anyone asked her out, she made up some lame excuse. Some of them were married, including her former partner. She certainly didn't want to go in that direction.

She picked up the phone and dialed her ex-husband's number. It had been at least two months since she talked with him. She knew it was his day off. The female voice from the other end answered, "Hello."

Hesitantly, Lois asked to speak to Joe.

"He's not here right now. This is his wife. May I help you?"

Lois pushed the off button. *That jerk*, she thought. *He didn't have the decency to let me know he'd moved on.* She knew that in reality, he moved on a long time ago and that she was the one stuck in the past.

Lois, it's time for you to move on too, she told herself. A tall New Jersey Italian formed a picture in her mind. *No way. I can't possibly be interested in The Kid,* she thought.

An hour later, Dee Jackson sat in the chair The Kid had vacated. She handed Agent Crandall an envelope. Lois pulled out the contents and shuffled through several sheets of drawings. It was obvious a child created them.

The calendar on the agent's desk reminded her of the many things yet to do. It made her feel overwhelmed. *And*, she thought, *the list doesn't include all the unwritten chores I've got to get done. How on earth am I going to tell Dee Jackson I don't give a damn about her precious little girl's artwork?*

"I know you feel you're wasting your time. These are copies of several of Sara's drawings. I think they'll help in finding out where James is. I'm certain he's seeing the same things that Sara's drawing," Dee's stubbornness kicked in as she looked directly into the agent's eyes. "Please don't discard this as simply a child's art. Sara knows things others don't know."

Agent Crandall wondered if Dee could read her mind.

Dee continued, "My aunt, on my mother's side, is a psychic. She's helped the police solve several cases. Under the right circumstances, I saw visions. My visions or ability to see the past or see what's happening somewhere else is nothing compared to Sara's."

Agent Crandall looked out the window, forcing Dee to accept the fact that she was making no headway. She thought she could get Dee out of her office when she heard Dee's cell phone chime. She also knew Dee was resisting the urge to answer it. The agent desperately wanted Dee gone. She pulled out the sheet with the clown on it and told Dee how interesting it was, but could not in her wildest imagination believe the drawing had anything to do with James' kidnapping. She stood up and looked across the desk at Dee with the sole purpose of letting her know the conversation had come to an end.

She knew her action would leave Dee with no choice – she had to leave. She noticed Dee's voice went up a notch with her parting words, "James may die because you aren't open about things you don't understand. Can you live with that?" She watched Dee walk out, leaving the door wide open.

Agent Crandall tapped her fingers on the empty envelope. Her fingers strayed to the pictures. She looked at each one, turning them over one by one – labeled with a title, signed and dated. She traced Sara's name on the one titled, "The Clown." She looked at another one with a face in the tree and vaguely remembered something she read about tree spirits.

TK came in as she stuffed the pictures back into the envelope and threw the envelope in the trashcan beside her desk. She couldn't help but notice how he acted as though their confrontation never happened. He said he saw Dee Jackson leaving the office and asked if Dee gave her any new information about James.

Agent Crandall retrieved the envelope with the pictures and handed them to TK. Dee's words had irritated the hell out of her. She thought, *Who is Dee Jackson to tell me how to investigate James' kidnapping? I was in my third year in college pursuing a criminal justice degree when Sara was born. Who are they to presume they can do my job?*

TK's accusation that prejudice was clouding her mind made her feel worse. He pulled the stack of pictures from the manila envelope and asked his boss what she was going to do with them. She told him he could take them if he wanted them. He could throw them in the trash or find out if such places existed. Once again, the pictures went back into the envelope and she watched him walk out the door with them.

This hasn't been a good day for me, Lois said to herself. The Kid didn't invite her to join him and the others after work. *Maybe. Just maybe, he took my words seriously and won't bother me again.* Her new best friend, loneliness, wrapped its way around her. The thickness of it frightened her.

Disappointment flooded Dee's thoughts as she made her way through the cubicles outside Agent Crandall's office. She pulled her cell phone from the side pocket of her purse as she walked toward her car. She missed her mother's call. Anna Marie's message said Connie stayed overnight in the hospital due to an unexpected respiratory problem that was preventing her from getting enough oxygen. She went on to say the doctor felt certain the condition was temporary and Connie would be discharged the following day.

The message made it clear. Aunt Connie wouldn't be available to help find James for some time. For Connie's sake, as well as James', Dee hoped the doctor was right that the problem would repair itself quickly. She called her mother, who often looked at everything through a gray cloud instead of rose-colored glasses. Anna Marie surprised her daughter with her optimistic outlook regarding Connie's recovery. That small factor made Dee feel better about her aunt's health. Her mother's attitude seemed to have gone through some kind of adjustment lately. Dee liked the change.

Dee concentrated on alternative options for finding James. She wanted to protect Sara and not pressure her for details about her drawings. She would have to find a way to get information without making Sara feel responsible for James' situation. Aunt Connie's help would be invaluable. She said a prayer for her aunt and sent good thoughts her way. Dee felt that time was running out for James. She knew she had to do something . . . soon.

As Dee drove home, TK sat at his desk in the open area he shared with several other low-on-the-totem-pole agents and research personnel. He pulled the copies of Sara's drawings from the envelope and looked at each one. The clown on a unicycle tugged at his mind. The wheel of the unicycle was slightly warped and the proportions in the drawing were far from perfect. He knew Sara's artistic efforts meant more than a few lines and colors of a drawing. He studied the clown – the red hair, the face – and marveled at how well Sara portrayed the balls in the air. He added the picture to the top of the stack and placed the pictures on top of the manila envelope before stashing them in a side drawer of his desk.

Later in the day, he opened the drawer and stared at the clown until one of his co-workers came by and tapped him on the head.

"Hey, Kid, it's time to hit the streets. I think you owe me a drink."

TK scowled. He hoped the others wouldn't pay attention to Lois' pet name for him. He felt branded.

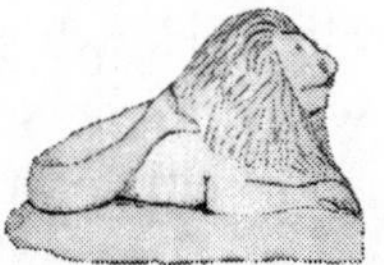

Chapter Nineteen – I'll Find You

Emily Jackson looked out her kitchen window at the empty pool. *Oh,* she thought, *it has enough water – just no children having to be reminded to walk, not run. No shouting kids, splashing and playing Marco Polo. No "Mom Jax, look at me." Empty and tired.* That's how she felt.

She recalled how Dan didn't do well handling Dee's visions and it was even harder for him to accept Sara's clairvoyance. She knew he felt threatened and was at a loss as to how to help him. She hardly slept or ate since his last call. She knew she needed to tell Dee about the baby. She didn't know how.

The night before, she'd been at Emmy's house helping take care of Marcie. With Hank spending a few days with his other grandmother, Emily expected to be able to leave early. She and Emmy ate dinner and bathed and fed the baby, who was sound asleep. Fred's dinner waited in the oven as she and Emmy waited for Fred. Emmy tried to rationalize his absence. She kept saying, "He's probably working overtime on a job that has to be completed tonight." She saw Emmy call him on his cell phone, several times, without getting an answer. A couple of times, her daughter went into the bedroom and paced back and forth.

A few minutes after midnight, she saw Fred's truck pull into the driveway followed by a deputy sheriff's car. She and Emmy got to the front door in time to see a deputy helping Fred out of the passenger side of the car. Fred, with shuffling feet and an unsteady gait, walked in front of his police escort. With support, Fred made it up the three steps to the porch, his head hanging low.

The man who drove Fred's truck home, held the glass storm door open. After Fred and the deputy entered, Emily recognized the driver as an old friend from high school. The friend helped Fred to his recliner in the den, pressed the side lever and placed the chair in a prone position.

The deputy explained how they found Fred walking in the middle of Highway 72 from Athens toward Sweet City. Like everyone else in town, he knew about the Rafferty family's crisis. He went on to tell them how they found Fred's abandoned truck. The two men agreed that Fred had not been driving his truck when they found him down the road; therefore, the deputy wouldn't press charges. Emily watched as her daughter's world continued to fall apart.

"Will anything ever be normal again?" Emily Jackson wondered out loud.

James sat at his small desk in the corner of the kitchen, refusing to look at Nan. She placed her hand on his chin trying to force him to look at her and acquiesce to her demand. "Timmy, look at me," she commanded. "I'm going to ask you one more time to say, 'Mommy, I love you.' A mother shouldn't have to ask her son to say that."

He pursed his lips tighter than before and pinched his chin. Her hand went into the air. He closed his eyes and waited for the sting of her slap. When it didn't come, he opened his eyes and found her eyes boring into his with a hatred that scared him more than the slap he anticipated. Trying to appease her he softly said, "Mamamommy, I lalalove yuyou." She stomped off in anger.

James tried hard to remember what his real mommy looked like. Each day his mommy's shape and form became fuzzier. Each day, her smell and the scent of her lotion became less strong. The feel of his daddy's arms as he picked him up became a distant memory. He questioned if they loved him. If they loved him, why didn't they come get him? When he saw them clearly, they were looking lovingly at the baby wrapped in a pink blanket in his mother's arms.

He reached down and pulled the Miss Pugg book from the space under his seat. He opened it, followed each word, and tried to remember how he felt when his real mommy read, "*I have to know where you are and where you'll be. I'm your mama, and I love you Oink Oink Three.*"

"Sasa," he cried that night. He wanted to ask her to tell him a knock-knock joke. In his mind, he promised to laugh at her silly joke. He thought about the Sea Lion and the face in the tree. He held the drawing Sara drew – the one that was in his pocket the day he went with his daddy to bring his baby sister home. It was the only thing he managed to keep. The clothes he wore that day disappeared. He hid the drawing by sitting on it when the mean mommy removed his clothes. Later, he stashed it inside his pillowcase. He still changed its hiding place every day to keep her from finding it. When he thought he would be alone for a while, he'd retrieve it and talk with his Sasa.

In his dream, he thought he heard her say, "James. I'll find you. Think of me. Think of me, and I'll think of you. Then, I'll find you." Her words gave him a feeling of hope that he'd eventually be free from his new mommy.

The dream disappeared with the night. The morning light brought back the mean mommy who complained about his stuttering, his lack of affection, and his manners. His begging to go to the park near the pier made his mean mommy angry. Most of the time she refused the request because he couldn't make it without stuttering.

He desperately wanted to see the clown. He felt sure the clown would make him feel better. He hoped to see the face in the tree on the way to the pier. Somehow, he felt the face in the tree wanted to help him. The last time he saw it, he imagined the rings around the face were the sun and moon. The mouth on the face opened and said, "James." The voice didn't scare him. It reminded him that he really was James – not Timmy. It made him feel safer. Sara's laugh warmed him when he tried to climb the tree and touch the nose on the face – the face of a princess.

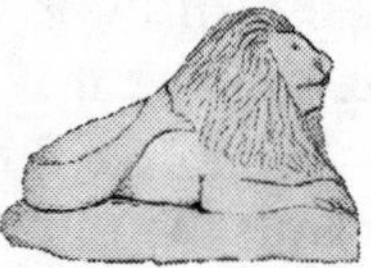

Chapter Twenty – The Whirlwind Visitor

Once again Emmy's side of the bed was empty. Fred pulled himself up and sat still for a few seconds before getting out of bed to check on his wife. Unable to sleep through the night since James disappeared, she often tried sleeping on the den sofa or in her recliner. Some nights she slept a few hours in James' bed.

He checked the den and kitchen without finding her. He peeked into Marcie's room where smells of baby powder and lotion wafted through to the hallway. He stepped toward the closet door with the intention of closing it, but found Emmy crouched on the floor. Her unblinking glazed eyes reflected the glow from the small night light on a nearby wall.

"Em," he said quietly, "Come on, honey. Come back to bed with me," he begged, holding his hand out to help her up.

He saw Emmy jump, grab Hank's bat from the floor, and cower backward.

Fred grabbed her arms and held them by her side before helping her up. "It's me. It's me, Em. You don't need the bat," Fred said, using all his strength to hold her arms down.

"Shhhhhhh. Listen. We have to be quiet. I won't let her take Marcie. You know she's coming here, don't you?"

Fred watched Emmy look at the bat; then she looked up at him. The bat hit the carpet with a thud. He could she was shaking.

Fred held her until the shaking stopped and led her to her recliner in the den before going to the kitchen to prepare a cup of Chamomile tea. As the teakettle heated the water, Fred wondered if the fear the kidnapper planted in their heads had completely taken over their lives.

Emmy's pale face, thin frame and flat expression when he returned to the den with the tea, made him think of the zombie movies he once loved. Zombies had lost their allure. Fred knew he would never see them as entertaining again – as long as he lived.

Janet's e-mail to Dee came at a really good time. Dee needed a diversion and Janet could certainly provide one – or more. No one could be around Janet long without smiling and laughing. They exchanged several e-mails since the phone call Dee made to Janet, letting her know Dan had left. Like almost everyone else, Janet didn't seem surprised.

Janet's latest e-mail surprised Dee though. She wrote that she would be in Atlanta the coming weekend as the pre-show opener for the Country All Around Band because the band's original opening singer had gotten sick. Janet's normal, high-strung personality kicked into overdrive and most of the message screamed in all caps. She asked if she could visit Dee and Emmy on Thursday and Friday before the show on Saturday evening. Dee quickly agreed and called Emmy. She couldn't wait to share the news, and felt certain Emmy needed Janet's visit. Janet would be a great distraction.

Janet arrived near midnight on Thursday, much too late to call or visit Emmy and her family. She pulled her small bag over the hump of the threshold at the front door. Her black pants fit like a second skin. The copper lamé backless top hung loosely on her tall frame. Her enthusiasm bubbled to a high pitch as she walked into Dee's living room.

"Girl, you look like a scarecrow," Janet said as she hugged Dee. "You okay, girlfriend?" Janet thought she had said enough and chose to ignore the dark circles under Dee's eyes.

"I'm fine," Dee said, determined to make the words real.

"I know you're happy to see your ole bunkie." For shock effect, Janet used the prison term "bunkie" instead of "roommate." Dee heard it before. She remembered how people looked at Janet in the past. Her college roommate had not abandoned her propensity to shock.

Janet bent down, placed her arms around Dee and continued, "It'll be okay. Girlfriend, this time next year, you'll be happy he's out of your life. You are fine. Just fine." She straightened to her full height and towered over Dee until she slipped out of her three-inch stack heels.

Dee thought about how the years had not changed Janet's beautiful features. Her tawny complexion, dark brown eyes and chocolate colored hair made her black lashes and eyebrows look as though she had been carefully painted by an expert artist rather than created by chance of nature. Janet's beauty reinforced the observation of Dee's father that women are their most beautiful in their thirties. The thirties looked good on Janet.

Before Sam died, he told Dee how proud he was of her. Dee's

daddy's words about her future now seemed like a premonition. He advised her to always know about the family's finances and always have a backup plan for surviving as a single mom. She assumed, at the time, he meant that Dan might die young. Now, she knew her dad recognized Dan's faults and lack of strength. Because she loved Dan so much she chose to ignore his faults and didn't see many of them.

"You may not know it now; but Dan will regret walking out on you," Janet continued. "You're the one who held this family together. How many times did he go out and buy something that blew your budget out of the water? Maybe out of the earth's atmosphere. The jerk."

Wound up and talking a mile a minute, Janet paused when she saw her old demo CD on the coffee table. She seemed impressed to find it on the table. She listened as Dee explained how the song, *It Doesn't Matter Anymore*, became her standby. Janet continued to listen when Dee described moving the chair from the kitchen, stepping into it, taking the fish off the wall above the fireplace, and how good it felt.

Janet's eyes widened, her voice went up an octave, as she shared how she and her producer were working on a video of the song when they hit a snag. They had tried several ways of portraying the importance of the unfaithful husband's fish on the wall.

Janet took her phone from her purse, pressed a button and waited.

"Hey, boss," Janet spoke into the phone. "I know you turned your phone off so you wouldn't have to listen to your number one, kick ass star. You know I'm your bread and butter for your old age. Just wanted you to know my Georgia Girl has saved our asses. The 'fish on the wall' thing? I know how to take it off. See you tomorrow night." She pressed a button on the phone and placed it in her purse.

She read the lines, "'*Take your stuffed fish off the wall, I don't want it at all. Like the fish, you don't matter anymore*.' It's called a 'bridge' and stops the flow of a song, changes key, reinforces the prior verses and prepares the listener for the ending verse." The glazed look she saw in Dee's eyes finally made Janet give up on explaining song writing.

The fact that Sara was spending the night with a friend in town allowed Dee and Janet hours and hours of girl time. They both looked forward to sleeping late the following morning and planned to skip breakfast since Emmy and Marcie would be joining them for brunch around eleven o'clock. Janet hadn't met the newest member of the Jackson clan.

Dee, with Janet's shoes dangling from her right hand and pulling her suitcase, led Janet down the hallway to the guest bedroom. They had talked for two hours.

The next morning, the smell of quiche wafted through the house, waking a hungry and slow-moving Janet. She wandered into the kitchen in a gray sweat tank top and matching pajama bottoms. "Ummm. That smells good enough to eat right now." She pulled a stool from under the edge of the island countertop and sat down.

"It'll be ready soon. I've talked with Emmy. She and Marcie are on their way." Dee said and placed a glass of orange juice in front of Janet. "Coffee's almost ready." The gurgling and sputtering noises of the coffee maker in its final dripping mode confirmed it.

"What if I say the wrong thing? I'm always freaked out that I'll say something stupid." Janet said.

"Don't worry. You can't say anything worse than what she's already heard. We've all goofed at some time or another. No one knows how to deal with the fact that James is missing." Dee talked as she placed a small bowl of peaches in front of Janet.

"Thanks, Georgia Girl," Janet decided to give Dee a new nickname, inspired by her help with the video. She added in an exaggerated Southern drawl, "Georgia peaches from the Georgia Girl."

"You're so welcome," Dee said. "Emmy just drove up. Excuse me. I'll help her with Marcie. She'll have a ton of baby stuff. I should've taken the food to her; but I wanted to get her out of her house for a while. She's been terribly depressed. The last time I was there, the whole house depressed me." Dee walked to the front door.

Dee saw Emmy leaning into the car and assumed she was unbuckling Marcie's baby carrier. Emmy turned when she heard Dee behind her. Dee, again, marveled at how much weight Emmy lost. Her loose khaki pants sagged. Even though Emmy's blue-striped shirt looked like a maternity top, Dee knew better. The first week Emmy and Marcie came home from the hospital, Dee helped sort and pack the maternity wardrobe. They were still in Dee's car waiting to be donated to a charity yard sale. Emmy wore her pre-pregnancy clothes.

Dee gave her a hug and welcomed her. She laughed and told Emmy to prepare herself for Janet – as hyper and animated as ever – as she took Marcie's diaper bag from the back seat and closed the car door. She reached the front porch in time to hold the door open for Emmy and Marcie.

Janet finished the last sip of orange juice, got off the stool, and made her way to the front door. To Emmy's surprise, she reached for Marcie before acknowledging Emmy.

"It's okay. I grew up taking care of babies. My mama and her sisters have lots of babies," Janet rambled on.

"Well, it's good to see you too, Janet." Emmy reluctantly placed Marcie in her friend's arms.

Janet leaned over and gave Emmy a kiss on the cheek. "Been thinking 'bout you lots, girlfriend, even if I didn't let you know."

"Thanks," Emmy said.

Dee broke the awkwardness. "Let's put Marcie near your place at the table, Emmy." She started to move a chair near the end of the table.

"That's okay. I'll put her carrier on the floor next to my chair. That'll work better." Emmy reached for her baby.

Janet handed Marcie back to Emmy and said her mama never let them come to the table in the clothes in which they slept. "I'll be baa-aack." She headed down the hallway to the guest bedroom.

"Do you have to pick up Hank from the theater?" Dee asked as she placed a glass of orange juice near Emmy's plate at the table.

"No. Fred is going to take Hank to an orthodontist. We may have to go the braces route. He's so handsome. I don't think he really needs braces. But Fred thinks he needs them, especially for the middle teeth on the bottom." Emmy bent over to look through Marcie's diaper bag for a pacifier.

"Then, we can spend the afternoon together. That is, if you brought enough formula for Marcie. Or, we'll go get more." She didn't want to give Emmy an excuse to go home early.

Dee removed the broccoli quiche from the oven as Janet returned to the kitchen, dressed in tight low-hanging jeans and a short rainbow-colored blouse. Her high heels tapped on the tile as she made her way to the table.

Dee placed the quiche, buttered grits, croissants, and a bowl of chopped peaches and blueberries on the table. The clinking of serving utensils, followed by munching sounds, filled the room.

The conversation picked up again as Janet asked for Dee's and Emmy's opinions about a song she was writing. She said her mama told her to never sing at the table and immediately broke that rule by singing a song about insurance fraud.

"It starts with the chorus." She sang, "*Grandmaw went swimming in the ocean. She swam way out into the sea. She swam so far I couldn't see her. She said she'd be sending love and kisses back to me."*

Janet stopped singing, "It's supposed to be funny. You know, like 'Granma got Run Over by a Reindeer.' Or, like that Ray Stevens' song about the squirrel that got loose in the church. You know, the one Dan sang at the Karaoke Bar in Carnesville. He was so . . .. Oooops." *Too late*, she thought. *I shouldn't have brought up Dan.* "Sorry Dee."

"It's okay. You started to say he was funny. He was. I hope no grandmother would really let her grandchild watch her swim away and never return. But, then again, I hope a grandma wouldn't really get run over by a reindeer, either." Dee looked at Emmy. "What do you think?"

"I like it. I'm trying to find something funny. Maybe the verses are funnier than the chorus. Go ahead, Janet."

"It does get funnier, I think." Janet sang the first verse of the song, "*At first Grandpaw seemed so very lonely, 'til the insurance check came through. He cashed the check and took the money. He said, 'Goodbye, so long, farewell, adieu.'"*

Janet added, "The chorus goes here, then the second verse: *Sev'ral years ago Grandmaw took lessons. She learned to swim so very well. She kept it all a great big secret. About the swimming she would never tell.'* The last verse goes like this: *We get postcards from exotic places. Love and kisses on the last line. They're all signed with two smiley faces. They say, 'We're having a mighty fine time!'* Then the chorus again."

Dee responded first, "Yeah. It *is* funnier. I can just see Grandmaw and Grandpaw standing on the deck of a luxury cruise liner, Grandpaw in a black tux and Grandmaw in a long blue evening dress, raising their wine glasses in a toast to the good life. Of course, a background of an island, palm trees, sandy beaches, and the first pinks and blues of the perfect sunset complete the picture."

"Yeah, and the family gathered around the living room coffee table looking at all the postcards from exotic places," Emmy added, absent-mindedly rocking Marcie's carrier seat.

"Hey, sounds like you two could help write the video of the song. Not that it's gotten that far. I haven't shown it to my agent or producer." Her long, tapered fingernails tapped on the wooden table.

Dee smiled and said, "I noticed your other song started with the chorus just like this one. I can't remember a song, other than yours, that starts with the chorus. It . . ."

"Georgia Girl, you got it. Not only am I trying to be the first African American woman to make it in Nashville's country music scene, I want to add my own touch." Janet lifted her right shoulder and turned her head as if she were posing for a celebrity photo shot. She meant to make Dee and Emmy forget their troubles for a second or two and she succeeded. They all three laughed.

For the first time in weeks, Emmy relaxed a little. Determined to give Emmy a break, Dee insisted on taking the task of changing Marcie. Emmy allowed Janet to hold Marcie for a short while, but when it came time for Marcie's bottle, Emmy refused to share the responsibility. She asked Janet not to take it personally and explained how she made it a point every day to bond with Marcie at feeding time. She told them how she worries she might not be able to give Marcie the love and care she needs while she deals with James' kidnapping.

Emmy went on to describe how Hank fell in love with the theater and how she couldn't forgive Fred for letting the kidnapping happen. Sharing her fears and frustration with a friend from outside the family seemed to be a good catharsis for Emmy.

Amazed at how time flew by, Janet moved quickly when she realized it was almost three o'clock. As Emmy gave Marcie a mid-afternoon bottle, Dee helped Janet pack. Dee tried unsuccessfully to get Janet to stay long enough for a snack before driving back to Atlanta. Janet insisted she would have an early dinner before joining the band for practice.

"By the way, my boss wants to meet you." Janet said to Dee as she got into her car. "And, tell Sara I missed her bunches. But, I'll see her next time for sure."

The fresh breeze that blew in with Janet left with her. Dee wanted to prolong the good feelings and suggested they go see Granny Nida. Emmy declined. Dee chose not to share that Granny Nida called the day before to say she felt left out of the loop. For several days, Mom Jax's migraine headache kept her incapacitated. Granny Nida had asked Dee what was being done to find James, and how Emmy and the baby were doing.

Dee insisted Emmy have a cola, cheese and crackers before gathering and packing Marcie's bag. Dee helped Emmy to her car. The pain of loss returned to Emmy's thin face.

The feeling of guilt grew as Emmy drove home. How could she have fun and laugh when her little boy was – where? Not knowing plunged her into depression. Guilt kept her there. Her mind went back to the day she was happy, preparing Marcie for the trip home from the hospital. She knew her mind traveled back in time in a vain effort to change the outcome. Her mind and her heart couldn't accept James' kidnapping. As she drove down the road, she ignored the neighbors' houses, their green lawns, and spurts of wild grasses that forced their way out of the hard red clay bordering the concrete roadway.

The beep from an oncoming truck startled her and made her realize she was drifting onto his side of the road. She jerked the steering wheel to the right just in time to avoid hitting the truck. She pulled over, gasped for air, and realized she almost killed herself and her baby. Hearing Marcie cry from her carrier, tightly buckled in the back, reminded Emmy of just how much she could lose. She got out of the car and assured herself that Marcie was okay. She inspected Marcie's car seat and placed a pacifier in the baby's mouth before returning to the driver's seat. Her weak legs threatened to collapse under her as she rested her forehead on the steering wheel and waited for a few minutes before starting the car.

The two miles from Dee's house to hers shouldn't have been a problem. Dee offered to drive her to and from her house for Janet's visit. Emmy insisted she could handle it since she drove to her mom's and to the grocery store the past few weeks. She looked around, shocked to find herself several miles away from her house. She didn't remember passing her driveway. She made a U-turn and headed home. Shaken and scared, she felt relieved when she saw Fred's truck in their driveway.

Chapter Twenty-One – I've Made a Mess

The day after Janet's visit, déjà vu kicked in as Dee let Suede out. He ran into the screened porch and made a beeline for two fat songbirds huddled low below a plant stand. Dee's heart raced as she chased him, trying to grab his collar. As before, the small birds seemed unable to fly high. Suede corned them, but they hopped out through the screen the dog tore when he captured his prize female cardinal. Before he could retreat or run through the screen after the birds, she grabbed his collar, clutching it with her left hand. She wrapped her right arm around his head, holding him in what she thought of as a death grip until the birds made their way to freedom. Again, they flew amongst low shrubs, making their way to the taller dogwood tree. Finally, they settled on a limb safely out of the reach of the resident dog. Dee let go of Suede and laughed as she went back inside, happy she had neglected to repair the screened porch. Without knowing it, Suede had provided the small birds their way to freedom.

Sara was at a friend's birthday party, leaving Dee with a couple of hours of free time. She decided to deliver the cheese straws she purchased for Granny Nida. After changing from pajamas to hot pink Capri pants and a sleeveless blouse in a lighter shade of pink, she headed out, thinking, *Okay. Hot pink should make me feel better. I've always gotten compliments with this color*. A great deal of her confidence left with Dan. She hoped to get it back.

She went through the drive-thru window at Wendy's and bought a chicken sandwich for the old woman she'd grown to love. Holding a bag with Granny Nida's favorite treats, she knocked on the door and heard, "Come in. Door's open."

Granny Nida sat in her lift chair dressed in a short-sleeved cotton dress with no waistline. Large bright yellow sunflowers covered her upper torso. The green stems and leaves marched their way to the hem, contrasting with her white skinny legs below the hem. Her brown bedroom slippers sat empty at the side of her chair, while her bare feet rested on the beige-colored linoleum floor.

Dee gave her grandmother-in-law the sandwich and the box of cheese straws she picked up at a specialty store in Athens. Granny Nida opened the box of cheese straws immediately, but couldn't tear into the foil package inside. She reached for the letter opener on the tray near her chair, punctured the foil, pulled it apart, and greedily ate two cheese crackers before offering any to Dee.

Dee smiled and declined the offer, knowing the old woman was being generous to share her favorite treat.

"Where's my Sara Lee today?" Granny Nida asked between bites.

"She's at a birthday party." Dee replied, smiling as the old woman ate and talked at the same time.

"She's such a purty little thang. Tell her I missed her." Before Dee could say anything, Granny Nida went on to ask, "What does she thank about being a big sister?"

"A what?" Dee asked – anxiety starting to grow in the pit of her stomach.

She saw Granny Nida's eyes widen. "I didn't mean to let the cat out of the bag, shug." Her hands shook as she reached out to Dee.

Dee took the old woman's hands and tried to calm her. "I know I won't be making Sara a big sister. So I assume Dan is."

"Oh, Dee Dee. I shore am sorry. I was at Em-ly's when he called. I thought you knew. Lordy mercy. I made a mess today."

Dee patted Granny Nida's shaky hands. "It's all right. I'd have found out sooner or later." Even though she was seething inside, she knew Granny Nida obsessed over almost everything and didn't want the old woman to worry about the awful slipup. "That boy was the apple of my heart." Granny Nida exercised her right to misquote clichés.

"You mean the apple of your eye, don't you?" Dee automatically tried to correct her, but immediately regretted questioning the old woman. Any effort to think straight ceased to exist after Granny Nida's announcement. Halfway listening to the old woman's explanation, Dee's thoughts jumped ahead as she tried to think how to get out of the apartment without leaving Granny Nida upset.

"No, sugar. He was more than the apple of my eye. He was part of my heart. And to thank he hasn't even called his old granny. It's partly my own fault. We spoilt him rotten. He was our first gran' baby. Cute little redheaded boy. He melted my heart. His granddaddy's too."

Dee took the wrapper off the chicken sandwich on the old woman's TV tray, added a glass of sweet tea, and stayed until she thought her grandmother-in-law would be okay. She walked out of Elsburg Towers wondering who else knew about Dan's baby. *Am I the last to know?* she wondered.

She drove across town towards the Jacksons' house. She hated confrontations. It was a lifelong weakness. Even when she thought her own mother had been unfair to her, she never confronted her. She never confronted Mom Jax about anything either. She drove by their house, a house she had learned to love; its brick veneer, large parking area between the house and matching brick garage housing Pop Jax's workshop, was a second home for her. Two blocks down the street, she turned around and made her way back to the Jacksons' house.

Dee's chin jutted out at the sight of her mother-in-law. She stood there until Mom Jax pulled her inside.

"How could you?" Dee said as her eyes narrowed. Her mother-in-law had never seen her cry. Dee, determined to keep it that way, took a deep breath and stood taller.

When her mother-in-law tried to give her a hug, she pushed her away. "Does everybody know but me?" Dee crossed her arms as she asked the question. She felt certain her mother-in-law saw the gesture and knew that she was asking about Dan's baby.

"Sugar, I'm so sorry. I knew I'd have to tell you. I just couldn't bring myself to hurt you. I loved you before you became my daughter-in-law, and I'll love you when you are no longer married to my son. Until I heard about the baby, I felt sure Dan would come to his senses and come back home."

"Does everybody know but me?" Dee asked again in a voice she didn't even recognize. The question sounded mean and hateful.

"Emmy doesn't know. I can't make myself add to her troubles. Oh, Lord, I know I'll have to, but it won't be easy. She'll have to know before What's-Her-Name has the baby. I don't know her name. The woman's having my grandchild and I don't even know her name. What is her name?"

"I don't know." Dee started laughing. It wasn't a particularly good laugh. She knew it sounded rather hysterical.

"Old What's-Her-Name." Mom Jax laughed.

Dee knew she couldn't stay angry with Mom Jax. She reached for the hug she'd turned down earlier.

"Old What's-Her-Name," they said in unison and hugged each other.

Later that afternoon, when Dee got home, she decided to e-mail Dan and tell him what she thought of him. But she had a habit of checking her incoming e-mail as soon as she started her computer, and that sidetracked her. She clicked on an e-mail from Janet instead.

The message read: "Hey GA Girl. Been thinking bout u. Heard a song 2day. I think it was popular a few years back. The lyrics r about a guy going 2 Maine or somewhere up north 2 often. Turns out he's got a girl friend there. Wife tells him that when he's finished, she'll be waiting for him. I just need u 2 assure me u won't pull that shit. Imagine a woman telling her man she'll be his doormat and then encourages him 2 keep wiping his feet on her. When u get 2 that point, come c me instead. Love 2 you and Sara."

Dee hit reply and quickly typed: "No problem. He won't be coming back. He and What's-Her-Name are having a baby."

The tears in Dee's eyes kept her from writing more. She knew she wouldn't e-mail Dan. He stopped the direct deposit of his paycheck without telling her. He cut off all communication with her and Sara. E-mailing him wouldn't solve anything.

She planned a visit to the bank hoping to set up a new account in her name. She forced herself to make a to-do list: create a new bank account, apply for a credit card in her name only, change the utilities to her name, and try to get Dan's new address from Mom Jax. She wondered if she'd have to sell the house. Both their names were on the deed.

Daddy, she thought, *I don't know how to do this. How I wish you were here. I miss you so.*

Dee called the lawyer who handled the closing of their house. He told her he would like to represent her, but as a real estate attorney he couldn't. Plus, he and Dan attended the same school and church for much of their lives. He felt sure there would be a conflict of interest. He gave her a name of a family law attorney, Felix Fannin, who recently moved to Elberton from Atlanta. Dee called Fannin's office and made an appointment for the following week.

She started her list of questions which included setting visiting rights for Dan to see Sara, the house payments, child support, furniture, and the car. She couldn't remember if her car was in her name or his. Making the list was overwhelming. She stopped, knowing the list was far from complete. The list felt like the official beginning of the end of her life with Dan. She would finish the list when the tears dried. She tried to remember where she filed the car title and tag receipt.

It never occurred to Dee that Dan would be unfair. Even if he no longer loved her, he'd eventually do what was best for Sara. Any question about Dan's fairness or lack of fairness arrived the next day in the form of their joint bank statement and the credit card statement. The automated draw for the house payment and several of Dan's ATM withdrawals totaled $2,500. Dan's credit card charges amounted to another $2,000. Its total would be taken out of the bank account in ten days.

Dee panicked. The bank closed in thirty minutes and she needed to pick up Sara within the hour. She called her neighbor to ensure Sara could stay longer, grabbed her purse, and made it to the bank before it closed.

Shock came with the knowledge that their joint bank account showed a zero balance and for several days, all withdrawals had been covered through an automatic withdraw from their money market account. She talked with a representative who helped her open her own account, using the remaining $2,000 from their money market account. Dee picked up the paperwork to take to the school board's office to ensure her paycheck would be direct deposited to the new account. She placed a hold on the savings account that required Dan's signature. He would have to fight in court to get any part of it.

Two thousand dollars. Two thousand dollars that should have been ten thousand left in the money market account *she* had struggled to maintain. Angry and frustrated, she left the bank ready to do battle. She had been told she was stubborn. Dan Jackson would soon find out just how stubborn she could be.

The next two days were dedicated to changing utility bills, the cable company, and phone bills to her name. Most of the changes were made online or with a phone call. She knew Dan didn't have any checks and probably wouldn't remember their checking account number. It would be a few days before he found out that not only was there no money in their joint account – it didn't even exist. She also knew he would never admit to taking four times more of the money than she took.

She found Dan's truck payment information in the same drawer as her car title and payment information. The car title carried only her name. Payments for both the truck and car were automatically withdrawn from their checking account. She typed in the changes for her car, ensuring future payments would come from her new bank account. The computer screen verified the change. She took Dan's paperwork for his truck and added it to the growing stack of mail she would eventually forward to him or ask his mother to forward. She wondered if he actually thought she'd keep paying his bills.

That evening Sara answered a phone call before Dee could get to the phone. With her hand hovering just above the kitchen phone, Dee noticed Dan's cell phone number on the display.

"Daddy." Sara's smile matched the excitement in her voice.

Dee backed away from the phone. When she walked into the den, she saw Sara's brow wrinkle and watched as Sara's chin quivered. Tears slipped down each cheek.

"Uh huh. No. I didn't know. Okay. Bye." Sara pressed the off button on the phone and laid it down.

Dee ran to Sara and tried to gather her in her arms; but Sara pulled away, ran to her room, and closed the door. Dee stood in the hallway a few seconds before knocking quietly on Sara's door.

"Sweetie. Is it okay if I come in?"

"Go away."

Dee turned the doorknob. It wasn't locked. Dee spoke as she entered the room.

"Let's talk. I guess your daddy told you about the baby. Right?" Dee asked.

"You knew. Mom. You knew and you didn't tell me?"

"I know. I thought it was Dad's place to tell you. I haven't known very long. I'm so sorry. Granny Nida let it slip. I was so angry with Mom Jax for not telling me, I should have known you'd feel that way, too. I'm so sorry." Dee tried to hug Sara and was met with less resistance. Sara's stiff body relaxed slightly.

"Daddy always called me his little woman. He used to say you were his woman and I was his little woman. I guess I won't be his little woman anymore." Sara's words poured out. "Mom, Dad's not coming back, is he?"

Dee knew she wasn't the only one who believed Dan would miss them so much he'd come back home. Sara's hope that he would return disappeared with the evening's phone call.

"Maybe the baby will be a boy and you'll have a little brother. That might be nice," Dee tried to paint a better picture for Sara.

"No. Dad said, 'You're gonna have a little sister.' They just found out today." Tears ran down Sara's face.

Dee couldn't think of anything to say to make Sara feel better. She held her daughter's thin body. Sara's arms found their way around her mother's waist. They rocked back and forth as Sara's head rested on Dee's chest. Dee's tears fell on Sara's red hair.

After a few seconds, Sara pulled away and looked into her mother's eyes. "I hung up on Daddy. I said 'bye.' He started to tell me something else; but, I heard enough, so I hung up."

Serves him right, the jerk, Dee thought as she smiled through her tears. She hugged Sara tighter.

Before she went to bed, Dee erased four phone messages, two from the financing company holding the loan on Dan's truck, and two from Dan asking Dee to call him. She ignored them all.

Her dream that night seemed so real she woke up startled. She remembered every detail. Leaning against the wall in the courthouse corridor, waiting to be called into the judge's chamber for the final divorce decree, Dee watched as an attendant pushed a stretcher down the hallway. As it came closer, she saw Dan with his body covered in a white sheet and wide gray straps across his chest and upper legs. She leaned over to get a better look at him. His auburn eyelashes lay against pale gray skin, the eyeballs underneath the thin eyelids darted back and forth. She touched his otherwise motionless body trying to get him to respond and jumped back when his eyes popped wide open. *What did this crazy dream mean? Even in her dreams Dan tried to manipulate her. Could ignoring his phone calls cause such strong guilt, she felt sorry for him on some level? Loyalty. Or lack of it. That's what it is. I feel disloyal – after all he's done – I feel disloyal. Go figure.* She drifted back to sleep.

Her first thought when she woke was the letter her dad wrote and gave her on her wedding day. She had placed it in the wedding album with her pictures. Quietly, she slipped out of bed, made her way to the den, and retrieved the album from the bottom shelf of the entertainment center. She didn't look at the photographs, knowing they would keep her attention for hours, and make her think back to a time she needed to forget. The envelope from her father, stashed in the back of the album, was easy to find. She opened it, pulled out the two-page letter, and spotted the paragraph on which she wanted to concentrate.

"My darling daughter, please understand that today, your wedding day, is a ritual. Rituals are good things, mostly. However, rituals come

from social needs. Leading up to the ritual is where you find the important things in life. A wedding is a ritual; the commitment you made to Dan came first. Today's ritual would be worthless without your prior commitment to love.

Today, I will have the pleasure of giving you, my precious daughter, to Dan for safekeeping. The ritual of taking your hand from my arm and placing it in Dan's hand will mean just that. It's a ritual. My arm will always be there in your time of need. Plan your rituals in life, but enjoy the process that comes before and after. And, always remember, I love you."

Her mind, seeking answers and a way to overcome the dark cloud of the dream, brought back the words her father said many times, "You're strong. You can do this, Deedle Bug. Take my arm. It's here for you." She smiled, comforted by the mere thought of her father.

The day after he called his daughter, Dan stopped by the ATM in Brownsville on his way home to the apartment he and Char shared. Dressed in a dark suit, white shirt and tie, he looked like a successful businessman. He punched the four digits required to access the checking account to make an ATM withdrawal. Surprised with the message that it was an invalid number, he punched it in again and received the same result. After the third try, he gave up.

He was aware that the Elberton checking account was linked to the money market account and ensured all withdrawals would be covered. Because he made more money than Dee, he considered any savings to be his money. He used the ATM withdrawals and his credit cards for everything when he traveled. It was an easy way to get money. He continued to do the same since moving to Texas. He hadn't kept track of how much he withdrew. He hadn't bothered asking for a receipt when he took the money from the ATM machine. He never had to worry about balances – one way or the other. He didn't bother trying to get funds from the account he set up for himself and Char, the new account to which his payroll check was direct deposited. Char told him earlier in the week the rent payment had bounced. He took money from the Elberton account to cover the shortage.

He realized he wouldn't be able to find out why he couldn't get into the Elberton accounts until the next day since it was after banking hours. He thought of Dee. *That bitch. She's responsible for this.*

He pulled out his wallet and thumbed through the bills. *A ten. A five. Three ones.* He knew $18 would barely cover the Chinese takeout Char ordered and asked him to pick up on his way home. *No problem. I'll put it on my credit card.* He left the bank and headed toward the Chinese restaurant.

Dan's name, printed on the green and white lined order form was stapled to the paper bag waiting near the cash register. Dan told the cashier his name and handed his American Express credit card to the old Chinese man. The cashier ran it through a machine, handed it back to Dan, and in broken English said, "No take."

Dan pulled out another card and handed it to the cashier who repeated the process. When he told Dan, "No will take," Dan became angry. He separated $15 from the $18 in his hand and threw them at the cashier before grabbing the takeout bag.

The cashier caught up with Dan at the door and gave him the credit card and a few cents in change. Dan pushed the card and change into his pants' pocket.

The two-block drive to their apartment didn't allow Dan time to cool off. He stormed into the apartment. Char took the takeout bag from him. If he had any doubts about her self-interest, they were laid to rest when he saw how much she enjoyed having her way. It occurred to him that she didn't know his resources were limited. He shook his head, knowing she still didn't know why he got so upset when she quit work after she found out she was pregnant. She had told him he was stupid if he believed she'd work until the baby came. She said there was no way she would let someone else take care of her baby. It finally registered with him that her working days were over.

He watched Char rub her baby bump before sitting down and didn't care if his unhappiness showed on his red face. He hoped his scowl left no doubt in her mind that something was wrong. He was surprised she had the nerve to ask him to get the plates from the kitchen cabinet. He wanted her to hear the slamming of the cabinet doors as he opened and closed them.

The plates rattled as he dropped them on the table. He noticed that she had already opened the takeout bag and placed the cartons of food in the middle of the table. Dan went back to the kitchen for a fork. When he returned to the table, Char had already started eating with chopsticks. They ate in silence. He knew she didn't care about his problems.

Janet performed another show at the Star Civic Center in Atlanta. The night before the show, Dee met Janet and her producer, Gary Bowles, for dinner at The Grit on Prince Avenue in Athens, before going to the Town and Gown Community Theatre for *The Rocky Horror Show*. Janet and Gary were already seated when Dee arrived at the restaurant. When Janet gave Dee a hug and introduced Dee to Gary, he hugged Dee, too, as if he'd always known her. His brown eyes twinkled as if he knew something funny that no one else knew. The slightly gray hair at his temples made him look distinguished. Dressed in jeans and a thin-striped shirt, he looked at home in the large old brick building housing The Grit.

Janet talked non-stop about the parts she played at the Town and Gown when she was a student at the University of Georgia. Her form-fitting dress, height and beauty attracted attention. A waiter hovered nearby, listening and watching every move she made.

Occasionally, Dee gave Gary a smile and received a silly grin from him. She sat quietly, contemplating the evening and wondering if she was attracted to Gary because she was already on the rebound.

When the food came, Janet stopped talking long enough to take a bite of her stir-fried tofu and vegetables. Gary immediately took advantage of the break and asked, "How's your cute little daughter Janet's always raving aboot?"

It took Dee a couple of seconds to realize he said "about." His Canadian accent would take some getting used to. Dee told him Sara loved knock-knock jokes and that she constantly drew pictures.

"I think she's going to be an artist." Dee purposely stayed away from talking about Sara's clairvoyance. Gary's question surprised her. The only man who asked her out after Dan left seemed to think she was sent by God to take care of his sexual fantasies. The man certainly wasn't interested in Sara, and wasn't particularly interested in her, if it didn't include sex. She learned all that without dating him. She didn't want to learn more. So far, being single or almost single proved to be very different from a decade ago. She hadn't really enjoyed dating then. Until she met Janet's producer, dating seemed rather dismal.

"She keeps you on your toes, eh?" Gary's question brought Dee back to the conversation. Again, his accent showed.

"All ten of them," Dee said laughingly.

Dee left her car parked in a lot across from The Grit and rode down the street to the theater in Gary's rental car. He left Dee and Janet at the front of the Town and Gown Theatre before parking the car on the side street.

As Gary parked the car, Dee took the opportunity to question Janet about him. "What's Gary's story? Is he married?" Dee asked looking back to be sure he couldn't hear the conversation.

"No. His wife and baby were killed years ago in a car accident. He hasn't seemed interested in meeting anyone. That is, until I told him about you. If he's asked me one question, he's asked me twenty."

Dee felt really good about Gary's interest. She smiled. Dee watched as Janet smiled and waved the tickets in the air to get Gary's attention when he entered the crowded lobby. As soon as Gary joined them, Janet ushered them to their seats, made it clear she wanted the aisle seat, and insisted that Gary go first, leaving Dee seated in the middle.

Dee knew the audience was expected to participate in the *Rocky Horror* play. The ushers and actors didn't have to coerce Janet. Gyrating in the aisle and dancing over to Dee, she pulled and beckoned until Dee joined in, moving to the sensual *Time Warp* dance. Janet tried to get Gary to join them. Eventually, he gave in. Soon most of the audience swayed to the steps of the *Time Warp* dance. By the time the actors gathered in the scary castle, the main character, a red-headed transvestite, made his first appearance. He played his part well. Dee laughed at his antics, until he murdered one of his creations without any remorse. The guy was amazing. She looked at Gary who winked at her. She thought, *He's flirting with me, and I like it*. Before the play was over, she decided she needed to get out more often. She had been too serious for too long. Gary made her want to get to know him better. He made her heart skip a beat.

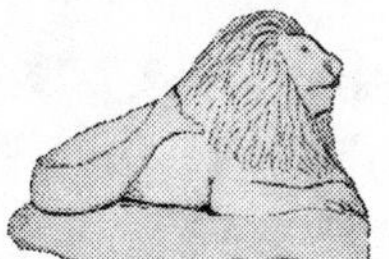

Chapter Twenty-Two – Riddles Piddles

On the island, James watched his mean mommy carefully, very aware of her disappointment in him. Every day he tried to appease her. His stuttering and nervous habit of pinching his chin became worse. As the stress built inside him, he stopped talking.

In Elberton, Sara tugged at her mother's shirttail. "Granny Nida says life is full of riddles and I should look for them."

"Why did she say that?" Dee asked, taking a pan of cinnamon rolls from the oven.

"It's 'cause her bottle of Vitamin C has rose hips. She asked me if I knew roses had hips. I told her I didn't and we looked at a rose. We couldn't see anything that looked like a hip." Sara hiked a hip toward her mother.

"Sweetie, I think it's the bump at the base of the rose after the petals fall off. Let's check it out." Dee placed her arm around Sara's shoulder as they made their way to Dee's small office.

"Now that Granny Nida said that about the rose hips, I've thought of a bunch of others." Sara looked up at Dee.

"Well, tell me about them while we wait for the computer to boot up." The computer sounded like an old man getting out of his rocker. Soft groaning and crunching noises filled the room. Dee longed for a new laptop. Every time she discussed it with Dan he said they couldn't afford it. *Don't go there, Dee Dupree,* she told herself. She realized she had already started thinking of herself without her married name. *You'll just make yourself miserable. Did that jerk buy What's-Her-Name a laptop? Stop it, Dee.* She made herself listen to Sara talk about riddles.

"I wanna know if a banana has a front or a back. I can't find one," Sara said.

"Ummm. Beats me." Dee said, looking up at her daughter.

"How about a pencil? I don't know the front and back of a pencil." Sara handed her mother a pencil she'd taken from a black and white container she made in an arts and crafts class at Bible school. The black fringe on top swayed as Sara's hand made the air move in and around the holder.

"Ummm. You got me there, too." Dee wondered if Granny Nida knew she'd opened Pandora's box when she asked Sara to find life's riddles. "Do you know the answers?"

"No. She didn't ask me to find the answers. She just asked me to find the riddles. Do riddles have to have answers?" Sara asked, leaning against her mother.

Dee read from the computer screen, "*The hip of the rose is usually orange or red and is the fruit left after the bloom has died.*" Dee looked at Sara.

"So. Some have answers and some don't. Right, Mom?"

"I think you're right and I think it's time you got ready for bed. You can think about riddles another time. Scat." Dee pushed Sara toward the door.

The riddle Dee couldn't answer was how on earth Dan Jackson could be so cruel to such a wonderful daughter. Sadness engulfed Dee every time she caught Sara looking at Dan's picture on the mantel. She really wanted to take all the pictures with Dan in them and throw them out. She resisted the temptation and thought, *Sara needs to know her daddy. The good and the bad.*

"Mom!" Sara screamed.

Dee left her office and ran to the kitchen table where Sara sat with a sheet of notebook paper.

"I'm scared for James. Mollie said James is a riddle, and we need to solve it." Sara was trembling.

Dee leaned down and hugged her daughter's shoulders. "Shhhh. It's okay, sweetie. We'll solve it. Just listen to Mollie. I know other people won't believe in Mollie. But, we do. She'll help us find him. Tell me exactly what she said."

"I was writin' down the riddles we talked about and my pencil fell out of my hand. When I reached to get it I heard Mollie in my head saying, 'Riddles, piddles, look at the island art. That's where you'll find James. You've had the key from the start.' Mom, Mollie is my friend, but sometimes I don't get her."

The door to the law office squeaked when Dee eased it open. Located in an old historic home on Elberton's Heard Street, it seemed appropriate for a family law office. Dee stepped into the large foyer with its wide wood-plank flooring, walked across the colorful Oriental rug in the center, never noticing its red-rust and brown colors, and made her way to the reception area. She signed a register and nodded to the young lady behind the desk. The woman looked at the clipboard and told Dee to have a seat in the front parlor.

While waiting, Dee opened her purse and pulled out a piece of paper and a ballpoint pen. She never got back to completing the list of things to discuss with the lawyer. Time had flown by. Quickly, she looked over the entries: visiting rights, house payments, child support, furniture, car, and truck. She struck a line through the word "car" since she found the title. It was in her name. She added Dan's bank account withdrawals along with the amounts.

Pondering over the list and lost in thought, Dee didn't hear an office door open or see a young dark-haired man walking her way. The sleeves of his white shirt were rolled up, almost to his elbows, and his tie looked as if he'd loosened it several times. His khaki pants had lost their crease.

"Mrs. Jackson?" he asked, all business.

"Yes. I'm Dee Jackson." She stood up, smoothed her sleeveless pink floral dress, and extended her hand to him.

"I'm Felix Fannin." He gave her hand a hardy shake. "Let's go into my office." He gestured past the registration desk toward a hallway.

The young lawyer's navy blue blazer draped the back of the desk chair. He motioned for her to sit in one of the two Victorian-style chairs across from his desk. He took notes as Dee described how and when Dan left Elberton to live in Texas and how he took most of the money from their checking and money market accounts. She explained that she paid the charges she made on their credit cards and requested that her name not be associated with his cards.

"My cell phone charges automatically went to our credit card. I changed to my own new card and left all his charges for him to pay."

"When did you hear from him last?" Fannin said as he leaned toward her, unconsciously moving a paperweight back and forth on his mahogany desktop.

"A few days ago. Actually, I didn't talk with him. Sara did. Sara's our nine-year-old daughter. He called to tell her she's … ah," Dee hesitated. She found it hard to put into words. "Dan told Sara she would have a baby sister in a few months."

"Have you been served yet?" he asked and leaned back in his chair.

Dee didn't respond.

Mr. Fannin asked the question in another way, "Has he filed for divorce yet?"

"No. At least I haven't been notified."

"We'll wait for him to file against you, unless you know of a reason we should file first. The advantage is if he files, he has to file in the county in which you live. If this goes to court, you don't want it to go before a jury in Texas."

"Oh. I didn't know that. I just want it over with." Dee leaned back in the comfortable antique chair.

"I'm surprised he hasn't filed. It seems to me, with a baby on the way, he would want a divorce sooner than later."

Dee watched the lawyer look down at his notes before asking, "Are you okay financially? We may have to file for support of some kind if you and your daughter are destitute."

She noticed that he had dropped the formal attitude he used with her earlier and seemed genuinely concerned about her and Sara.

"I'm okay for a couple of months. If his expenses aren't coming out of my account, I'll be a lot better off. He never knew or cared about bank balances. He spent whatever he wanted." Dee explained how she lost count of all the times she moved money from their savings or from Sara's college funds to cover down payments on trucks, boats, lawn mowers and cell phones. She told him how Dan replaced major purchases soon after buying them, often before all the payments were made.

"We can go ahead and file for child support." Felix Fannin explained how temporary child support almost always sets a precedent on permanent child support. Most judges use the temporary guidelines in setting permanent support. He asked Dee to bring him Dan's records of income including paychecks and any bonus information.

"Oh. One more question. Have you changed the locks at your house?" he asked and looked up from his yellow lined legal pad.

"No. Just the utility building. I didn't want him to take the lawn mower. I need it."

"You should change them. If you can't do it, get a locksmith or a friend if you know someone who can do it for you. I've known of several cases where the one leaving thought he had a right to everything. Don't take any chances, change the locks," he warned. He also advised her to change all codes to the alarm system.

Mr. Fannin told her he'd try and get an address for Dan and asked her to bring Dan's mail, payment schedules, and other information for his truck. He wanted to send a certified letter letting Dan know he was representing her.

"If this goes to court, I want you to be unimpeachable. I'll file papers of abandonment and then start working on a legal separation. You'd think his having a girlfriend with a baby on the way would leave you free to do whatever you want. I've seen this backfire. Are you involved with anyone?"

"No," Dee responded with a frown.

"Good. Don't get involved with anyone. He and his lawyer will use anything and everything against you. Don't date or spend a lot of time in the company of single guys." He laughed. "Or married guys either. It'll make our lives easier down the road." He stood up, waited for her to join him, shook her hand, and walked her to the door.

Dee stopped by the receptionist's desk and made an appointment for the following week. She thought about Janet's producer, Gary and wondered if she should have told her lawyer about him. She knew she'd have to stay away from the Canadian until the legal separation was filed.

"Eh?" She said out loud as she unlocked her car. She imagined Gary's twinkling brown eyes teasing her.

A huge red tow truck with a Fulton County tag was idling in the paved turnaround beside the driveway when Dee returned from the lawyer's office. Dee took out her cell phone, ready to press 911 if she felt threatened. The man dressed in jeans and wearing dark sunglasses reminded her of a bounty hunter she saw on a television reality show with his bald head and stocky build. Cautiously, she walked toward him, dreading the confrontation that was sure to come.

"Mrs. Jackson?" the man asked.

"Yes." She looked at her phone, her thumb hovering over the keypad. His bulk, blood-shot eyes, and redneck attitude gave her the creeps. She felt his gaze checking her out, making no effort to hide that he liked what he saw.

"I'm looking for Dan Jackson. No one answered the door. I was fixin' to leave when you drove up. Is he gonna be home soon?"

"I don't know," she answered, purposely evasive.

"Oh. Will you have him call me?" the man asked as he took a step closer to Dee, continuing to stare at her cleavage as if he envisioned her without the floral sleeveless dress.

"Why are you looking for him?" She placed her finger on the number 9 on her keypad.

"He's missed a couple of truck payments and the credit card attached to the file is closed. Our office left several messages on your home phone. No one returned the calls," he said, accusingly.

"I didn't call you back because I don't have any information to help you," Dee replied. The anger in her voice was unmistakable. "He's not here." She almost added that Dan wasn't paying any bills and that with a daughter to take care of, a job, a house, and everything that goes with keeping a house, she had enough responsibility. She didn't want to give the stranger too much information. She continued, "His truck is not on my list of priorities."

The man took a step backward. He realized he wouldn't be intimidating this woman. "Sorry to have bothered you, ma'am."

The truck's gears made grinding sounds, and its axle creaked as the man drove away. As soon as the truck was out of sight, she went inside, gathered Dan's mail, pay records and truck payment information, and rushed into town. She made it to the lawyer's office just before closing time. She smiled as she walked out of Fannin's office. Dan Jackson gave her freedom – now she was ready to use it.

When she got back home, Dee checked her e-mail and clicked on the one from her Aunt Connie. It read: "Your mom and I have decided the best revenge you can get on Dan is to live well and be happy. By the way, did your mother tell you she sold five paintings to a hotel chain? They plan to duplicate them and use them in their hotel rooms."

Leaving Dan's papers with her lawyer made her feel free. Aaaaah. *Makes me happy. Now, if I can just get the "living well" down pat, I'll have it made.*

Her mother's voicemail picked up when Dee called to congratulate her on selling her artwork.

"Hi, Mom. Congratulations on the wonderful sale of your paintings. I'm so proud of you. Call me when you get in." Dee could hardly wait to tell Sara. She wondered which of her mother's paintings were included in the sale.

It was almost eleven o'clock when the phone rang that evening. Sara had been asleep for a couple hours, leaving Dee time to finish reading the last section of the upcoming lesson plans for her history class.

"Hello."

"Hey, Dee. Thought I'd call and see aboot you."

Dee smiled, "Hi, Gary. I'm so glad you called."

"I just need a Southern fix and I know just the bootiful girl to help me out."

Gary's Canadian lilt made Dee smile again.

"How's Sara?" he asked.

"She's okay, She's such a sweetie pie. She's dealing with a lot right now. We both are."

"I know. I just wanted to check in. I love Southern expressions. I'll have to remember that one." He laughed.

"Pardon?" Dee couldn't think of what he meant.

"You know – Sara being a sweetie pie. I love it." Gary tried to explain. He wondered if he had offended her.

"Well. Yes. That's what I call her when she's been really good. Today, she was especially nice. Never thought anything about it actually. Most of my family, except for my mom, calls each other 'sweetie.'" Dee laughed when she realized he wasn't making fun of her.

"Dee, it's like sweet tea. I think it's a Southern thing. I love Southern."

"Actually, my husband's, well, soon-to-be ex-husband's family, calls us all 'sugar.' It's a nice term of endearment." She wanted him to know she liked his loving Southern.

"Terms of endearment are good. Remember the movie?" Gary asked.

"I love that movie. Sad, but poignant." She sat sideways on the chair in the den with her legs hanging over the cushioned side.

Dee asked Gary about Janet.

"She's dynamite. I've never seen such energy. You coming to Tennessee any time soon?"

"I hope so," she answered, settling deeper into the chair.

"Let's make it happen."

They said their goodbyes. Dee sat in the chair thinking about how her mother didn't use terms of endearment. Dee couldn't remember a time her mother called her sweetie or honey or sugar, much less sweetie pie. Hugs and embraces were rare. For the first time ever, Dee wondered if her independent streak or her closeness to her father affected her relationship with her mother. She wondered, *is it possible I made Mom feel left out? Maybe she couldn't deal with my stubbornness and my need to avoid confrontations.* Dee forced her mind to a more positive place. She decided to study her own actions, instead of placing all the blame on her mother. The handsome Canadian slipped back into her thoughts. Her mother didn't know about Gary.

When she went to sleep that night she expected to dream about the Canadian. Instead, Mollie's ghostly white face appeared. In the dream she asked Mollie why she didn't warn her about Dan's weak character. Mollie's black hair blew in the wind.

"You told me not to let my stubbornness get in the way of my happiness. You encouraged me to give Dan another chance when he wanted to make up with me. I wouldn't have to go through the pain of losing him again if I just walked away back then." Dee's words sounded weird in the dream.

"Ahhhh. Remember when you were a little girl and you said you wanted to get married and have red-headed children? Sara wouldn't be Sara if you hadn't married Dan. She'd have someone else's genes. I think you'll agree, Sara is worth all the heartache." Mollie's form faded slowly away.

The dream stayed with Dee for days. It made her feel differently about Dan. Mollie was right on target. Dee knew she wouldn't change a thing about her little red-haired daughter.

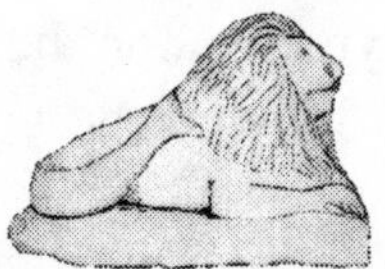

Chapter Twenty-Three – The Key

The mail carrier's vehicle pulled away from the mailbox at the end of the driveway just as Dee caught sight of her house. She parked the car in the garage, got out, and made her way to the mailbox. As soon as she held the stack of mail in her hand, she shuffled through the envelopes, sorted according to priority, and placed the junk mail and magazines behind the first class smaller envelopes. She placed the envelope from her mother on top of the stack.

With an hour before she needed to drive into town and pick up Sara from the piano teacher's home, Dee sat on the living room sofa to open the mail. When she pulled out a folded sheet of paper from her mother's envelope, two checks fell to the floor. She bent over to pick them up.

"Thirteen thousand dollars? No way," she said out loud. She looked again in disbelief. The check was made to Delores Dupree Jackson. When she took another look, she saw the word "gift" written in the bottom left side of the check. She hugged it to her chest before looking at the second check.

The second check was made out to Sara Jackson for the same amount of money. Dee placed both checks side by side. *Another gift,* she thought. She reached for the sheet of notepaper. Her mother's beautiful cursive writing explained: "Dee, I've sold, for a great deal of money, five paintings. A New York company in charge of decorating for several upscale hotels chose five of my paintings. One is the Knock Out Roses inspired by Sara. She chose those roses for our art project. Remember the paintings? My inventory already included paintings of hydrangeas, azaleas, dogwood blossoms, and camellias. I've checked with my accountant and he says I can give you and Sara up to $13,000 a year as a gift without you having to report it as income. So, there. I'm doing it. Love, Mom." It was dated and mailed before Connie told Dee about her mother's great sale. Now Dee knew why her mother hadn't called back.

Dee made the decision to deposit Sara's check into her college fund. Her check would go into her checking account to help her pay bills, including the John Deere lawn mower Dan bought the year before. She refused to make the payments for the boat he took to Texas. She needed the mower since she mowed the grass the past several months. He'd have to fight to get it.

Her mother's kind gesture temporarily took the financial stress out of the picture. Dee jumped up from the sofa and danced around the room singing, "Living well. Living well. Dan can go to hell, 'cause I'm living well." She sang it several times to get it out of her system before driving into town to pick up Sara.

Dee wished she had recorded Sara's reaction to seeing the checks. As soon as Sara buckled herself in the back seat, Dee passed the checks to her and watched from the driver's seat. She saw Sara's large blue eyes widen. Dee passed her the letter that came with the checks.

"If Mama Anna can sell her picture of the roses for this much, maybe I could sell mine, too," Sara said wistfully. "Woo-hoo. Wouldn't that be great? Daddy would be so proud of me."

"Not to worry, honey. I'm proud of you in so many ways. I'm sure your daddy is, too. Mama Anna sold several paintings, not just the roses. I'm planning for your money to go into your college fund." Dee hoped she handled the zinger well. She had no idea Sara was trying to find ways to make her daddy proud.

"You mean I don't get anything?"

Dee saw Sara tilt her head and look at her in dismay.

"What do you want?" Dee smiled. She loved how Sara didn't try to hide how she felt about the money.

"I want a laptop. And, I want you to have a laptop. We could do our homework at the same time," Sara said as she hugged the check close to her chest.

"Okay. You and I will get laptops. Good idea." Dee didn't bother telling her daughter that she already decided to use some of her money to buy herself a laptop. She'd let Sara think it was all her idea for both of them to have new computers.

As soon as they arrived home, Dee called her mother to thank her for sharing her good fortune. When they finished chatting, Dee gave the phone to Sara, walked into the laundry room, shifted clothes from the washer to the dryer, and returned to the kitchen.

Dee heard Sara trying to explain the Georgia Guidestones to her Mama Anna. A lapse in Sara's side of the conversation made Dee wonder if the call had disconnected.

"Okay, Mama Anna. Thanks again for the great gift. Mom says I can buy a laptop, but after that, it all goes to my college money." Dee assumed her mother's last comment involved an "I love you" because Sara ended with, "Me, too," and hung up.

"You two talked a long time. Does Mama Anna want you to give her a tour of the Georgia Guidestones?" Dee asked.

"No. She saw them on the History Channel. I told her about the words on the stones that said we shouldn't have so many people. Mama Anna started telling me about a ZIP . . . or something like that. She said before you were born she worked at the place where they planned families. She said if a family replaced the mommy and daddy, we wouldn't have so many people. Something about population." Sara shrugged her shoulders.

"ZPG, sweetie. I remember Mom talking about it. She worked for Planned Parenthood. They helped people plan families. I think they were the ones who had the idea for Zero Population Growth by replacing only existing people, you know two children to replace their parents. Somehow, that formula was forgotten."

"I'm hungry," Sara said, letting her mother know she'd lost interest in ZIP or ZPG.

Other than the dream where Dee questioned Mollie about not warning her about Dan, she hadn't seen Mollie in years until the night Dee woke from a deep sleep and saw the ghostly young woman at the foot of her bed. Mollie held Sara's drawing of the whales. In a strange low voice she said, "The key, Dee, is here." Mollie slowly and deliberately moved the drawing toward Dee's face. The picture faded away. Dee felt Mollie's frustration as she and the picture faded into oblivion. Certain that Mollie wanted or needed to say more about the picture and what it meant, Dee was confused. She moved to get out of bed and check on Sara. Before her feet touched the floor, she remembered that Sara was spending the night with Mom and Pop Jax. She drifted back to sleep.

When she woke up a couple of hours later, she wondered why Mollie decided to contact her instead of Sara. Dee assumed Mollie preferred communicating with Sara. She knew Sara's strong ability to receive information from Mollie made communication easier. With Dee's limited ability, Mollie had to work much harder to get a message through. Dee got out of bed and made her way to the kitchen.

Her copy of the painting of the *Whales in the Park* and the poem lay on the island countertop. She could have sworn she left it with Emmy's wrapped gift on the shelf behind the table. *Could Molly have moved it?* Sara's hand-drawn picture of the whales lay beside it. Dee picked it up and wondered when Sara had drawn it. After puzzling over the picture for several seconds, a memory surfaced. *Could it be the rocks Sara drew at Emmy's house?* She put it back down on the countertop beside her copy of the picture of the whales with the poem and realized their importance. The unsophisticated lines of Sara's drawing outlined a large whale with a smaller one on its back. Dee changed clothes, grabbed the pictures, her purse and car keys, and ran out the door.

She drove a couple of miles when she called Emmy from her cell phone to make sure she was home, only to find she was at Mom and Pop Jax's house. She said, "Stay there. I have something I want to show you." With no traffic coming towards her, she did a U-turn and headed towards Elberton.

Mom Jax met her at their back door. Holding the door open for Dee, she asked, "Sugar, you look like you've seen a ghost. You okay?"

Dee held up two sheets of paper. "I'm okay. It's just that I think I may have a clue here as to where James is."

Dee saw tears in her mother-in-law's eyes as her hand moved to cover her heart. "Emmy's in the den, rocking Marcie." Mom Jax raised her voice so Emmy could hear, "Come to the kitchen, Emmy."

Dee helped her mother-in-law move several snack dishes from the table to make space for Dee's copy of the poem and the picture of the whales. When Dee placed Sara's drawing beside it, neither Emmy nor her mom seemed to get the connection. Dee traced the outlines of the animals from Sara's drawing to show them the commonality of the two pictures.

Emmy read the poem. She looked at the picture in the book and looked back at the poem. She ran her finger under the words, "*it was worth the trip to the South to birth this wondrous creature in the warm waters off St. Simons Island.*" Emmy picked up Sara's drawing of the mother whale and her baby. "The Whales in the Park at St. Simons Island. Dee, are you sure?" Emmy was unable to control her shaking hands. The sheets of paper rattled.

"No. I'm not certain. I just want us to check it out. I think we should go to St. Simons – now." She told them about Mollie's visit and how Mollie said Sara's picture held the key.

Dee was quiet as Emmy stood there staring at the pictures. After a few seconds Emmy said, “Fred’s working in the yard. He probably doesn’t have his phone with him.”

“You know there’s a storm down there?” Mom Jax interjected. “It’s nice here today; but there’s nasty weather on the island.”

TK planned the trip to St. Simons Island weeks before the hurricane threatened the area. When his sister confirmed the unlikely chance of the hurricane hitting the island, he didn’t cancel the trip. He arrived on Thursday before the rain, just as many residents were leaving. His sister, a shorter version of himself, with dark hair and an olive complexion, greeted him at the door of the family’s condominium.

TK hadn’t seen Robert since the family reunion in New Jersey two years before.

By Saturday morning, TK’s visit was almost over. The hurricane was downgraded to a tropical storm forcing them inside for hours. TK planned to leave the next day after the storm moved North. When Robert asked him about his work, he felt that his nephew was trying to be a good host and make conversation with him while his mother made sandwiches. TK told him how he became interested in police investigative work, how he started in New Jersey, and moved to Atlanta before taking the assignment in Athens. He became really excited when Robert told him about the strange woman and the little boy, and how he was certain something wasn’t right.

“How old is the boy?’ TK asked.

“About five or six.”

TK remembered Sara’s drawing of the lion’s face. “Is there a lion’s face in a tree around here or a face within circles?”

“No. No lion. There are five or six trees with faces, though.” TK could tell that Robert was trying hard to think about where they were located.

“You know, the one near the Dairy Queen has rings around the face. I think there’s another one that has a mustache and long hair. He kinda looks like a lion. I can’t remember where it is.”

TK paced the floor, deep in thought, and walked toward the mantel. Just before turning around to talk with Robert, a bright picture caught his attention.

“Who’s the clown?” he asked.

“Me. Grandpa gave me his clown stuff.” Robert responded.

"You ever wearing that outfit when you saw or talked ta the boy?"

"Yeah. In the park near the pier."

"My God, Robert. Where do they live?" TK asked as he pulled his phone from his pocket.

TK cut him off before he could answer. Speaking into his phone, he said, "Lois, I'm on St. Simons Island. This is a poor connection. Can you hear me?" He barely waited for a response.

"Okay. He's here. James. James is here. Yes. No. I don't have proof, but do you remember Sara's pictures?" He waited.

"The clown. He's my nephew. Sara's pictures were on target the whole time. And the faces in the trees? They're here too." He waited for Lois to respond. The connection was breaking up.

"How fast can you get here?" TK listened for a second or two, then said, "The local police may not be of much help with this storm still raging, even though it's on its way out. Some people have evacuated, but should be coming back soon. I'll get back to you as soon as I know where she lives. If she's left the island, we won't be able to find her for days." His phone went dead. He didn't know how much she actually heard. He now knew why Sara's clown picture seemed so familiar. His father told him how he rode a unicycle and dressed like a clown when he was a teenager back in the '60s.

TK remembered his dad's story about wearing the clown suit the day he met his future wife. His father bumped into her in the grocery store while he was riding the unicycle and juggling apples. The first time he met her, he knocked his future bride to the floor. The unicycle scooted across the store's black and white linoleum floor. The clown landed on the young dark haired woman. TK wondered how he could have forgotten his father's clown stories.

He put his arm around his nephew and said, "Come on, Robert. It's a small world. Show me where you've seen this woman."

Getting ready for the six-hour trip to St. Simons Island required more time than Dee and Emmy would have liked. Dee heard her mother-in-law say she didn't mind keeping Marcie, but thought it was too soon for Emmy to make the long trip. In the end, Emmy agreed the children should stay with their grandparents; but she would make the trip.

Dee kept listing the pros and cons of why Sara should or shouldn't go to the island. Could she expose her daughter to more of the dark side of life? And, what about the weather? And what if they found James and he . . .? *Ummmm.* She couldn't bring herself to think that James wouldn't survive this. Sara could be invaluable on site if her psychic abilities helped them know exactly where to find James. The dilemma presented more questions than answers. She knew she'd have a battle with Dan if he found out about it. Making the decision for Sara to go would give Dan ammunition in a custody battle. Her concern for Sara's physical and mental health left her wanting to leave Sara safely in Elberton. She wouldn't call Dan. She would make the decision on her own. She talked with Sara, who insisted she needed to go with them.

It would help if she could discuss this with Emmy; but it might sound as if she were placing more worth on Sara's life than James' life. Her cell phone rang. She looked at the display, and didn't recognize the number. She answered, "Hello."

"Hi. Dee Jackson?"

"Yes. Who is this?"

"Agent Crandall. I've tried the Raffertys' numbers, the Jacksons' number and finally got through to you."

"That's because they've been on their phones. We're . . ."

"I need to talk with Mr. or Mrs. Rafferty, please. I have some information," Agent Lois Crandall said.

"Hold on." Dee handed her phone to Emmy and mouthed Lois Crandall's name.

"Yes." Dee heard Emmy say, knowing Emmy didn't have time for pleasantries. Dee was thankful that Emmy pressed the button on her phone to make it possible for everyone to hear.

"Mrs. Rafferty, I just talked to TK. He's on St. Simons Island with his family. I want to know if you have family there. TK mentioned a nephew, but the connection was breaking up badly. I think he said his nephew lived there. He mentioned leads to James' case. Do you have family on the island?"

"No family. Where are you?" Emmy asked.

"Just pulling out from the gas station on the Atlanta Highway."

"Are you going to St. Simons?"

"Yes. Why?" the agent asked.

"We're going, too. If you want to ride down with us, we'll pick you up somewhere in Athens and go down Highway 15. I'll explain the sudden trip when we see you. We may need your badge to get on the island. I believe James is there."

"Let me encourage you not to. It's . . ." Dee wondered if she was going to say "inappropriate." The agent said, "The weather is unpredictable right now."

Before the agent could say another word, Emmy broke in. "Agent Crandall, we are going. I don't care. The hurricane has been downgraded to a storm. If we can't get on the island, we'll stay nearby. I believe my baby's there and I'm going. James needs me."

Dee knew Lois was dealing with FBI rules and regulations they wouldn't know or understand. She felt they were putting her in a bad position.

The agent asked, "How quickly can you get here? Maybe I could help with the driving as well as getting you on the island."

Emmy told her they could meet her at Cracker Barrel near Walmart on Epps Bridge Road in forty-five minutes. She ended the conversation, pressed the end button on the phone, and handed it to Dee. Dee placed it in her purse and looked around the kitchen to find Mom Jax pulling a bag of deli turkey and sliced cheese from the refrigerator.

"Hand me that loaf of bread." Mom Jax pointed to the counter near Dee's elbow. "I'm making sandwiches. Y'all don't need to be stopping. Hank," she called out, "go to the garage and get the largest cooler."

They left Mom and Pop Jax's house with an ice chest full of drinks and sandwiches. The chest and a large bag of snacks fit into Long John Silver's storage area behind the bench seat. Mom Jax loaded pillows, blankets, and rain gear around the ice chest. Emmy got through to Fred to let him know the plans.

Sara kept insisting she needed to go. They all knew Sara might be the only one with enough information to save James. At the last minute Dee caved in and allowed Sara to make the trip. Dee asked her mother-in-law for her most recent photograph of James to share with the Glynn County authorities.

When they stopped on their way out of town to pick up Fred, he took over the driving. He and Emmy sat in the front with Dee and Sara behind them. On the way to Athens, Sara kept touching her mother, on her hand, her leg, or her shoulder, each time giving her mother a nervous smile. At one point, she whispered, "We're going to get James, Mom. We're going to get James."

Dee whispered back, "Yes, love," and blew Sara a kiss. She worried that she'd given Sara too much hope. If this didn't work out well, Sara would be devastated.

When they stopped in Athens, Fred added the agent's single

suitcase to the stash already piled behind the bench seat in the back of the van. Sara climbed onto the bench seat, making room for Agent Crandall to sit by her mother. She propped pillows all around the bench seat, pulled a small unicorn from her backpack, and stepped into an imaginary world of her own making.

A few miles south of Greensboro they came upon the side road where Nan stopped to remove the handmade dealer tag and the Florida decal from the bumper of her car the day she kidnapped James. In her mind's eye, Sara could see the black Honda parked on the side of the road. The woman pulling off the decal turned around for a second, just long enough for Sara to catch a glimpse of the face in the picture she drew of the woman morphing from a brown haired woman, to a blond, and to a small person with red hair. The thin lips and narrow empty eyes looked too familiar. Sara's head turned and watched the side road as her Uncle Fred drove the van farther down the road. When the side road was completely out of sight, she closed her eyes. A vision of James sleeping in the back seat of an old black Honda slipped into her mind. Sara shivered.

While the wind and rain blew in and around the buildings on St. Simons Island, Robert told TK he thought he knew the area in which Nan lived. He described how he and his friend lost her trail many times, always in the area near Dairy Queen on Mallery Street. Without success, TK tried several times to get through to the Brunswick's FBI resident agency in Glynn County and finally decided to go to Robert's dad's shop in the Village to find a local authority to help find James. On their way to the Village, they rode slowly down Mallery Street, looking for any clue that might help them find the house that had become James' prison.

Nan waited for the car to pass. It was the second time the SUV crept by, the vehicle's lights barely visible through the thick trees and shrubs she had planted to hide the house a few blocks off Mallery. She waited long after the SUV stopped driving by. The blowing rain – the same rain she planned to use as cover while she carried Timmy to the pier – wouldn't last forever.

The sleep aid she gave Timmy did its job well. He was still breathing. Not that it mattered to her. She gave him enough to sleep through anything. She blamed him for the action she was taking. *He wasn't the little boy she brought home. He didn't cuddle with her. He called her Mommy only when she forced him to do so, and then stopped talking altogether. He didn't talk plainly anyway. He wasn't her Timmy. He didn't even want to hold her hand when they walked to the Dairy Queen. He never thanked her for all she did for him. He didn't deserve her love.* Each thought made her more determined to follow through with her plans.

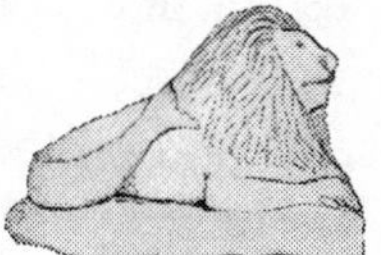

Chapter Twenty-Four – My Hero

Nan wrapped James in a thin yellow and white striped cotton blanket, tied the ends together, and laid him in the back seat of her car. She didn't see anyone as she drove through the village – the deserted pier barely visible. She parked as close as possible to the walkway and took James from the backseat. The rain lashed out. Large drops of water stung her face when she raised her head to check on her progress. The wind pushed her backwards, impeding her efforts to move forward. The soaked blanket made her bundle heavier as she trudged through the storm. It was perfect. The storm would soon be over. Just as she predicted, most of the locals left the island two days earlier, and the others were boarded up in their houses waiting. She thought no one would see her.

It was late afternoon. Focused on getting her bundle to the pier, Nan missed seeing a light in the window of one of the stores. She had no idea that Robert, his Dad and TK waited at the family shop for backup from the Brunswick FBI office.

Robert was standing inside near a large window protected by an overhang and partial wall when he saw Nan's black Honda slowly making its way to the pier. He screamed for his Dad and TK to join him, grabbed a rescue ring off a stack near the counter, and ran out the door.

Fred made the trip in record time – less than five hours. He got turned around when he drove onto the island. He missed the turn toward the village. When he got to the traffic circle near the airport, he didn't know where to turn. As he made his second loop within the circle he heard Sara.

"Uncle Fred, take that turn. Turn right. Right here. James needs us now. He's sleeping in a blanket his mean mommy . . . hurry Uncle Fred."

Fred took the next right and passed an airport sign to the left. The sheets of rain blocked a view of the tarmac and hangars. Within a few minutes, he turned on Kings Way towards the village.

"I see James. His blanket is getting wet." Sara, deciding to get closer to the front to make sure her uncle could hear her, pushed the red button on her seat belt, freeing herself. Her mother caught her as she stepped between the middle seats and pulled Sara onto her lap.

"It's okay, sweetheart. Fred heard you. He's doing his best."

The wind and rain kept Fred from seeing the pier. He first saw the black Honda at the entrance to the pier and stopped the van behind the car. He and Agent Crandall jumped out and ran to the pier. Dee, Emmy, and Sara weren't far behind with Dee trying to place rain ponchos on everyone as they ran. She barely got herself and Sara covered before throwing one over Emmy's shoulders.

At the end of the pier Nan shook her head, trying to clear her vision. The heavy bundle, her dripping hair, and wet face caused her to stumble. "Two yards at the most," she muttered as she lifted her load. She felt the metal railings before she saw them. Her evil laughter floated back across the pier. She knelt down, placed the blanket on the wet boards, and pushed it and its contents through the railings and into the water. She took a couple of steps back before TK tackled her from behind. Her knees buckled.

Robert and Fred focused on the falling bundle. It was almost impossible to see anything. They both screamed to the others to look at the blanket caught on a piling underneath the pier. Fred jumped in and Robert followed with the float he had taken from his dad's store.

Nan crawled forward trying to be sure the boy had fallen into the water. She felt TK grab her arms, trying to lift her. She screamed, "I didn't hurt him. I didn't hurt him. He's just sleeping just like her. I didn't hurt her either. Did I, Mama? I didn't hurt any of them." She pushed TK away, kicked him, making contact with his right knee.

TK heard her words in bits and pieces as Nan rolled away from him. Halfway on her feet, a gust of wind knocked her into a railing. She fell backward, reeled forward, slipped through the railings, and fell against the metal safety bars before descending into the water. TK saw the churning black water pull her under and heard haunting screams die away as the storm quieted slightly.

The bright colors of the soaked blanket stood out against the gray water and helped the men keep James in sight. Mother Nature calmed the raging storm and allowed Fred and Robert to get to the bundle and separate it from the piling. Fred took his son as Robert pulled the blanket away. The wet heavy blanket sank immediately.

TK threw a rope down to the rescuers who used it to secure James to the float. As soon as TK and Robert's dad pulled James up, TK started CPR. With his head to the side, James coughed and sputtered as the seawater spewed out.

Robert's dad threw the float back in the water. With Fred's help from below, Agent Crandall and Robert's dad hoisted Robert up to the edge of the pier. The agent pulled from one side of the float while Robert's dad pulled from the other side. Finally, Robert's exhausted body lay on the pier, his head resting on his dad's chest.

Fred's weight and size made it difficult to lift him up high enough for the others to grab. Half way up, the wet rope slipped through his hands. His head made contact with the wooden piling that had trapped James and kept him from going under.

A few rays of light slipped through the dark clouds and made it easier for TK to see Fred's head hit the piling. He dove in and was trying to keep his strokes steady when Fred disappeared. TK plunged underwater searching for Fred, resurfaced once for air, and went down again. On the second trip, TK found Fred near the base of the piling. He grabbed Fred from behind and lifted him to the surface. He managed to get a hold on the float and used it as a bumper each time the waves pushed them against the concrete piling.

Again, the waves slowed enough for TK to get Fred to the rocks lining the shore. When TK looked up, he saw two strong young men from the Glynn County Rescue Unit making their way over the rocks. He managed to place Fred on a jutting rock, and held him there until the first responders got to them.

Sinking into the churning water frightened Nan. She knew she couldn't surface anywhere near the pier. Too many people were watching. She held her breath and forced her muscles to relax, letting the undertow of the storm carry her out into the ocean. When she felt her lungs would burst, she straightened her body just as the current moved upward, buoying her up to the surface. She managed to bob up and down in the ocean far away from where the waves broke on to the huge rock boulders that jutted out at the ocean's edge. She couldn't see the pier.

Just when she thought she didn't have the strength to move, she saw trees and shrubs south of the larger rocks. With no sand in sight, she knew the landing would be rough. The force from the ocean alone might kill her. Without choice, she gave into the wave of water as it engulfed her, riding the current until her body fell with the spray of water on to the rock before rolling into shrubs, briars and dead wood. Blackness engulfed her as the water receded, drained into the rock, and made its way back into the ocean.

James and Fred rode to the hospital in different ambulances. The EMTs allowed Emmy to ride with James, who looked at his mother only one time and kept his eyes closed during the rest of the ambulance ride. The EMTs worked constantly to keep him from going into traumatic shock. Emmy held his hand and whispered comforting words.

The EMTs called ahead and asked that a pediatric doctor be ready to evaluate James. The doctor met them when they entered the hospital and helped move the stretcher to a large room divided into cubicles.

Agent Crandall drove the Raffertys' van to the hospital. Dee sat in the front passenger seat with Sara behind the driver's seat. The agent looked in the rear-view mirror and saw Sara chewing on her bottom lip.

"Sara," Agent Crandall got the little girl's attention. "Please don't worry about James. I saw him breathing. I really believe he'll be okay." Agent Crandall forced a smile.

She saw Sara smile back.

Agent Crandall parked the van and the three of them arrived in the crowded emergency room as Fred was being wheeled in. Dee asked Agent Crandall if she minded sitting with Sara. The agent agreed to wait with Sara in the family's waiting area and tried not to show how intimidated she felt around the little girl. As soon as she sat down, her cell phone rang.

"How are they?" TK asked.

"We don't know yet. Sara and I are waiting. They've just gone back."

"Call me when you know something. We finally got some local help here – Agent Brad Cook. His people ran a check on the car registration and it came up with Nannette Jones, along with her address. When we went to her house, a neighbor called her Nan. So far, she hasn't been found."

Before saying goodbye, Agent Crandall promised she would call when she knew something about James and his daddy. Through the entire conversation, Agent Crandall was well aware of Sara's presence and saw the little girl's head nod several times.

The agent asked, "When did you eat last?" She'd never seen a child go through such trauma without whining and complaining.

Sara shrugged her shoulders and said, "I don't remember."

"Want something to drink?" Agent Crandall asked, unsure of what to say or how to act around the gifted child. *Does she know what I'm thinking? She's just a child,* she told herself, *probably a hungry kid.*

The next time she saw Sara's head nodding, Agent Crandall went into a nearby hallway and pulled money from the small wallet she kept in a jacket pocket. She could see Sara's head resting on the arm of the chair as she fed money into the machine and bought two bottles of water and two packs of crackers. She didn't bother waking Sara when she returned. Instead, she sat beside the lanky thin girl and lifted her head just enough to let it rest on her shoulder. She knew Sara was exhausted. She watched her sleep and smoothed the red hair spilling over the arm of her short-sleeved jacket. Sara's complexion seemed fairer in the stark fluorescent lighting, making her freckles more obvious. She studied the features of the strange girl who saw beyond the norm. She knew Dee was right all along about her daughter's clairvoyance. She also knew she'd never again dismiss Sara Jackson's abilities as an artist or a psychic.

Not far away in a small emergency room cubicle, Emmy's fingers touched James' cheek. Unable to keep her hands off him, she smoothed his brown hair, as she watched a nurse check his pulse.

When James opened his eyes, Emmy smiled. He didn't reach out to her. But, she pulled him to her, hugged him, and kissed his forehead. He didn't hug her back. His limp body didn't respond at all.

She looked at the nurse and asked, "Is he okay? He doesn't seem to know me. I . . . I'm his mother." Tears filled her eyes. She hugged him to her chest and continued stroking his brown hair.

"The doctor will be here soon, Mrs. Rafferty. He's checking on some test results." The nurse said, then turned and walked out.

Emmy saw James pull away. She thought his green eyes looked empty of feeling. She sincerely hoped it was from exhaustion and would be temporary. She wondered again if he'd forgotten her and questioned if the awful woman had given him drugs. The relief she felt in finding him seeped away as panic took its place.

She turned toward the door when the pediatrician came in carrying James' chart. "Mrs. Rafferty, James' tests show a residual amount of sleeping medication. It was probably an over-the-counter drug. When the EMTs got there, they were told that he threw up the salt water he ingested before they arrived on the scene. I believe it might have saved his life. The drugs would have exited his stomach along with the salt water."

"Thanks. I wondered if she drugged him. He seems not to recognize me." Emmy looked back at James, hoping for a response.

"Your friend, Dee, told me about the kidnapping. It's been a while since he's seen you. It may take some time for him to understand he's safe. Physically, he's going to be fine. My advice is to get him help when you get him back home. Your family doctor can recommend a good therapist. There's no telling what this little fella's been through. Give him time."

Emmy watched as the doctor placed the clipboard on the tray table, turned to James and asked him to follow his finger. James' eyes looked from one side to the other as the doctor's fingers went right to left and back again.

"James, stick out your tongue," the doctor commanded. James responded. The doctor checked his tongue and throat, and asked, "Can you say 'aaahhh'?"

It made Emmy glad to see James following the doctor's directions, knowing he at least heard the doctor and responded to him. She lost that good feeling when he opened his mouth and no sound came out.

"He seems to be fine. Congratulations. It's good to see a family reunited. I'd like to keep him overnight to be sure everything's okay."

Emmy couldn't speak. She gave the doctor a hug, then kissed James' cheek, and watched his lips tightened into a frown.

Dee saw that look as she entered the small cubicle. She walked to the opposite side of the bed and told Emmy, "Let me stay with James. The doctor needs to talk with you about Fred."

Engrossed with James' condition, Emmy had forgotten about Fred, who lay motionless in a cubicle two doors down from their son. Full of guilt for not thinking of him, Emmy walked in expecting to apologize, but Fred's gray complexion and white bandages around his head made her wonder if he was dead. His still form under the white sheet frightened her until she saw his chest move.

She didn't notice the doctor until he stepped closer to the foot of the bed. He put his hand out and introduced himself before telling her that Fred's severe concussion could lead to lasting problems. The next few hours would be crucial in determining the damage. The doctor wanted to run another test. He left Emmy holding Fred's hand.

Without thinking, Emmy prayed out loud, "Thank you God for saving James. Please take care of Fred. He's my hero. I can't make it without him." Her tears fell on his forearm.

Emmy's cool hand touched his forehead. The nurse came in and told Emmy they were getting a room with two beds so Fred and James could stay together. Emmy thanked her for thinking of it.

The nurse said the doctor arranged it for Emmy's convenience. As the nurse walked out, Emmy looked back at Fred, whose eyes were barely open. His forehead wrinkled and his puzzled look scared her. It made her afraid that he, like their son, didn't recognize her.

"Em, did you say I'm . . . I'm your hero?"

She saw him making the effort to lift his head. "Yes, my love. You stay still and rest now. You gave me back my baby. James is going to be okay." She leaned over and kissed him on the lips.

She liked the smile Fred gave her before closing his eyes.

As soon as Fred was moved to a room, Emmy made her way to James' cubicle. Dee stood by his bed, holding his hand.

Emmy filled Dee in on the plans to spend the night in the hospital. Dee, worried about Emmy being pulled between her husband and her son, was relieved to learn they would share a room.

Within twenty minutes, James was moved to the room where he would spend the night with his parents for the first time in months.

Dee found Sara munching on the crackers Agent Crandall bought.

"Thanks, Lois, for sitting with Sara. Fred and James are in a room. Emmy will stay with them tonight. I know we're all exhausted, but I think we need to get something to eat, then find a place to stay tonight." Dee didn't even realize she called Special Agent Crandall by her first name. The exhaustion showed in Dee's voice.

"I'll drive us back to the island," Agent Crandall offered. "TK reserved a room for me at The Inn before he knew you all were with me. I'm pretty sure he said their only available room has two beds. Some of the tourists didn't leave in time to get off the island before the storm hit. You and Sara are welcome to stay with me. We can order room service."

"Thanks. I'm glad you're here. I'm so tired I don't think I could make one more decision." She smiled at Lois, took Sara's hand, and led her out of the hospital.

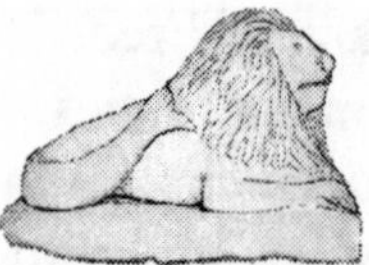

Chapter Twenty-Five – The Girl of My Dreams

The storm had roared its way up the coast, leaving the island drenched in morning sunlight. Dee could see the ocean from their room. *A new day. A new start*, she thought. She and Sara left the room while Lois finished getting dressed. TK arrived in the lobby at the same time Dee and Sara stepped off the elevator. He lifted Sara up and swung her around until she laughed.

"Sara, my favorite artist. You're the girl of my dreams." He sat her down and ruffled her red hair.

"Then, you'll have to meet Mollie. She's in my dreams, so she'll be in yours, too." Sara laughed as she smoothed her hair down in an effort to undo the damage he caused.

TK frowned, "Who's this Mollie?"

"Mollie's a different story for a different time. I'll tell you about her someday," Dee answered, noticing the huge smile Sara flashed at TK. She knew her daughter was trying to keep his attention.

The elevator opened. Lois stepped out and walked toward the group with a bright smile.

Dee spoke first. "Thanks, Agent Crandall, for taking care of us last night. We would've been stranded without you. I talked with Emmy. The doctors are releasing Fred and James. I'll drive us all home. Emmy will have her hands full. I hope she'll be able to take a nap on the way home. Want to ride to the hospital with us, or should we come back for you later?"

"Thanks. It's okay to call me Lois. I think we've all been through enough to be on a first-name basis. I'll stick with my partner. Please be careful. We've all been stressed to the breaking point. TK and I hope to tie up some loose ends before we head North. It might be late tomorrow before we get away from here." Lois looked at TK for affirmation.

"Right on target, Lois. Agent Cook is meeting us after breakfast to go ta Nan Jones' house. So, ready ta roll? I want to introduce you ta someone before we meet up with Agent Cook."

TK took Lois by his sister's house where she saw the clown picture on the mantel and remembered Sara's drawing of the clown on the unicycle. *Hell, I've been wrong before, but this is a big wrong*, she thought and reached for the picture.

Lois knew that Robert, his mother, and TK watched as she took the picture from the mantel.

"You know I hate to admit it, but you were right to give credence to Sara's drawings. I'm so sorry I couldn't see how they could have helped us. James almost died because of my doubt." She knew she'd beat herself up over this mistake for a long, long time.

"It's okay, boss. We all do the mistake thing." TK gave her a smile.

On the way to North Georgia, Dee sat in the driver's seat with Fred in the front passenger seat, fully reclined and covered by a blanket with pillows under his feet and head. Emmy sat behind Dee with James across from her. She touched him often without any response.

Sara sat on the bench seat in the back playing the knock-knock game, but answering for James and herself. "Knock. Knock. Who's there? James. James who? James Rafferty. That's you, James. That's you. I'm so glad you're you." She reached over and patted his arm.

They stopped at McDonald's in Metter for a restroom break. Fred didn't wake up until Dee shook him. She helped him out of the van and to the door of the men's restroom.

Emmy held James' hand and insisted he go with her to the women's restroom. She couldn't bear to let him out of her sight. Sara finished first and traded places with her mother at the entrance to the men's restroom. When Fred came out of the restroom, she held his hand until Dee returned. They helped Fred as he made his way across the parking lot. When they all were back in the van, James climbed in beside Sara on the bench seat. Sara buckled his seatbelt. Emmy passed out drinks and tried hard not to be hurt by James moving away from her. She decided to drive for a while and be near her husband.

Fred woke up when he needed medicine for a headache. While Emmy drove, Dee handed him his pills and a bottle of water. Even though Fred was mostly sleeping, Emmy held his hand as she drove west on I-16. She took Highway 15, the Adrian exit, heading north.

They stopped for a late lunch at Zaxby's in Sandersville. Except for the restroom stop in Metter and lunch at Zaxby's, Fred slept the entire trip.

They finished the trip home with Dee driving, Fred in the passenger seat sleeping, Sara and James in the middle seats, and Emmy stretched out napping on the bench seat in the back. Emmy fought the constant need to touch James and tempt him to talk. Knowing the fine line between mothering and smothering, she knew she'd have to control her impulses. *Mothering. Smothering.* She thought, *I'll have to watch that little s.*

Back on the island, Lois and TK accompanied Agent Brad Cook to Nan Jones' small house. The three agents put on plastic gloves and stuffed evidence bags in their pockets before entering the house. Standing near the coffee table in front of the sofa, Agent Cook motioned for them to join him. Lois walked behind the table and sat on the sofa. Agent Cook held a picture of a child with the face missing. The scissors, placed nearby, left no doubt in their minds that the face had been removed recently.

Lois stated, "I'm quite sure it's a picture of James. If y'all want to take a room each, I'll finish the living room. Maybe she put the cutout of the face in a trashcan." Lois shook her head, wondering just how sick Nan Jones had been.

TK offered, "I'll take the front bedroom." He stepped into the short hallway.

"Okay. I'll start with the back bedroom," Agent Cook said and headed in the opposite direction.

Lois couldn't find the face cutout from the photo in the living room's small narrow trashcan. Before checking the entire living room, she chose to look into the kitchen trash container and found it almost empty. Looking around the room, she realized that Nan Jones more than likely suffered from an obsessive-compulsive disorder. She walked into the laundry room and checked out the dirty clothesbasket. She pulled out underwear, blouses and slacks. The underwear on top was slightly rumpled, but further down, the clothes were folded and neatly stacked. She pushed the basket against the wall.

After checking the pantry, Lois knew Nan Jones suffered from OCD. All the grocery items, stacked neatly in rows with half an inch of space between each row, showed the labels facing forward. It looked as though Nan Jones used a ruler. Lois looked through each shelf, opened and closed the electrical box on the back wall, used a small stepladder to look through the items on the top shelf, and left the room amazed at how well the house was organized, especially with a child living in it. She walked back into the living room and heard TK say, "Hey guys, you might want ta see this."

When Lois walked in, she found TK sitting on the edge of a queen-sized bed holding a paisley patterned fabric covered box, about the size of a shoebox. The matching top lay nearby on the bed. He held a picture of a woman, with the face missing. "I found this box under the bed. What do you think? Her mother? See the hands." He pointed to the wrinkled, veined hands, one crossed over the other and resting in her lap.

Lois pulled a smaller picture from the box. Like the others in the living room, the face was missing, leaving a picture of the torso of a small boy. Lois opined, "It looks exactly like the same round cutout. She suffered a bad case of OCD. He looks too young to be James."

"What makes you suspect OCD?" Agent Cook asked.

Lois laid one picture on top of the other to show how the circles were the same. "Obsessive Compulsive Disorder. Just the way the kitchen is arranged. These pictures. Notice they're not cut out in the shape of the head, but perfectly round circles. It's almost like she used something to make sure she cut them the same."

She added, as she picked up the picture of the small boy, "The old woman's picture is larger. Look at this. The circle is the same size as the circle in the picture of the old woman as well as this boy's."

She looked at the back of the boy's photo. "It's dated. This one isn't a picture of James." She sat on the bed across from TK. She placed James' picture beside the small boy's and pointed out, "Taken several years ago. James wasn't kidnapped until a few months ago."

TK's silence puzzled Lois. She looked directly at him, "The old woman's picture doesn't have a date. A photographer probably took hers. What do you think?"

"Damn, Lois. I think we've got ourselves a serial killer here."

Lois handed Agent Cook the pictures. He turned them over and looked at each one. "I think you're right. The boy in this picture has a brown mole on his left hand. See how small the wrists are? He's a lot younger than James, and James' left hand doesn't have a mole. This can't be James." He handed the picture back to Lois and said, "I'll have the office start checking on missing boys around the date stamped on the picture. We need to find out where she lived the last ten or fifteen years, then, maybe we can find evidence to validate our theory of a serial killer."

Lois looked toward TK when he turned the box upside down and picture fell out. He held it up. "Here's another reason I think she's a serial killer. This wedding picture. This is a much thinner woman, but it's her and the poor schmuck who had the misfortune to marry her." He held the picture up, showing the man's missing face. "Same size hole. I've not seen anything that makes me believe a man lives here."

"Maybe he was the first one she killed. Maybe she didn't kill him. We need to find her Social Security number. Surely she worked somewhere." Lois added, "Her OCD is a small problem considering what she's done. But, it may help us here. When we find her pattern, we'll find out a lot more. She obviously took what she wanted and justified the means of getting it. Any other pictures in that box?"

"No. That's it. Maybe Sara Jackson can help us," TK offered.

Lois didn't argue with him. She asked them to think back and reconstruct the order of the pictures. "I believe she stacked the pictures in a particular order. For instance, her mother's picture was on the bottom, wasn't it?"

TK took the pictures. "I thumbed through these as I called you guys. The wedding picture was on the bottom; then the small boy's; then the mother's. I expect she planned to add James' picture after she killed him. I'm certain of it."

"That's it," Lois said. "It makes sense. She killed the husband first; then kidnapped the little boy that looks like he's about 4 years old. I wonder what went wrong that made her kill him? … Assuming she killed him. Why did she kill her husband? … Maybe she wanted her mother's house." She thought a second and continued, "Why did she marry the man and then kill him? She obviously became disenchanted with the little boy, just like she probably did with James."

"She needed something from the husband," TK offered. "I agree that she needed her mother's house."

Agent Cook picked up the wedding picture. "I'll bet she took out an insurance policy on the old man. He doesn't have the look of money. He looks like a cleaned up druggie. His clothes don't fit well and his fingernails are dirty."

Lois spoke up, "Hey, guys, I'm thinking we may not have the full picture here. Has she always been a killer and just never got caught? And, are these all of her victims. She's methodical." She thought, *Is this the tip of the iceberg?*

A few yards away, in the overgrown trees and shrubs, Nan watched with tired eyes and waited in wrinkled and torn clothes. Her stringy hair clung to her head. Turmoil raged inside her bruised and bloodied body. Anger grew as she envisioned strangers going through her personal belongings. The coldness of her eyes had nothing to do with the weather. Exhausted and determined she watched her house.

As soon as the intruders left, she entered through the back door, made her way through the kitchen to the pantry, and opened the electrical box. She pulled a wire handle at the top and lifted the entire metal box with its fake switches from the wall. As the panel came from the wall, she smiled. Her stash of money stacked neatly between the studs and resting on a two by four, survived the police search. She double bagged two grocery store plastic bags and filled them with the money. She removed an envelope and took out a driver's license with the name Mary Brown. She smiled and moved from the pantry to the laundry room, where she pulled clothes from the bottom of the dirty clothes hamper before taking off the wet and ragged clothes she was wearing when she fell from the pier. After dressing in clean beige pants and a long sleeved shirt, she moved the hamper six inches from the wall.

Nan believed in backup plans. She knew they looked through the hamper by the way the clothes on the bottom were disturbed. She left some cleaned and folded in case she needed a change later. Dressed in the clean clothes, she pulled a thread at the top of a denim jacket pocket. Her blind stitching worked perfectly. She pulled out a card with a different identity from Mary Brown. Like the first card, the picture was missing. The game of deciding her new look was her favorite part of deceit. She placed the dirty damp clothes into a plastic bag and left with more clean clothes, the money, and her new identity cards.

Via cell phones, Mom and Pop Jax and Hank kept up with the crew making their way back to Elberton. Emmy waited for James to fall asleep to call her mother again and tell her about James' dyed hair. The brown hair had shocked them all. They weren't prepared for all the changes in James – the hair color was minor compared to his silence, and the new habit of pinching his chin. Dee could see Emmy's heart break each time James narrowed his eyes at his mother.

A large homemade sign hung above the garage welcoming them

home. As soon as Sara saw the sign she touched James' arm and said, "We're here. We're here. Look, James. A sign – just for you. It says 'Welcome Home James!'"

The Rafferty van pulled into the garage. Tired and exhausted, the passengers got out slowly. Pop Jax opened the front passenger door and helped Fred out. He placed Fred's arm around his shoulder. He used one arm around Fred's waist and used his other arm to steady him. Pop Jax managed to get him inside and seated in a recliner in the den.

Everyone else's attention was centered on James. Mom Jax ran to James' side of the van and slid the side door open. She hugged him so hard, he grunted. She swooped him up and carried him inside.

Reluctant to let everyone know he was on the brink of tears, Hank stood in the background, waiting as everyone circled James. When Sara saw Hank leaning against the kitchen door jam, she walked over, took him by the hand, and led him to James. To everyone's surprise, James wrapped both arms around his brother. They held each other tight.

Finally, Hank said, "James, we've got cake and ice cream." He led his little brother to the kitchen table.

Emmy left the room while her mother cut the cake. When she returned, she carried a squirming baby girl. The family members took a few steps back, making room for Emmy to reach James in his chair at the end of the table. The large bright-colored helium balloon attached to his chair swayed above his head as his mother and baby sister came closer.

"James, remember Marcie? You're Hank's little brother and Marcie is your little sister." She held Marcie close to James.

James scooted himself backwards in his chair. He pulled his shoulders in, making himself as small as possible. He pinched his chin and pursed his lips together. Emmy watched as his eyes narrowed before he looked down at his lap.

Dee saw the look and managed to get around the table quickly. She took Marcie from Emmy's arms.

"James, here's your ice cream, darling," Mom Jax handed Emmy a bowl of ice cream. Emmy took it and placed it on the table in front of James before sitting down beside him. Sara sat on the other side.

That night Emmy tried to get James to cuddle with her. She hoped he could go to sleep easier if she slept with him his first night home. Stiff as a board he lay in his bed not making a sound. She finally gave up and slipped out of bed, hoping he could relax and go to sleep. An hour later, she went into the boys' room and found them sleeping in the same bed with Hank's arm draped across James' sleeping form. Wascal slept on the floor on James' side of the bed. She watched James breathe. She couldn't get used to his brown hair and distant personality. She wondered if James would ever trust her again. She checked on Marcie, even though she'd been asleep for hours. When she walked into the kitchen, her eyes went to the crinkled helium balloon. It almost touched the floor, its limp string still attached to the back slat of the kitchen chair. Emmy lifted the half-filled balloon, held it to her chest and cried.

After finishing the search of Nan Jones' house, Agent Cook asked Lois and TK if they wanted to join him in checking out the old Honda that had been locked in the police impound yard to ensure Nan or anyone else couldn't have access.

He handed out plastic gloves and evidence bags. He assigned Lois to the driver's area, TK to the passenger area, while he started a search of the back seat.

"My forensic crew has already dusted for fingerprints and DNA samples. I don't know if we need to have them take the seats out or go beyond the testing they did earlier today. You guys got any ideas on that?" Agent Cook asked as his fingers probed the areas around the cushions of the back seat. Before the others could answer he said, "Bingo. Found something." He pulled a small folded and wrinkled piece of paper from under the cushion behind the car seat.

Lois and TK watched as Agent Cook slowly unfolded the sheet of paper. A drawing of a statue with the head of a lion and the tail of a fish appeared. It also had a tree in it with a face carving. He handed it to TK.

"That's a Sara Jackson drawing. I could tell before I saw her name in the bottom right corner." TK pointed to the name in the corner and continued, "See how she has his full name in larger letters here?" He handed it to Lois and pointed to the left top corner. "I think she deliberately made his name large."

"You're probably right. It was well hidden from Nan Jones," Lois said and handed the drawing to Agent Cook.

"He must have used the drawing to help him remember who he really was. Poor little fella," TK surmised.

Agent Cook placed the drawing in a plastic bag, said his goodbyes to the Athens agents, and drove to the Brunswick FBI office to file the evidence from the car.

TK drove Lois to the Island Inn. On the way, he told her he would be treating his sister and her family to dinner at the Crab Trap and asked Lois to join them, telling her a little about the menu.

Lois wasn't sorry she agreed to go to dinner with TK's family. His sister was a shorter, female version of TK and her stories about the island fascinated her, making her want to spend her next vacation there. Her choice of local seafood and a salad gave her back the energy she lost the last couple of days.

On the way back to The Inn, she asked TK if Robert was adopted.

"No. Why?" he responded with a frown.

"You and your sister can't deny your Italian background. Robert's red hair and freckles made me think he might have been adopted."

"Nay. Robert took after Dad's side." He told how his father wore the clown suit, rode the unicycle, and ran into his mother, knocking her on the floor. TK finished the story. "She fell in love with him right then and there. Her family didn't approve for more than a decade – but they finally came around."

Certain TK would want to spend the night with her at the Inn, she hid her disappointment when he walked her to the door of the lobby and asked her where she would like to have breakfast the next morning. They agreed to eat at the restaurant on the corner of Mallery and Kings Way. He kissed her cheek and left.

She went to sleep thinking of him. She woke up in the night thinking about Nan Jones. Her thoughts kept going back to Nan Jones' house, teasing her with snippets of yesterday's visit – the pictures with holes, the laundry room, the pantry. *Something didn't make sense. What was it?*

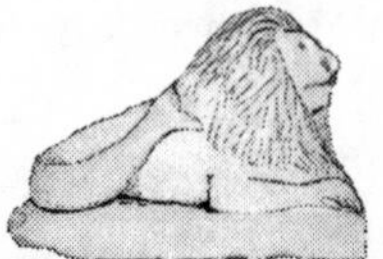

Chapter Twenty-Six – Nan Jones' House

The following day, TK drove into The Inn's almost empty parking lot, located under the building, just as Lois walked out of the lobby. He parked the car and suggested they walk to the Village for breakfast. Lois' navy blue blazer and matching dress pants – her work outfit – soaked up the heat like a sponge. Humidity caused her normally straight hair to curl a little. Within a couple of blocks she took the blazer off, exposing a white blouse with narrow straps. She pulled a hair clip from the purse hanging over her shoulder and with a quick twist, swept her long hair off her neck and clipped it in place. If she'd worn shorts instead of long pants, she'd have looked like the summer tourists filling the streets and shops. TK looked cool and comfortable in jeans and a red cotton shirt with a UGA logo on the pocket. As they walked, Lois adjusted the slightly raised collar at the nape of his neck. She resisted the temptation to smooth his unruly black hair.

"Thanks," he said.

She saw his mischievous smile and how he used the opportunity to give her a slight hug without missing a step.

When they arrived at the Fourth of May restaurant, TK held the door open for her. The bright sun outside made the inside of the restaurant seem dark until their eyes adjusted. Lois pretended not to notice how he used it as an excuse to place his hand at the small of her back and guide her to a table near a window.

She watched the waiter pour her second cup of coffee, her mind puzzling over the findings at Nan Jones' house. Something about the clothes basket in the laundry room kept creeping into her thoughts. She wondered why the clothes on the bottom were folded and clean, while the other clothes were worn and wrinkled. She wondered if Nan Jones had a backup plan. What if she survived the churning waters?

She looked at TK, pulled her cell phone from her purse and said, "I want to go back to Nan Jones' house before we leave."

"Okay," TK agreed. "We have all day to get back to Athens." He watched as she pressed the numbers on her phone.

"Agent Cook. This is Agent Lois Crandall." She waited for his response. "Yeah. I know. We're not leaving yet. I want to go to Nan Jones' house again before we leave." Again, she waited. "We'll meet you there in about 20 minutes. We're finishing breakfast in the village. See you there." She pressed the off button and placed the phone in her purse.

When they arrived at the house, Agent Cook's empty car sat in the driveway. The front door of the house stood open. TK knocked on the door casing and called out to the FBI agent, who came into the living room just as they entered. After they exchanged greetings, Lois headed to the laundry room. The dirty clothesbasket sat six inches from the wall in the same place she found it the first time – not where she left it – against the wall. Nan Jones' OCD would not have allowed her to leave it in what she considered the wrong place. Lois moved the basket to the right, exposing several pieces of dead skin inside the circle where the basket had rested.

"Hey, you guys. Look at this." They came in from the kitchen and she continued, "When we were here yesterday, I left this basket against the wall. It's been moved. The clean clothes in the bottom underneath these wrinkled clothes? They're gone."

"Are you sure?" Agent Cook asked. "Are you sure the clothes were clean?"

"One hundred percent certain. Her OCD would have kicked in, making her have several backup plans. I'm also certain that Nan Jones didn't die in the ocean."

"I don't know how she could have survived. Look at Fred Rafferty. He almost died trying to get out of the water." Agent Cook raised his eyebrows in disbelief.

"See the dead skin here?" Lois pointed to the scaly pieces of crust on the floor. "These fell off her arms after she moved the basket away from the wall. She changed clothes; causing her psoriasis to flake off more than if she just walked by. Look closely. There's also some debris here that wasn't here before." She gathered particles of dirt and leaves and placed them in an evidence bag. She followed the same procedure with the skin flakes.

"Let's check the area outside before we leave. If this matches anything between the house and the beach, it will help confirm that she survived," Agent Cook said.

"Yesterday, we each took rooms to search. Let's walk through the house, all of us together, and see if there's anything out of place. If she came back, she surely took more clothes or something from the other rooms," TK suggested.

They looked through everything in the kitchen and the laundry room. The pantry, too small for all three of them, required each of them to go in separately.

Lois went in first. "Shit," she said. "Wasn't there an electrical box in the laundry room? You know, on the wall away from the washer and dryer. Because it's beige, like the walls, it doesn't show up much." She left the pantry to check out the laundry room only to find that TK beat her to it. He opened the painted electrical box, turned to Lois and said. "Yep. It's here. Why?" He flipped several switches, cutting electricity off and on in different parts of the house.

"Why would a house have two electrical boxes?" she asked and motioned for them to follow her.

They all headed back to the pantry. Lois backed up and let Agent Cook through. He opened the metal door of the electrical box. He flipped a switch and nothing happened. When he pulled on the heavy wire handle at the top inside panel the entire box moved. It almost fell into his hands. "This one is fake." He passed the box to Lois and TK. They each took turns looking into the space behind the box.

"The perfect hiding place. What would you hide if you wanted to start a new life?" Lois asked TK and Agent Cook.

"Money," they replied in unison.

"Important papers. Maybe new identification," TK added, stepping backwards, forcing the other two to leave the pantry.

They walked from room to room and found nothing else to make them believe she returned. Agent Cook locked the house.

"Let's check around out here," Lois suggested, heading away from the cars, and making her way to the back of the house.

They found fresh tire tracks on the vacant lot next door, just yards away from Nan's backdoor. Agent Cook called his office to get a forensic team to take tire-track samples as well as anything else they might find to back up their assertion that Nan Jones survived.

A pathway from the house to the beach led the agents to a spot where weeds and leaves were pressed into the ground as if some person or animal had slept there. Skin flakes showed up on a magnolia leaf, which were bagged along with hair samples. Lois noticed several spots of blood near the hair samples.

"She survived, but she was banged up. Look at the blood here and there." Lois pointed to a mound of brown leaves and pine straw.

Agent Cook talked with his forensic team before joining Lois and TK at TK's car. "This case is not closed. Y'all want to stay another day or two?"

"Thanks, but no thanks," Lois replied. "We'll be checking with you. She's smart enough not to hang around here. She's gone. We just need to find her before she finds another victim."

TK and Lois followed Agent Cook to the Brunswick office, and signed off on the paperwork that would forward information about Nan to all 13 Georgia FBI resident offices as well as the national network. Lois was disappointed they couldn't give anyone a recent photo of Nan. It was difficult to describe her since she often changed her appearance. They left several pictures with a sketch artist with the hope of having a good likeness of her soon. After having coffee with Agent Cook, they headed back to Athens. Both were quiet as TK's SUV headed north on I-95. TK pressed the button to make the CD player start. He watched Lois' look of surprise when she recognized the soundtrack to the Jersey Boys' Broadway play. Her look puzzled him.

"Hope that look means what I think it means." He raised an eyebrow.

"I'm surprised. That's all," she responded. She was impressed he remembered how much she loved that particular soundtrack. She added, "Surprised, about the CD."

"You sure? I hoped it meant you'd hauled off and buried the garbage from your divorce." His hand found hers. He pulled her hand to his lips and kissed the inside of her palm. He lowered both their hands and rested them on the console, waiting for her reaction.

She spoke quietly, "Ummm. I think I have gotten rid of that garbage. I certainly held on to it long enough."

"By the way, how is it you know so much about this OCD stuff? You seemed ta know an awful lot about it back there at the house."

Lois hesitated before she answered. "My sister has it. We've dealt with it for years. It showed up in kindergarten. The symptoms changed daily at first. Saying it was difficult would be an understatement. Her life was … is … hard."

TK took her hand, pulled it to his lips and kissed her palm again. The sweet gesture was not wasted on Lois. Her chin trembled. She looked away when her eyes moistened. They traveled in comfortable silence for several miles. By mid-afternoon, TK's stomach was growling. Without asking Lois' opinion, he took the Metter exit.

"Now that's a place for a good triple bypass," TK said as he moved his head and looked toward the right side of the road.

Lois followed his gaze to a Burger Bar. "You mean a hamburger?"

"Well, not just any burger. I like it with everything, extra pickles, extra onion, and extra cheese. Takes all that to make a gut bomb."

"Uuuugh." Lois' mouth turned down. "Any appetite I had just disappeared."

"Awww. Come on. Don't be such a sissy. You could never make a Jersey girl. They know us guys have to have a cholesterol fix occasionally. You gotta be zinc, kiddo."

"You sound like you're speaking a foreign language." She frowned.

"Jersey talk. Sorry, babe. You talk so tough. Can't believe you let a little Jersey get to ya." He looked disappointed.

"Turn here," she said with authority.

He did as she ordered and pulled into the parking lot with a big barbecue sign.

"This'll do. It's a Southern-style cholesterol fix," he said with satisfaction.

"What's zinc?" She asked as they sat in a booth waiting to order barbecue sandwiches and Brunswick stew.

"Means cool."

"Cool?" She laughed. "I had no idea."

"You probably won't find it in Webster's dictionary," he said. "It's like your Southern words – "over yonder." Not all Southerners use it, but you all know it means over there. Ma hated it when we made up words. She thought we were trying ta hide something from her."

Brownsville, Texas seemed like a haven for getting away from Elberton and the responsibility of catering to his family. Dan couldn't remember how infatuated he'd been with Dee. He wasn't sure when his love for her dwindled; but he knew it had, until there was nothing left.

Char's beautiful Asian features captured his fancy soon after he started traveling to Brownsville. The thought of running his fingers through her short black hair, feeling his way down her naked body, and caressing her tight small ass, created more than one hard-on even though he resisted her flirting for years. He gave in to temptation three years ago. She possessed no sexual hang-ups. He told a friend and colleague that Char was a *tiger* in the sack. Until recently, the ride the tiger gave him had been exciting and worth forfeiting his family in Elberton.

He was entertaining second thoughts as he walked out of his apartment and saw a large red tow truck parked behind his pickup truck. A burly muscular man with thick brown hair walked around Dan's truck checking cable hookups.

"You the owner?" the man asked without looking at Dan. He turned and walked to the front of his truck.

"By God I am," Dan screamed at the man and pulled his cell phone from his pocket.

He watched the man drop a cable he'd pulled from his rig, reach in his shirt pocket, pull out a sheet of paper, and calmly hand it to Dan.

"No use gittin' mad. Yore sorry ass wouldn't be in this fix if you kept up the payments, buddy."

Dan couldn't argue with him. He didn't know how many payments he missed. He left the package from Dee's attorney on the kitchen table without bothering to open it. He figured it contained legal documents trying to get money for child support. He decided to pretend he didn't receive the package and had no idea that Char signed a receipt. He chose to ignore the envelope.

Finding a way to and from work without his truck wouldn't be easy. He hit the wooden railing with his fist as he walked on to the porch outside the apartment. The sound of the tow truck's gears shifting and the groaning – metal against metal – followed him into the apartment.

The first thing he saw when he walked into the kitchen was the manila envelope. He picked it up, turned it over and looked at the recipient's portion of a receipt. He opened the envelope and shook out the contents. His truck payment coupon book lay on top of the stack.

The tone of his voice as he walked into the bedroom, made Char cringe. When he questioned whether she had accepted the envelope, she admitted she signed the receipt.

Char's carefree personality wasn't so great when he needed her to take some of the responsibility. Her recent actions confirmed that Char cared only about Char. His needs were insignificant.

The first week after James' rescue, Mom Jax met Dee at the car when

Dee stopped to pick up Sara. She told her that Sara was on the phone with Dan. Dee told her mother-in-law she wanted to wait outside, so they sat at the glass picnic table – waiting.

"I'm so sorry, Dee. I know Dan has a lot of problems. You were the best thing that happened to him. For the first time in his adult life, I felt he made a good decision when he married you. He was more stable than any other time." Mom Jax leaned over and patted Dee's hand.

"It's not your fault. I'm sorry you and Pop Jax have to go through this too. He's not good at communicating. Something must be wrong." Dee said.

"You're right. He's broke. Evidently, What's-Her-Name is less responsible than Dan. They're having to move in with her parents in a small town near Brownsville." Mom Jax pushed her bangs away from her forehead. Her look of defeat bothered Dee.

Dee knew the family was hurting and remembered the advice she was given: *The best revenge you can get on Dan is to live well and be happy.* More than ever, she was determined to move on and make a new life for herself and Sara. She really felt sorry for Dan's family. They didn't deserve this kind of hurt.

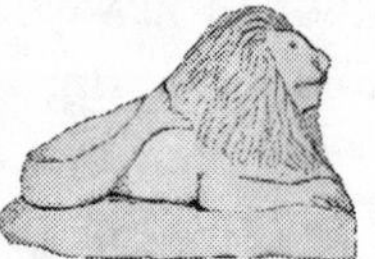

Chapter Twenty-Seven – People Watching

James sat in the barber's chair watching his brown hair fall to the floor. Emmy watched James. He hadn't spoken at all. He waited. He observed. His lack of emotion bothered Emmy. His toys didn't interest him. He never had a huge appetite, and now, food seemed even less important. She knew the boy sitting in the barber's chair wasn't the same little boy kidnapped in June.

The night before, she found him in Marcie's room staring into the crib at the pink bundle propped on her side with a wedge pillow. His hands, hanging by his sides, made tight fists, then the rest of his body tensed. His fists relaxed. He repeated the process until Emmy got on her knees beside him and hugged his entire body.

"James, I love you as much … I love you so much." She almost said, "as much as I love Marcie." She stopped herself just in time. She pulled back to look into his face. She saw no malice. In fact, she saw no emotion. She picked him up and carried him into the den. She sat in her recliner rocking him and felt his body relaxing against her as she told him how she felt. "Sweet little boy of mine. I love you all the time. I love you when you're awake. I love you for love's sake. I love you when you sleep so sound. I love having you around. Sweet little boy of mine, I love you all the time*."* She repeated it until he fell asleep in her arms.

Emmy wished James' memories of the bad experience could go away as easy as the brown hair piling up on the floor. Soon, the hair would be swept into a dustpan and thrown into the trash where it belonged.

She wanted desperately to sweep all the hurt into a pile, and throw it away. She knew there would be times ahead when she would have to hold him as she held him the night before. She couldn't bear to think about what the kidnapper had said and done to her little boy. She knew that kidnappers often told their victims how their families didn't care about them. She also knew she would do whatever it took to let James know she still loved him.

When she told Fred how tense James seemed while he was watching Marcie, Fred put into words what she had been unable to say. "We can't leave him alone with her. He might hurt her if he believes that Marcie took his place. That bitch may have told him that Marcie took his place."

The thin sophisticated woman traveled with the laptop in the computer bag at all times. It was much better than the old computer left in the house on the island. The old one had served its purpose. She used it to pull up a list of the most common surnames. That's how she chose her current name of Brown. It was listed as the fifth most common name with Mary being ranked number one for girls' names. Except for the white van, the laptop represented the most expensive purchase Nan had made with the money she retrieved from behind the electrical box in the house on St. Simons Island – *her seed money.*

The old pickup truck she had hidden on a vacant lot not far from her house helped her get to Brunswick where she sold it, using her new identification, and replaced it with a white service van that held everything she owned. The double rear doors opened from the middle. She chose to keep the identification numbers, zero, one and five, left by the previous owner on the bottom corner of the right door panel. She stenciled ATL above the numbers to make the vehicle look more official, giving validity to the van's presence at Atlanta malls and in neighborhoods.

When she needed to connect to the Internet, she parked near stores offering a free connection, sat in cafes with wi-fi service, or roamed around town with her laptop open as she searched for an unprotected account. The van served her well.

She had no trouble finding a store with copying services, making it possible to create and print any paperwork she needed to help with identification papers. Different cafés provided her access to electrical outlets to charge phone and laptop batteries. Updated reports from newspapers in Northeast Georgia confirmed the imposter had survived. No one saw the temper tantrum she threw when she saw that the boy had been rescued. She pulled her hair, screamed, and tossed a bottle of water against the dashboard of the van.

The woman with red hair, long enough to stuff behind her ears, and the dangling pearl earrings, didn't resemble Nan Jones from St. Simons Island. Dressed in a slimming black pantsuit, she fit in with the shoppers at the Mall of Georgia without standing out in any way. Mary Brown sat on a bench participating in her favorite activity – people-watching. Many of her mannerisms, hair styles, and clothes choices came from ideas she got while observing women in malls and restaurants.

Her obsession with motherhood had not diminished. Finding her real Timmy ranked high on her list of things to do. The only obstacle in the way lived not too far away in Elberton. That boy, James, could identify her. She'd tied up all the loose ends of the past motherhood failures, except for the ungrateful little boy who never appreciated the life she had given him. His existence meant she failed in her well-laid plans. She couldn't abide failure, especially her own. Her OCD wouldn't allow her to leave even one loose end. Contemplating how to remove the horrible boy who pretended to be Timmy drove most of her thoughts and actions. Only when he was out of the picture, could she pursue her dream. She was confident her new look could fool anyone.

A plethora of consignment shops and thrift stores in and around Atlanta gave her access to inexpensive outfits. Her right hand smoothed the silky black pants that had hung on the clothes rod behind the front seats of the van. The clothes gave her privacy at night as she snuggled into her sleeping bag in the back of the van. The work van had no back seats, leaving her able to create a small mobile bedroom. New carpet covered the entire back area of the van. At least once a week, she checked into a motel room in order to shower, color her hair if needed and prepare for the coming week. She always paid cash and used a different name each time. Mall and restaurant bathrooms made daily hygiene possible. She often took her makeup bag with her and experimented with different looks.

She had a real fright two nights before when she chose to park the van behind a small strip mall in Buckhead. After checking behind several stores, she thought she found the perfect place to hide. A number of white service vans filled the spaces near a ramp to a plumbing company's back door. She pulled in between two of them.

The evening had been uneventful. Her right hand brushed against several pieces of clothing hanging on the rod above, as she lifted the top of the ice chest she kept behind the front passenger seat. She took a cup of yogurt from the chest with her left hand. The confined space challenged her OCD, making her determined to have all the comforts she wanted in an organized small area. She sat cross-legged on her sleeping bag thinking and planning the next step toward her goal. She looked at the empty space in front of the ice chest, opposite her sleeping bag. Soon, a second sleeping bag would fill up the empty space. The little boy who would sleep in it would fill up the empty space in her heart. She felt certain her Revised Plan would succeed this time. Before the weather turned cold in Northeast Georgia, she and Timmy would be living in a small bungalow by the ocean. She felt certain Timmy would love Florida.

She unzipped her sleeping bag and pushed the top layer aside. The warmth of the night made any cover uncomfortable. Her body relaxed and sleep came quickly.

A noise woke her around three o'clock in the morning. The door handle on the driver's side of the van squeaked. She heard footsteps as someone made their way around the van, checking the back doors and the door on the passenger side. Whoever was out there checked the other vans. She lay still for the longest time and finally dozed off after an hour of quietness. The next morning she purchased a gun from a pawnshop a block away from the Buford Highway. As always, she provided fake identification. The storeowner never questioned the middle-aged woman's credentials.

She didn't consider herself homeless even though she created a sad story to use, if questioned by mall security personnel. She planned to shed a few tears to go with the sad story, if necessary.

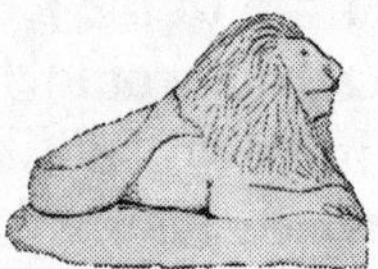

Chapter Twenty-Eight – It's Okay

With the exception of Granny Nida, who didn't like going out at night, and Dan, the entire Jackson family attended the first production of *Our Rocky* at the old Elbert Theatre. As a history buff, Dee never tired of telling the theater's story. Built in 1940, before air conditioning was common in homes or businesses, the theater enticed moviegoers to leave the summer heat behind and cool off in the large comfortable chairs while enjoying cartoons and a movie. The magic eye water cooler provided its own novelty. Repairs made after a 1950 fire ensured the theater's operation for several decades. It became a teen center in the late 1960s. It sat vacant for several years before the city and community supporters raised the money in the 1990s to restore it to its original art deco style. It reopened about the same time Dee moved to Elberton.

Fred took Hank to the theater an hour before the play started. On the way back home, he stopped at a neighbor's house to give Marcie's babysitter a ride. When he pulled into his drive, Dee's car was parked to the side of the driveway. He parked Emmy's van, went inside and told Emmy and Dee how Hank talked or sang non-stop and couldn't sit still all the way to the theater. Fred said Hank sang "Ma, I Wanna Be a Man" so many times they both knew every word. Fred's mother and stepfather arrived just in time to follow them into town.

Fred and Emmy sat in Long John Silver's front seats with Dee in a middle seat behind them. Fred's right hand lay on the console while his left hand guided the steering wheel. James and Sara sat together on the bench seat in the back. Dee smiled each time Emmy reached for Fred's free hand. Mom and Pop Jax walked to the theater since they lived only a couple of blocks away. They waited in front of the theater as Fred drove by on the way to the parking lot.

The crowd made it difficult for the family to get through to their reserved seats six rows from the front. On stage, the play started with three boys, dressed in blue denim overalls, talking about a mentally challenged man as they climbed a ladder to their clubhouse. The boys found creative ways to make fun of the young man. They entered the clubhouse and waited for Rocky to walk by.

Dressed in a light khaki colored shirt and darker khaki pants, Rocky entered the stage from the right, his awkward gait slowing him down. His large shoulders slumped as he made his way to the middle of the stage and turned toward the façade of the gray wooden house in the background. Taunting him by pretending to be ghosts, the boys moaned and groaned. The noise from the tree house didn't seem to bother Rocky at all. He trudged on, making his way home.

The boys came out of the clubhouse, disappointed that they hadn't irritated Rocky. They sat in front of the tree playing a game of marbles and making plans for the next opportunity to bother The Retard, as they called him.

The following day, they tried tripping him on his way home, by stringing a wire across the road. They waited behind the tree. Rocky's labored gait made him cautious and almost always caused him to look down at his feet as he walked. When Rocky walked by, the boys raised the wire they had attached to a small shrub on the other side of the road. Rocky's big work shoes stomped the wire into the pavement. He walked on down the road and went into his house without looking back.

Disappointed again, the boys plotted and planned, coming up with the idea to throw rocks from the window of the clubhouse. The lights dimmed and the quiet of night took over the stage to show the audience that another day ended. When morning came, the boys filled a bucket with rocks and placed it under a window in the clubhouse, facing the side street – the one Rocky used on his way home every day. The large door facing the audience stood opened, allowing the audience to see each boy pick up a rock. The boys hid beside the open window overlooking the street. The actor playing the part of Rocky slowly made his way toward the clubhouse. To make sure Rocky didn't see them, the boys waited until he turned the corner and headed away from them before they threw the rocks. When Rocky heard the rocks hit the road, he jumped around awkwardly. The boys huddled under the window and giggled.

The character named Bob said, "Now we know how to make The Retard dance. We showed 'im, didn't we?"

The Hal character chimed in, "We did. We did. We made 'im mad, too."

"I've never seen The Retard mad," Hank's character, Bert, said.

Rocky gathered the stones and walked down the street to the flower garden in front of his house. He placed the stones in a line with other stones he gathered to outline a flower garden. He stepped onto the porch and walked through the front door.

In the meantime, the boys' mothers stood on the right front stage opposite the tree house, gossiping. One told the others that someone said their boys were throwing rocks and calling Rocky names.

The mothers walked down the street to the tree house and found a small mound of rocks at the base of the tree, partly confirming their suspicions. Not knowing their mothers were waiting below, the boys came down laughing and talking about how they made The Retard angry. The mothers grabbed their sons, the first one by a collar, the second one, Hank, by the ear, and the third one by the arm. One by one, the mothers issued some form of punishment against each boy, as they marched them to the right front side of the stage and made them sit down. Pointing and shaking a finger in each boy's face the mothers sang a song about the Golden Rule. At the end, Bert's mother said, "If you want to be a good man you have to start when you're a boy."

The boys slowly got up from the floor, singing: *"Ma, I wanna be a man. I wanna grow up as fast as I can."* They stretched up on their toes and continued the song, *"See how tall I stand. Ma, I wanna be a man."*

The mothers shook their heads and turned their backs to their make-believe sons.

Hank's character, Bert, strutted across the stage with his thumbs under the shoulder straps of his blue overalls. He sang the first verse: "*I wanna grow up and drive a fire truck every day; stop and put out fires along the way."* He lifted his fisted hands into the air and shouted, *"I wanna be a fire man."*

All three boys sang the chorus together, *"Ma, I wanna be a man. I wanna grow up as fast as I can. See how tall I stand. Ma, I wanna be a man."*

Bob, with his hands pushed into the back pockets of his denim overalls, sauntered toward Bert and sang, *"I wanna grow up and put all the bad guys in the jail; read their Miranda rights without fail."* Like, Hank before him, he lifted his fists into the air and shouted, *"I wanna be a law man."*

The boys sang the chorus again. Then, Hal stepped into the foreground and sang the last verse: *"I wanna grow up and fix houses all around this town; put smiles on faces instead of frowns."* He thrust his fists in the air and ended with a loud, *"I wanna be a handy man."* The three boys all shouted, *"Ma, I wanna be a man!"*

The stage curtain came down and theater lights came on. Almost everyone in the theater knew the Raffertys' troubles. During intermission, many theater-goers stopped by to say how happy they were to hear that James was home. James' silence caused some awkward moments. News traveled fast in a small town, and it was common knowledge that the trauma left him unable to speak. James didn't like the attention. He did like helping his daddy and Sara pass out drinks and popcorn.

Fred sat in the aisle seat with James to his right and Emmy in the seat past James. A brown-haired woman Emmy worked with a few years before stopped to speak with Emmy. Her shape and size reminded James of his mean mommy. He spilled popcorn as he scrambled away from her. The lighting left the woman's face in shadow as she leaned toward Emmy. James saw her coming closer and closer.

Shaking and huddled in his seat as far away from the woman as possible, James' small whimper caught Emmy's attention. She took his popcorn and handed it to Sara. Emmy helped James out of his seat, pulled him into her lap and held him close. He curled into a fetal position within her arms. She whispered, "Shhhhhhhh. It's okay. Mommy's here. Shhhhhh."

In the meantime, Fred saw how the woman affected James. He stood up, forcing the woman to step away, back into the aisle. He apologized to her and tried to explain how James continued to have problems. He promised that Emmy would call her later.

Thinking he needed to help Emmy with James, Fred reached to take him from her. She shook her head back and forth as she continued comforting her little boy. Fred sat in the seat James vacated and rubbed his son's back. He understood. He knew Emmy needed to replace James' fear of another mommy with her own love and caring. With the love and understanding from his parents, James slowly relaxed.

The light dimmed and the play resumed. James peeked out from his safe haven in his mother's arms to see Hank and the other two boys as they continued torturing Rocky day after day. On one occasion, they used their water pistols. Streams of water shot out from the clubhouse window leaving water spots on Rocky's light blue shirt. The boys left their clubhouse, laughing and nudging each other as they made their way off the stage. Again, stage lights dimmed, indicating nightfall.

When the stage lights came back up, the boys walked on stage with ammunition and slingshots. They climbed up the ladder and waited by the window for Rocky. Small pebbles flew from their homemade slingshots, seldom hitting their target. When the stones hit Rocky's shoulders, the boys laughed. Rocky swatted his arms and pranced around trying to get away from the pebbles flying through the air. The boys said in unison, "Look at 'im dance." They laughed again. Rocky walked away shaking his head. The lights dimmed and the quiet of night took over the stage, again.

The stage lights became bright again. The boys sauntered across the stage and chatted about how they put marbles on the road to Rocky's house and made him slip and fall. Mimicking Rocky, they fell on the ground twisting and squirming. Their laughter filled the air. When they stood up, each boy pulled out marbles from the pockets of his overalls and placed them in a bucket at the foot of the tree. They climbed the ladder, entered their clubhouse, and closed the large front door behind them.

James gasped and turned his face away from the stage when he saw smoke coming from the entrance of the tree house. His mother whispered into his ear, "It's okay. It's just pretend. Hank won't get hurt."

On stage, the boys couldn't get out of the tree house. Smoke billowed around the closed door. The boys looked out the window on the side and down to the ground. They talked about how they were afraid to jump. They screamed for help just as Rocky turned the corner opposite the tree house, headed home.

Rocky placed his strong stout body under the ladder at the door and pushed and pushed until it fell free. He moved the ladder underneath the window and helped each one of the boys down to safety. He became the boys' hero. The play ended with the boys helping Rocky finish the flower garden in front of his house. They took their stash of rocks to finish the outline of his flower garden. They planted pots full of bright summer flowers between the rock and the porch. The play ended with huge applause and a standing ovation.

The actors waited in the lobby to greet the audience. Hank beamed as compliments flowed all around him. All the way home, he talked about the standing ovation.

On the trip back home, Emmy's smile warmed Dee's heart. The play gave all of them hope and a break from the guilt, helplessness, and hopelessness that enveloped them the past few months. Dee thought

Emmy's depression seemed to be lifting.

Dee felt certain that Emmy continued to worry about the trauma James' kidnapping caused the entire family. Plus, Nan Jones' body had not been found, leaving them all to question if she would come back to get James or to get revenge or both? Dee hoped Lois and TK were wrong. She hoped the kidnapper had drowned in the stormy waters off St. Simons Island. It was an on-going investigation. For the Jackson family, it would not close until Nan Jones was behind bars or in a morgue.

Emmy promised Granny Nida that she and Fred would take her to the third and final show of *Our Rocky* on Sunday afternoon. Mom and Pop Jax were babysitting Marcie at the Raffertys' house. James chose to spend the afternoon with Sara. When they arrived, Sara ran to the fence and opened the gate for James. Suede almost knocked James down trying to give him a sloppy wet kiss.

"James always loved that dog," Fred said. "Nothing quite like seeing James doing ordinary things, is there?" He looked in his rear-view mirror before backing out of the driveway.

Emmy smiled in agreement.

At Elsburg Towers, Emmy moved from the front seat to the passenger seat behind Fred, since it was easier for Granny Nida to get in and out of the van from the front seat. Fred fastened Granny Nida's seat belt before walking around the van and getting in the driver's seat. His eyes widened as Granny Nida made a comment to Emmy.

"Lordy mercy, that Tammy gives the best blowjob of anybody."

Fred peeked around at Emmy. The twinkle in Emmy's eyes was priceless. She winked at him. He hadn't seen that mischievous look in months.

"Hey Fred, Granny Nida had her hair done yesterday in honor of seeing her great-grandson on stage today. Doesn't she look wonderful?"

"Ummm. Yeah. Sure. Granny Nida, you look good today," Fred said.

"Thanks Fred-er. I was just telling Emmy Lou that Tammy didn't use the rollers in my hair yesterdy. She gave me a blowjob instead. I like it, even though I don't thank it'll hold up quite as good as the rollers."

Fred knew from experience about Granny Nida's propensity to tell dirty jokes and wasn't sure this time if she was as innocent as she acted.

Her sweet angelic face didn't give him a clue either way.

Late that afternoon, and after James left with his family, Sara asked her mother if she could call her father. Dee agreed, took her cell phone from her purse, and handed it to Sara.

Sara pressed the number three, the direct dial number for her daddy's cell phone. Almost immediately, she handed the phone to her mother.

"It says I've reached a number that's not connected."

"That's the only number I have for him. Maybe you should call Mom Jax and find out if he has a new number," Dee suggested. She thought *if I were a betting person, I would bet Dan Jackson has reached the maximum on his credit card that covered the cost of his cell phone charges.* Dee felt relief knowing she had moved her phone charges to her own credit card.

Dee knew her stubbornness and aversion to confrontation kept her from facing the truth. She thought about the nightmare she had with the black hole and the monsters trying to pull her into it. She wondered if they were caused by her subconscious mind trying to make her deal with her problems. The creepy nightmare had not returned since she faced the fact that Daniel Jackson wasn't the person she fell in love with. She realized *her Daniel* existed only in her mind. He disappeared with the lies and deceit, leaving the real narcissistic Daniel to his new wife and child. She never knew how much of a burden he'd been, until the burden disappeared.

The FBI's Research Technology Team in Atlanta obtained Nan's mother's name through the real estate records of the closing of the St. Simons Island house. Using her mother's surname led them to Nan Jones' birth name - Nannette Jamie Rantz. She spent most of her life in Fulton County, Georgia. Her medical records showed a stillbirth at the age of thirty-one. There was no father's name listed on the paper work. She lived in Decatur at the time of the baby's birth and death. The pieces of the puzzle were falling in place.

Lois' and TK's interviews with the Decatur neighbors gave them new information. The neighbors never knew that Nan's baby died at birth. They thought she was somewhat odd, but saw her many times with a baby. The old lady, who lived next door and was dressed in pajamas and slippers, answered the door after several knocks. She remembered Nan well and invited the agents into her home. Full of surprises, she told them about the casserole she took to Nan when her 10-month-old baby died. She told them Nan was distraught and her sister came to live with her about a year later. The old woman said Nan told her she just couldn't handle living with her sister's two-year-old boy while her own baby was dead. The old woman said, "I guess it was a constant reminder of her baby, so she left. The sister moved out a few months later." The old woman talked on, "Those two girls sure did favor each other. They were twins, you know."

The woman said she didn't know why the sister moved. She added, "She was there one day and gone the next. Those girls loved their mama, who was frail. She couldn't even be around her grandbabies 'cause they might give her a virus that would kill her. I babysat for Nan once a month so she could go see her mama. When her sister moved in, I kept her little boy, Jimmy, so she could visit their mama until their mama retired and moved away. To the beach, I think. Yeah. They loved their mama."

The team quickly found the documentation of Nan's marriage to Joe Jones. Lois and TK talked with the minister who performed the ceremony. He told the agents, step by step, all the good things Nan did for Brother Jones. The pastor and the congregation showered her with sympathy when Joe went back to drugs and alcohol. Many of them gave her money. A look of disbelief crossed the pastor's face when he heard their theory that she may have killed Jones. He told them he didn't believe it. At the time, they couldn't prove she killed her husband. They didn't bother telling the pastor that they were certain that Nan kidnapped and murdered several children.

When they got to the office, they filled in some blanks on the history wall they were creating for Nannette Jamie Rantz Jones. So far, the sequence indicated that Nan Rantz, a thirty-one-year-old woman delivered a baby that didn't survive; shortly after, she kidnapped an infant who died before his first birthday; at thirty-three she pretended to be her twin sister and kidnapped a two-year-old whose remains hadn't been found; and she married Joe Jones at the age of thirty-four and killed him within the year – that's when she started keeping pictures of her victims.

TK added the picture of the boy with a mole on his hand. "She was probably thirty-five when she kidnapped this four-year-old boy and was thirty-six when she killed him. She killed her mother shortly after she killed the four-year-old – just before her thirty-seventh birthday – two in one year, and almost thirty-eight when she took James. She's been a busy woman."

Looking at the board, Lois asked the staff psychologist what he thought.

"I have no reason to believe that Nan Jones was a serial killer before the death of her baby. More than likely her mind was fragile all her life, but she didn't become a killer until after the baby's death. The hospital's paperwork described the baby with words like 'abnormally disfigured.' It was more than her mind could handle." He looked thoughtful for a few seconds and continued, "Something happened to make her start documenting with pictures – like maybe she wasn't happy with the way she handled her victims in the past and she needed these pictures to fulfill her goal. Her OCD may have kicked in, making her feel the need to be more organized."

"We'll go with a crew and check out the house and yard in Decatur. If she disappeared in the night, she might have left without the boy. If his remains are there, we'll find them," Lois said, wondering what she would say to the old woman next door who babysat for Nan.

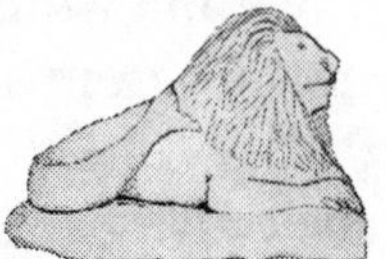

Chapter Twenty-Nine – The Pretender

With a cap pulled down low on her forehead and a tight fitting undershirt to flatten her breasts, Mary Brown looked more like a skinny teenage boy than a thirty-nine-year-old woman. The entire outfit, including shoes and socks, were from a local thrift store. Her new phone could take pictures and allowed her access to the Internet. It was perfect for taking pictures of unsuspecting families as she searched for Timmy. She sat on a bench in front of a fountain in the mall.

She saw the woman with the small blond boy walking toward her. Last week, a man was with them. The phone hid her smirk. They walked past her, unaware that she took their photograph.

Mary put on sunglasses and walked in the opposite direction around the large fountain and green plants. She slowed down as she circled the fountain. When she reached the other side, the woman and boy were a few feet ahead. An adrenaline surge gave her extra energy. The excitement racing through her body was more potent than any drug she could have taken. Chasing her dream to be a mother always gave her a rush.

She followed the boy and his mother to the escalators and watched as they exited on the parking garage level, allowing more distance between them before she followed them through the glass doors. She almost danced with joy when she saw them get into a deep blue Lexus near her van, parked one row over. They would have to pass her van on their way out of the parking garage.

Almost running, Mary made it to the van, jumped in, and started the engine well before the Lexus drove by. She backed out and pulled forward, letting a small car pull in front of her, just before the Lexus stopped at the pay booth. She felt certain that the woman in the Lexus never saw her white van.

Mary Brown reached for the notepad in the passenger seat. Luck stayed with her as the car in front of her took a left. Mary turned right and pulled in behind the blue Lexus at a red light. She made a note of the information on the tag. *Gwinnett County. That's good*, she thought.

With any luck at all, she would see them again in the mall. Next time she'd be able to get a name when the woman became careless with her purse or a bag with a credit card slip from a recent purchase.

She followed them until they turned into a subdivision. Satisfied with the progress she made, she drove back toward the mall, looking for a place to park for the night. She could hardly wait to check out the Internet to find the subdivision and get a map with street names. As soon as she found a name for the family, she'd find their home address.

Her thoughts went to the blond-haired, green-eyed boy from the mall. *Timmy will love living in the van until I find us a small house in Florida. All little boys like camping out and moving around. I'll buy him the sleeping bag next week.*

As she drove around the back of a strip mall she thought about the trip to Elberton she would have to make soon. The little boy who pretended to be Timmy had to be punished. In her mind, he became *The Pretender*. The real Timmy lived in Gwinnett County. Soon she would have her little boy with her. They would have such a good time. Her Timmy will know how to appreciate a mother who would do anything to make him happy.

She knew the imposter would be in school on Friday. The map, folded and ready, would take her straight to his school. She'd get there early. She'd surprise him.

James visited a children's therapist in Athens each Wednesday afternoon for thirty minutes. Each week Emmy and Fred waited, hoping their little boy would talk with them. After Emmy found James in Marcie's room balling his fist, she told the therapist that they worried James might hurt Marcie in some way. The therapist assured Emmy he would talk to James about Marcie and James should be able to understand that the baby didn't cause any of the bad things that happened to him.

The doctor asked Emmy to continue observing James' behavior around the baby and let him know if the aggression escalated. After the consultation, Fred went back to work. Emmy, Hank, and Marcie waited in the lobby area while James finished his one-on-one session with his therapist. On the way home, Emmy stopped at a nearby Burger King.

Hank, the pre-teenager, lounged in the background, away from the little kids' playground at the restaurant. He leaned on a fence and appeared not to notice James trying to take his turn climbing the ladder to the slide. A muscular boy dressed in camouflage shorts and T-shirt, pushed James aside, looked back, and taunted, “Poor little boy, can’t say a word. Poor little boy, looks like a turd.” He climbed the steps with a swagger. Just before sliding down, he looked at James, made an ugly face, and laughed.

Hank moved to the end of the slide, followed the boy’s progress, and grabbed him by the back of his T-shirt as soon as his feet hit the ground. He forced him to stand by the slide until James made his way up the ladder and finished his ride down. He whispered into the boy’s ear, “You’re nothing but a bully. You say ‘I’m sorry’ right now to my brother. Nobody bullies my brother.”

With his head hanging, and in an almost inaudible voice, he said, “I’m sorry, little boy.”

“You’re what?” Hank’s voice lifted above the chatter of the children playing nearby and caught the attention of several grownups. “Say it again, and mean it. Look him in the eye and tell him why you’re sorry. Tell him you will never bully him again.”

“I’m sorry I called you a turd and made fun of you ‘cause you don’t talk. I … I won’t pick on you again.”

“Now, shake hands with my brother.” Hank loosened his hold on the boy’s shirt.

The boy did as Hank ordered.

“Now, I want you to tell your mother what you did. I want her to know what you said to my brother.” Hank watched the boy turn toward a woman at a nearby table.

When the boy reached his mother and told her the name he called James, she looked at James. When he told her he made fun of James because he didn’t talk, his mother took his hand and walked the boy to the table where Emmy sat with Marcie in her lap.

“I believe my boy learned a good lesson today. I don’t know why your boy don’t talk, but it’s not right for my boy to be ugly towards ‘im. I’m sorry.”

Emmy accepted the apology and the woman walked away with a tight grasp on her son’s wrist. Emmy spotted Hank and James coming from inside, each carrying an ice cream cone. She knew James had no money. “Who paid for your ice cream, sugar?”

James pointed to Hank, who shrugged as if it was no big deal. They sat in silence at the table with Emmy while they finished their ice cream. Afterwards, Emmy gathered her purse and Marcie’s diaper bag.

Hank took the large diaper bag from his mother and handed Emmy's purse to James. Emmy picked up the baby carrier with Marcie in it and started toward the parking lot. She buckled Marcie in the back seat of the van and saw her purse that James placed on the console between the two front seats. She heard James' seat belt click. As soon as Emmy made herself comfortable in the driver's seat, they headed home. She smiled at Hank and called him her co-pilot.

Except for the sound of Marcie sucking her pacifier, silence filled the car as they passed the old houses on Prince Avenue. After driving several miles on the bypass, Emmy brought up the playground confrontation, "Hank, you . . ."

"Mom. I know that boy shouldn't have bullied James. But, I felt like a bully when I stopped him. How do you stop a bully without being a bully?"

Surprised at the unexpected question, Emmy couldn't think of an answer. She said, "I don't know. I've dealt with it from more of an adult's point of view. I see now that it's different for a child to correct another child – not that you're as young as that boy," she added quickly. "Let's read up on it. I'm sure there's some help out there. I just want you to know how proud I am of you. You're the best big brother ever. I think you did the right thing when you made him shake hands with James. Nice touch." She held her hand out for a high five.

Worry about how James was interacting with Marcie stayed at the forefront of Emmy's thoughts. She was thankful he hadn't shown any more animosity toward the baby, but knew that could change quickly. In her rear-view mirror she could keep an eye on Marcie and the middle part of the back seat. She saw James' index finger pointing at Marcie and moving toward the baby's seat. She was slowing down, preparing to stop the car, when she saw Marcie reach out and grab James' finger. The pacifier dropped from Marcie's mouth. Emmy saw the smile Marcie gave her big brother. When Emmy looked in the rear-view mirror again, she saw James return the smile.

When they arrived home, James jumped out of the car and waited at the back door until Emmy arrived with the key. Since he returned to the family, James never showed excitement – about anything. Before she could get through the door with Marcie, James scooted under her arm and ran into the house.

Emmy saw him run through the kitchen and disappear into the hallway. She placed Marcie in her crib and went looking for James. She found him in the room he shared with Hank. He was looking through the books on the lower shelf and stopped to pull out *Miss Pugg Rescues a Hummingbird* and placed it to the side. The pile of books on the floor grew as he added books from the Miss Pugg series: *Stars and Stripes: Raccoon Brothers,* and *Michael's Shadow*. When he found *Some Little Oink Oink*, he handed it to his mother.

Emmy leaned against the propped pillows at the head of James' bed. With an arm around James, his head resting against her chest, she read, *Some Little Oink Oink.* When she got to the end, she understood his need to hear the story. She read, *"I'm your mama and I love you Oink Oink Three."*

James turned and looked up expectantly. She put the book down, pulled him to her, and hugged him tight.

Dee recognized Aunt Connie's phone number on the display of her cell phone.

"Aunt Connie, how are you?" Dee asked as she sat down at the kitchen table.

"I'm fine. In fact, that's why I called you. It's been a few weeks and I seem to be better than ever. I didn't know a gallbladder could make me feel so poorly. How are you, sweetie?"

"I'm okay. Busy since school started. I'm happy to know you're better." Dee hesitated, wondering if she should broach the subject of whether Connie could help find James' kidnapper.

"How are Emmy and her family?" Connie asked.

"Emmy's so much better with James home. She's one busy mama." Dee, excited about the energy in her aunt's voice, hoped it meant she felt up to helping find Nan Jones.

"Do you think the FBI agents would be open to me trying to help find that awful woman?" Connie asked. "I wouldn't insert myself into this situation, except I know from experience and from what you told me, she's still out there. Even if she doesn't come back for James, she's working on kidnapping the next child."

"Thank you so much. Yes. I feel they'll welcome any help they can get. At first, Special Agent Crandall was completely against any help from Sara. But, Sara made a believer out of her." Dee smiled when she thought about Lois Crandall admitting that Sara's drawings presented many clues in the search for James.

"I'll need something of hers. I assume they have some articles belonging to the kidnapper," Connie surmised.

"I don't know if the FBI Brunswick office kept them or if the Athens office is holding them. What do you think about going to the house where she lived? Would that be even better?"

"Probably. Any personal items might be just as good. Would you mind calling them? Or, if you'll give me their number, I'll call."

"I'll call Agent Crandall, the lead agent. Her partner is TK … I don't remember his last name, but I'll get it for you." Dee's heart raced at the thought of finding the monster and putting her in a place where she could never hurt anyone again. "Oh. I remember. It's Agent Kidd. Goes by TK."

"Thanks. I don't know if I can help. I just want that woman found soon. Want to go to St. Simons Island with me if I can't get what I need otherwise?"

"That would be great. Do you think I should mention this to Emmy?" Dee didn't want to leave Emmy out. But, she didn't want her worried needlessly.

"Please don't. I don't want to get her hopes up."

"Okay. I'll call you as soon as I get in touch with one of the agents," Dee promised.

"You do know that Sara is capable of doing this, right?" Connie asked.

"I thought about that. I just don't want to put too much on her until she's more mature. Hopefully, she'll learn to handle this gift as well as you have," Dee reflected.

"That's why I offered. She'll have plenty of time to help others when she's older. I just wanted to let you know I consider her ability to be very strong." Connie remembered how many people doubted her when she was a child. She didn't want Sara to run into the negativity she experienced.

"Thanks. I agree completely."

"By the way, let's ask them for Friday. Let's do lunch after we've met with the agents." Connie suggested. "I don't want to put this off."

"Sounds good. I actually have a scheduled day off. It's a date." Dee thumbed through several business cards looking for Lois' information.

"Great. Talk to you later. Thanks, sweetie. Bye, now." Connie waited for Dee to say goodbye.

"Bye. And, thanks again." Dee pressed the off button on her phone, raised her fists in the air and said, "Yes." Her next thought was, *With*

Aunt Connie working on James' kidnapping, the chances of finding the culprit just got a lot better.

Dee's call to Agent Lois Crandall went well. Lois agreed immediately to see Dee and Connie on Friday morning. Since all the evidence was stored in the Athens regional office, she told Dee she would have several items available from the evidence room.

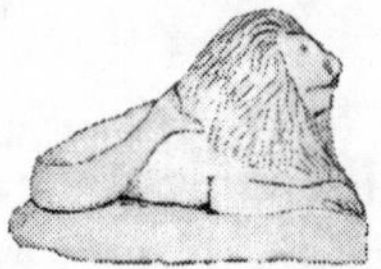

Chapter Thirty – The Evidence Box

With the boys in school and Marcie napping, Emmy remembered her promise to Hank about finding out more about bullying, particularly about how to stop bullying without becoming a bully. Her teaching experience gave her insight to most bullying tactics. She knew from experience how the fine line of positive aggression could cross into bullying – negative aggression. Emmy had a good start on her list before Marcie demanded her attention.

After changing Marcie's diaper and before leaving to pick up James at school, Emmy checked her notes and finished an outline for Hank. By the time he got off the bus, James was home enjoying an afternoon snack and Marcie played nearby.

The outline she handed Hank gave him ideas, while allowing Hank to do the work. She asked him to fill in the blanks. The first line of the outline identified four types of bullies. She asked him to describe each and finish with a summary.

Hank sat at the kitchen table while she went with James to the den to help him with his homework. Emmy could hear the tap, tap, tap of the laptop keys as Hank recorded his research information.

Hank filled in the blanks, took the paper back to his mother, and showed her his first draft: *1) Violent = The meanest of abusers who hurt kids with there fists and words. They sometimes threaten to hurt other members of there family. 2) Aggressive = Almost as mean as the violent ones. They mostly hurt with words and like to get someone else to fight for them. 3) Assertive = Don't hurt as much as the first two, but enjoy taking part in bullying. 4) Secondary = the bully who walks beside or behind the stronger bullies, carrying out there orders, causing fear. Follows orders.*

Summary: Sometimes the first three will start something and get the secondary bully to finish the job. Like threaten to punch a kid but gets another kid to do it. That way the secondary bully gets the blame. The meanest bullies like this a lot. Kids that bully don't have real feelings. They don't know how to feel sorry for other kids. They'd do anything to get there way. Boys and girls don't always bully in the same way. Lots of boys use there fists and bully right out in the open. Mostly girls are more secret. They'll say anything about another girl just to make her cry. It makes a bully feel good.

Emmy read Hank's work out loud. She complimented him on his understanding of bullying, helped him correct a few errors, and explained how *their* and *there* should be used correctly. Emmy made it clear to her son that his interference with the boy on the playground did not make him a bully and his intention to stop a bully was successful.

Hank and Emmy didn't notice how intently James listened to Hank's words. His thoughts went back to Nan Jones who didn't care if she made him cry. In his mind, the mean mommy was the worst kind of bully. He slipped out of his chair and walked to the bedroom, curled up on his bed, and closed his eyes tightly, hoping the picture in his head of the mean mommy would disappear forever.

The evidence box sat on the small conference room table. Special Agent Lois Crandall was standing at the head of the table when Agent Kidd walked in with Dee and Connie.

"Hi, Dee. This must be your Aunt Connie." Lois started the conversation.

Dee introduced her aunt to Lois and then commented on the box. "I've never seen so many labels and stickers on a box before."

"It's called the chain of evidence. Agent Kidd and I both have to be present when the seal is broken. When we finish, we send it back with a record of who touched it, the times involved, and any other pertinent information to ensure no one changes or exchanges anything in the box. The seal we will use when we send it back will ensure the authenticity of the evidence." Lois nodded to TK, who took a pair of scissors from a nearby cabinet.

Lois thought about Sara and how much she contributed to finding James. She asked Dee, "Where's Sara today? I thought she might come with you."

"She's at school. Emmy is picking her up when she picks up James. I think—"

Connie interrupted, "Actually, Sara probably could do this as well or better than me. However, Dee and I want her to be more mature before she tries handling more of the darker side of life."

TK asked, "Shall I let you take the items out one at a time so you can see which ones you're gonna need? I'm not sure 'bout how this psychic process works." He held the scissors underneath a two-inch strip of yellow tape with the word "EVIDENCE" repeated again and again in black lettering.

"It's okay. I'll take out the items. I know you or Agent Crandall will have to record each item as I take it out." Connie said and waited for TK to cut the tape.

As soon as TK opened the box, they all watched as Connie pulled out several pictures and held them for a few seconds. Her fingers lovingly touched each hole where a face once peered out. She placed them on the table beside the box and pulled out a bag holding something that looked like crumbs.

TK opened his mouth to say they were flecks of skin when Connie said, "She obviously has a bad case of psoriasis." She held one hand underneath the bag and placed the other hand on top.

She continued, "These belong to someone who's in her mid to late thirties. She also has a bad case of Obsessive Compulsive Disorder." Connie closed her eyes. When she opened them, they all saw that her pupils were enlarged and she looked pale.

Lois left her chair and walked to a credenza against the wall behind Connie's chair, poured a glass of water, and placed it in front of Connie.

Connie smiled her thanks, took a swallow and pulled another item from the box. They all seemed to hold their breath as Connie's hand shook. She pulled out the plastic bag with Sara's drawing of the Sea Lion and the tree face. She held it to her chest and leaned forward.

"The spirits of the Sea Lion and the face in the tree kept James' mind from slipping away. He managed to hang on to this when everything else he had the day of his kidnapping disappeared." A tear slipped down her cheek. She didn't even try to wipe it away even though Dee slipped her a tissue.

TK and Lois exchanged glances. They never told James' family about finding Sara's picture of the Sea Lion and the tree.

Connie reached for the pictures she pulled out first. "You do know she kidnapped and hurt others before James?"

"We feel certain she killed her mother. We talked with her mother's neighbors. Three of them said Nan told them her mother had a heart condition. When we checked with the doctor, there was no record of it. The evidence we secured at her house leads us to believe she killed at least one child before she kidnapped James," Lois said.

"Let's deal with this later. I suddenly feel the need to find something to help me know where she is. Time is running out." Connie pulled another bag from the box. It held a hairbrush and makeup from Nan Jones' dresser. As with the other plastic bag, Connie placed the bag between her hands. She lifted the hand that had been resting on the top and slowly moved it in a circle over the bag.

"Is it okay if I take the hairbrush out? I have worked with cases that didn't allow me to open the bags."

The agents said in unison, "Yes, it's okay."

Connie took the brush from the bag and rubbed a strand of hair between her fingers. She swayed so far to the right that Dee put her hand out to stop her from falling.

"He's on the move," Connie said.

"You said he. Did you realize you said he?" Dee asked.

"The cap. The short hair. The boy's clothing. She looks like a boy. He . . . She's driving a van. The hood is white. She's driving north." Connie stopped talking. She took long deep breaths.

"She's driving north," Lois repeated Connie's words. "Can you tell if she's in Georgia?"

Connie took a gulp of water as if her body and brain couldn't keep working without more fluid. She picked up the bag with skin scales and again asked Lois if she objected to taking out a piece of crusty skin.

"Sure. I'll record the amount and size. You take what you need." Lois said. They all were mesmerized by Connie's actions and words.

"She's watching the traffic on her right, trying to change lanes." Connie's brow wrinkled. "She's on I-85 northbound. She just passed Pleasant Hill Road. She's looking at the 316 Exit. She's in . . . north Atlanta."

Lois, TK and Dee watched Connie's energy level decline.

Connie continued, "She keeps looking at the passenger seat. There's a picture there. I can't make out what it is. Maybe the next time she looks, I'll be able to see the picture more clearly." Her hands dropped to the table as if the muscles in her arms stopped working.

TK couldn't stay quiet longer, "Is she headed towards Athens or Elberton?"

Connie forced her hands back to the table and continued rubbing a piece of crusty skin between her fingers. "I'm not sure. There's something behind her. It appears to be a rod with a curtain or something hanging just behind the driver's seat. It has a small opening, like something's been pushed aside to give her a back view of the van. Maybe it's so she can see the traffic behind her."

Dee put her arm around her aunt, hoping to give Connie some of her own strength.

"Thanks, sweetie." Connie removed Dee's arm. "I know you mean well. I'm okay. I see more clearly without distractions." She patted Dee's hand.

Connie held the hairbrush in one hand and a sample of the flakes of skin in the other hand. She closed her eyes. A strange loneliness enveloped Connie as she sat holding Nan Jones' hair and skin. Her body sat in the chair across from Lois and beside Dee. A part of her rode with the kidnapper as she exited I-85 and passed Boggs Road.

"She's going to Elberton. It wasn't a picture on the seat. It's a map. It's clearly marked with a wide blue line from Atlanta to Athens, around Athens to Highway 72 to Elberton. There's a star marked at a school. She's on the move and determined."

Stunned, the others sat quietly for a few seconds.

TK asked, "Where does James go to school?" He looked at Dee.

"Just before you get to the Elberton city limit sign. It's not far from our house. If she's just getting on 316, we can get to the school before she gets there. I'll call Emmy." Dee's heart was racing. She pulled her phone from her purse.

Lois put her hand in the air. "Stop. Not yet," she commanded.

Everyone in the room looked at Special Agent Lois Crandall.

"We've got to think this through. We need to get there before she does. If she gets any idea that we know about her, she'll disappear, and we may never get another chance to catch her." Lois stood up and walked around the table. She sat down beside Connie.

Connie didn't acknowledge Lois. She sat in a daze.

"Thank you, Connie." Lois touched Connie's hand. They all saw that the touch seemed to bring Connie's mind back to the room. Lois continued, "Now we know she's disguised as a boy. Without your information we wouldn't know she's in Georgia, much less dressed like a guy."

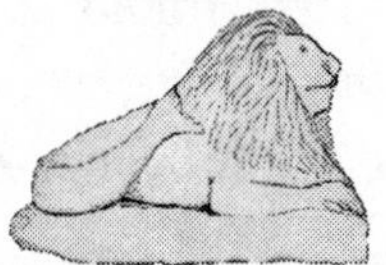

Chapter Thirty-One – Those Wonderful Blue Eyes

Lois felt she needed to take Connie along as they chased the kidnapper. If they lost track of Nan Jones aka Mary Brown, they would need Connie's psychic ability to find her.

TK drove Lois' work car while Lois called the Elbert County Sheriff's office. They followed Dee and Connie from downtown Athens, drove through the small towns Dee called the three C-towns, Colbert, Comer, and Carlton. Not long after crossing the river from Madison County into Elbert County, Dee pulled into her driveway.

Dee and Connie got into the back seat of the unmarked sedan. TK sat in the driver's seat, leaving Lois free to question Connie about the case. She turned to speak to Connie. Connie's deep blue eyes gazed straight at Lois.

Before Lois could ask her a question, Connie asked, "Have either of you ever met Nan Jones?"

"No." Lois replied, wondering why Connie asked.

"Has she seen you anywhere?" Connie continued her questioning.

"No." Lois replied again, even more puzzled. She usually asked the questions. What was Connie trying to accomplish?

"Think back. If she's ever seen either of you, she'll disappear. She's cunning. Has a memory like an elephant. If she gets her hands on James, he won't survive. The smallest detail could ruin our chances of catching her," Connie said.

TK asked Lois, "You think she might've seen us at her house going through her stuff?" He ran his fingers through his black hair.

"Nope. I don't think so," Lois' thoughts went back in time – to the island and Nan Jones' house. She looked again at the setting. Walked through the back door. Searched the yard. She could almost see Nan Jones' crumpled and bruised body lying in the leaves – leaving crushed vegetation and traces of blood.

"I think she may have been watching and waiting when we were at her house. Remember? She came in after our initial search?" TK said. Like Lois, his thoughts took him back to the small white house on St.

Simons Island.

"Oh crap." Lois sounded frustrated at herself for not thinking that Nan Jones may have seen them. Of course, at some time she left her bed in the undergrowth of the huge trees. She watched and waited until they left her house.

"Whose car were you using that day?" Dee asked.

Lois opened her mouth to answer. But TK beat her to it. "Mine," he said.

"Isn't this your car, Lois? The one you left in Athens when we stopped to get you to go to St. Simons?" Dee thought she'd seen the car before.

The conversation continued. They all four agreed that Nan Jones wouldn't recognize Lois' car but might recognize one of them.

TK looked at Lois, "Hey, you could let your hair down, and she wouldn't recognize you. Your hair was pulled back into a tight twist in the back. You really look different with it down."

Dee and Connie smiled at each other noticing how TK enjoyed taking out the long clip holding Lois's black hair. Her long dark hair fell around her shoulders.

"That works for Lois. But, how about you, TK?" Dee asked.

"I guess I'll have ta stay in the background." TK sounded disappointed.

"Or – I've got a cap that belonged to my ex-husband. I'll run in and get it." Dee jumped out of the car and hurried inside. She took the hat off the rack in the laundry room and realized she truly thought of Dan as her ex-husband, even though the official papers remained unsigned.

TK placed the hat on his head, looked into the rear-view mirror and said, "This'll do. Thanks."

Lois, short on time, had been unable to place FBI agents in strategic places. She informed Connie and Dee that the local sheriff agreed to use their unmarked cars. He also promised he wouldn't make a move until he got a call from one of the agents. The first unmarked car waited at Nickville Road near the Elbert County line, giving them the advantage of knowing when the white van crossed over into Elbert County. He gave orders to his people to ensure the van didn't leave the county. County deputies were staked out at the other roads exiting the small town.

They all saw an empty silver SUV in the circle at the entrance to the school as TK drove past the school and parked several yards away.

They sat in silence while Connie held two bags of evidence. All eyes watched the road leading to the school.

Twenty minutes later Connie said, "She just crossed the river. She's in Elbert County."

Lois' phone rang. She smiled as she heard the sheriff repeat Connie's words, "She just crossed the river. She's in Elbert County."

"Thanks," Lois responded into the phone. She reminded the sheriff of his promise not to use sirens of any kind. Lois knew from experience how quickly a suspect could get spooked and run.

Lois looked back at Dee and Connie and said, "She should be here within ten minutes if I calculated the miles correctly on our way in."

They all looked at their watches.

Dee said, "School will be out soon. Children will be everywhere. Nan Jones will have to make her move before school lets out, otherwise, Emmy will be here to pick up James and Sara."

They watched as two school buses pulled into the parking lot beside the school not far from their car.

Lois asked TK to take the evidence they brought with them and lock the box in the trunk to keep the chain of evidence secure. While he was out of the car, Lois explained to Dee and Connie how the evidence would be needed when the case went to trial. It had to be in their presence or secured at all times.

Ten minutes later Lois' phone rang again. She listened for a few seconds before announcing, "She's turning off Highway 72. She's almost here. I'm certain she didn't know school was getting out early. If she had, she would've come earlier. We wouldn't have been here."

As planned, Lois got out of the car first, made her way to the front of the school and disappeared. A couple of minutes later TK left the car and walked down the sidewalk past the entrance to the school. More buses pulled into the parking lot. A man and woman with a small child exited the front door of the school and got into the silver SUV.

Dee reached over and held her aunt's hand when Nan's white van rolled slowly past a couple of parked cars. She knew it wouldn't be long before the line of cars with mothers and fathers waiting to pick up their children would snake around the entrance and back down the street.

The silver SUV pulled away from the front entrance. The white van took its place. A young boy wearing a cap got out and sauntered toward the door of the administrative building. Lois opened the door and greeted Nan Jones. Large and small circles of psoriasis dotted the top of the hand that held a note giving permission for James Rafferty's cousin to pick him up early.

By the time Lois took the note, TK stood behind Nan Jones with handcuffs. Several squad cars drove in from the entrance and the exit to the school, blocking traffic.

As soon as Dee saw TK handcuff the disguised woman, she jumped out of the car, ran to the entrance, and made her way through the group of people. She heard the shrill voice of Nan Jones insisting she came to pick up her cousin. She said she'd done nothing wrong and screamed, "Look at the note. I have permission."

Dee found Lois showing her badge and issuing an order for the school principal to make an announcement for all teachers to hold their students in class. Lois assured him that everything was under control. The sheriff walked in behind Dee, nodded and made his way to the administrative offices. Dee could hear him verifying Lois' request.

The fear and the exertion from running to the front desk left Dee winded. She gulped for air as she looked around trying to locate the receptionist.

"Mrs. Jackson, what's going on?" the wide-eyed young woman asked as she made her way to the counter.

"It's complicated." Dee said.

Lois, the sheriff and the principal walked toward them. The principal addressed the receptionist. "Have one of the aides cover the desk. Take Mrs. Jackson to Sara's class, then to James Rafferty's class. I want both students to be outside and waiting by the time Deputy Manning escorts Emmy Rafferty to the front entrance. She's been through enough." The principal nodded to Dee and walked out behind the sheriff and Lois.

Relief filled Dee's body. It almost killed her to leave Emmy out of all that just happened. She knew in her heart it was the right thing to do. Emmy needed to stay away until Nan Jones was caught. Dee felt certain Emmy wouldn't have been able to stay away if she knew the kidnapper was anywhere near James.

As she and the receptionist passed the front entrance, Dee saw Nan Jones' head being pushed into the back seat of a squad car. Until her stomach made growling noises, Dee forgot she'd skipped lunch. A huge dose of adrenaline gave her plenty of energy to hurry down the corridor towards her daughter's room. She welcomed Sara with open arms.

Sara's worried look disappeared when her mother explained that

James' kidnapper had been caught. Her smile widened as she looked at her mother. They made their way to James' classroom.

Dee carried James in her arms as she and Sara walked to the front entrance of the school. Dee realized she left Aunt Connie without any explanation. She put James down, held his hand and practically ran the last few yards to the front door where she found Connie sitting quietly on a concrete bench, her back resting on a brick wall. The sweet smile on her face said it all. Hardly anyone knew how Connie saved the day. Dee knew her aunt didn't want accolades. She knew her aunt got exactly what she wanted – a happy ending.

Sara saw her great-aunt and said, "Hey, Aunt Connie. I knew you'd be here today when Mom said James' kidnapper was caught." Sara gave her great-aunt a hug.

Dee watched as a silver van pulled up to the entrance. Emmy jumped from the passenger side of Long John Silver. She didn't bother closing the door. She ran straight to James, picked him up and kissed his cheeks. She seemed unaware of the others.

"Emmy, we meet again," Lois said.

Emmy held on to James. She looked at Lois. "Thank you, Agent Crandall. Thank you. I'll never be able to say thank you enough." Her hand trembled when she touched Lois' arm.

"Just doing our jobs," Lois said. "I have to tell you that Agent Kidd and I couldn't have pulled this off without some special people." Lois nodded toward Connie, Sara and Dee.

Still holding James, Emmy walked to Connie and gave her a hug. When she pulled away, Connie's face glistened with Emmy's tears of joy.

Emmy put James down. She took his hand in hers, bent down to Sara, cupped Sara's face in her other hand and said, "You're the bestest ever, Sara Jackson. You and your Aunt Connie are my heroes. I can see what you've been saying for years, Dee. Sara and Connie are so much alike. Those wonderful blue eyes!" Emmy stood up. Keeping a tight hold on James' hand, she continued, "My wonderful sister-in-love who's just stubborn enough to hang in there until anybody and everybody has to listen. Without your pushing to keep this case open, I would be looking over my shoulder for the rest of my life. Or, worse, I'd have lost James forever. Thank you."

Dee's eyes filled with tears. Emmy's happiness meant a lot to her. She could only imagine how she would feel if someone kidnapped Sara.

The deputy who explained the situation to Emmy and got her car out of the line of waiting vehicles walked up and handed Emmy the keys to her van. Emmy smiled and thanked him.

Lois made her way to Dee's side and reminded her that none of them had eaten lunch. She asked Dee where they might find something to eat.

"Any good pizza in town? I'm starving," TK said.

"Me, too. Let's go to the pizzeria on the Square," Dee suggested. "Hey, wait a minute I don't have a car."

"Dee, can Sara go home with James and me? We've eaten lunch and I want to get back home to Marcie. Mom's with her. Oh my God. I forgot to call Mom and tell her about that crazy woman coming back. When I left home I had no idea today would be such a monumental day." Emmy looked around and realized she didn't have her phone. Her phone was in her purse in the car.

"Just wait and tell Mom Jax when you get home. I'm sure she rather hear it in person than on the phone anyway," Dee said.

The agents sat on one side of the table with Connie and Dee across from them in a booth at the pizza parlor. News traveled fast and the owners had heard that James' kidnapper was caught at the local school. The pizza prepared for the day's lunch buffet was all gone, but the owners insisted the new customers have a salad while they prepared fresh pizzas.

TK ordered a pizza with all the meats from the menu, adding hot peppers. When he referred to the gut bomb effect, Lois rolled her eyes.

Dee, Connie and Lois chose to share a pizza with bell peppers, onions, mushrooms and tomatoes. They enjoyed their salads as the aroma of their baking pizzas filled the dining room.

"Do you mind if we talk about one of Nan Jones' other victims?" Connie asked the agents.

"Not at all," Lois answered for both of them.

"Before Agent Kidd locked the evidence box in the trunk I held a picture of a little boy – about four years old. Even though the face had been cut out, I know he looked like James. Green eyes. Blond hair. Somehow he's connected to the area where there's a big peach in the air. Not a picture, but a sculpture of a big peach." Connie took a sip of sweet tea.

Lois, TK and Dee waited for Connie to continue.

"I know of two such peaches in this part of the world. There's one below Macon on I-75 and one in South Carolina, above Spartanburg. You probably need to start with the one in Georgia, near Macon."

"Thanks Connie. We'll start working on that as soon as we get back to the office," Lois said. She looked up to see a waitress hefting two large pizzas to their table.

Silence filled the booth as the foursome devoured the hot pizza. When they tried to pay at the cash register, the owners refused to accept any money. They walked from behind the counter and gave Dee a hug and shook hands with the others.

"I like this town," TK said as they walked out the door.

"Yeah. You'd like any town where you can get a loaded pizza free. You're such a bum," Lois said. Her fist hit TK on his upper arm.

TK grimaced and pretended she hit him too hard. "Where's this granite bowl the sheriff talked about?" he asked as he held the door open for the three women.

Dee smiled and answered, "See the courthouse?" Dee gave TK time to look down the sidewalk toward the newly renovated courthouse. "It's behind the courthouse, near the sheriff's office."

"TK is going to drop me off at the sheriff's office before he takes you and Connie to your house. I want to see Nan Jones' van. I just got a text message from the sheriff saying they found a huge stash of money behind the front passenger seat. The inside of the pocket behind the passenger seat was cut and put back together with Velcro at the bottom where no one could see it. She removed the stuffing from the seat and replaced it with a cloth bag filled with hundred-dollar bills," Lois shook her head and added, "The woman is resourceful, to say the least."

Dee directed TK as he drove past the courthouse toward the Elbert Theatre where she told him to turn right at the traffic light. TK could hardly keep his eyes on the road when he saw the big hole in the ground with granite seats on all sides.

TK paid no attention to the exit arrow as he entered the drive between the Granite Bowl and an old granite building on the hill. He stopped three times to look to the right into the Granite Bowl, before he asked about the rock building on the left.

"That's the rock gym. It's vacant now. Hopefully, it will be renovated soon. I think it may be a museum for the military. Before it was a high school gym, it was the armory for the National Guard unit here in Elberton." Dee told TK to turn left and drive up the hill beside the rock gym.

TK stopped the car near a granite bust of Franklin D. Roosevelt. Lois got out and headed toward the sheriff's office. TK backed out, pulled forward and stopped to get another view of the Granite Bowl.

"The Granite Bowl was made of more than one hundred thousand tons of granite with approximately twenty thousand seats," Dee told him.

"Zinc," he said.

Puzzled, Dee and Connie looked at each other.

"Means cool." TK told them.

After Lois got out, Dee moved to the front passenger seat and gave the agent directions back to her house where they said goodbye. Dee insisted that Connie rest before they drove to Athens to retrieve Connie's car.

Soon after finding the remains of the two-year-old in the backyard of the Decatur house, Agent Crandall decided to pursue Connie's advice regarding the picture of the boy with the mole on his hand. She and TK made a trip to the Peach County sheriff's office, south of Macon, to check out a three-year-old cold case. The sheriff's file contained several pictures of a four-year-old blond-haired, green-eyed boy.

Lois pulled her file from her briefcase, removed the photograph with the face missing, and compared it with the pictures in the sheriff's file. Only one of the sheriff's pictures included the boy's hands – his left hand rested on top of his right hand as he sat at his desk for a school photograph. The size and placement of the mole on the left hand matched her photo taken from Nan Jones' house.

The next step would involve locating the boy's body. The agents felt that wherever Nan lived when she kidnapped the four-year-old boy, they'd find his remains. Otherwise, the boy's family would never have closure. They talked about how she planned to get rid of James. If she succeeded, James' body may never have been found.

It was late Friday afternoon when they left the sheriff's office. As they walked to the car, Lois shared her thoughts about the murders. "She seems to be all over the map in the methods of disposing of the bodies. Usually, serial killers use the same mode of operation. Her MO is all over the place."

TK shared his thoughts, "Maybe it's how she fights OCD. You know, by making a point of changing things. Plus, circumstances are different in each case. Like, she's been able to make some of the deaths look like natural causes. Her mother. The Jones guy. She may have OCD, but she's also an opportunist."

Lois gave TK the keys to the car and asked him to drive. As he backed out of the parking space, TK looked at Lois and asked, "Got any weekend plans?"

"Not really," Lois answered absentmindedly. "Thought I'd let you take me to a movie tomorrow night."

"Then, let's go ta the island for the weekend."

Lois, intrigued by the offer, asked, "Which island?"

"St. Simons. We're half way there. And, we can check in with Agent Cook and find out what's new on their end and give him our update."

"Are you crazy? I can think of several reasons not to. Like, I don't have a toothbrush, change of clothes . . ."

"Don't matter. There's a Walmart around here. We passed it coming in. You can get all the things you just named." He gave her a big grin. "I'll call my sister. She'll loan you something ta wear if you can't find anything ta buy."

"Men. You amaze me. You think I'd fit into your sister's clothes? She's at least four inches shorter. I don't wear petites. Or, have you noticed?" Lois shook her head and looked out the window.

"I noticed. Thought you'd look zinc in short skirts," TK said, trying desperately to turn a mistake into a compliment.

She thought for a second, looked at TK, grinned, and admitted she'd like to go to the island. They found the store on their way to I-16. After buying toothbrushes and other personal hygiene products, TK went to the men's department while Lois made her way to the women's area.

Lois could hardly concentrate on what to buy. Giddy with excitement, she chose a red low-cut ribbed tank top and a pair of jeans.

At the last minute she added a lacy low cut pair of panties to her shopping cart. Sexy. She kept the pink comfy low hip cotton briefs she already chose. She'd use those when they walked around the island when comfort would be an issue. A display, full of colorful flip-flops, distracted her and kept her shopping longer than she intended. *The brighter, the better*, she thought as she placed a bright colored pair in the cart. *The swirls of red go well with the tank top.*

When they got back in the car, TK said he spent some time on the

Internet a few weeks before and found several things he wanted to do and see. He pulled out his phone and sent a text message to a friend from New Jersey who owned a condominium near the beach, asking if they could use it for the weekend.

They were almost to the Golden Isles exit when TK's friend called with his approval to use his condo. He gave directions to a realty management company near the village. Within twenty minutes, TK held a key to a gorgeous condo on Ocean Boulevard.

The elevator took them to the top floor. As soon as TK opened the door to the condo, Lois walked straight down a hallway, through the well planned and furnished kitchen and sitting room, to the sliding glass doors that opened to a wonderful view of the ocean. The old live oak trees' limbs near the building almost touched the balcony. She watched two red-headed woodpeckers hop from one limb to another as they pecked insects from the lichen encrusted tree limbs.

"Hey. Come look. It's like living in a tree house." As soon as he came through the door she added, "I'm in love." The sound of the ocean waves beyond the trees and the beautiful landscaping warmed her heart.

TK said, "I hoped you'd say that. I just thought it might come after you've enjoyed the master bedroom suite."

"No, silly. Look at this. What a view." She chose to ignore his racy comment. She continued, "I forgot how much I love the beach. Mom and Dad brought us here. I was a teenager the last time we came. We stayed at the King and Prince."

"They must have liked the beach a lot. You said they moved ta St. Augustine when they retired. Did you get the beach bug from them?"

"Yes and no. I have thought about a beach place when I retire. But, for now I'm happy where I am. Mom and Dad moved to Florida to be near my sister and help her with her two kids. She went through a divorce just before Daddy retired. It works well for them that she lives near the beach. Mom made this incredible sandwich she called her beach sandwich. Want me to make it for you?" Lois turned slightly to hear his answer.

"You didn't give the kitchen a glance. Did you see how it's got everything? A blender, a microwave, a coffee maker." He took a step closer to her as she looked toward the ocean. He put his arms around her, clasping his hands together beneath her breasts. He pulled her against him. With his cheek against hers, he continued, "We'll just have ta make a run ta the grocery store. What's in that beach sandwich?"

Lois turned around in his arms. She forgot the question. His lips were too close for her to ignore them. Her kiss made him forget about the sandwich. He backed into the living room, taking her with him, and guided her to the master bedroom – a room she didn't actually see until the morning sun came through the partially opened wooden slats over the bedroom window. She looked at him sleeping beside her and said, "I'm in love."

Half awake, he heard her and answered, "Me, too."

A couple of hours later, the phone rang. TK grabbed his cell phone off the nightstand before he realized it was the condo phone.

"Who the hell knows we're here?" he asked.

Lois shrugged.

"TK," He said loudly into the phone.

"Hey, boy. You awake?" his New Jersey friend's voice could be heard from across the room.

"Am now." TK sat up on the edge of the bed.

"Shit. Did I get you at a bad time, buddy?" His friend laughed so loud Lois heard it.

"Not really. Thanks for the loan of your place. Zinc is not a strong enough word for this mansion."

"Glad you asked." He added, "I just want ta give you some good advice on seeing the island. I've got a great girl you should look up."

"Wait a minute. I got my own girl. I don't need one of your leftovers." Before TK could say anything else, his friend interrupted.

"I know you got your own girl. I could tell that from yesterday's conversation. After all, how many times does a guy need digs at the beach? Bunny's the best tour guide on the island. She does this trolley tour you and your girl will love." He told TK he could find the trolley tour brochure in the middle drawer of the sideboard in the living room.

After he ended the conversation, Lois reminded him to call his sister and make arrangements to have dinner with the family. She gathered her Walmart bag and headed to the bathroom for a shower. He got the answering machine at his sister's house and left a message.

TK found the tour brochure and called Bunny the Tour Guide. He discovered the tour started at eleven o'clock from near the pier, leaving them short on time. His plans to join Lois in the shower would have to wait. They parked at the pier and walked toward the trolley as the driver pulled the cord and rang the bell announcing their departure.

Bunny stood at the trolley's door, dressed in a white low-cut sundress. Her lime green sandals matched the bracelet dangling from her right hand. "I wouldn't let him leave without y'all." She batted her lashes at TK and waited for them to step into the trolley. She moved in behind them and removed a bag from the front right seat; she'd very discretely saved them a seat up front.

The headphones sat snugly on her blond hair as she told her audience about the Sidney Lanier Bridge and the Johnson rocks, named for President Lyndon B. Johnson and placed on the St. Simons Island beaches to prevent further erosion.

Bunny openly flirted with TK. Her friendly manner and Southern hospitality were in full force. Lois knew Bunny's personality was part of the local tour package. Occasionally, Bunny's sexual innuendoes caused both TK and Lois to laugh out loud. Lois punched TK several times when she saw him openly admiring Bunny's cleavage.

Lois thought, *Bunny may advertise herself as a fading Southern belle in the tour brochure, but I can see she's a woman who knows what she wants*. Lois felt certain that Bunny was on top of her game. Underneath the pretty Southern lady, lived a well-informed woman who knew how to read each and every person on the tour. Lois sat back and enjoyed Bunny's entertaining stories.

The trolley made its way through Neptune Park, named after a slave who grew up with the plantation owners' children and accompanied their older son to war, bringing him home – by pulling a make shift stretcher hundreds of miles – to be buried in the family cemetery. Shortly afterwards, he went back to war with the family's younger son who survived. The King family honored him with the gift of land for his love and loyalty.

The trolley traveled to Ocean Boulevard toward the King and Prince Hotel. As with everything else on the island, it boasted a good story. Two guys, dubbed "The King and The Prince" due to their features – one tall and large and the other one small and short – often hung out at the Cloister on Sea Island where celebrities and the rich vacation. Once, they imbibed too much at the bar and were thrown out. They built their own hotel – with a bar.

The trolley slowed down for the crowd to see the Marshes of Glynn, an important part of the island's ecosystem with the tides moving in and out of the salt-water marshes. Bunny's words made Lois think of the last two stanzas of Sidney Lanier's poem: *"And I would I could know what swimmeth below when the tide comes in - On the length and the breadth of the marvelous marshes of glynn."*

The tour included the Bloody Marsh where the waters around the marshes ran red with Spanish blood when they attacked General Oglethorpe and his band of Highlanders; Redfern Village shopping center, named for Paul Redfern, the aviator who attempted to fly from Brunswick to Brazil, in the late 1920s; the first African Baptist Church where the slaves worshipped and buried their own; and a well-kept park with a Celtic cross honoring John and Charles Wesley, founders of the Methodist church. Lois remembered a magazine she saw about the making of the cross and told TK the cross was made and processed in Elberton.

At Christ Church, the couple stayed close to Bunny as she told a love story about a pastor buried in the church cemetery between his two wives. During plantation times and without a post office, Christ Church served as the site for mail distribution. Bunny made her way to TK and Lois and talked with them as she led the group back to the trolley. The last stop was a slow ride through Retreat Plantation. Lois imagined carriages making their way through the tree-lined entrance to the plantation house during the years before the war. The trolley headed toward the village.

TK looked at the playground as the trolley pulled into its parking spot near the pier. He couldn't take his eyes off the bench near the walkway. He could almost see James watching the clown ride by on the unicycle.

Chapter Thirty-Two – Back Where You Belong

Opening the new silver laptop brought a smile to Dee's face. Her mother's generous gesture brought the two women closer than ever. Dee placed the cursor on her browser icon. As soon as her homepage came on the screen, she clicked on the small envelope giving her access to two new e-mails. She immediately clicked on the one from Special Agent Lois Crandall.

The message, addressed to Dee, Connie and Emmy, read: "*Hi All – Just thought I'd update you on our progress regarding Nan Jones. Our investigation shows she grew up in South Atlanta. Her mother purchased that small house on St. Simons Island after she retired as a nurse. Nan's first victim may have been a baby. We aren't sure about its death. We're still looking into it. The records are confusing, showing she delivered a stillborn baby. There's a death certificate for that baby and another one dated a few months later for a baby that wasn't hers. The remains of a two-year-old have been found in the yard of the same house she lived in after the second baby died. The next victim appears to be a recovering alcoholic from the Atlanta area named Joe Jones. This is when she started keeping pictures. He was an easy target. He gave her a common name. The insurance policy she took out on him financed her quest to kidnap the son she couldn't have. Remember the stash of money hidden in the back of the passenger seat? Joe Jones' contribution to her cause.*

Her four-year-old victim was from Peach County, below Macon – just as Connie predicted. We found his remains buried in the back yard of a house she rented.

We believe, but can't prove, that she murdered her mother in order to have a house for the son she was determined to steal. I suppose we could prove it if we exhumed her mother's body; but, we don't think it's necessary in order to prove she's a serial killer. The stillborn she had when she was in her early thirties left her unable to conceive again. Our psychologist seems to think the loss of her own baby was the catalyst that led her to try and find him or replace him. He said that when each boy she idealized in her mind didn't measure up to her sick standards, she got rid of him.

She hasn't confessed to murdering any of them. She says she 'put them to sleep.' She did just that. She put them to sleep permanently.

The pictures on her cell phone and the information on her computer confirm she had picked another victim, very similar to James. Hopefully, he and his family will never know how close they came to disaster. I sleep better at night knowing this serial killer is behind bars. We couldn't have done it without you. Tell my favorite little redhead that her FBI admirers say 'hello.'"

The second e-mail, from her attorney, let her know the judge had signed the legal separation papers. It also stated that he heard from Dan's attorney. The divorce proceedings had started.

Lois overheard a colleague talking about how TK let the cougar catch him. She fumed all day. That evening, as soon as TK stepped through the door of her condo, the words she held in all day came pouring out.

"A cougar. He called me a cougar," Lois said, pacing the floor. Each word fueled her fire of resentment. "You don't understand!"

"Not ta worry Lois. You're not a cougar. I'm much too close ta your age. You'd have ta be a lot older ta be a cougar." A quirky little smile played around the edges of his mouth. Trying to avoid smiling at her while she was upset made his dimples deeper – a lot deeper.

Lois couldn't help but notice he was trying to hide a smile. She swore his Jersey accent became thicker when he teased her.

"You're not the one they're talking about, Jersey Boy. I don't hear them calling you a Barracuda." She took a step closer – getting in his face.

"Well, they would if you were fifteen years younger than me. Don't matter. You're not getting off the hook that easy." TK took her hand and led her to the sofa. He ran his hand over her smooth hair and removed the elastic band holding it back. Her hair fell loose. Her body automatically moved to fit his. As he continued stroking her head, she made a purring sound.

"Think you can handle a cougar tonight, Jersey Boy? Purrrrrrrr." Her hands slipped down the muscles of his shoulders and made their way to his waistline. He laughed out loud when she squeezed his buttocks and meowed like a kitten.

"Hurry up, slow poke," Dee called from the kitchen as she gathered a stack of graded papers and stuffed them in a tote bag. She pulled the book of poems titled *Ekphrastic Collection* from the kitchen shelf and placed it in the bag. The painting of the Whales in the Park at St. Simons Island had been instrumental in finding James; it was time to give the book to Emmy. She would cherish each page, especially the page with the painting and poem that helped them rescue James from the evil kidnapper. She'd deliver the book to Emmy after school.

Sara walked out the back door in front of her mother. She turned her head and said, "Mollie is so funny. She said I should get ready for a wedding." Sara laughed and slung her book bag over her shoulder.

"Don't you think you're too young to be thinking about a wedding? When did she say that?" Dee asked as she locked the back door.

"Last night. She didn't mean my wedding, silly. She said I'd be a little bride's maid. What does a bride's maid do?" Sara climbed into the back seat of the car.

"Not too much. I think she meant a junior bridesmaid. So, who's getting married?" Dee's curiosity was getting the best of her. She placed her purse and tote bag in the front passenger seat.

The conversation continued as Dee backed out of the garage. "It's TK and Lois. I thought I was the girl of his dreams. I guess he couldn't wait for me to grow up." Sara added, "You think he won't wait for me 'cause of Mollie? Sometimes, Mollie scares people."

"No, honey. TK loves Lois. I could see it as soon as I saw them together." Dee pushed a button above the mirror, waited for the garage door to close, and drove to the highway. "Put your seat belt on." Dee waited for a car to go by before pulling out into the road.

Sara's seat belt clicked as the car gained speed. "I like Lois. 'Sides I don't want to get married. Nobody's ever gonna want a girl who talks to a ghost."

"Not to worry. You've got plenty of time to work on that. You've got a special gift, my love. Not all guys are threatened so easily."

A few miles down the road, Sara asked, "You think Lois will let me dance with TK at the wedding?"

"I'm sure she will, sweetheart." Dee smiled at the thought.

"Won't I get a new dress for the wedding? A long one that touches the floor?"

"Oh yes," Dee answered – a smile in her voice.

Later in the day, Dee checked her calendar. *Nashville* scrawled across the four-day weekend and marked her trip for Thanksgiving weekend. Janet practically insisted that Dee visit and November was the only time that worked for Dee's teaching schedule. She hoped they would be able to celebrate the finalization of the divorce. She crossed her fingers and smiled. In her mind she could see the funny grin of a certain Canadian's face.

"Eh?" she said out loud. He called her several times each week since Janet's last concert in Atlanta. They learned a lot about each other and looked forward to learning even more. She started gathering papers to grade. Life was good.

As Dee contemplated her Nashville trip, Sara and James sat at Mom Jax's kitchen table. The hotter-than-normal September sun beat down on the waiting pool. The yardstick that hung above the back door proclaimed their grandmother's rule – "Homework before Swimming."

With their homework on the kitchen table, Sara moved in front of James and forced him to look straight into her blue eyes. "James," she said, "tell me why you're not talking. You can write it on this paper." She pushed a page of notebook paper in front of him and handed him a pencil.

He looked at the pencil, pinched his chin and replied, "Mamamommy wowowon't lililike meme."

"Is it 'cause you don't talk plain, like you use to?"

James shook his head up and down.

"Oh no, James. Aunt Em loves you whether you talk or not. She won't stop loving you just 'cause you don't talk plain." Sara smiled at him.

"Yuyuyou ththink sso, Ssasa?"

"I know so, James." She gave him a hug.

"Mymy uh uh other ma ma mommy … " James stopped trying to finish the sentence.

"That wasn't your mommy. She was a stranger who didn't know you. She didn't really love you. She may have wanted to be your mommy, but she wasn't." Sara went back to her chair. "Aunt Em is your only mommy. She loves you a lot."

James smiled.

Tears rolled down Emily Jackson's face as she stood at the kitchen window looking out at the shimmering pool and listening to her grandchildren. She wiped the tears away with a dish towel.

"Hey, you two. I'm going to break my own rule. Swimming before homework today. Let's swim." She gathered cookies and juice as Sara and James changed into their bathing suits.

Mom Jax took the time to place her new cell phone in the pocket of her blue and white striped seersucker pants. As soon as she celebrated with James and Sara, she planned to surprise Emmy and Dee with a text message. Not only would they be surprised that she learned to text, they would be delighted that James had talked with Sara.

Sara said goodbye to Mom Jax before she and James ran out the back door. "Can we take James to the museum?" She held the car door open for James to get into her mother's car. "He wants to see the Sea Lion." She scooted in beside him in the back seat.

"Sure, sweetie," Dee replied as she waved goodbye to Mom Jax. "Don't let me forget to give Emmy this book when we take James home. Okay?" Dee showed her daughter the wrapped package. "It has the original picture and poem of the Whales in the Park at St. Simons Island."

"Okay," Sara responded, looked at James, and asked if he remembered the story of the Sea Lion that was carved from rock.

"Uh huh," he said, shaking his head up and down. He thought, *Someday I'll tell Sasa how I kept the picture she drawed of the Sea Lion and the tree. I'll tell her how I hid it to keep it safe. Someday I'll tell her how the faces in the trees talked to me and made me feel better.*

Sara's blue eyes sparkled. "Like the Sea Lion, James, you were stolen. Because we love you so much, we found you. Just like the Sea Lion, you're back home where you belong."

RECIPES

Pocket Bread Toasted Cheese: Slice a pita (any flavor – my favorite is onion) pocket bread in half. Smear insides with mayonnaise (optional) and stuff with cheese. Spray the outsides of the bread with liquid butter or olive oil. Brown in a non-stick fry pan until cheese melts and bread is crusty brown. Yields two single servings.

The Beach Sandwich: Slice a pita bread circle in half. Place each half in a small bowl to keep its shape, standing upright. Cover both insides of the pocket bread with Provolone Cheese. Layer the following between the cheese: thin sliced turkey, shredded cabbage, thin sliced cucumbers, and onion. Add a few sliced green olives. Pour two heaping tablespoons of Ranch Dressing over all. Heat in microwave oven for one minute or less, allowing dressing to drip through ingredients. Take out as soon as you see the cheese melting. Do not overcook – it makes the bread chewy. Yields two single servings.

Quick Green Beans: Place three tablespoons of olive oil in a skillet, letting it cover the entire pan. Add a medium sliced onion, spreading them evenly as a bottom layer. Drain two cans of cut green beans and spread over the layer of onion. Let them cook uncovered until the onions look clear. Stir beans and onion and let them cook until all the liquid is gone. Yields four single servings.

Mozzarella Capresi: Layer - one slice of tomato, broken basil leaf, and a layer of soft Mozzarella cheese. Sprinkle with balsamic vinegar and place a basil leaf on top. Yields one serving.

Feta Greek Dish: Spray an 8"x8" casserole dish with olive oil and layer the following: Two cups of diced raw chicken – enough to cover the bottom of the dish; sprinkle with oregano, salt, and pepper; press a layer – one large bag – of fresh spinach over the chicken; add a layer of sliced onion; and add more seasoning. Spread a can of drained petite, diced tomatoes, and top off with feta cheese crumbles. Place foil over the dish and cook for forty-five minutes at 350º. Take foil off and cook fifteen minutes without a cover. Feta cheese should be crunchy brown.

Martha Phillips grew up in North Georgia. After retiring from the University of Georgia School of Law in 2005, her love of writing songs and poems expanded to novel writing. "Writing this sequel to *Written on a Rock*, felt like going back to Elberton and visiting with old friends," she says. "When one of my nice characters became a jerk, I actually got angry with him. Imagine that!" Art, including her love of painting, allows her creative spirit to soar.

Carved Landmarks (Photos and Painting) by Martha Phillips

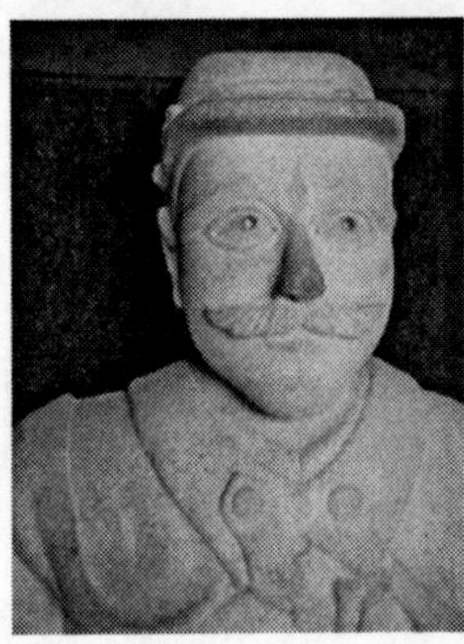

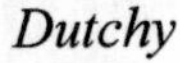

Dutchy

Acrylic Painting of Whales in the Park
St. Simons Island, Georgia

CPSIA information can be obtained at www.ICGtesting.com
Printed in the USA
LVOW10s1110100913

351769LV00003B/9/P